MW01616630

Sophomore
Sophilosophy

A Novel by
Victor David Giron

Curbside Splendor Publishing

www.curbsidesplendor.com

CURBSIDE SPLENDOR PUBLISHING

All rights reserved. Published in the United States of America by
Curbside Splendor Publishing.

First Edition

Copyright © 2010 by Victor David Giron

ISBN 978-0-615-40443-1

Book design by Karolina Faber

Drawings by Gabriel Hurier

Edited by R. A. Miller

www.curbsidesplendor.com

Table of Contents

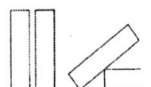

Dedicated to the big bird and the little monkeys.

Thanks to Karolina Faber, R A Miller, Gabriel Hurier, Garett Holden, Jim Klise, Gina Kapsimalis, Vadim Dadiomov, my 4th grade substitute teacher that convinced me to read The Hobbit, my 6th grade teacher Ms. Sackley for demanding I admit I could do well in school, my mom for inspiring me to love literature, my sisters and brother, and my dad (may he rest in peace).

Writers and Fighters

I consider myself a Chicagoan now, having lived in the city since I graduated from the University of Illinois at Urbana-Champaign with a degree in accounting. I came here often when I went to Maine West High School out in Des Plaines, which is a short drive west on the Kennedy or a short Blue Line ride toward O'Hare airport, the next-to-last stop in fact. My friends and I would take the Blue Line downtown and then transfer to the Red or Brown Line up to Belmont and Clark, our favorite part of the city when we were 16 and 17, mainly because of The Alley—a store that sold concert shirts, posters, spiked bracelets and stuff like that—and Gramophone Records, the electronic music store that took my virginity, so to speak.

A few years ago I moved to an area of the city called Wicker Park because I at times aspire to be some sort of artist and wanted to be surrounded by more artistic types. I didn't realize that the artists had pretty much left because people like me and companies like Starbucks made it too fucking expensive to live here. So now, I live just a few blocks north of the Damen Blue Line stop in this nice, refurbished, overpriced loft with all the "right finishes," surrounded by retail chain stores and countless other yuppies—the people I was trying to escape from and swore to never become like.

I wake up as late as possible before going to a job I can't stand although I tell everyone I meet, especially girls, that I love it, because girls want to hear that you love what you do for a living, are doing something you're "passionate about." I'm not the type that gets up extra early to do push-ups or sit-ups, make coffee or lunch for the day, walk his dog or read the newspapers. No, I leave just enough time to drag myself into the washroom, take a shower, maybe shave, put on my black socks, v-neck undershirt, boxers, slacks, dry-cleaned button-down dress shirt, black slip-on shoes, and black belt—untuck the shirt, grab my MP3 Player, keys, wallet, corporate ID, and make my way down Damen Avenue listening to something loud. Hoping not to break that bad of a sweat, I get my coffee at Half and Half, right at the corner of Milwaukee, Damen and North Avenue, am served by the art student kids who live in the area, am called "sir" by them, wish I was them on many occasions but not on others after thinking of how little money they must make. I climb the El stairs, wait there at the top, (trying to calm my sweat), and stare off at the pretty girls on the platform in their pretty work suits, skirts and pumps, and pretend like I'm not staring. If I'm lucky, I'll leave the office around 6 p.m., make it home around 7 p.m., and go to the Bally's down by the Webster Street movie theater and run a bit. If not, I just sit home and watch something like Chris Matthews or Keith Oberman blabber on MSNBC. Or, if I'm extra motivated, I'll read a book and fall asleep doing so.

When I have extra energy, I'll go to one of the many great venues here in Chicago to see live music—places like the Empty Bottle on Western and Augusta, the Metro down the street from Wrigley Field, the beautiful Vic Theater up on Sheffield and Belmont, where they show movies and sell beer when there's not a band playing, or even just down the street from me to the Double Door, a small club right there across from the Blue Line. I used to have a few friends who would go with me, but they've long since moved, and now I usually go by myself.

I've had a few opportunities to move away from Chicago. I thought about moving to places like New York, San Francisco, Madrid or Mexico. I worked in San Francisco for a summer, thought it was a beautiful city, but after a few weeks of walking around it, I felt that I found everything there was to discover and, although it was nice, I was bored of it already. And New York, however vast it is—diverse, busy, exciting—I never could move there, it's just a bit too dirty, too busy, and the people, yes, they come off as a bit too cold, especially to a shy Midwesterner like me. I've thought about moving to Mexico where my parents were born. I've been there many times, as a child growing up and recently as an adult, to visit the countless number of relatives we have. I've been to the small city in the mountains that my mother is from, and to other beautiful cities like Guadalajara, Zacatecas, Oaxaca, Puebla, Puerto Vallarta, and Cuernavaca. I've even thought about marrying a nice-looking Mexican woman and bringing her back here to live with me, like so many of my cousins have. But I concluded that she probably wouldn't find my peculiar tastes in music and other stuff all that interesting, realize that I can't dance worth a shit, especially for a Latino, and eventually find me dull. I decided to avoid what would probably have been a disaster.

The music scene in Chicago has kept me here, and I don't even go to that many shows anymore, only a few a year probably. I like to know that the venues I've loved are close by and if and when I want to go, I can, and that all sorts of people, young and old, are going to them every weekend, every night, having fun, getting high, getting laid, "expanding their horizons," meeting new friends, falling in and out of love, shit like that.

I went to see Sonic Youth at the Metro once, by myself, and I got there early to get a spot upstairs against the balcony rail in the center. Although I grabbed a great spot, I didn't know how I was going to get drinks because as soon as I left my spot it would be gone. Luckily the man standing next to me, his name was Ron, was also by himself. He was in his 40s, a father of two girls. He was glad to be able to get to the show, as Sonic Youth was one of his favorite bands. He was going to bring one of his daughters, but she and her mother had something else to do. He told me how they used to play The Flaming Lips or They Might Be Giants for their daughters when they were babies. We ended up taking turns going to get drinks, while one guy fought off the crowd and held the spots. Sonic Youth played great that night. Kim Gordon did her circular dance in high heels, and the band was loud. I want to be like Ron if I'm ever a father.

The day after September 11, I went to see PJ Harvey play at the Riviera. Again, I was by myself, up in the front, and she came out alone with a guitar and spoke to the audience saying that the band had talked about whether or not they should play in light of the circumstances, whether it was in some way not respectful to the victims. But she said that they decided there was really no viable option other than to play because they were nothing more than musicians. For them not to play would be insulting to those who died or were injured. So, she strummed a slow song from their new album at the time, *Stories From the City, Stories from the Sea*, about someone who had fallen in love and was observing New York City from the top of a building on some early morning. When the song finished, the rest of the band members slowly joined her on stage, and suddenly they ripped full force into one of her powerful, hard, thumping songs called "Meet Ze Monsta," playing while silhouetted in blood red. The rest of the show pretty much kicked ass like that.

I know that most any city has its great music venues, and I've been to some, but for some reason, maybe a selfish one, I like to think they're not like here in Chicago. Chicago is comforting to me. I like its streets, the low buildings, all of its neighborhoods. It has lots of trees, wood decks with chairs, tables and barbeques. During the summer, my cute newlywed neighbors can often be found eating out on their little deck in the evenings, sharing a bottle of wine; you'd never know you were in the middle of a metropolitan area.

Alex Kotlowitz captured Chicago in a fantastic way through his book *Never a City So Real: A Walk in Chicago*. He describes Chicago through his descriptions of individuals from different areas of the city—from Ed Sadlowski, a Unionist in Chicago's Southside, Millie and Brenda, two African American ladies he has lunch with regularly on the West Side, to Robert Guinan, an artist who painted scenes from Chicago's underbelly: one-legged prostitutes, a mother and boy sleeping on an El train, and a decrepit Polish bartender smoking cigarettes at a local Wicker Park pub.

Nelson Algren wrote: "It used to be a writer's town, and it's always been a fighter's town" when describing Chicago in his poem called *Chicago: City on the Make*. I think he wrote that in the 1950s. He lived in Wicker Park, on a street called Evergreen, close to the actual park called Wicker Park. I've read that in the 1990s the city tried to change Evergreen to Algren Avenue in his honor, but supposedly the residents complained because they had to change their addresses, so the city changed it back. I'd never heard of Algren until recently; he's one of those authors that was never really recognized in his home town but was recognized elsewhere, by like the French. He's known for writing novels like *Walk on the Wild Side*, a book about New Orleans in the 1930s and the pimps and prostitutes who lived there, and also *Man with the Golden Arm*, set in Chicago, about a card dealer, drugs, and more pimps and prostitutes. I guess Frank Sinatra played the character in the movie by the same name, but Algren didn't like it.

It was amazing, or at least I thought so, when I read these authors and realized that they were describing Chicago not through recounting its famous history or events, but through the stories of not-so-famous inhabitants, and even fictional ones, who embody the attitude and spirit that now make Chicago what people perceive it to be.

If I had any talent, I would make a movie of Chicago. I would team up with Alex Kotlowitz and make a movie about its people, maybe the people he describes, and the regular people I've come to know or see here in this city. I'd like to team up with Nelson Algren, but unfortunately he's no longer alive, and he would probably think I was a poser.

Unlike the sissy way Woody Allen started *Manhattan*, my movie would start with a still shot of Chicago's skyline during the early morning, shot from the lake, with Navy Pier, the Hancock Building, the Sears Tower, looming in the distance. After a few silent seconds, a song would start to play in the background, a rock and roll song, maybe a Smashing Pumpkins song, like "Cherub Rock" from their *Siamese Dream* album. You would hear the drum roll start, the bass, and when the song kicked into full gear with rolling guitars and Jimmy Chamberlin banging on the cymbals, the viewer would be treated to scene after scene of Chicago—shots of the skyline from the vantage point of a car coming up the Dan Ryan, from a plane flying into Chicago over the lake at night, a shot from a camera whizzing down the "Magnificent Mile" full of shoppers, beggars, musicians, and tourists. And then a shot of someone like me, or better, a cute girl with pumps or boots, gotta love those boots, walking down Damen Avenue on her way to the train, looking all cool and city-like with her ear plugs plugged in. And then to a scene of a young Latino couple having sex in their stuffy apartment in a building across the street from Humboldt Park, to a shot of young Middle Eastern and European immigrants playing soccer on Montrose beach, to another group on the adjacent beach there smoking a joint and drinking Old Style. Then to a shot of a black family having a birthday party in one of the last standing Cabrini Green housing projects, followed by a group of yuppie 30-somethings having a kitsch dinner party at someone's condo in the city.

I would layer on shots of our sports teams—the Bears running through the orange and blue Bear head at the corner of Soldier Field, the Cubs running onto the field in Wrigley on a sunny weekday afternoon, saluting the drunk bleacher bums sitting just above the Ivy, the White Sox finally winning the World Series again, and a shot of good old Michael Jordon hitting his last game winning shot against the Utah Jazz.

I would follow that with shots of hipster music lovers waiting anxiously in line at the Metro to go see the latest hipster band, a shot of the Flaming Lips playing a New Year's Eve show at the Metro, and shots of Lollapalooza along the lake.

The last scene of the intro would be of a backyard party in Des Plaines, the American salad bowl of a suburb, where a 17-year-old Mexican-American boy is drunk and about to recite his "Green Shit Machine" poem to his cheering Maine West classmates, members of Generation X, who are also sons and daughters of the Greek, Polish, Mexican, Cuban, Puerto Rican, Asian, Italian, Irish, Indian, German, Russian, Jewish and whatever-else, immigrants that make Chicago what it is.

American Latino Wimp

To get some facts down and out of the way, my name is Alejandro Lopez. I am a 30-something-year-old Latin-American male no longer comfortable saying exactly how old I am. I was born in Chicago to immigrant parents, still live in Chicago, and work as a certified public accountant ("CPA") for a large corporation. My mother, Maria, was born in a small town in the mountains of western Mexico, and my father, Manuel, was born in a small Mexican town further south. They separately immigrated, illegally, in their early 20s—ran across the fucking border, crawled through pipes, were stuffed into vans, etc.—and eventually made their way to Chicago to become proud American citizens. I say that my parents met on some park bench, where my father saw her and put the moves on, although I'm not really sure that's what happened... but it makes for a good story. They started dating, got married, had me and my sister and eventually divorced when I was about 11 and my sister was about 9 because my father was a raging alcoholic and beat all of us.

I've been single for most of my adult life, aside from a few really fucked up relationships. I have countless CDs of bands that never see the light of day in a mainstream radio studio, and countless others that I'm ashamed to admit I own. I draw pictures using charcoal pencils and try to paint abstract images. I have a lot of my own art up on my walls, some which is fairly good, some not so much. Whenever I've had work friends over at my place they've looked around in a sort of bewilderment and usually ask me, "How come you're an accountant?" I've often wondered that myself, and I still don't quite have an answer...

I remember much of the time when I didn't know English, back when we lived in Logan Square, in an old red-bricked building that had urine-sprayed hallways. A large percentage of Chicago's Latino population lived nearby. We were surrounded by people from Puerto Rico, Mexico, and South America, most here illegally like my parents and unwanted by most of the American population—except to fill shitty jobs. English wasn't really required in our neighborhood, which is why I didn't learn it until I went to school. For these immigrants, coming to the United States of America was supposed to be the answer, the opportunity to make more money than they would at home by working the jobs that no one else wanted. Many of these people have children who make the news because they steal something, shoot someone, or beat their spouse. They have children at an early age, who then barely graduate from high school and have children themselves at an early age. Others go back to their parents' native countries and show off their American money, or, like mine, move out to the suburbs and put their children through the crazy process of assimilation—and then usually become Republicans. Yet others are successful, true pioneers, but I can't elaborate on this part of the American Latino population because, well, I just don't know any.

My earliest memories of Logan Square are playing in puddles with my little sister, who was two or three at the time, on the sidewalks surrounding the Logan Square Eagle column where Kedzie Avenue, Logan Boulevard and Milwaukee Avenue all intersect—the "Logan Square Circle." It was a scary area back then and still can be. But now you can go see a hipster concert at the Logan Square Auditorium, eat a fancy meal made with organic ingredients at Lula Café, buy nice flowers and candles at Le Fleur, and attend the farmer's market right there by the circle every Sunday morning during the summer. Now the area is "up-and-coming." But up and coming for whom is the question. Most of the locals are so worried about being run out of their neighborhood by people like me, like the residents of neighboring Wicker Park and Bucktown have, that they have been able to convince the Alderman several times to issue a temporary moratorium on condo development—temporary being the operative word.

It makes me sad to think of my mother and father meeting here. Not really because of what eventually happened to them, but more because of all the promise that was there. They were two illegal immigrants in their early 20s, escaping a life of poverty in their home countries to live a life of poverty here in the hope of finding something better and trying to fulfill their dream of raising a family.

They both worked two jobs. My father made furniture during the day, as he still does, and at night he was the janitor for the building we lived in—which helped with the rent, but led to him getting beat up by the gang that lived in the basement of our building. They called themselves the Orchestra Albany, or the "Crazy OAs," and were mainly Puerto Rican. Why the hell they called themselves that I'm not sure, but I guess it had something to do with their operations being based on Albany Street, the street we lived on. They were a small gang in comparison with the other local Latino gangs like the Latin Kings and the Spanish Lords, but I guess they were well respected. There were 20-or-so kids who basically lived in the basement of our building. The owner of the building, some old Polish guy, always wanted my father to kick them out. Every time my dad tried he would get his ass kicked really bad. I can still see the blood running out of his nose, his bruised eyes and torn up shirt and hear my mother frantically screaming and crying, and the sounds of the gang-bangers taunting us right outside the door. My father had to send my mom and us to Mexico when it got too bad so he could find a new apartment for us to live in.

My parents tell me they worked hard to move us to Des Plaines. Although Des Plaines had a large number of immigrant transplants from the city, we were the only Mexicans, or spics, on the street we lived on. I was held back my first year of school there because I didn't know English. I vaguely remember being in English as a Second Language classes with a bunch of other Latino and Indian kids. My father told me that we would play with our neighbor's little girl Janice and we would talk to her in Spanish and she would answer in English. But then her father complained to my father that his daughter was getting confused and asked that we only speak English to her. My father told him to fuck off and a fight almost ensued. Janice moved away not long after that.

I also remember the many nights that my father wouldn't come home and how my mom would freak out when he finally showed up drunk—when he would beat us with his belt. My dad had it all going for him, a beautiful wife, two kids, and a house in the suburbs with a big yard, but for some reason—I guess the same as any other person with an addiction problem—he couldn't fend off alcohol and drugs. After many nights of crying, violence, and suicide threats, my mom finally did the unspeakable (for a Latin American woman) and divorced my father. And despite my father being such a monster to us, we hated Mom for it.

My dad eventually agreed to leave us and went back to live in the city in an apartment with some Mexican guys that he knew from work. They all worked in an upholstery shop on the Southside, getting paid little for making and maintaining the furniture of the rich people who lived in the North Shore suburbs. When we dropped him off at the apartment, my sister and I sat in the back of the old blue Chevrolet crying and crying as my dad, also crying, waved good-bye to us while holding his bag of clothes. It was drizzling that day, and it seemed like we were the only people on that street.

My dad is now remarried, has three younger children, and has been a devoted member of Alcoholic's Anonymous for several years. He has a type of Hepatitis and cirrhosis of the liver, and always asks me how my sister is doing even though he now hasn't talked to her for many years. He's not too far away from death. I recently had to spend a few days with him in the hospital, sitting there and watching as he lay incapacitated with needles and tubes in his arms and stomach. He always talked about starting his own furniture shop, once even made business cards, but he never pursued it. My dad is in his early 50s, but he looks way older and much more fragile. Despite all he's done, I love him, and I guess I feel that it is my responsibility now to continue loving him until he dies.

I like to say that I am an amateur philosopher. I studied philosophy in college but gave it up in order to major in business so I could make steady money. I say I still practice it, study it on the side, but I haven't read a real philosophy book in years now. For work, I read boring contracts, analyze prospective transactions of a soulless corporation, and tell my bosses what the right accounting treatment should be. I write research papers, and "manage projects." No matter how interesting I try to make it sound, how proud my parents are of me, I find it all to be quite miserable. I get paid well, but it's in return for sacrificing every bit of creativity I might once have had.

It seems like my childhood friends and I are finally settling into our destinies. We're receiving steady paychecks and have jobs with "good benefits." Most of my friends have moved back to the suburbs where we grew up, with their wives and their children, to have more and more children, to be conservative parents like their parents, to start going to church again, and to watch the Bears and Cubs season after season in the hopes that maybe, just maybe, one will finally win a championship again—justifying all the time spent watching the games on television.

I also struggle with the fact that I'm Latin American, but hang out mainly with white people. I can speak Spanish pretty well, can read it ok, but I always think in English. I worked so hard to assimilate in high school that I almost destroyed any linkage to my heritage.

My friend John once said that I'm 90% guy and 10% girl. People have asked me whether I'm gay, and I've even thought about it, but I always come back to the one thing I do know— that I've been obsessed with women as long as I can remember. I like them a lot. More than the normal guy? Probably not, but certainly just as much—which is a lot. I haven't had many long-term relationships, really only like three, but I've had quite a few short-term relationships, have gone on lots and lots of dates, and have had lots and lots of sex. In fact I don't like to admit anymore how many times I've had sex. I seem to have a keen sense of picking out women who are desiring sexual attention, and somehow they always end up coming on to me. But like everyone else, I tell people that I "long for something real," that I "want to settle down."

I'm about 5'11" or 6'0" tall (depending on who I'm talking to), thin framed, and somewhat athletic looking—although I could be a lot more athletic looking if I didn't drink as much beer or smoke as many cigarettes as I do. I normally have long, wavy, dark hair, but I've been known to buzz it down every now and then. I've been told that I'm an attractive looking guy, on certain occasions by people other than my mother or sister, and I've often been told that I look like the boxer Oscar De La Hoya, though I don't believe it. Besides, who would want to look like an old, washed-up boxer anyway?

I think my penis is too small. I've read that the average erect penis is about five inches long, which I find pretty hard to believe. That means guys out there actually have two- or three-inch penises, when they're hard. I guess Asian, Irish and English guys are supposed to have small penises. But only two inches? I don't believe it. I don't see how anyone could have sex with a penis that small. I've had a hard enough time with mine in certain positions, especially like from the side—I can't keep it in that way.

(The thing about Irish guys having small penises might be true though. Miki—a friend, ex-friend, ex-lover, or whatever you want to call her—once said after we were done having sex: "Why are you so good? It's because your dick is so big..." I knew that her ex-boyfriend was an Irish guy, so for her to have said that my dick was big must have meant that he had a really, really small one. She was drunk, of course, when she said that.)

I seem to think that if I really was as attractive as some people try to lead me to believe then I would have girls throwing themselves at my feet. But I don't, or not as much as I would like. This is one of the ways that I'm 10% girl I guess— I expect to be hit on by the opposite sex. I know this is not the norm, so I probably do have a chemical imbalance of some sort. But I've just never been good at picking up girls; I struggle at what to say, especially in places like bars, so I've had to rely on girls initiating contact with me. Either that or the girl has to be one I'm able to get to know over time, like at work.

I've been a big wimp for as long as I can remember. It happened when my parents divorced. I used to be pretty cool... in the fifth grade. The girls back then all loved me. I was Michael Jackson in one of our school plays, doing the freaking moon-walk across the stage, wearing a red jacket, sunglasses, fake diamond glove, black pants that were floods, white socks, and black shoes. I then signed autographs afterward for the fourth grade girls. I was a stud, I think, or at least it seemed that way.

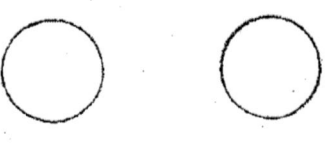

Jackie and the Outsiders

I remember the nights my father would go to the parent teacher conferences at our elementary school. My sister and I were terrified when we heard him coming home because we knew he was going to hit us with his belt. We would run to our rooms crying, our mother would be screaming, and our father would come into our rooms with his belt in hand in order to give us our lashings for not getting the best remarks from our teachers. God that fucking hurt. It was true that my sister and I were bad students, I was constantly getting in trouble and had bad grades, but he never seemed to care until those nights for some reason. Besides teaching me how to play baseball and his belt beatings, I don't remember much else from my father in terms of parenting—except I guess for his advice on picking up girls, which was pretty much to hit on anything and everything I saw and liked. It wasn't until after my parents divorced that I became the semi-nerd that I was in high school.

My parents each remarried within a few years of their divorce. My sister and I hated the divorce, hated our mom for kicking our dad out—even though he was terrible to us—and we hated our stepfather Doug, who in hindsight was a very nice man. My sister and I were little assholes, in fact, to my mom and Doug. We said all sorts of nasty things, stuff so bad that I've never wanted to date someone who had children already. I guess I admire them for sticking through it all.

That, above anything else, is what I had in common with my little group of friends when we first moved to Des Plaines. We all hated our lives at home, so we'd spend countless hours just hanging out in the streets of our neighborhood, causing trouble, breaking windows, and bullshitting about wanting to be sports stars, act in movies, be archeologists, or be astronauts.

When I was little, just after we had moved to Des Plaines from Chicago, my first friends were John Jankowski, Matt Ostrowski and Carlos Arroyo. They were from dysfunctional and immigrant families like mine. John's were from Poland, Matt's were Jews from Poland and Russia, and Carlos' from Mexico. We were also friends with Jig Patel, whose parents were immigrants from India, but his family was fairly intact and strict, so he never went around causing trouble with the rest of us, and instead we all usually picked on him.

It's funny to think of the conversations children have. You've barely been alive; you're not educated enough to talk about politics, fashion, sex, etc., yet you still do. But I guess that's not much different than me and my adult friends now.

I've known my core Des Plaines friends now for over 30 years. These friends today are, for the most part, consumed with jobs that are boring as hell during the day—so much so that when we meet up there's almost nothing to talk about, so we mainly talk about sports. We talked sports when we were little too, but mainly we played them. Now, instead of playing, my friends memorize all sorts of statistics for their "fantasy" leagues and criticize players and coaches as if they could somehow do better themselves.

What the fuck is it with "fantasy" sports, anyway? A bunch of guys sit around a room and hold a draft, select professional players to be on their team, and based on how well they do, their team either wins or loses. Like it's not enough to just watch the damn games, or bet on them or something. There's a whole market devoted to fantasy sports now—magazines, talk shows, and Web sites. I once was in a fantasy football league. I called my team the "Gatos Negros," and went to a draft meeting and everything. Guys brought their magazines all marked-up and highlighted with notes. I didn't know what the hell I was doing, so my team started getting its ass kicked right away. I didn't spend the time during the week to keep up on how the players were doing, didn't make any changes to my team, and eventually I had guys playing who were injured. I finished in dead last and wasn't asked to play again the next year.

My friends and I talk about our jobs, but mainly about how stressful they are, the boring meetings we have, our asshole bosses, and how busy we are—so busy that we don't have time for personal stuff like our friends, families, or hobbies. The people I work with at my corporate job talk the same way; they all struggle because they're at the office all day and usually have a spouse who's pissed because they're taking care of the children all the time. They constantly talk about how if they don't start working less, they're going to end up divorced, but they don't change, and most of them do end up divorced. The older men usually tell me to not make the same mistakes that they did, to not let work be more important than family, to take advantage of my time now because before I know it, it'll be gone, and then I realize that they're talking just how my dad used to talk to me.

My friends and I also talk politics sometimes, but we're generally not informed enough, or we're too thick-headed to have an intelligent conversation on the topic. We're either Republicans or Democrats and get upset at listening to the other point of view. We can't talk about things like music, books or movies because, besides me, no one else really is into these things anymore, and I somehow feel immature because I am. Whenever I bring up a new band or movie I'm into, most of my friends respond by saying, "Man, I'm so out of the loop, I haven't bought a CD or anything in years now..."

After exhausting our conversation on topics such as sports, our jobs, and sometimes politics, we usually resort to talking about the girls we used to score with and how we used to get fucked up. They're all old stories though; no one has any new ones, no original ideas.

Fyodor Dostoevsky wrote in his book *The Idiot* that we all have thoughts that at times illuminate us, give us certain guidance that result in dramatic epiphanies. However, many of us never share these thoughts with each other, or even if we try to, the translation is lost in the communication, therefore leaving the original idea we had lost in the back of our minds forever. It seems like that happens to me all the time. It seems to me that children express these thoughts with greater ease than adults. Children tend to express their thoughts without much revision or interpretation, just purely through simple words, simply by asking "Why?" I've read that four-year-olds ask about 400 questions a day. Maybe all the great original ideas are truly communicated by children, and if someone walked around with a tape-recorder taping children's conversations we'd be able to make true philosophical breakthroughs…

There's some crazy statistic that Des Plaines has the highest amount of railroad footage for its size, or something like that. Some tracks carry large freight trains that would chug through a few times a day, always stopping traffic, and other tracks haven't seen any use in years. A river called the Des Plaines River runs though town; it has a bunch of little creeks and woods running alongside its eastern bank. All this was right next to where we grew up and provided for fun turf to play on. Along the tracks and the creeks were all sorts of bridges and dirt paths that we called "the trails." There was also a big viaduct that we hung out under all the time.

Of all my childhood friends, the one I had the most substantive conversations with was my little Polish friend John. It seemed like my other friends, like Matt and Carlos, were always more interested in causing trouble and later finding girls. My most fond memory of Matt when we were little is of the two of us standing in my living room watching the scrambled "On-TV" feed of late night porn and laughing at our hardons, which, at that time, we didn't know how to use—they were just funny to us.

Hanging out under that viaduct in Des Plaines, John and I used to say stuff to each other like, "Man, I don't want to grow up to be boring 'n shit. I want to be remembered, do something cool with my life."

"Yeah, like make movies, write books."

"Be an athlete, go on trips, see the world. Fuck being an ordinary person like our parents, watching TV, sittin' around, you know?"

"Yeah, fuck that. That sucks. I mean, doing that is boring as shit. Look at us, man, we're not boring. We're not going to be boring either when we grow up, no way."

And then we'd talk about God, like all the time, saying stuff like, "John, what do you think God looks like?"

"I don't know, I guess like a big old man, but I'm not sure."

"Why would God make himself look ugly though, you know? If God's always been alive, then why would he look old? If I were God I'd make myself be beautiful, you know?"

"I don't know, I guess you're right, maybe he's not old, or he doesn't even look like us."

"Do you think he's lonely?"

"No, well, maybe. But if God's the most powerful, then he could never get lonely; powerful things don't get lonely, do they?"

"I guess not, it's just weird that's all. I mean, what did he do all that time before we came? Did he create other people that have since gone? Does he just keep creating different people over and over, for the hell of it? Did he create the dinosaurs?" During my Sunday bible school classes I used to love asking who the hell created the dinosaurs, and if they went to Heaven or Hell like we did. It just always bugged me out, the whole concept that dinosaurs existed and "ruled" the Earth for supposedly such a long time.

John is married now and has children in a big old house out in the suburbs, and I don't talk with him that much anymore, especially not in the way we did back then. I miss those conversations. Now as 30-something adult friends, we dare not ever talk like that anymore—it's like almost taboo to bring up substantive issues like religion and death as an adult. But the thing is, I still think about these things all the time. I wonder what "God" really is. Does it really exist? Why do we even believe in such a thing? I still think about the damn dinosaurs, and it still bugs me out—gives me the chills even. I can't help it. The problem is now I really don't have anyone to talk to about this sort of stuff. Now it's just all in my head.

Sometimes John and I will talk in terms of us not having accomplished much yet and we're not satisfied, but mainly because we don't make more money than we'd like. Besides making more money, sometimes we talk about how we'd like to do something different with our lives other than our boring corporate jobs. However, the conversation never really dares go beyond that, to what it is exactly we want to do. We usually end these conversations by saying, "Oh, well, that's life, that's how it is." My friends and I seem to have lost that early childhood desire to explore dreams. We all have safe, secure jobs and seem to be heading down the road to normalcy. We're getting tired, ready to give it up, whatever "it" was. John and his wife Amy will raise their family and probably never think of what they possibly are missing. I think people in that situation draw a barrier between their lives and alternatives around them. It's almost as if those alternatives never really existed, or if they did they were quickly stomped out as purely delusional, imaginary wishes.

Or maybe I'm just the one that's fucked up. Maybe raising a family like that is perfectly fine—a valid dream in and of itself. And in order to focus on raising your children, you have to abandon any wishes or goals you had as a selfish adult. But abandoning all creativity, adventure, just seems like a nightmare to me. I think that's why there are so many bored people in the world who do nothing but watch TV. If I become a parent, I'm going to try and not lose my sense of identity.

Even as an adult John used to have dreams—before he got married and had his first child at least. He once bought a guitar, started trying to teach himself how to play. I also bought a guitar. I was a slow learner but eventually taught myself, was able to get a point where I didn't suck that bad. However, John pretty much dropped it right away due to Amy's complaining about it, or that's what he blamed it on anyway. He said that she thought his trying to learn how to play a guitar was stupid because, well, he was an adult now. I'm not trying to say that there's something better about learning an instrument, practicing an art, but, well I guess I'm not sure what I would do with my free time if I didn't pursue such things. I wonder whether John ever thinks about trying something like playing the guitar again, or what might his life had been like had he continued pursuing such hobbies.

When we were little, when the movie *The Outsiders* came out, it was like a gift from God. We were able to see a bunch of kids on the screen who were also from shattered families. We watched the movie over and over and then would go to the viaduct and act out scenes to our own imaginary movie, which was similar. Our favorite scene to act out was a big gang fight, in which our gang prevailed with one of our members, played by Carlos, tragically dying. During the scene, John was taken down, losing his knife, and was about to be stabbed by his assaulter. Carlos would come running into the mix and take out the rival gang member, wrestling him to the ground, stabbing him heroically. But just as he's successful, he would take a knife in the back, deep enough that it killed him. John, of course, would get up and avenge Carlos but then would turn back to find him on the ground dying. Carlos would remain conscious long enough for us to thank him and hug him as he died. For little kids we acted out a pretty decent death scene. The last scene was after the funeral and we would all walk underneath the viaduct with our heads held high knowing that new days lay ahead with more battles to be fought in the mean cold streets. And as we walked, we would blast Survivors' "The Eye of the Tiger" through a boom-box we brought with us. I was the director, but also played one of the gang members who was the quiet, mysterious one, yet was feared and respected. I only wish we had a camera back then, who knows what would have happened?

A lot else happened under that viaduct. We learned to swear, started smoking cigarettes, had our first drinks of alcohol, and first started getting excited about girls. We used to get cigarettes from John's older brother who was 13 but hung out with all these older head-banger kids who smoked. They all had long hair and listened to heavy metal, which we eventually got into. I think I was about eight when I first started smoking, though we didn't know how to inhale until much later. Besides smoking under the viaduct, we would sit underneath this railroad bridge by the Des Plaines River, act all cool with our cigarettes lit, and talk our little-kid philosophy. It was cool when the trains would come by, especially the big cargo ones taking shit off to who knows where. They were slow but loud as hell. We always talked about jumping on one and seeing where it took us, maybe somewhere far away, until one of John's brother's friends tried and he got his foot run over and ended up in the hospital. So we said, "Fuck that."

When we first started smoking we thought we were tough, and during the summer we walked around the elementary school with our smokes lit. The school was close to my house, so soon my sister and her friends saw us smoking. When she said she was going to tell our parents, I told her to fuck off, and we just kept smoking. That night when I got home, my dad already knew, and he threatened to burn my hand on the stove. He actually lit the stove and dragged me over there screaming and crying and put my hand inches away from the flame, so close I could feel it. I promised never to smoke again, but soon we were back at it, only now we knew to be more discreet.

My first kiss was with a girl named Jackie. In grammar school we used to play on the swing sets and jungle gyms during and after school. Eventually, we started exchanging little glances. Next, we started telling our friends who we liked, and then rumors would spread about who liked who. Jackie and I started talking and walking together after school, just literally walking around and around the school. One of those days as we were walking together, barely talking, I was nervous as hell because I wanted to kiss her. I didn't even know how to do it. (The anxiousness I felt was a sign of things to come.) We'd all seen adults do it in movies, on TV, and we'd also seen our parents do it. At first it was revolting, but eventually, as with me and Jackie, it became intriguing and we wanted to do it. Out of nowhere, as we were walking and about to say goodbye to each other, I leaned forward and gave her a quick little kiss on the lips, and we both walked away nervously. I remember how red in the face and embarrassed she was in the moments leading up to the kiss, as I'm sure I was. I still get nervous as hell when I think about it.

Eventually the innocent little kissing and flirting led to make-out parties in John's basement on Saturday nights when his mom was either out for the night or too drunk to give a shit. The basement would be full of couples all spread out on couches, pillows, with music like Prince's *Purple Rain* playing in the background. The making out was fun. I was still with Jackie—for a first girlfriend she lasted a really long time, probably my longest relationship to date. Jackie was generally considered the hottest chick in the 6th grade back then. She had short brown hair, a curvy little body and large boobs—she had blossomed early. We never had sex at that age, thankfully, but pretended to. A few years later, though, she let me have it.

It happened on an afternoon during the summer when her parents were gone. We used to spend afternoons at her parents' house floating on rafts in her pool, listening to music. My mother, even at that age, was talking like we were going to get married. It seemed like it, and we were always together and had been for years now. We had a long-term relationship before we even had gone through puberty. I liked her; she was the only girl I knew who actually liked cool bands like Metallica, Iron Maiden, AC/DC. She went with me and Matt to concerts that his mom would take us to—like Iron Maiden at the Rosemont Horizon during their *Somewhere in Time* tour, or AC/DC with Megadeath opening—and I was in love with the fact she could go to these shows and rock out harder than any of my guy friends—and she knew all the words.

I remember us laying there, our naked bodies on white sheets in the dim-lit room, hearing the rain outside beating against the windows with Fleetwood Mac playing through the speakers of her record player as we un-wrapped the condom that I was to use. We were nervous, we didn't know what the hell we were doing, and it didn't last long at all. I also remember seeing a tear come down her cheek when we finished. I asked her what was wrong and she responded with, "Oh, nothing, I just like you a lot and am glad you're here with me." I wondered whether she was ashamed or something, but I just laid there with her, and we fell asleep as the record started to skip.

Jackie helped me through the divorce of my parents because she was really the only person I could talk to—although we actually didn't talk that much about it, we mainly sat in her room and listened to music. Suddenly, though, Jackie had to move away, and I was fucking devastated. Something happened with her family, I never knew what exactly, she didn't talk about it. I never really talked to or knew her father, and her mother always seemed quite nervous. They moved somewhere down south; I don't remember where. We tried to stay in touch, but suddenly she stopped returning my calls, and I gave up. We were way too young to have been in a relationship and having sex anyway. So it faded away. Sometimes I wish I would've stayed in touch with her. I wonder what has happened with her life, what happened with her family, whether she kept rocking out to cool music or eventually became bitter at something and is now unhappy. Maybe I would rather not know what hap-pened with her life in order to keep the image I have preserved of that beautiful young rocker chick with short brown hair, fair skin, and a mischievous little smile.

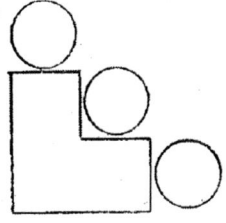

Halloween Tricks

When I was little I had the typical Halloween outfits like Dracula, Frankenstein, and the werewolf. The werewolf costume was made with the stuff you were supposed to put on your face to make it look like you had hair but ended up sticking to your hands and your clothes. My mother would take us to the K-Mart and buy our little pumpkin candy-holders and cheap little outfits and dress us up before school or before taking us to our babysitter who lived across the street.

Other parents of Latino children in our school wouldn't let their kids dress up for Halloween because they thought it was Satanic or un-God-like. Unlike the Mexican holiday "El Dia de los Muertos," Halloween was not about paying respects to dead relatives; it was seen in the Latino community as some sort of sacrilege—kids dressing up and running around like monsters or demons. That's what the other Latino kids at school told me anyway, when I would ask them why they wouldn't dress up. My mother was religious, and we attended church, but she never mentioned anything about sacrilege. My sister and I just wanted to do what the other kids were doing, so my mother went along with it. She would try to take that evening off from work to take us trick-or-treating, but many times we would have to go with one of our friends' parents because she needed to work nights and my father was out drinking.

I often think of my mother waking up early to dress us on Halloween—to put our little costumes on us while she struggled through her marriage, and how she worked so hard to pay for our house and keep us away from the shit we lived with in Logan Square. I don't remember my mother ever dressing up for Halloween, and I'm pretty sure she never has; it has probably never occurred to her.

My favorite costume was this big green dragon suit I wore when I was like 11. It was a full-body, cloth costume with a yellow belly, big green flippers for feet, and a tail with white soft spiky things that ran along the back. The head had big round eyes and a mouth with white spongy teeth that opened for my face to stare out of. At that point I was already working a little—delivering newspapers—and for some reason I felt like wearing something different that year, so I bought it. My father called me stupid for spending so much money on something like that, but he laughed in his drunken way and told me again how stupid I looked when I put it on for my family the night before. My mother told him to shut up and told me I looked good, that it was the best costume she'd ever seen and that I would probably win a prize in school for it. My sister also said I looked stupid and laughed like my drunken father did, and our little dogs barked at me and tried to bite the tail when I ran around the house.

On the way to school the next day, I was happy that everyone stopped and said "Wow," or the parents walking their kids would tell them, "Look, there's a dragon," and little kids would run behind me trying to grab the tail as I wagged it while my sister laughed at me and told me how stupid I was.

When I arrived at school, everyone was amazed, laughing, looking into the head to see me and ask where I got it. For some reason, I said that my mother had made it. The costume was made out of simple cloth and sponge-like material, so I'm sure someone could have made something like that, but the teachers looked at me sort of like, "Oh, ok Alex, that's great, your mom did a real nice job," like I was full of shit.

I made up stories all the time growing up. I would say things like my mom made me steak and eggs for breakfast every day, that my father played the guitar and sang our family songs from his home town at night, that we had a very rich uncle in Wisconsin who was murdered one day and that's why I was really sad at school, that one of my cousins who lived in Chicago was a Latin King wanted for several gang-related murders. My lies were never about me, they were always about the people around me, mainly my family.

That Halloween went great; I won first place in the Orchard Place Elementary School costume contest. Some kid that had a freaky looking Jason costume from *Friday the 13th*, with a facemask and an ax going through it, took second, and some girl with a witch costume took third. Those costumes, though, were truly homemade, and they were cool, and it made me feel a little bad. My costume was a bullshit one bought from

K-Mart. But no matter what, everyone liked it—I liked it, and it was green and fucking fun—so maybe I deserved the first-place prize. We had a dance at school that day, and again, I was a hit. All the girls wanted to dance with me, and I led this big dance line that ran across the gym, with a girl behind me holding my tail. I wiped out when some kid stepped on the tail, and everyone was talking about the wipeout and the whole dance for days after.

I loved that costume. I never wore it again; don't know what ever happened to it. It was probably thrown away.

My sister and I loved scary stories and movies—plentiful around Halloween every year. We watched them all: *Halloween*, *Nightmare on Elm Street*, the *Friday the 13th* movies, *The Texas Chainsaw Massacre*, *The Omen*, *the Exorcist*, and *The Amityville Horror*. I think *The Amityville Horror* was our favorite, the scariest for some reason. We would watch it over and over, and each time it would freak us out. We would not be able to sleep; my sister would wake up screaming and crying, which would wake me up, and I would start screaming and crying, which then caused my mother to have to run into the room, and then she would get mad at us for "watching those darn movies." I watched that movie recently, and now it sort of seems cheesy, but it still gave me the creeps—especially the beginning scene with the scary music and the scary white house with windows that look like eyes, and the fact that every time the clock turned 3:15 a.m.—the exact time that the Defoe family was supposedly killed by their possessed son—some really scary shit happened. I still can't look at the clock whenever I wake up in the middle of the night.

I loved Edgar Allen Poe as a kid, especially *The Tell Tale Heart* and the *Fall of the House of Usher*. Or all the Stephen King books my sister and I would read, like *The Tommyknockers*, *The Shining*, and *Cujo*. When I was little, I even wrote a scary short story that won a prize, about a freaky little monster that arrives at our babysitter's house and stabs the hell out of her in the kitchen with a butcher knife as my sister and I watch, and the monster turns and laughs at us saying we're going to get in trouble. The teachers loved the way I wrote it, but they probably should have thrown me into the psychiatric ward right then and there. I've always wondered whether the way my sister and I liked those movies and books, and the freaky-ass shit I wrote, was an indication of the problems we had. Or maybe it was just us being kids, right? Or maybe it was visiting the little Mexican village our mom grew up in, where our grandmother would always tell us scary stories about ghosts like *La Llorona*, the ghost that would wander small villages screaming for her lost children, and if you saw her you would die. The scary part was that if you heard her scream really loud, like she was right next to you, it was ok because that meant she was really far away, but if it was soft and faint, then you better close your eyes, bury your face in your pillow, and pray to God.

Besides the green dragon costume and the scary movies and stories, the other good memories I have of Halloween are of ones that I can't believe I didn't serve some time in jail for, like my senior year in high school.

Before high school, our fun consisted of walking around at night and ding-dong-ditching houses, throwing rocks at kids riding by on their bicycles, running out into the middle of the street and acting like we were putting things down in front of approaching cars and then running off like hell. The worst was when we actually started breaking people's windows, which was terrifying but caused a huge rush. Each time it was Matt who would throw the rock, after Carlos, John and I egged him on. As he would prepare to throw, Carlos, John and I would take off running, laughing, scared as shit, and then all of a sudden you would hear the smash of a window breaking and then we would really freak out, turn around and see Matt running, waving his hands at us with his blond hair waving in the air. We would run across streets, into backyards, and then finally choose some good bushes to hide underneath. This was always at night of course, often during the week. My babysitter didn't give a shit, as long I was back in time for my mother to be there and pick us up, which wasn't until late. John's, Matt's, and Carlos' parents obviously didn't give a shit either. Carlos' dad was an alcoholic who ran off with a woman at some point, leaving Carlos and his five brothers living with his mom in this tiny house. John's parents were equally as fucked up—in fact, I never met his father, even though John insisted he lived with them—and his mother always walked around in her underwear smoking cigarettes and drinking vodka. Matt's father worked with the carnival—so he was never around, and he had some sort of major gambling problem.

You supposedly get smarter as you grow up, but in high school we started drinking, smoking pot, and driving, so it all got worse. I wasn't planning to dress up for Halloween my senior year, but my friends were planning to go out egging kids after school and thus decided to wear all black. This sounded fun, so I decided to join in. We wore black pants, black long-sleeved shirts, with black sweaters or hoodies, black hats or ski masks, and our black Reeboks or Addidas indoor soccer shoes. My friends were talking about how it was our right that year, being seniors, to go out and egg the freshmen—it was a tradition. The strange thing was, I never remembered me and my friends getting egged as freshmen. But suddenly it was a tradition and we were going to do it.

We talked John into driving his dad's car, and I was going to ride in it along with Matt and this guy Tony. Tony was more Matt's friend than ours. They were both on the wrestling team. Like Matt, Tony was built like hell, a good wrestler, and he was good looking and got laid a lot, or so he always said he did.

Matt and I ran out of the house when John pulled into my driveway to pick us up. Matt was all excited, and we told my mother we were going trick-or-treating. She was no longer working double shifts when I was a senior in high school and was generally home when we came home from school.

"Hey polack," Matt yelled as he approached John's car. Although it seemed like Matt used these racial slurs the most, we all generally used them on each other. Growing up in a salad bowl like Des Plaines there were plenty to go around. John was the polack, Jig the Hindu, Matt the Jewbag, Carlos and I were the spics (Tony was also technically a spic although no one but Matt ever called him that), Patrick was the mick, George the gyro, Eric and Nick were the wops or dagos.

All of our parents were born in their respective countries, grew up in their own traditions, came here at early ages, and struggled to learn English and American customs while living in Chicago. They first lived in one of the ethnic neighborhoods—like Logan Square, where we lived, or little Italy in the near southwest side, or Hinduville up north on Devon Avenue, or Jewville in Rogers Park, or Greektown just west of the Loop, or Polish town up on Central and Belmont. They then managed to move out to Des Plaines where we kids were free to mix it up. Des Plaines was a common destination for immigrants because it was close to the city, and back then it was affordable because it was so close to the airport, unlike the rich northern suburbs along the lake like Highland Park and Winnetka. When our parents set us loose in Des Plaines, we didn't know what the hell was going on and had little supervision because they worked all the time. So I guess we sort of made up our own traditions.

I remember learning about the "melting pot" versus "salad bowl" debate in our American History class. We would debate which metaphor best described America. Well, to us, growing up in Des Plaines was living proof that the "salad bowl" concept was indeed reality. Though we all generally got along, we constantly reminded each other of how different we were through the names we called each other.

Besides our group, there were plenty of other spics, polacks and Hindus in Des Plaines that hung out in their own little groups, lived in their own areas of the town, and spoke in their own languages. We barely ever talked to these kids. It was probably circumstantial; I mean, the friends that I had were simply because they were the kids in my neighborhood—my parents just happened to get a house in a part of Des Plaines where a bunch of other people were mixed in. I guess if we had lived in the part where all the other Mexicans lived, I would have been hanging out with them instead, and I'm sure

I would have had entirely different experiences. I had opportunities to hang out with other Mexican kids. I played soccer
with some of them and would speak Spanish with them, and
on some occasions went to their birthday parties—where we
would eat *carnitas* and *tamales* and there would be a *piñata*. But I
would more often than not shy away from these invitations and
they eventually got the hint. I was trying to assimilate so hard
that it got to the point that I, in turn, was being prejudicial. I
would even get called out on it. Once, this guy Manuel said to
me in broken English, when I didn't want to go with him to a
party with his Mexican friends, "What, you don't think you're
Mexican or something? Too cool to hang with us?"

By senior year, the similarities and differences between eth-
nicities among my friends blended in with the day-to-day noise.
"Al, get in the shotgun, I'll get in back and ride here with the
other spic Tony," Matt said to me outside of John's car before
he got in back.

Tony was of a mixed background, his mother apparently
was Cuban or something, and his father was white. I never met
his parents or talked much to him about them, and he didn't
know a word of Spanish. We only interacted with him when
we were with Matt. And then those interactions were limited
to greetings and conversations like "Who the hell are you guys
fucking nowadays?" or "Did you see that shit Noreen had on
the other day? Holy fuck man, I wanna tear that girl a new asshole," or "Drink up you pussies!! I didn't get this beer for you
fuck-wads to stare at and jack-off to."

"What's going on fuck-tits?" Tony asked us as a greeting.
Tony was one of those guys, of which there were many at
Maine West, that combined the word "fuck" with other words,

generally body parts, to make up swears.

"What about those fucking freshmen?" asked Tony.

"Yeah, we're going to egg their asses," Matt responded.

"Fuck yeah," said Tony.

"Where the fuck are we going?" asked John as he began to pull back out of the driveway.

"Dude, we're going to fucking Dominick's first. We gotta pick up some eggs 'n shit," responded Matt.

"You guys don't have any eggs yet?" asked Tony, acting surprised.

"No, you spic," said Matt, "we waited for your spic ass or else we knew we wouldn't get any money from you."

"Dude," said Tony as he was punching Matt in the arm, "you better stop calling me that or I'm gonna kick your Jew ass, me and Alex over here will, fucker."

"Yeah right, and then I'm going to fuck your girlfriend in the ass with my big Jewish cock," Matt responded and then they both punched each other a few more times in the shoulder while laughing. I always wondered whether those two would ever hook up.

So we were on our way to the Dominick's grocery store a few blocks away from Maine West. As we drove down Mannheim, past the Rosemont Horizon, and down further toward Leigh Street, Tony was telling us the plans. Certain freshmen were supposed to be trick-or-treating down by the school, off of these streets that were in between the McDonald's and Maine West, which would be perfect because the Dominick's was down the street from there. Tony knew where this group was going to be because some girl named Clarissa, who was a super cute freshman he was trying to "get on," told him. Apparently, he had worked it out so our car would hit this group over there, and then our other friends Pat, Eric, Nick and Carlos were going up to an area called the Villas to hit a group of freshmen there, with some others going over by Central Junior High. I had no idea such a plan had been laid out. We were off in our separate groups to make sure we hit a good portion of the freshmen fuckheads we wanted to get, and then we were supposed to meet back up at some park in the Villas—after which we were going to head over to our friend Pat's house for some beers and smokes. All this planning, and we didn't even have cell phones back then. We arrived at Dominick's on Oakton Street, and pulled into the huge parking lot that also served a Little Caesar's Pizza and other stores typically found in suburban strip malls. After we parked, Tony and Matt got out of the car and offered to go in and get the stuff. Matt had his black ski hat on the top of his head, and I think Tony had his tucked in one of his back-pockets. How stupid, I thought; it couldn't have been more conspicuous, more obvious. It looked worse when they both came out of the store with big smiles on, each carrying four cartons of eggs, Matt with a bag of other stuff hanging from one of his arms.

"Dudes," said Tony as they were getting up to the car, "open the fucking trunk." John smiled, shaking his head, and popped open the trunk. They put the eggs in, and then got back into the car.

"What you got in the other bag?" John asked them as they got in, as he was starting up the car.

"Dude, we got some fucking balloons and whipped cream," Matt said as he and Tony were laughing, snorting, and taking the stuff out of the bag.

"What are the balloons for dude?"

"Here, we're gonna fill them up with whipped cream and then smash them over some freshman's head," said Matt as he starting demonstrating for us, as John yelled back at to him to be careful and not get any on the car seat because his dad would get pissed.

"What about those condoms?" I asked as John drove out of the parking lot and toward Maine West.

"Those are for when Matt fucks John later on tonight," said Tony, and we all started to laugh, except for John, who put up the middle finger sign at them, shaking his head as he continued to drive.

"No asshole, don't worry about them, I had to pick some shit up for the side," and then Matt put them away. So they continued blowing up balloons and filling them up with the whip cream.

We parked behind some other car, next to some bushes, and then Tony and Matt got out of the car and went around back to the trunk and came back with plastic bags filled up with eggs. We were on a normal side street lined with little ranch style houses typical of that area of Des Plaines.

At first, the plan was that we would all proceed on foot carrying our bags, and as we saw freshmen we would egg them and then circle back and meet at the car. But we debated what to do if we didn't get back at the same time, and what to do with the balloons—and also, if we needed to run, we would likely break the eggs. We were leaning toward staying with John and the car, driving around and throwing shit from the car as we saw kids, or having a few of us get out, hitting them, and then getting back into the car so we could split. Then all of a sudden Tony saw some freshmen walking down the sidewalk on the other side of the street.

"Holy shit, look, it's that little Mac fucker, and his little fuck buddies, and those little bitches…"

"Where?" Matt asked.

"Over there, fuck-tit, on the other side of the street," Tony responded, now whispering, and we all looked over, watching them walk down the street. It must have been 7 p.m., but it was completely dark. There hardly were any more trick-or-treaters out. Most of the young kids had already gone home with their parents, and now it was just the older kids—like these freshmen—out walking around just for the sake of staying out late on a school night.

"Here," said Tony, and he started to gather eggs in his hands and in a plastic bag and said to Matt, "I'll get some fucking eggs, you grab some of these balloons and some eggs; let's go." Matt then grabbed a bunch of the balloons and a bag of eggs and they got out of the car with Tony whispering, "We'll be right back, John you fuck-shit. Keep the car running and get the car over to that street there and get ready to get the fuck out of here." And so they got out and scurried across the street like two undercover spies or something. They both had their masks down, and John and I put our masks down also.

John backed up and slowly turned the car around to head to the spot where Tony said to go and slowed to a stop on the corner. You could hear the car running, the radio slightly although it was turned down low, and really nothing much else. The street was dark, lit only by the lights from peoples' homes. A few minutes went by, maybe five, and we heard no sounds.

I kept looking back but saw nothing, so I decided I would get out and see what was up while John stayed in the car.

I slunk down like a burglar as I got out of the car, stopping to look if anyone was around. I then went past the car and out to the corner of the street and looked to where Matt and Tony had gone. It was dark down the street and at first I couldn't really see or hear anything, but then I started hearing various voices and other noises and all of a sudden I saw a black shape up ahead. It was Matt running down the street toward me, waving his hand motioning to go back, like when we were little kids after smashing a window. So I turned around and ran back to the car, got in and slammed the door shut, and looked back around to the street.

John was asking what the hell was going on as Matt suddenly came around the corner and did a roll-over across the front hood—like people do in action movies—which was completely unnecessary, but he landed on his feet on the other side and got in, and John shook his head.

"Holy shit," he was saying, turning back looking for Tony. His mask was halfway up his face, some of his blond hair sticking out, and he was covered in whipped cream and maybe some egg as well, but I couldn't quite see.

"Dude, what the fuck?" I asked, "What happened? Where's Tony?"

"John, back the car up, let's see if Tony's coming, otherwise we might have to take off," said Matt, ignoring my question.

"What the fuck's going on?" asked John as he backed the car up, but Matt continued to ignore us as he looked back out toward the street. As we got closer to the intersection, we saw

Tony sprinting down the sidewalk, full steam ahead. It wasn't clear if anyone was running behind Tony but we heard other noises, even sirens or something. John kept asking what the fuck was going on, when suddenly Tony came running closer to the door, not slowing down, and then jumped up and dove straight through the back window, which was only half-way down, shattering it. He landed on Matt, and John and I looked back in shock.

"Holy shits" and "what the fucks" were being thrown around by all of us, with Matt holding onto Tony.

"Get the fuck out of here!!" yelled Tony as John kept asking what the fuck was going on. "Just go, you moron!" Tony yelled and then we started taking off down the street. We were finally cruising down the street when John was like "Where the fuck are we going? Dude, you fucking broke my dad's car window!!"

"Holy shit, man," was what Tony kept saying in the back. "We need to get somewhere to clean this shit up," he said as they were both wiping off the glass and shit that was all over. Surprisingly no one got cut.

"Dude, go to the McDonald's," was Matt's idea where to go and clean off. So, in our grand wisdom, we headed back out toward Oakton and toward the McDonald's.

From conversations that occurred later and after that night, we discerned that Matt and Tony decided to follow the freshmen down the street as the kids stopped at houses to trick-or-treat. When they felt like they hit a good spot, they both busted out yelling "Fuck you, freshmen!" and Tony started throwing eggs and Matt balloons—the first smashing this kid on the head, and the next exploding in his hands as he was getting ready to throw it.

After Matt ran out of the balloons, he started throwing eggs. The kids started running down the street with Tony and Matt chasing after them winging eggs as they ran, when all of a sudden a bunch of other freshmen turned the corner and teamed up with the first kids and held their ground. Although heavily outnumbered, Matt and Tony, who were much bigger, continued throwing eggs. All of a sudden Matt and Tony realized that the freshmen were throwing rocks—one hitting Tony on the shoulder as he ducked.

"Motherfuckers! I'm going to kick your mother-fucking asses!!" Tony said he was yelling as he started coming out onto the street, dropping the remaining eggs, walking toward the kids who were still throwing rocks, but now they crept backwards, some of them starting to run. Then Matt decided to pick up a big-ass rock he saw on the ground and whip it across the street at the group of kids. He threw the rock way too hard and over the kids' heads and straight back into the windshield of a parked car.

"I just started fucking running man," Matt said.

"I saw the fucking rock go over my head and into that fucking car," Tony said, "but I was fucking pissed, so I started running after those fucking freshmen who started running like little pussies when they saw that fucking rock smash through the fucking window, little fuckers, it was Carl and Sam those little fucking pricks, I can't wait to kick their little fucking asses..." Tony said that he started chasing the kids but then stopped when he thought he heard sirens in the background and turned around and started running back to the car.

As we were pulling into the McDonald's parking lot, John was in shock, shaking his head with a perplexed smile on his face, which he usually had when he was annoyed—and this must have really fucking annoyed him.

We pulled into a spot right across from the drive-through lane, next to the K-Mart parking lot—totally visible from Oakton which was fairly busy at that time of night—and got out to start cleaning the glass out of the car. Tony and Matt were full of eggs and whipped cream; we were all still dressed in black, with our black hats on the top of our heads, and with John cursing out loud about how fucked up this all was, how crazy it was that Tony had jumped through the window, all we had to do was stop and quickly open the door, which wouldn't have taken him that long, and Tony telling him to fuck off, that he had no idea it was half way up and that anyway, he would take care of it. As we did this—with the suburbanite adults and teenagers going through the drive-through, and the kids working it staring at us—a cop car pulled in and flashed its lights and made that obnoxious siren sound.

We stared at the cop car, then at each other, as the two police officers got out asking us to move away from the car. The thing I remember most was looking at Matt, who was softly saying, "Holy shit," as the cops arrived, almost oblivious to the fact he was still wearing his black ski mask. It was so stupid, but funny. I almost started laughing right then and there. I always want to laugh when something bad is happening, to me or people with me—I can't help it. The funniest thing about that night was that no one objected to the fact that we decided to go a public place like the McDonald's parking lot literally a few blocks away from where the egging and the car window smashing took place to try and regroup and clean our shit up. We might as well have driven straight to the damn police station. There were friends' places we could have driven to, even to one of our houses, anywhere, except where we went. I guess we were shocked and panicked or something, or maybe it was just that we were 17 and stupid.

The two police officers interrogated us individually to get our stories. I don't quite remember what I said; just that we were out trick-or-treating, and that yeah, we were egging some kids, but that they were also egging us and that it was all in good fun. I didn't mention the car windshield that Matt broke with the rock, and neither did anyone else. When they asked about John's window I said that a kid threw a rock at it as we were driving to the McDonald's, which is why we pulled over there. I remember Tony and Matt trying to give us the big wink of the eye as John and I were taking our turn being interrogated. It must have worked, because after calling us dumb and lucky because no one had gotten hurt by the broken window of John's car, they made us finish cleaning up the glass from the parking lot with brooms and shovels that some of the McDonald's staff brought out for us. They made us throw the remaining eggs away and promise that we would go home. It was embarrassing as the people going through the drive-through stared and pointed at us, some of them people who we knew—and thus the whole episode made for good conversation at school the next couple of days. But nothing ever happened about the car window Matt broke. The cops didn't ask about it. Apparently one of the cops knew Tony's older brothers from his old high school wrestling days, and maybe that helped.

As we were leaving, we were all in higher spirits because we didn't get our assess dragged into the police station. Tony continued to reassure John about the broken window, telling him to "chill his Polish ass down," and we decided to go meet up with the rest of our friends at the originally scheduled spot.

"My dad's car window is smashed!" John yelled, to which Matt started saying that we would figure out a way to put something on it that night over at Pat's so it could be driven the next day. Tony also said he knew this guy who would put on a new window for cheap and that he would take care of it. I even started chiming in that it was ok, we only live once, it was our senior year, and next thing you know John was hesitantly agreeing to go—so we headed in the direction of the Villas. John even offered the idea that we should take side streets and try avoiding the major thoroughfares, to which we all agreed was fucking smart, with Tony patting John on the shoulder saying, "That's fucking smart thinking dude, let's go man, fuck those cops."

Pat, Carlos, Eric, Nick, George, and a few others were all at the park when we pulled up, most of them with beers in hand. We got out, all excited, especially Tony and Matt, who ran up laughing, telling them what had happened. They huddled around the broken window to check it out, and some of them patted John on the back as he shook his head. Although it was a school night, it didn't matter, because none of us really knew what the hell the concept of a curfew was. We agreed to go back to Pat's house so they could try to tape up cardboard over the broken window in order to at least block out the cold wind so his dad could drive the car to work the next day. John was still bothered about what he was going to tell his dad. We all told him to say the same thing we told the cops, that some kids through a rock through the window, and we tried to chase them down but that there was nothing we could do.

After crafting the story and seeing the cardboard up and taped to the door, John felt better about the whole thing and even started to drink a beer himself and started laughing about the whole incident. We all did, with Tony and Matt telling the story from different perspectives, how crazy it was that Tony was horizontal as he leapt from the sidewalk and through the window, like he was fucking Superman. If the window really was down it wouldn't have been as sweet. It was like a stunt shot from a movie. Then they all started talking about how much money could be made in doing stunts, that, as Tony had proved that night, it was pretty damn easy, and for a little bit, there brewed a serious discussion about how we should fuck college and instead pursue careers as stunt doubles, or at least models or something.

After a few beers and a joint in Pat's garage, we decided to head back out and see what kind of shit we could start, possibly kick the asses of those little freshmen if we could find them. Instead we did some ding-dong ditching just for old time's sake. Now that we were grown, we were faster and thus were willing to take more risks—like having one of the guys ring the doorbell then go and hide in the bushes and wait for someone to open the door, then jump and scream—freaking the hell out of the person and then taking off like hell down the street, with the rest of us hiding across the street behind cars, trying hard like hell not to laugh our asses off.

The worst was just before the night ended.

Someone had the great idea to take a garbage can, partly fill it with garbage, piss, beer, water, shit, and stuff like that, and put it up against someone's door, tilted against it, so when they opened the door the can would fall inside the house. And we were all like, "No fucking way man!! That's awesome!!!" Well, most of us were, especially Tony and Matt who started immediately looking for a can and suggesting we also fill it up with windshield wiper fluid, oil, anything from the garage.

The idea sort of bothered me, and I wanted to voice my opinion against it, but I didn't. I mean, having the can fall inside someone's goddamned house? John was opposing this idea—he was always the sensible one—saying that it was stupid and we should just get out of there and call it a night, but he was called a pussy and told to help gather shit up and help, which he did.

We decided to try this on Mr. Olsen's house. He lived near Pat and was the father of this girl Vicki that was a stuck-up bitch, and he was considered to be an old fucking asshole for calling the cops on Pat's parties and just being a son-of-a-bitch in general. "That son-of-bitch," Pat was saying as we were filling the can up in the back of his garage. We put all sorts of shit in there, water, beer, car fluids, garbage. Carlos was asked to take a shit for it, but he refused to, so then Pat decided to go get some dog shit from his neighbor's yard and throw it in. We then realized we hadn't thought about how to get the thing over to the house. Someone suggested putting it in a car in the back seat or trunk, but no one wanted to volunteer their car. We then decided that two of us would carry it down the street and put it outside the door and ring the bell. Pat and Tony volunteered to do it. And so they started off down the sidewalk, with the rest of us walking on the other side of the street, then as we got to the house, we hid right across from it so we could watch. We got there ahead of Pat and Tony, who stumbled along with the can, going quietly, and having to duck out of the way a couple of times as cars drove by. I remember sitting there and suddenly seeing them stumble along the sidewalk with the can in between them, each one with a hand on one of the handles. It's amazing that no one busted us preparing all this, but then again, those suburban streets were so quiet and dark at night that you could fucking hold a drug sale and no one would notice.

They walked right across the front lawn toward the house. We could see lights from the living room window and the faint glare from a television, so someone was home for certain. We were all nervously laughing to ourselves as they got up close to the door. Pat opened the screen door with one hand, and they set the can on the welcome mat and leaned the top of the can against the door as planned. We were all planning to sit there and watch what happened, but after Tony rang the bell a couple of times and Pat knocked on the door, they started running like hell along the bushes back the way they came; we all, without even talking about it, also got up and started running like hell. We didn't see what happened. I remember just running, as fast as I could, pulling ahead of everyone and not even looking back until I turned into Pat's yard and the side door of the garage that we had left open. I went in and found Pat and Tony inside, gasping for breath. The others soon came in after me. Pat and Tony asked us if we saw Mr. Olsen open the door and then called us pussies for having run, and we told them to fuck off. We then decided to get into someone's car and take a drive around the block, past the house to see what was going on.

We took Nick's car, and I rode in the back with Pat and Tony, with Matt up in the front, but all of us crouched down so we couldn't be seen. We drove down the street, and nearing the house we started laughing under our breath with Tony saying, "Dudes, just look straight ahead." I remember having a sick feeling inside as I saw Mr. Olsen standing in front of his house with a robe and slippers on. You could see his wife-beater, beer belly and hairy chest. His gray hair was all disheveled, and he was looking pissed as hell and holding a baseball bat in his one hand, just standing there as if surveying the land to get a sight of the fuckers who did that to his house. He stared at the car as we drove by and kept staring at it as we drove off, sort of walking toward it. As we got farther away, everyone was like "Holy shit, did you see the look on that fucker's face?" but no one was really laughing anymore. We decided to get back to Pat's and to get everyone the fuck out of there before the cops came or something.

After getting back to Pat's, Matt, Tony, John, and I loaded into John's car and headed home. I sort of felt sick in the stomach thinking of Mr. Olsen standing there looking at our car driving by. I thought we would get pulled over again but we did not. Tony and Matt kept laughing about the night. I felt like a big fucking asshole, I mean, what the fuck? That must have felt like shit to that old man, you know? He had probably been asleep on his recliner watching the news or something and had to put a robe on and open the fucking door, only to have a garbage can full of a bunch of shit come falling down, possibly on him, and onto his floor.

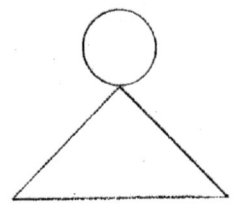

God, Books, and Good Looks

So, why the hell don't adults talk about anything inter-esting anyway? Or maybe it's just the ones I know, but really, what the fuck?

Why can't we talk about things like religion, death, life, aliens, or planets and not be considered weird? Why do we al-ways have to talk about sports and the weather instead? For once, I would love to have a conversation with someone about something substantive, like we did when we were children. I'd like to discuss questions like: Does death scare you? Do you really believe when you die you are going to Heaven or Hell? What is Heaven or Hell? When you die are you going to have a split second, or maybe a few minutes, to scramble and remem-ber as much as you can about your life, the impact you had on others, your secrets, your regrets, your accomplishments and abandoned dreams? Are you going to fear that your life was empty and that you're leaving nothing for anyone to truly re-member you by? What are you going to do with the minutes, if you're lucky enough to have any, leading up to your death? Will you be courageous, or will you freak out and end this life like a crying baby enters it? What if there is no eternal being there waiting to greet you, and all of sudden every moment you've lived, every laugh, every tragic encounter, is forgotten except by the few friends and family that are left to remember you—but who only remember a relatively small percentage of your moments, only the ones they had the opportunity to share with you, and soon they will forget them? And think about the small percentage that your remaining family members and friends comprise of the five or six or seven billion people on the planet—it's such a small percentage that you might as well not ever have even existed. How does your perspective on these thoughts affect the way you live your life? If this is what you believe, does it make you cower and want to give up and think that nothing matters, or does it somehow inspire you?

Or maybe there really is a God waiting, and we'll live for-ever and ever. I've often wondered how many people actually believe that they continue on in an eternal life, even the ones that say they do. I'm sure there are people who literally believe this, so much so that it becomes a reality for them, allowing them to let go of petty desires like sex, drugs, alcohol so they can concentrate on doing all the good things. For the majority though, people like me, belief in a religion seems more like an excuse to lead a mediocre life, full of human vices, and justify that it's okay because there's nothing to be afraid of because there will be something better after we die. It's almost as if we secretly know that the notion of eternal life is bullshit, or something we can't comprehend, so instead of trying to understand whether it's real, we live on and just kind of hope that there's something better afterward.

When asked if they believe in God, most of my friends usually respond by saying, "Sure I do, why not? You have nothing to lose by believing in it. If it's true, and you're a believer, you go to Heaven and it's great. But if you're not a believer, you go to Hell and that would suck, right? If it's not true at all, then none of it matters. So you're better off just believing and hedging your bets."

They have a certain point. But the problem with this position for me is that only believing in God as a way to "hedge your bets" prevents you from making the most of life. Why? Because if you really, really believed in Heaven, and were concerned about not making it there, wouldn't you live every moment conscious of that, trying your hardest to make it there? I sure would.

It kills me that we all have similar concerns about this kind of stuff, but we barely talk about them. It pisses me off that the only real conversations I can remember having like this were when I was young.

I know I fail to take strong positions on these topics. I like to think that I'm taking chances, but here I am—a fucking accountant, on a plane from Chicago to Philadelphia to work with some more accountants, all scrambling and working really hard to prove a point to our supervisors and make more money.

The thing is, I think I know what I believe in, but I have a hard time sharing it with others. I tend to believe that this is our only shot, and we need to grasp on to this life and live it, let go of petty issues and desires because in the end they're not important. I also like to think that if there is something like God, or a "higher power," that we'll never be able to fully understand it and therefore we shouldn't try to interpret it because it's a completely different form of existence. It's like trying to explain yourself to a cockroach; it'll never be able to understand what you are. Therefore, it makes sense to not believe in a singular religion, let go of petty shit, and just focus on enjoying our creativity and working hard.

But I can't take the full plunge. Soon after I have such thoughts they fade away, and there I am, back to worrying about stuff like girls all the time. And I can't stop enjoying simple things like cigarettes, food, alcohol, weed, and sex. I'm way too fucking vain. I keep thinking I'm too shy, too dim-witted, too dull, that my arms are too skinny, my head too big, my stomach too flabby.

I'm told that I dwell too much on the negative; I don't give anyone, or even myself, enough credit. I'm basically a crabby bastard most of the time.

The world does have its nice qualities, and I even have some good qualities myself, I suppose.

I'm generally nice to people although I'm a bit quiet.

I like to read, but I hardly ever remember what the hell I read. I say that *The Sun Also Rises* is one of my favorite books, but the only character I seem to remember is The Lady Brett Ashley because I thought she was hot and wanted to fuck her. And I remember the young Spanish Matador, Pedro—whom she hooks up with—because I wish I was him. But I don't remember the poor sap that is the chief character, the American guy who had his penis blown off during the war and is in love with Brett. She sort of loves him too but can't have a real relationship with him because he doesn't have the goods to deliver what she really wants.

And then there's *Love in the Time of Cholera* by Gabriel Garcia Marquez, probably my favorite book. It's a classic, funny love story about a young man, Florentino Ariza, and his lifelong dedication to his love for Fermina Daza. They fall in love, but she's from a wealthier class and marries the prominent Dr. Urbino. Regardless though, Florentino dedicates his life to waiting for her and it's not until they're in their 80s and Dr. Urbino has died that he finally renews his courtship of her. In the meantime, in order to preserve himself, he has the best diet and has sex with countless women, with the justification that he's keeping his body intact for when his reunion with Fermina has arrived. I like that philosophy, have often declared Florentino to be my role model.

My favorite line of any movie may well be John Cusack's line when he played Rob Gordon, the neurotic record store owner in *High Fidelity*, when he's reflecting on his intelligence and the books he has read: "I've read books like *Love in the Time of Cholera* and *The Unbearable Lightness of Being…* they're about girls, right?" Well, I think he was right, they were about girls.

I like to think of myself as having many interests in music, the arts, literature, philosophy, but really, much like Rob Gordon, I always end up thinking about girls.

You know, what really fascinates me about girls, and guys for that matter, is trying to understand what they are really looking for in a mate. In my experiences, it seems like most guys and girls I know are generally interested in looks at first.

However, when asked what they're looking for, people will usually say that they're not interested in looks, that personality matters—even good-looking people say that. However, the good-looking people that say that, in my experience, are generally ones that have been hurt by other good-looking people.

I've known many good-looking girls who, at any first sign of adoration from a good-looking guy, fall for them as well. No matter what background, such as the barely-out-of-school, struggling-salesman guy my beautiful sister married (he's good looking and funny, but a total idiot), and the great-looking-but-fucking-asshole guy that this girl Heather I knew dated. Heather used to always tell me that maybe they weren't soul mates because she felt uncomfortable talking to him about things like life or death, but she had never met someone who adored her as unselfishly as he did—and she always talked about how hot he was. So she continued to date him, until he finally left her pregnant for someone else. The whole point is that she and my sister, both smart and beautiful, fell in love with guys just for their good looks.

This hot Polish girl Asia I worked with used to tell me that that's what girls see in me, my great personality; I always interpreted that as her telling me I wasn't good enough looking for her. There are quite a few guys I can think of that have great personalities that are not the best looking guys but have pretty good-looking girlfriends. However, now to think of it, the guys I'm thinking of really aren't that bad looking at all. They might be a little overweight, short or something, but they seem to have a degree of those certain features that are the core to being good looking: a well proportioned face, narrow eyes, etc.—and they're usually pretty successful in some sort of way.

Either way—looks or personality—I feel like I always fall short. Girls that are into personalities don't like me because I'm really dry when they first meet me. I'm the worst small-talker I know. When people around me are cracking jokes and everyone else around is responding with laughter and jokes of their own, I force myself to laugh because half the time I don't catch on to what the fuck was funny. I'm just not interested in what people are usually talking about and am usually drifting off to who knows where while everyone else around is chatting away about who knows what.

I often try to play off the image of the sensitive guy, who is interested in all sorts of things, like I'm a modern renaissance man or something. Half the time I get called out on it. Like this time I was at a bar the night of John's bachelor party. I was drunk and talking to this girl, and she was not in the mood to talk, particularly to me. But she was there, and I thought I would try and talk to her anyway. When she wasn't having any of it, I tried to pull out the sweet talker, with my pouting face and all that. After a bit, she simply said, "Oh, please don't give me any of that shit. Your 'sweet sensitive' face. Sorry honey that simply doesn't work for me." And that was that.

However, there have been plenty of times where the act has worked, starting in high school. I honestly think I'm more sensitive than the average guy. I know this due to my conversations and experiences with all my guy friends. For example, I like the book and the movie *The English Patient*, which is generally a big no-no with guys. I loved *Lost in Translation* by Sophia Coppola, which most of my guy friends thought was stupid. Carlos, one of my few Des Plaines friends who still lives in Chicago, hated it and fell asleep during it. Then again, I'm comparing myself to guys who are destined to be the heart of suburban America, members of the Republican Party, and heirs to the torch of conservatism. I'm sure there are plenty of other dudes out there who like stuff like *Lost in Translation*—I just don't know many of them.

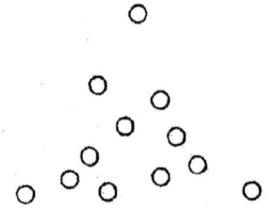

Theme Songs

"I am, I am, I am Superman, I can do anything," goes the R.E.M song, "Superman." I've liked to say that should be my theme song, you know, the song that should play the instant I enter a room, any room, especially at a party or something like that. It's pretty simple, with a catchy beat and chorus. The person singing is in love—in a kind of love that makes him feel invincible, so much so that he would do anything, travel any distance, do any heroic act to be with the person he's in love with. I guess I like that song because I wish I could be that way. I wish I could've done whatever was necessary with girls I've wanted to be with, or in the many other instances when I've seemed to share a glance with a pretty girl on the El or at a bar, but instead of trying anything, I've just looked the other way.

Everyone should have a theme song, or a few of them for different occasions. One for when you feel like shit, or depressed, like after you've been dumped or have had your heart broken, which in my case would be "Don't Know What You've Got" by Cinderella, or "Pictures of You" by the Cure, or any Elliot Smith song. You should have a song for when you don't give a shit—when you feel like everything around you is all bullshit, commercialized, like "Signs" by Tesla. I love that line "Signs, signs, everywhere there's signs, fucking up the scenery, breaking my mind…"

Other songs would be appropriate for when you're just feeling good, glad, as in my case, to be a heterosexual male and that women are as beautiful as they are. Songs that fall under this category for me would be "All Right Now" by Free, "Sweet Cherry Pie" by Warrant, "She's Got the Look That Kills" by Motley Crue, and "Girls" by The Beastie Boys.

In my days as a financial auditor, I worked with this girl who was a manager like me. I told her that "Sweet Child of Mine" by Guns N' Roses was her theme song one time when we were out drinking and that it should play whenever she walked into a room. She giggled and thought it was cute. I told her it was appropriate because she's a sweet, blonde, wholesome Midwestern girl from a small town in downstate Illinois, but that the song also has this, you know, hard-rock edge, and so it rounded her out. I more thought it was appropriate because of how pretty she was. She had this warm face and the most perfect set of teeth that you'll ever see, true pearly whites. She had bright blue eyes; that's why when Axl Rose sings: "She's got eyes of the bluest skies that if they thought of rain, I'd hate to look into those eyes and see an ounce of pain," I swear he was writing about her. I obviously had a crush on her, but I never told her nor did anything about it because I never thought I would be her type; she needed someone much more straightforward and disciplined than I could ever be. She was much smarter than me, took her job way more seriously, will probably be a CEO or some shit like that some day.

Some of my friends have named classic theme songs for themselves. Like Jig, who is Indian, used to say that the song "Black Betty" by the band Ram Jam should play every time he walked to the plate to bat on our championship softball team. I don't know why this was his song, but I guess it has something to do with Jig being dark skinned and having a big butt. One of our friends back in Des Plaines had Jig be one of his groomsmen and actually had "Black Betty" play as Jig and his counterpart made their entrance, which I thought was pretty fucking funny. My friend John always said that "Eggman" by the Beastie Boys was his theme song; I guess it had something to do with the fact that he was a little white guy who liked rap, but I always preferred "Shorty the Pimp," by Too Short for him. Matt would say that his theme song was "Ride the Lighting" by Metallica because that's what girls would feel like while they were having sex with him.

My old boss—a former college football player for the University of Alabama, a big southern boy who became a CPA after his bid for a professional football career never materialized, one of the smartest-yet-silliest accountants I've ever met— used to say that his theme song would be either "Fat Bottomed Girls" by Queen, or "Baby Got Back" by Sir Mix-a-Lot. Both of which I thought were appropriate; you'd understand if you met him.

He and I used to joke around that we should have a boom box in his office in order to play different songs for different meetings we were having, like have sleek dance music playing softly, as an undercurrent, as we had our meetings to discuss which accounting pronouncement was more applicable to this or that scenario, kind of like we were being filmed for an *Alias*-like TV series on the days and lives of accountants. We would also pick theme songs for different people as they came walking into his office. You know, like we would have "Iron Man" by Black Sabbath play when the angry, crew-cut, die-hard-George-Bush-supporter, accounting manager guy would come into his office all angry about something.

(I later found out that the angry accounting manager's favorite band was the BoDeans, the fucking BoDean's! Apparently that's all he listens to in his car.)

We also liked "Touch Myself" by Divinyls or "Look What the Cat Dragged In" by Poison whenever our long-legged, big-breasted, southern blonde assistant would come in, and "I'm Too Sexy" when the gay vice president we worked with walked in.

The long-legged southern blonde talked with quite a southern twang and told me that her theme song was "Legs" by ZZ Top one night while we were in bed—which I agreed was definitely appropriate, better than my initial selection for her, "You Shook Me All Night Long" by AC/DC. She dated me, or rather slept with me a few times, while my former boss was still married and unavailable. She dumped me as soon as my boss started having marital problems. I'm not bitter about it at all; they make a much better couple than she and I would any day.

Asia, the hot Polish girl I used to work with, had come to Chicago from New York to work at our company. She was born and raised in Poland, had her MBA from Columbia University, and was smart as hell. Asia was a real Eastern European beauty, with long black hair, big arc-like eyebrows, and almond-shaped, entrancing eyes with long eyelashes. She always had this smirk on her face that told you no matter what you said or tried, she already had you figured out. I went through pains to try and get her to talk to me. We finally started hanging out, going out for drinks, going out to dinners. I finally told her one night that I was crazy for her, really enjoyed her company, hoped it would continue and would evolve into something else, to which she responded in her semi-broken English "Oh, I'm sorry Alex, I didn't mean to lead you on, I only thought that we were friends, that's all." I then said that my feelings were meant only in the sense of friendship, so she shouldn't worry—then I felt like an ass the rest of the night. I gave her "Lucy in the Sky with Diamonds" as her theme song.

The crazy thing about working in a corporate office is you're forced to be with all sorts of people from all sorts of different backgrounds, all day, sitting in front of a computer, with a phone to one side, drawers and cabinets to another, pencils and pens in a cup thingy, pictures of dogs, family, friends, or whatever, hanging up to remind you of why you're there, staring off at another person who is sitting next to you all day also, and sometimes you catch them picking their nose.

You go to meetings to discuss all sorts of mindless, boring stuff, where people take notes, agree to hand out tasks, debate over and over about who knows what, take turns writing on the stupid whiteboards. The most exciting part of the day is discussing what should be ordered in for lunch or dinner—whether to have sandwiches from Potbelly's or salads from So-prafina, or get crazy and order Chinese. Everyone then goes home, often late, to their families, by themselves or to another person, and comes back the next day to do it all again, just to earn a living. In fact that's usually what we say to each other before leaving: "Ready to do it all again tomorrow?" All day we write memos, create spreadsheets, graphs, flowcharts, and PowerPoint presentations. We review these materials over and over, debating whether the bullet points are succinct enough, getting to the point fast enough, drawing in the audience's attention, whether we should use italics here or bold font there, a colon here or semicolon there. We then have to get up and present this stuff to a room full of highly overpaid white males, with women and minorities sprinkled in for good taste.

We have these "teaming" meetings and events in which we think of ideas as to how make everyone feel more involved, part of a family, I guess in order to increase morale and thus productivity. I mean, what the fuck, right? When not in meetings, I sit there and stare at the screen half the time, look at the cursor flash, move the mouse around, stare at my online calendar, at the clock, open up Internet browsers and see the same headlines over and over again on CNN, about the President saying this or that, more soldiers and militants dying in Iraq or Afghanistan, and then go back to my flashing cursor. I know I should feel blessed to have the career that I have, the money I have, but it's a miracle I haven't picked up my laptop and thrown it against the windows of our 55th floor as I've daydreamed about many times.

When I leave my corporate accounting job, if ever I do—but I hope to God I do—I'd want "Give Me the Beat Boys" by Doby Gray playing as I'm leaving and saying goodbye to the good corporate people I've known, wishing them well on chasing down their dreams, finding that perfect accounting standard, running that perfect meeting or writing that masterpiece memo. I'd relish those lyrics: "Give me the beat boys that frees my soul, I want to get lost in your rock and roll and drift away," as I left one last time.

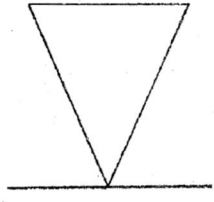

Steady Benefits

I was not as cool in junior high school as I was in grade school, and I was not that cool in high school either, though I had my moments. This Mexican girl, Monica, who had big boobs, especially for an 11-year-old, used to grab my ass in the sixth grade and say things like "Alex, how come you have such a big bulge in your pants?" But later in junior high school, after my parents divorced and I was not so cool anymore, she said "Man, you used to be so cool, and now you're such a nerd, what happened to you?"

Kids are rough.

Losing my confidence as a result of my parents' divorce might have saved me, or that's what I like to think. I could've skipped college, had children with different women, been married and divorced a few times by now. I think I was always susceptible to those kinds of tragedies, but I did things like study, read, listen to music, draw, paint and write—and for the most part stayed out of trouble. On the other hand, maybe I didn't experience all that I could have if I let myself go a little more. I often feel that I could have been successful in an artistic role. However, it seems like every time I start to veer toward those pursuits, I'm pulled back by my need to be accepted and to be "normal." It's like being born into a blue-collar, middle-class society is like being born with a leash around your neck that always tugs at you, then at last you become tired of pulling and settle down in your suburban home with its big fat grill, or you completely freak out and have a midlife crisis.

While John, Amy, Jig and I were in California on a trip to see the Cubs play, we started speaking with this guy at a restaurant in Santa Monica who was a freelance graphic designer. He was on his lunch hour at the time, drinking what appeared to be his fourth beer of the afternoon. We spoke about his job and life there. He recently worked on the *Nemo* film and was currently working for Honda, helping to illustrate advertisements.

"You know, moving pixels around and shit," he said, and then asked, "So, what do you do?"

After staring at each other for a bit before responding to his question, as we usually did when people asked us what we did for a living, I said, "Oh, the three of us are accountants, and John over here, is well, we're not really sure."

It seems like we always pause when asked what we do for a living, perhaps because we're all ashamed of what we do—except when we're around only each other. With each other we can talk about our careers for hours and you'd think we worked for the government as secret agents or some shit. But around others we're always ashamed to admit we are accountants. In public settings, like at a comedy club, I always dread being called on and asked what I do for a living because I know how boring it sounds when I describe it. It sucks to have a career that you're ashamed of. I've more and more felt a yearning to do something more tangible, like be a contractor, to build stuff. But a contractor friend of mine always says he'd love to do what I do, to sit in a nice office in front of a computer all day. So, who knows, right?

"I work for a large benefits plan administrator. We manage the retirement and health benefits plans for some of the largest companies in the country," answered John, in his proud tone. After the guy kind of stared at him quizzically for a bit, John added "I manage project teams."

"Yeah, pretty much boring shit like us accountants," I interjected trying to make fun of what we did.

"I see," answered the California dude. "But hey, you know, there is something to be said about a steady check and benefits man."

"Is that all we do, us people who are accountants and stuff like that?" Amy asked out loud as she took a sip from her beer. "We just work for corporations to get money, steady money, and hope for the steady progression, with hopes of making more money?" It was like she had a grand epiphany there on the shores of the Pacific.

And that's just it. As part of the middle class, we work to scrape out a decent stream of money so we can find a partner and reproduce, to keep the body of the human race going. It's like the brains of the human race are held by the few individuals who are able to express what we all think and feel, and John, Amy, Jig, and I—and all those other CPAs, heath plan administrators, human resource managers, executive recruiters, blue collar laborers—just keep the body up and keep it going, and we collect our steady paychecks and benefits.

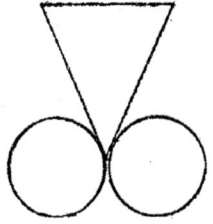

Miki

On a winter night in 2000, after we survived the turn of the century and the imminent collapse of society, I was at the Field Museum in downtown Chicago with a crowd of other CPAs and finance "professionals" from PricewaterhouseCoopers, where I worked. We were all dressed in our suits and dresses, drinking wine, mixed drinks, or beer, and talking with big smiles on our faces about all sorts of shit, like bad work stories and happy hour drunken escapades, without any notice of the treasures that the museum holds. I was with my girlfriend at the time, Erica, whom I didn't really like but was too much of a wimp to break-up with. I always dwelled on how I would be breaking her heart if I did. We knew each other because we both worked at the same firm, saw each other at the same after-work drinking events, and frankly she was blonde, cute, and seemingly harmless. At first I thought she was fun—she liked to cook and drink beer, watch football, have sex and all that. I was lonely, horny and thought I wanted to have a girlfriend—it had been a long time.

Next thing you know we'd been dating a year; people began asking me when I was going to propose, and I thought that my worst nightmares were coming true.

So there I was at the Field Museum with Erica, answering questions like, "So, what are you working on nowadays? Are you and Erica going anywhere nice this spring? When are you guys getting engaged?" Blah, blah, blah…

While we were standing in a group of people, this girl Miki, who I had known for a while through work and who was a good friend of Erica's—and who was tall and striking—came walking toward me. Her big watery eyes locked directly on mine.

She sort of glided up next to me, put both arms on my shoulders, leaned in and whispered directly in my ear, "Do you ever feel like we never tell each other what's really on our minds?" Although I knew exactly what she was talking about—I had fantasized about something like this happening for a long time but never dared to do something about it—I was taken off guard, shocked that she actually had the guts to say something like that right there in the middle of the party. I mean, that was something that people in soap operas or cheesy paperback romance novels say, right? I knew that Erica was just a couple of bodies away from me. I could see her back over Miki's shoulder, and I could hear her voice amongst the clutter of noises. But I still reached my hand up and grasped one of Miki's hands, slightly at first and then slowly tightening as she solidified her grasp. There we were, surrounded by mindless, drunken chatter among a bunch of accountants and shitty lounge music, firmly holding each other's hands, steps away from my girlfriend.

I eventually responded to her question with an "I know." After a few seconds of standing there, staring at each other and glancing away to see if anyone was noticing, we let go, and she faded back into the crowd. Downstairs in the museum where they had more drinks and food and dancing, we had a few more encounters. Like when I was getting drinks for Erica and I, and Miki was also standing there in line. I walked up behind her knowing that she had seen me approach and then stopped just behind her, waited in line there, close enough that our bodies touched and my hand found its way on the small of her back. I then slid my hand down to the point of where her bottom half started curving away from her body, where my fingers could feel the band of her panties through her black dress.

Erica and I eventually left, she was tired and wanted to go home, and nothing more happened with Miki until a few months later.

Miki graduated from the University of Southern California and was about 5'8" and had short dark brown hair with tints of blond, as did most girls back then. I liked the way it curved down the side her face, in what I liked to call her "Uma Thurman 'doo." Her parents were German, but like second- or third-generation. She had big turquoise-green eyes, wide and with that innocent watery glare that only female eyes can have. She had soft skin, with a slightly darker tint, and irresistible long limbs. Miki exuded a sweet feminine grace in all her mannerisms, was very womanly, but had a hint of a hard edge to her. Miki also, more than any normal girl, seemed to be disposed to crying at any given moment.

Originally from Pasadena, Miki's parents moved to Chicago when she was in college. Miki was a girl out of control with her emotions and sexual drive. She told me that she had sex with 11 guys her junior year at USC. Yeah, 11 guys in one year. Most guys are repulsed by that concept—in a girl that is...

We worked as auditors, financial accounting auditors, to be more precise. At that time there were four major public accounting firms, down from eight and then six. They were called the "Big Four" and were like the Ivy League of the accounting profession. Getting a job at one of the Big Four firms in Chicago is sort of a reward for going to a Big Ten school or Notre Dame and majoring in accounting, drinking a significant amount of the time, and not knowing what it is that you want to do with your life except to graduate and start making money. You had to be able to memorize and regurgitate useless facts, such as that a debit goes on the left and a credit is always on the right, and all these accounting rules that we would rattle off to each other to show how smart we were, like, "I think that's FAS 97, paragraph 8.b.4..." I used to listen to all of us talk and think, "How fucked up have we humans made everything we do?" (The only thing worse than talking about them, in some cases, were the accounting rules themselves. Like so-called "Mark-to-Market" accounting rules, where experts are supposed to determine the value of financial instruments companies invest in so they can be recorded to the financial statements. CPAs, who know nothing about valuation, are supposed to then determine if the valuations are "reasonable." They don't know what they hell they're doing, so it's no wonder when companies have to admit their accounting was wrong, it's usually because these very valuations were full of shit.)

I loved going to the conferences the accounting profession would have a few times a year, like the annual AICPA conference in Washington D.C. Everyone got into a tizzy about that one. I would sit there in a daze, staring at some overweight, balding, white male accountant with a mustache standing behind some podium babbling, and I would stare off at the attendees furiously taking notes, whispering to each other, or falling asleep. The best was the drinks afterward. You could always spot the older accountants telling what appeared to be really funny stories to all sorts of aspiring younger accountants, stories that were generally about being able to go out drinking all night only to wake-up bright and early and meet with the clients—all to ensure the appropriate application of "Generally Accepted Accounting Principles." I always wanted to videotape a room full of accountants standing around drinking and talking, though I'm not sure anyone else would be interested in seeing it.

Once you make it to a public accounting firm, you are paid to repeat mindless tasks over and over and drink a lot of coffee during the day and alcohol at night—which is pretty much what you did in college while preparing for such a life. It's almost as if the college curriculum is set up that way because the schools and the public accounting firms know that's what's required for someone to succeed in the accounting profession. It's no wonder that a firm like Arthur Anderson completely fell apart when its auditors started screwing around. It's like working on the assembly line of the financial world. Individuals with true mental ability, sharp personalities, and good looks, go on to work for investment banks or consulting firms.

The first time I heard of Miki was when I was 22, my first year out of college. We were at our company's annual party. I saw her and was blown away at once. "Who's that girl?" I asked my friend Rick who was standing next to me.

"Oh, she's with Eric. Eric met her last New Year's Eve, I think. She's still in college, but she's coming to work for us next year." He responded as he sipped his drink. "I think she told him she liked butt sex."

As was typical for most young males at a Big Four firm, Rick's train of thought never really strayed from a certain few topics—sex, alcohol and cigarettes. We talked further about Miki, and he introduced me. Our introduction was brief, we exchanged a few pleasantries and she told me how she was going to start with our company in the fall and we should hook up for drinks. She left and Rick stared off as she walked away and said, pretty much to himself, "God I would love to fuck her." I agreed in silence as I also stared off and took another sip of my drink.

We met again when she started her job at our firm, and we would talk a little at the happy hours we attended. At that point I was in a relationship that seemed somewhat promising but never went anywhere. Miki started dating this Notre Dame graduate named Andrew Walsh. Andrew was not a bad guy, but I always resented him for going out with Miki; I thought he was a lucky bastard. They would end up dating for a few years.

Besides the happy hours and stuff like that, I never really saw her until we were scheduled to work together on a small biotech client in the western suburbs.

I felt anxious when I saw that she was on the job. I had to psyche myself up that Sunday night before going to work the next day. I pulled through and despite a few nervous moments that first morning, I was fine, and we talked a lot that week. Our manager wasn't around much, so it was mainly Miki and I. I told her a lot about the books I liked to read, the music I liked, and how I liked to paint and draw. I made mixed CDs for us to listen to, and she loved them. She would always remark how "interesting" I was. We laughed a lot, making fun of the nerdy controller that we worked with and his bad outfits. On the last Friday afternoon we were together, we had this long philosophical conversation for a few hours about God, death, and romance there in the client's office long after everyone had left. It was one of the rare times that I've ever talked about that kind of stuff with someone at work. We shared our thoughts that maybe God isn't something we can ever understand and trying to fit the concept of God into just one of the world's religions almost seemed futile. She said she loved our conversation as we said goodbye that night and said that we should meet up for drinks. So we met out a few times after that; her boyfriend was really jealous, and they started having some hard times. I was able to act like the consoling guy friend, and eventually they broke up, but by that time I already had found myself in a relationship with fucking Erica.

While Erica and I dated, I continued to keep in touch with Miki. We e-mailed all the time. I would talk to her at work-related parties, keeping track of whether she was still single or not. Erica and Miki became better friends, then best of friends, so I saw Miki all the time at places we went to. We had these awkward moments, but I didn't know how to interpret them. I thought about breaking up with Erica but I couldn't do it. I wrote Miki letters and e-mails while drunk expressing my feelings to her, telling her I was in love with her, but I couldn't get myself to send them. I was almost ready to let it all go until she came up to me that night at the Field Museum.

Later that week, after the party, I called Miki to talk about our "situation." I called her from work, from a conference room at a client's office. The conversation was pretty awkward. After some light conversation, asking each other how our weeks were going, that kind of stuff, I said something like, "So, do you think we need to talk about this? About what happened?"

"Yeah, I guess so," she responded. And we went on like that for a few minutes with no real direction or conclusion, except that we would try to get together sometime, or at least keep in touch and see what happened. I've had a few of these conversations, and they're always the same. It's hard to have a sober discussion with another person after you've had an awkward intimate moment while intoxicated. Although these conversations are dry, timid, they're always on the brink of chaos. It takes just one of the people involved to speak up about how they're really feeling—either feeling utter disgust or true desire—and move the conversation away from the security of nothingness to the uncomfortable position of admitting there is a problem that needs to be addressed.

We didn't meet up right away. I was nervous about what to do, so I didn't call her back. I just kept hanging out with Erica and acting as if nothing happened. When Christmas came around, and Erica went back home to Memphis, I found myself alone for about a week and finally worked up the courage and called Miki. We agreed to go out for dinner and drinks, just to catch up. I picked her up, she was wearing dark-grayish slacks, black boots, a nice purple knit sweater, and she looked as beautiful as she always did. We went to Rosangali's, an Italian restaurant very popular with the yuppie crowd of Chicago.

After Rosangali's we went to a bar across the street called the Blue Parrot, where we had more beers. Conversation was pleasant, and we avoided the topic of what happened back at the museum. I couldn't bring it up. It freaked me out, the possibility of cheating on my girlfriend, even though I didn't really like her. We went to the Wrightwood Tap after for more drinks, sat close to each other and talked about who knows what.

We were drunk that night, and as I dropped her off, you would've thought something would happen between us. But it didn't. I'm sure she was waiting for me to put on the moves, and I was thinking that she would, especially after she was the one with the balls to start something in the first place. But we just said goodbye in my car, with a soft hug. We went out like that a few more times, off and on for months, but again, nothing happened. It was almost like a game of chicken, but no one buckled. I wasn't sure where, if anywhere, it was all headed, but then before I knew it she was in a relationship with some other lame Notre Dame guy. I almost had a jealous fit at a party in front of Erica and our friends when I saw them together. Everyone thought I was sick, or upset about something. Miki knew though. I think she thought it was funny and made out with him in front of me at the party several times. Erica thought I was mad at her for some reason and couldn't figure out what the hell was wrong with me.

After that night of my near breakdown at the party, I refused to go anywhere I knew Miki would be and refused to even talk about her with Erica. But then I heard that Miki and her boyfriend had broken up. I thought about contacting Miki right away but decided to try and hold off. I soon ran into her at a party I was at with Erica. Miki came up to me as I was standing with Erica and asked how we were doing. She looked at me specifically and smiled, as if nothing was ever wrong, and said that it had been a long time since we last spoke. She even went so far as to say that we should meet up for drinks some time when we were both in the office, to which I agreed. Erica gave her blessing and said that although she had been traveling for work a lot recently, the two of us should still get together because, well, Miki and I had been friends long before Erica and I got to know each other, which was true. After that night, I debated and debated with myself whether I should call her. Based on the way she looked at me that night, I had the feeling that her aggressiveness was back—the Miki from the museum had returned—and it intimidated me for some reason. It felt like she had figured me out over the last few months and had decided she was going to make the first move because she knew I wouldn't. I hesitated calling her because I knew I would end up cheating on Erica. I couldn't make up my mind, I had decided to let it go for a little bit and maybe try to break-up with Erica first, which I didn't do.

On a Friday afternoon weeks later, I was sitting in my cube staring at my computer and waiting for the day to end. That morning when I came into the office I specifically checked to see if Miki was in, as I always did, but she wasn't, so I was at ease. Toward the end of the day, though, Miki came walking by my cube and stopped and smiled at me. I felt the sweat begin to gather at the top of my forehead immediately. She, however, seemed completely cool, almost in mockery of my nervousness. I tried my best to collect myself. She made conversation about what we were working on and what was up with people we knew as she leaned on the side of one of the cube walls and gently slid one of her bare feet in and out of its shoe, acting as natural as could be. Goddamn did she have cute toes, I thought, nice little womanly toes with red nail polish. As we talked, I remembered that I had plans to go to a show at the Double Door with my roommate Caleb later on—and Erica was not coming home until late—so if there was a night to have drinks with her, this would be it. I thought about whether I should say something about grabbing a drink, wondered if she was thinking about it although she didn't mention it. She told me that it was nice to see me and that I should have a nice weekend when I all of a sudden said, "Hey Miki, ah, well since we're both downtown, you know, why don't we just go and grab a few drinks together after work tonight, like we talked before, because, well, I'm not doing anything tonight, you know, and if you're not either, then…

So we agreed to meet at Fado's at 5:30 after work.

Fado's is the Irish bar chain that in Chicago is located downtown, at LaSalle and Grand, close to where we worked. It's a decent replica of an Irish pub, with a dark interior and wood throughout. The crowd on a Friday night is typically dense, filled with 20- and 30-something professionals and a slew of other types, like college students, suburbanites and out-of-town visitors.

Miki and I sat on two wood stools close to one of the bars and had several glasses of heavy European beer. These beers are my favorites because of their full texture, warm feel and heavy alcohol content. Miki loved to get drunk, which is another thing that intrigued me about her. After a few beers, amidst the surrounding layers of music and voices, we transformed out of that uneasy state of sobriety.

There are certain moments you read or hear about that you imagine happening to you. You see them up on a movie screen, and imagine what it would be like if something like that ever happened to you, how you would react. These might be moments of success, of fame, of despair, of experiencing the death of a loved one, of falling in and out of love or experiencing intense erotic passion, even if at least for just a night or a moment. You never know when one of these moments will come upon you, but when one does, you feel as if you were witnessing it like a bystander would. You know that it's happening to you, yet at times there's a reluctance to allow yourself to fully participate.

Miki and I had been in these situations together before, like at the museum party when she came up to me or the few times we went out when Erica was out of town. We could have done something dramatic like gone to a secret corner of the Field Museum and made-out, had sex, but we both had the composure to behave like proper adults. For whatever reason, this particular encounter at Fado's was more accessible. Maybe it was because our prior meetings had just been warm-ups for this one, or the lighting at the moment was perfect, or all the heavy European beer we were drinking, or that a song came on at the right time. Bur for whatever reason, we found ourselves more and more at ease with staring at each other for longer and longer periods of time, holding on to those glances that usually last only a couple of seconds.

In male-female conversations between individuals that are not intimately involved, direct eye contact when words are being exchanged is permitted as it exemplifies attention. However, once words cease to be exchanged, during those pauses, continued eye contact is prohibited, unless either of the individuals wants something more than friendship. If you stare longer, you face the risk of the stare not being returned and the other person feeling invaded and it all becoming awkward and weird. However, if you do offer an extended stare and the stare is returned, and held, then you've crossed the line.

As the night wore on, we held our stares, longer and longer. During the first chords of U2's "Beautiful Day," we held a longer stare followed by both of us turning to gaze off into the crowd. We knew what was happening. Underneath the influence of fucking U2, we had finally started to let ourselves drift off into a moment; that P.M. Dawn song might well as have been playing in the background.

At around 8:30, I suggested that we leave because I had to meet Caleb back at my apartment by 9:30. We were going to see a band called The Toadies that night at the Double Door. Miki and I managed to get our long black coats on, pay the bill, and make our way outside to a cold Chicago night.

We were standing in front of the bar's entrance saying our goodbyes. When we went to give each other a hug and kiss, as our faces were approaching, I caught her eye. I turned my head from left to right so that our kiss turned into a full-frontal meeting. Our lips held for a moment, and then we took the plunge and pressed forward with the full weight of our bodies. We let go and then kissed again, our tongues meeting, our kisses becoming hard, and fast. We grasped each other tighter and started to sway in unison away from the corner and back against one of the walls next to the entrance. Our arms were wrapped around each other so hard as if to save each other from falling. Her head tilted down to one side with mine tilted to the other, down upon hers as our lips opened and we consumed each other. Underneath the city lights, at the corner of LaSalle and Grand, bathed in the stares of the Latino valet parkers, taxi cabbies, and the curious, envious or disgusted individuals passing by, we became two souls lost in a moment.

We finally released our lip-lock, and she pressed her head on my face so that I could feel her hair on the side of my cheek, could smell it, and could feel her breath on my neck. I felt myself breathing rapidly. During that brief pause she looked up at me, turned toward the street for a second, looked back and said to me, "Maybe we should go somewhere else, or at least out of the way, someone might see us." I thought about taking us to the alley that was nearby, maybe I would've if it was warmer, but then she said that this was bad, kind of to both of us. We kissed again though right after that. At that point the realization hit me, that I finally had cheated on Erica, and with one of her best friends. I responded with soft, muffled replies such as: "Shh…don't worry. We'll figure it out." Then I suggested that we get into a cab and head north toward her neighborhood.

From the moment we got into the cab, we smothered each other in kisses, fully embracing, her legs wrapped around mine. The cabdriver never looked back, but he must have felt uneasy. Ultimately that's what cabbies do. They are paid to transport us to and from locations, from idle spaces and insufficient lives to what we hope will be promising destinations. In the cab, in between muttering our regrets and expressions of lust for each other, with her back to one of the corners of the backseat and with me half on top of her, we breathed heavily and our kisses went from our mouths to our necks and our hands reached down to feel each other's bodies—me feeling the warmness between her legs through her suit pants and her feeling the stiffness between mine. She wanted me to come in, but I had the fucking composure to insist on meeting Caleb.

Although I had no composure with respect to cheating on my girlfriend, rock 'n roll was waiting, and I wasn't about to abandon Caleb. Caleb, though, would later remark that I was a fucking idiot for not staying with her, and I kind of agreed, but in the end it worked out.

Caleb and I shared a few cigarettes and drinks back at our place as I played for him the new High on Fire album, *The Art of Self Defense,* and laughed as I recounted the evening's story. Caleb and I had that bond. He understood, as did I, the thrill of allowing oneself to be trapped in crazy moments.

The Double Door was the prime escape for me that night, and we lost ourselves in the crowd of 20-something hipsters. The Toadies are a hard-rocking band from Texas, who kind of suck now, but that night they were fun as hell. We made our way toward the front, close to the stage, and enjoyed the sound. Not much was said between us at the show, which was the treat of being with Caleb. Nothing has to be said when it's all good, when you're watching a kick-ass band, drinking beer and smoking cigarettes, and absorbing the warm feel of the surrounding bodies and pretty faces of hipster-girls. I especially felt good standing there knowing that not long before I had a beautiful, young, yuppie girl who would have done anything that night to have been with me. After the show we smoked a joint on the rooftop of our apartment building in Wicker Park staring off at the Chicago Skyline, and it was a good night, though I started freaking out a little as to what I was going to do with Erica.

Miki and I talked a little during the week, but not too much because I wanted to avoid awkward conversations and instead have another face-to-face. I wasn't so apprehensive about her anymore; I knew what I wanted. So that Friday night, I told Erica that I was going out on a pub-crawl with my co-workers. Instead, I made plans to meet Miki at a restaurant called John's Place at the corner of Webster and Racine, close to where she lived, where we would talk things out and see what was going on.

We were sober at first and didn't talk much while we consumed our drinks. I was worried that in our sober state she would freak out and demand to know what we were doing, etc. But that fear subsided as we started getting drunk. And I felt like Miki knew what was going on, that in getting drunk we would avoid any awkwardness. After John's Place she suggested we go to a nearby bar, which we went to and did a bunch of Irish Car Bombs (a half pint of Guiness, a shot of Baileys and Jameson) until we were both drunk. Walking hand in hand toward her place after we left the bar, she said, "So, do we just make ourselves drunk so we can do what we're going to do?"

"Maybe, I don't know," was my response as she stopped to kiss me, and I squeezed her hand. When we got to her place, she opened the door and we made our way in, quietly in order to not wake her roommates, and headed down the stairs to the basement where there was a living room along with Miki's bedroom.

I made my way to the couch and she asked if I wanted something to drink, so I asked for a beer, and she made herself a cocktail. She eventually went to her bedroom and changed into "something comfortable," came back and we threw in *Groundhog Day* and settled onto the couch.

Movies, alcohol, music, marijuana—they're all sedatives we use to forget about things, to make the most of moments we'd like to be great and memorable, to help us expand how we experience things, and make getting laid easier. With the lights down, *Groundhog Day* started and she lay back and placed her feet on my lap. Not wanting to waste any time, I quickly finished my beer and started caressing her feet, moving to her ankle, and slowly across her calf, sliding my hands up her pajama pants. I then lay down next to her, nestling myself in between her and the back of the couch. She adjusted to allow space on the pillow and rested herself back against me. In the dark with the flashing television providing soft, vibrating illumination, I continued my caressing and worked my way from her hips slowly up her side, feeling the soft skin of her lower back underneath her sweater and eventually across toward her belly. As my touches steadily quickened and became concentrated, she sighed and rested the back of her head firmer against my chin. I then moved my lips through her dark hair and slid down so I could kiss the back of her neck. The soft kisses I placed on the back of her neck led to her turning her body so that her lips met mine and we maneuvered so that our kisses became open-mouth embraces. My body then found its way firmly on top of her as she spread her legs.

Before I knew it, she had taken my pants off and there I was in my boxers with my pants down to my knees. I then started to grab her pants to do the same when she said, "Wait" and stopped me. "I don't think we should take our clothes off just yet… I mean, shouldn't we talk about this first?"

"Well, I guess you're right," I responded with that dissatisfied guy kind of response, and thinking to myself that my clothes were already practically off. "Talk about what? What the fuck?" I thought but didn't say it. Girls just always seem to throw that kind of shit in when something is getting good. At that point we were breathing heavily as the movie played in the background. Quickly, I pulled my senses together and responded, "Miki, I understand. Why don't we just go to your room and talk this over, shut this movie off and put some good music on." With the movie off and us on her bed, I could then use the next sedative, music, to my advantage—if only I had a joint I knew I would be golden, but I didn't. Unlike a movie, music has that beautiful quality that, as you can't see it, allows you to be lost to yourself or whomever you're with.

Her room was kept nicely, had those soft covers, sheets and pillows that make sleeping with a woman so awesome. Conveniently, she had a clock radio with a CD player to the side of her bed and CDs that you might expect to find in the bedroom of a young yuppie girl: U2, Coldplay, Janis Joplin, and REO Speedwagon. I thought the REO album was the best, so I put that in, their greatest hits album in fact. "Heard it from a friend who, heard from friend who, heard from another that you've been messing around…"

We lay there and commented on the music. "I love this CD," she said, and I firmly agreed. "What are we going to do? This is so bad."

"I know, but I can't help it," I replied. This was the kind of conversation we had as we kept rubbing each other and kissing. As the kissing went on I kept trying to take her pajama pants off, but she wouldn't let me. Finally, after more of that, I realized it wasn't going to happen just yet and slowed things down. We cuddled, and drifted off into sleep.

Some time in the middle of the night, we woke up with her body pressed hard against mine. I reached my right hand over and cupped her vagina through her panties. I groped her from behind, and she turned her head and our opened mouths met. The harder we kissed, the harder we pressed. This time there was no resistance to me pulling her pants down over her waist and hips, down her legs as she lifted her feet out of their openings. There's nothing better than finally feeling the pants come off a girl, especially for the first time. I took off my boxers and turned to get on top of her as she positioned herself. After a few moments of trying, I entered her with such a rush that after my full insertion and pulling back out to go back in again, I felt that gut-wrenching feeling of unavoidable premature ejaculation and came all over the bottom of her stomach.

Not only did I come immediately, but I came with intensity. There was apparently a lot stored up. It was pretty awesome actually. We both laughed, and she said "Are you always like this Alex?

Time, as we understand it, has existed approximately 15 billion, 16 billion, 18 billion years, depending on which scientist you ask. Or if you believe in the steady-state theory, you'll conclude that time has existed forever, which is even more mind-boggling. But whatever it is, it's a long fucking time. And I've only been alive for approximately 30-something years of it, which is an insanely small percentage of time that has passed.

Our existence is so fleeting that it's gone before we know it, and at times all the individual pain and suffering we endure seems inconsequential. But the sex that Miki and I had that morning, even if that would have been the last time I ever had sex, would have made my whole inconsequential life worth it.

We woke up with our bodies already intertwined, moist with morning sweat, underneath the covers with the sun shining through one of the windows onto the bed. As I made my way on top of her, she kicked the cover off the bed, leaving our naked, coupled bodies exposed to the morning light and silence. I thought of the T.S. Elliott poem that starts with "The morning comes to consciousness of faint stale smells of beer" for some reason. Her long legs naturally propped to allow me deep access as my arms took hold of the back of her thighs, propping her calves and feet up off the bed. Without any speech, we concentrated on that position as my strokes became faster, harder, eventually causing the headboard to hit the wall. We made no effort to calm the noisy thuds. In fact, as the thuds became louder, it seemed like we hit our bodies harder, as if to amplify the sound. Nor was there any effort or thought of switching positions. After what seemed like an endless moment, her hands clasped onto the back of my shoulders and she pulled my head down to the side of her neck and, almost in a panic, and she muttered that she was coming. At that point I let all concentration to restrain myself go and buried my face deeper into the side of her neck and we settled into a slow, throbbing motion. When all was still, except for the steady beating of our hearts and our breathing, we turned to look at each other and exchanged soft kisses.

"That was much better, Alex," she whispered after a minute and we both laughed. I rolled over and placed her head against my chest, with one of her legs wrapping itself around my waist. The whole bed felt drenched as we lay in silence, breathing slowly for a few moments.

I eventually left. We didn't have any sort of conversation as to what we were going to do. I just got ready and we agreed to see each other again soon. As I walked away, she watched me leave from the doorway. I made my way down the street toward my car, lit a cigarette, and took a drag—inhaling the sweet smell on a cool Chicago morning. And, within an hour, I was on my way to play golf with my girlfriend and her friends.

We had a scramble with Erica's friends that day, one of those games where you always play the best ball, along with some other rules that I never understand. I hate freaking golf, so I normally have to force my way through these things, and that morning was worse. I went through the motions, talked the aimless bullshit conversation that I always had with Erica and her friends, and I drank beers and kept reflecting on the previous night. It's amazing to think how anyone in their right mind could've gone and played golf after having such an encounter. I should bring that up in a job interview when asked to describe my most challenging moment and how I handled it. I don't quite know if you can say it's resiliency, or pure lunacy, probably a combination of both.

Time went on, with Erica and I going through the routine of a relationship and Miki and I and continuing to meet up for crazy, crazy sex.

We would meet up for drinks and secretly make our way back to her place for sex. We had sex in my car several times, right in front of her apartment. We both would leave work for lunch and meet back at her place to have sex all afternoon. On many nights I would go out to dinner with Erica and afterward I would make an excuse and drop her off, only to then go straight to Miki's. I never entered through the front door, though she desperately wanted me to knock like a proper gentleman, meet her roommates, and then take her out for a "normal" night on the town. However, what we were doing wasn't "normal." It was crazy from the beginning. I stayed in my relationship with Erica, never having the balls to break it off because—besides being a wimp—I was reluctant about what, if any, kind of relationship Miki and I would have. I liked looking at her, liked having sex with her, but she kind of freaked me out. I always thought about how she supposedly had sex with 11 guys one year in college.

Miki made repeated efforts to curb what we were doing, to try and prevent us from having sex until we had a better road map for our future. One time we met out after work at a bar called River's, an outdoor place along the Chicago River. It had been a while since we had seen each other—a week, maybe. The conversation was mild, as was the cool breeze coming off the river. That night I was trying to play it civil and purposely did not make any advances. But the next thing you know, we were walking back to my car and on the way she started holding my hand. As soon as she did that, we stopped and made out. On the way back to her place, we stopped and made out at every red light, and even a little in between. As my car sat in front of her place, we kept making out and then when I wanted to go inside, she insisted that I not because it wouldn't be a good idea. I then tried to have sex with her there in the car again but she wouldn't let me. I had the opportunity there to make another one of those "moments," and I think that's what she wanted. I could've insisted and shut her mouth with a strong kiss, grabbed her hand and told her that I loved her and wanted her more than ever. I could've done all that. She even looked back at me as she was opening her apartment door, paused for a second, and then walked in. Without doing anything, I left.

Miki insisted that I break up with Erica, but I couldn't. Although Erica and I continued to date, I became distant. We stopped having sex altogether. I thought she would break up with me but she just didn't. We even went away to Mexico together for a week. That trip, as I look back, was really pathetic. From her perspective, it must have been a last attempt to make the relationship work. We didn't kiss each other the whole time, both conveniently agreed at night that we were tired and needed a good night's rest and so we never had sex. I didn't want to have sex with her, and she must have known it. I couldn't, in my right mind, given what I was doing with her friend.

Miki always accused me of being weak and not being able to make up my mind. I would say that I wanted to be with her but needed time so that things with Erica would work themselves to their natural end. Then we would need more time to let things settle, after which we could focus on a real relationship. That, I think, was honestly my plan. Sure I could've taken more of an aggressive stance and forced the end of the relationship if I really wanted to be with Miki that bad. I thought I had a sound strategy. I thought it was patient and pragmatic—and eventually, after many months of waiting, Erica finally broke up with me.

Erica told me we needed to talk, so I went to her place after work. After I walked in, I found her in bed crying, and to my surprise, she started in with a whole break-up conversation. It was traumatic, much harder than I ever thought it would be. She cried; I cried; we hugged.

"Maybe another time it could've worked out. I love you, but right now I need to be with someone who makes me feel like they love me. I've loved you so much since we met, Alex, but I just don't feel that back from you," she said. You know, although I had wanted it to happen, I wanted her to break up with me because I thought it would be easier for me, I left her apartment that night with a heavy heart and a sick feeling in my throat. I walked all the way home from her apartment by Lincoln and Wells to mine in Wicker Park. I was pissed at myself. I realized that playing with someone's emotions, like I had with Erica's, is a dangerous and borderline-evil thing to do. I knew for the longest time that we needed to break up; I was even sleeping with her friend, but I thought that I was being noble by not breaking up with her and letting her come to that decision on her own. But that was just reckless on my part. Letting her go on, grasping and thinking that she could salvage our relationship, wondering what was wrong, and making her come to grips and do what was needed to be done, was just plain irresponsible of me. To this day it is one of my single biggest mistakes.

That night I went home and listened to Radiohead's *OK Computer*. In my bummed out state, and aided by that album's beautiful sadness, I kept thinking about something my dad always told me. My dad always told me not to let my youth go to waste like he did. He always told me not to give a shit and talk to whatever pretty girl I wanted to because, as I'll someday figure out, we never have anything to lose. Like any good Latino dad, he also taught me that it was okay to stare at any good-looking girl that walked by, no matter how obnoxious, because as a guy it was my right to. But that I night I wondered to myself whether we all end up with regret—is it inevitable? I had followed my dad's advice and had taken advantage of my youth by hooking up with Miki, but I still felt wasted and empty that night after Erica broke up with me.

That night I also listened to The Flaming Lips song "Do You Realize?" that asks "Do you realize that someday, we all will die?" I kept thinking about how every time you see someone, a parent, a friend, a lover, it really could be the last time you see them. I'm scared to wonder what we would be like if we really took this notion to heart. It's probably some sort of internal conditioning that lets us flirt with these kinds of thoughts but never for too long. For most of us, we think these thoughts long enough that maybe they are inspiring for a brief period, but then we usually let them slip away and come back to our comfort zone and continue living our life as we were. It's like a cycle, right? Like when you get drunk, so drunk you wake up with a terrible hangover that maybe lasts for days, but you soon get over it and there you are, back at some party or bar, getting just as drunk.

Soon after Erica and I broke up, things between Miki and I started to change. We both weren't as eager to see each other as we were before. She went on a month-long trip to Asia with her friend. We thought that the time apart would help let things settle down. Miki and I decided that we would take things slowly, let things play out naturally and with time, we would be able to have a public relationship and everyone would think it was something that happened after the break-up. Upon Miki's return from Asia, we met at BIN 36, downtown. We hugged and were excited to see each other. It was there that Miki unveiled her great plan she devised while off on her trip. She no longer wanted to wait and let things cool down. Instead, she was prepared to tell Erica that she had tremendous feelings for me, wanted to date me and wanted her to be ok with it. She was willing to take all the blame, lose her friendship in order to have an open relationship with me. "Are you crazy?" was my immediate response. I mean, I'm way too indecisive, way too much of a coward to handle that kind of a plan. And she was serious about it too. I wanted to keep it secret, but that meant having more secret meetings until enough time went along where I would no longer be worried about the impact it would have on poor Erica. It all tied back to the horrible feeling I had that night with her. After seeing her cry like that when she broke up with me, I didn't want to make it worse.

Miki and I had sex again, anyway, that night and also a few more times after that. One day we skipped work and had sex all day at her place while her roommates were at work, and we fought about Miki's plan in between sessions. I couldn't believe she would do that to her friend, openly admit what was going on and destroy their friendship to be with me—I mean, how could someone be that honest? It turned me off, so I started convincing myself that she wasn't the right one for me. I started to shy away, not making much of an attempt to see her. I convinced myself even more that she wasn't my type, that she was too shallow, not really interested in anything. I decided I needed to tell her that we just weren't going to work out long-term. I started by not returning her calls. But I couldn't resist calling her to try and hook up, especially when I was drunk, lonely, and horny. She wouldn't let me hook up with her, though, until we had a plan for us. I then freaked out when she stopped returning my calls altogether.

She took my indecision as a sign that I didn't feel the same way about her and decided she didn't want to talk to me anymore. I called and I called, leaving messages, saying things like "Miki, I don't understand what's going on. I just wanted some time, um, just some time to let things, you know, settle down with Erica and everything. If you could only please return my call we could talk it out, figure it out."

Finally, on a Saturday night as I drove up to a friend's party in the suburbs, I called her and she picked up the phone. We had it out, and she all of sudden was pretty forceful that we needed to stop seeing each other, and I became bothered by the sudden sense of direction on her part. I kept prying until I finally got it out of her that she had met someone else, and although she had strong feelings for me, probably was in love with me, this guy wanted to be with her. He wasn't a big fucking wimp like me. She was ready to let everything else go for me, her friendship with Erica, being ridiculed by their mutual friends for what she had done—she was prepared to take all the blame and I didn't react. Everything she said was completely true, and I was pissed off. What pissed me off more than anything, I convinced myself, was that it took meeting another guy for her to tell me off and put me in my place. But really, I was pissed because I knew she was right.

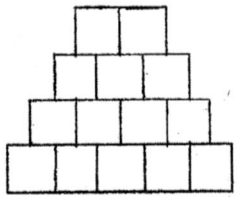

On Being Mexican American — Part I

My grandfather Alfonzo Arturo Gonzalez Lopez and grandmother Maria Concepcion ("Concha") Lopez Ramirez ran a ranch together in Michoacan, a state along the western coast of Mexico where it curves, where the Monarch butterflies migrate to every year, and where my mother was born.

Alfonzo and Concha had a lot of children, which was typical for ranching families back then, though it's not clear exactly how many they had. I've heard they had anywhere from 9 up to 16. My mother Maria is the youngest, and she's a supporter of the higher number, because that's what her oldest sister Nadia claims (and according to Maria, out of the brothers and sisters, Nadia would know best).

Nadia claims that the grandfather had 16 children, 4 that died as infants and 4 that were borne by his mistresses that lived in a village on the other side of *el cerro* (the mountain).

Of the four bastard children, they never knew three, and the one they know supposedly doesn't know he has a different mother. My uncle Javier says Nadia doesn't know what she's talking about, *esa pinche india no sabe de lo que esta hablando* ("That damn Indian doesn't know what she's talking about."), but he's supposedly the one that doesn't know he has a different mother.

Though my mother was born on the ranch, she doesn't remember living there as the grandfather sold it and moved the family to the nearby town of Ciudad Hidalgo soon after she was born. I've never been to where the ranch used to be, but it's supposedly about 45 minutes from Ciudad Hidalgo. They say it's no longer used as a ranch because the ranches in that area were eventually closed down due to competition from bigger farms closer to Morelia, the capital city of Michoacan, and south in the state of Guerrero. Some of my cousins now run ranches in Guerrero, where they harvest the cannabis plant, Mexico's cash crop, though no one in my family openly admits it. Also, it's said that many of the young people who would otherwise have worked the ranches chose to instead make their way up north and pay a *coyote* to take them across the border, like my mother did in her late teens.

I'm not really sure what my grandfather did for a living after he sold the ranch. Whatever he did, it seems to have involved him traveling to a nearby village, where he had the mistresses. But the grandparents seemed to have been well-off, as they had the biggest house and largest plot of land in the town and were well respected. *Todos conosian al abuelo*, "Everybody knew the grandfather," Javier used to say to me. He used to also say the grandfather was very tall and strong, and that he was *muy carbon*, which literally translates to "He was very male goat," but is slang for saying he was a bad-ass, or a pain-in-the-ass. Like many words in Spanish, the word *cabron* has multiple meanings.

Alfonzo Lopez died when my mother was about 15, for causes that are not clear—my mother just says he was old, though he was relatively young, in his 60s I think. Back then in those small villages it seems that people always died for un-known reasons—they were just old or sick. It's similar to how everyone's birthdays are always disputed. My mother says she was born on Valentine's Day, February 14, 1950. That's what her birth certificate says. However, Javier says that she was ac-tually born four months earlier, in November, but the grand-parents were not able to make it to Morelia to record the of-ficial documents until February, and February 14 coincidentally happened to be the day they went. I'd argue with him saying that surely she was born in a hospital, and so surely they re-corded the date right. He would look at me funny and say *como te crees?* ("What are you thinking?"), and that back then you'd be lucky if there was a pan and some wet towels and hopefully a nun there to pray for you, and also do the delivery. My mom would slap him on the shoulder when he said that, calling him a *sin verguenza*, a "without shame."

Though he might have been exaggerating, what Javier said was true, to a certain extent. Based on my own accounts, in Ciudad Hidalgo no one ever seemed to go to a hospital. If you were sick, the village "doctor" would come to the house and treat you, usually give you a shot, and if you were re-ally sick, there would be a bunch of old ladies there praying for you. I hated getting sick there when I was young. It just

seemed like I would end up getting a shot in the ass for everything—for a cold, a bump in the head, or too much sun.
Every time we were playing and I'd get hurt, my sister would
say she was going to tell our mom so they would come give me
a shot. I have nightmares of seeing the ladies pulling massive
looking syringes out of their bags. I'm not even sure what they
would give us shots of.

Concha died when I was like 16, again for reasons that are
not clear, except that she was old. We used to visit her every
year, during our summer breaks, and sometimes during Christmas break. The land Alfonso left her had shrunk over the
years, being parceled off (some say illegally) to other members
of the extended Lopez family, some who sold off to others, at
what some alleged were sizable profits. The dealings with the
grandfather's estate always seemed to cause a rift in the family,
between those that took the parcels, and those, like my mom,
Nadia, and Javier, that claimed the grandmother was taken advantage of.

Mexicans seem to like that kind of drama; they always
think someone is conspiring against someone else. They always think that everyone is rich but hiding it. Years would go
by when my mother wouldn't talk to certain of her brothers
and sisters because they thought she was rich, and wasn't being open about it. As of now, my mother has made up with all
her brothers and sisters about their previous feuds, but there
are still certain cousins that will not talk to me because of the
feuds that once existed between our parents, or because they
now think I'm rich.

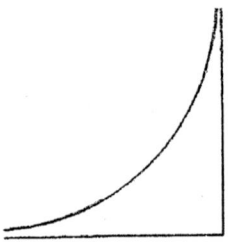

History

Every high school has its beautiful, all-American girl that every guy—even guys who never had a real chance with her, guys like me—has a crush on. When I was in high school, that girl was Candice. Candice was tall, slim, long-legged, blonde, and so sweet that when she talked to you it was like everything happened in slow motion.

Candice was on the pom-pom squad; her family was well-to-do, and she always dressed great—never slutty, just really fucking great. She was smarter than most of the other girls that were in her category of being hot and popular. She wore glasses often to read, black-rimmed, rounding out this smart and sexy-but-sweet look. Thinking back on her, the song "Crimson and Clover" by Tommy James and the Shandels jumps to mind, especially the beginning "Ahhh…. da da da da da dah… now I don't hardly know her …. da da da da da da dah… But I think I could love her…" Knowing that women like her exist makes me really glad I am heterosexual and, if God really exists, then it's a man because who else would create such an exquisite beauty for us guys, you know?

I never knew Candice during my early years in high school. She was just an idea I'd fantasize about. But in my junior year, her boyfriend, the all-American high school football guy, Jaime, had the same history teacher as I did. I had the first class of the day at 8 a.m., Jaime had history at 9 a.m., and Mr. Powers used to give these quizzes and tests in the multiple choice format—the same test in each class. I used to always ace them. I mean I wouldn't miss a question. I was definitely a history geek.

I always thought history was fascinating because what's cooler than knowing the story of all stories—where did we come from and where are we going? It's crazy shit, especially to study history combined with cosmology (the start and evolution of the universe), biology, and chemistry. I don't think I'm that good in history anymore—like when you used to play an instrument but haven't in a long time. I've forgotten a lot of what I learned, but I think I retained enough to appreciate its significance.

It just bugs me out, all of it, from the beginnings of civilization, to ancient civilizations, to supposed lost civilizations like Atlantis, to later civilizations like the Greeks, and then the contemporary ones like the British, Spanish, and now the Americans. And all this has occurred when humans have been on the planet, which has been like less than 1% of its history.

I love how major discoveries, from the discovery of fire to the current information explosion, keep coming on faster and faster. My crazy anthropology professor used to tell us that these "paradigm shifts" have come and gone faster and faster because we were in essence spiraling toward a point of infinite expansion culminating in the year 2012, the year the Mayans predicted that time would end.

GWF Hegel, a German philosopher, wrote on the Philosophy of History (not to be confused with the History of Philosophy). He tried to identify patterns in historical events and understand what they meant and to understand why there was such a thing as history. He argued that there was logic behind history—that all events are leading to the self-realization of mankind, like a state where us humans finally "get it," whatever "it" is. Therefore, there are points in time in which fundamental changes in the things we believe occur. They take a relatively long time to happen, and those living through a period of change often don't realize it except for maybe a few who lead the change in ideas. For example, at one point almost all cultures believed in multiple Gods; now most believe in only one, though how that one God is interpreted varies by culture. At one point most people believed the world was flat, and now most believe it is round. I like what Hegel was trying to get at, and I thought that maybe if more of us tried to think in such terms, we would feel less pressure to hang onto our biased views; we'd challenge why we believe certain things and contemplate the results of our actions.

Back in high school, though, I just pretty much thought it was cool to read about these different stories, cultures, and how we've changed so much, or how we've maybe not changed at all, in certain respects.

During my junior year Jaime somehow got word that Mr. Powers loved me and that I always aced his quizzes and tests, and one day during lunch he waved me over as I was walking through the cafeteria with my lunch tray.

"Hey Alex, what's up man?" he said leaning back as I was walking by, sort of like we'd always been good buddies.

"Hey, uh, Jaime. Not much…"

"Hi Alex!!!" said this cute girl named Colleen who was at the table, across from Jaime. I barely knew her either although I did have a class with her my sophomore year. Up until that year, I didn't talk to girls that much, I just mainly read, played sports, or hung out with my stupid friends and got drunk.

"Hey man, how was that quiz today; it was kind of tough huh?" said Jaime continuing to talk to me. Standing there I started getting anxious, thinking the whole cafeteria was looking at me, wondering why the hell he was talking to me.

"Yeah, it was, I guess. You know, but I studied 'n stuff."

"Yeah, I'm sure you did. You probably fucking aced it, didn't you?" he said laughing, and then got serious. "Hey, man, let me ask you something. What was the first question on your quiz man?"

"Um, well it asked which French political group was considered to be the 'theorists or thinkers' versus 'men of action' during the French Revolution, the Girondists or the Montagnard? With the answer being, you know, the Girondists." I answered, now really perspiring.

"No shit; that was the first question on ours. I didn't fucking know that man. You're a smart dude, huh? I hear you always ace Mr. Powers' tests…"

"Yeah, Alex, you're so smart," chimed in Colleen. There was a bunch of chatter going on at the table, and I noticed that Candice was sitting there talking to a girl next to her. I was desperately trying to hold my composure and act cool, wondering if they noticed that I was sweating. I was doing the thing with my hand, rubbing my forehead pretending to fix my hair—something I've always done when I'm nervous—holding the tray with my other hand, hoping that I wouldn't drop it or something.

I got good grades in high school, As and Bs mainly. I always wanted to get straight As but never seemed disciplined or, maybe, smart enough. I had a few classes each year with the truly smart kids who did get straight A's, so I never thought of myself as a very good student, but I guess compared to my friends and some others at Maine West I was.

"Hey, what was the second?" asked Jaime.

"Something like 'What was the name of the English general who defeated Napoleon for the first time?' or something like that."

"Yeah... fuck, fucking Mr. Powers must give the same quizzes to every period, huh? I thought he was kind of slow with it, but fuck man... crazy, huh?"

"I guess man... well I gotta get going," I said after standing there for a minute, wanting to get the hell out of there.

"Yeah man, all right man," finished Jaime, turning around and saying something to one of the guys at the table as I walked off.

The next day in the hallway as I was walking off to a class, Jaime came walking up behind and yelled out: "Hey Al, what's going on?" acting all friendly, putting his arm around me and smiling. He stood about 6'4, so he was kind of looking down at me.

"Not much Jaime, what's going on?"

"Oh nothing man, fucking school, you know? Hey man, I

was thinking, you know we have a quiz this coming Friday in history, right?"

"Yeah, I think we do. I don't think it'll be very hard though, you know."

"Nothing's hard for you dude, right? What the fuck. I'm getting killed in that class man. If I don't get at least a 'C' I might get suspended from football.

"That sucks man."

"No shit, that sucks. I have to play you know? Hey, I was thinking, would you mind doing me a favor, you know, a real favor, man?

"Well, yeah, but like what?"

"You know how we were talking yesterday at lunch, that Mr. Powers seems to be giving the same tests to his different periods?"

"Right, that's what it seems like, unless he mixes it up after a while, I mean we only discussed the first two questions."

"Yeah, well, I was thinking man, on this next quiz, if you could write down your answers on a piece of paper, flip 'em to me on your way out, you know? It would be huge, man."

"I don't know man; I mean that's kinda cheating right?"

"Dude, don't worry, I'll get some wrong and I promise I won't say anything. I just need a decent score, man, you know."

I agreed, and that Friday as I was taking the quiz, I had a piece of paper out and took down my answers. Mr. Powers never really paid attention, and it was known that he would often fall asleep during tests and quizzes. In fact, it was common for kids to pull out notes in class, sometimes even textbooks, in an attempt to get some additional answers right. No one ever got busted, and that day I didn't either, but I was nervous as shit. That was really the first time I tried something like that. I kept looking up at him and seeing that he was nodding off, and I looked around to see if anyone was looking, but no one really was. Anyway, I handed the piece of paper to Jaime in the hallway after class as he was walking down the hallway toward me. The handoff was pretty cool; he was strolling along in his usual strut, baseball cap on backwards and his blond hair sticking out down his neck in the standard white guy mullet for those years. We both didn't really look at each other, just kind of walked by, and my hand brushed up against his and he grabbed the piece of paper from my hand and we kept walking, like a scene in a Tarantino movie—there should've been some old 70s music playing in the background.

The operation was a success; Mr. Powers was indeed giving the same questions, and Jaime got a B+. Mr. Powers was impressed with Jaime and spoke to him after class, telling Jaime he was surprised but pleased, and Jaime told me he answered, "Thanks boss; I studied... I guess studying pays off?" To which Jaime said Mr. Powers responded with, "Yes, Jaime, it does. Keep it up, son."

So, this whole thing continued on, and Jaime started paying me. Then he proposed that these other jock guys and some other burnout types pay me also in exchange for my answers. And so it became a lucrative little business, for a while anyway.

As Mr. Powers was slow, this went on for over a month but eventually he had to realize that all of a sudden all these guys in the 11th grade that absolutely sucked as students were beginning to get good grades in his class. I think at first Mr. Powers thought it was his teaching. He started acting a lot more animated in class. When he announced, "These grades were surprisingly good, I'm impressed," it was as if he was stunned yet happy that his teaching was paying off—poor guy. Classes became fun; they always are when a teacher becomes engaged like that.

Suddenly one morning, a much more somber Mr. Powers came walking into class and said, "Hey everybody. Something's been going on. I know that someone, in this period, has been passing test scores along to people in the other periods. I want to know who it is, and I'm giving that someone an opportunity to confess now and let what's coming come a little easier."

No one answered and we all sat there in silence for a while with Mr. Powers looking around the room. Although I sat pretty much right in front of the class, Mr. Powers looked over my head and around to the rest of the room as he gave his ultimatum. I think he never in a thousand years believed that it was me who was giving away the scores. I was too good, too revered by the teachers to do something like that. Although I did have my own way of causing trouble, I always did it in a way so that I would not get caught. I probably drank and smoked more than most of the kids in my classes, but no one knew. After a little more of standing there without any response, Mr. Powers kind of backed up a bit and said, "Well, don't you worry; I will find out, and when I do, that person will have hell to pay. From now on, I'm going to make sure this doesn't happen again, and the next person I catch cheating will face my wrath." He never found out though. Apparently, he gave a similar speech to the rest of the periods, and the whole affair stopped. My first entrepreneurial endeavor was over.

The Green Shit Machine

The first time I remember getting really drunk was when we raided John's father's liquor cabinet when we were about 15 years old—doing shots of Christian Brother's and Johnny Walker Black Label, the nasty shit Polish and Indian fathers drink. We did shot after shot, until we eventually ended up rolling around on the floor laughing and then crying. I remember crying and saying stuff like I never wanted to end up like my alcoholic father and that I would make something of myself. Jig would cry when he was drunk and talk about how he was picked on by everyone when he was little because he was Hindu and how we all thought that his house smelled like shit (which it kind of did).

But that's how we got fucked up, just in our own little group of guy friends, stumbling around in someone's basement or out in the woods. There were never any girls, a trend that continued on through high school and after. I always hated being in a group of just guys, standing around getting drunk and talking bullshit, and looking over at another group of guys that had a bunch of girls with them, laughing, dancing around. I was never sure if the girls with these guys were their girlfriends, or what, but it just looked like a lot more fun than the stupid shit we were doing.

In high school we eventually started going to parties. At first it was just a thing we heard the older kids did along with some of the kids our age that were cool enough to go. You had to be invited, or know someone there who could get you in, especially when you were a freshman or sophomore. It was embarrassing to have the door opened for you at a party and have the person say, after looking your group over, "Sorry guys, we're not letting anyone in anymore." This situation exists today. Every time I've gone to a dance club it's been like that, which is primarily why I don't go to that many. You wait in long lines, and it's humiliating when the doorman lets in girl after girl and guys that are with girls. Eventually you're forced to just walk away saying that they're a bunch of assholes.

The day after Mr. Powers busted up my cheating business, Jaime came up to me in the cafeteria and said, "Holy shit man, I can't believe that fucker caught on. I guess it was about time; we had a good thing going. I know he'll never find out so don't worry about it."

"No problem man, don't worry about it. I don't think he has any idea, so it's all good."

"Cool man. Hey, thanks a lot, that's pretty cool of you, you know."

"Yeah man, no problem."

"Most of these smart kids are a bunch of little assholes,

you know," he said looking around the cafeteria. "But you're different man. You're pretty cool."

"Again, no problem man."

"Hey man, what are you doing this Friday night? Andy's parents are out of town and he's having this fucking bash man. His older brother is having people over also; it's going to be cool, you know?"

"Oh really, that's cool man," I said, trying to act all cool. Andy was one of Jaime's friends, another beefy jock guy.

"Yeah man. You know, you should come. It'll be great."

"Cool, sounds good," I said, still trying to act all cool.

"Yeah, all right… I'll get you nice and fucked up, sort of like a last payment, you know?" he said, patting me on the back.

"Cool."

At first I wasn't sure if I'd go to the party because my friends and I had not gone to the parties thrown by Jaime and his friends, or if we tried to, we weren't let in. I thought about it, going back and forth, but then I finally talked John and Carlos into going.

I immediately saw Jaime when we got to the party, and he was like, "Alex!!! What's up?"

"Hey man, what's up?" I said; he then greeted John and Carlos and took us to get beer cups. I saw that all the popular kids of Maine West High School were there, along with a bunch of older kids we didn't know at all.

Maine West is actually one of three high schools in the Maine Township School District, which includes Maine East and Maine South. Maine North existed at some point—I think it was where they filmed the movie *The Breakfast Club*—but it closed. Maine South is in Park Ridge, a wealthy suburb bordering Des Plaines, and the kids that went there were generally better looking than us and kicked our asses in most sports. (People like fucking Hillary Clinton went to Maine South.) Maine East, on the other hand, is in Niles, another bordering suburb that back then was lower on the social continuum than Des Plaines—but they still kicked our asses in sports.

Andy was from a well-to-do family in Des Plaines, so the house was big. It had two stories and a basement, unlike the single-floor houses most of my friends and I lived in. It was packed that night, kids moving back and forth among the house. There were some older people there I somewhat recognized from when I was a freshman who were still hanging around Des Plaines working or doing whatever kids that don't go anywhere after high school do. The year was 1990, so the 80s' hair styles were still around; with big sprayed-up bangs and perms, guys with mullets or shaved sides and the Brian Bosworth shaved lines. There were tons of rolled-up jeans, with plenty of black or white Reeboks, along with a handful of "houser" outfits.

Carlos had a houser outfit on that night. The houser outfit was worn mainly by the Latino, Italian, and Greek kids—along with a handful of white kids who were generally considered to be posers—and it basically consisted of IOU sweatshirts or white turtle necks, cardigans, gold chains on the outside of the sweatshirts, and rolled up black Z-Cavaricci pants (basically saggy black slacks that were rolled up at the ankle). Housers wore slicked back hair, long in the back and spiky on top with shaved sides, and black "Zodiacs," which were sort of like loafers but funkier. House music, which gave rise to the name of the outfit, is dance music—soulful but with a heavy, constant beat. It was supposedly invented in Chicago in the late 1970s—an off-shoot of disco—and they say it got its name because it was first played by DJs in a Chicago gay dance club called The Warehouse, but that's disputed. We didn't know that. As teenagers we called any sort of dance music house music; we didn't know what we were talking about, so we misused the word. Carlos went through a fad of liking to dance to house music, and he wasn't bad, but unfortunately he overdid it sometimes. I was really hoping it wouldn't get to that tonight, for his sake. I always thought that dancing to house music was peculiar. It was a faster sort of way to break-dance, without many of the moves like spinning on your back or head, but with other moves like the "Air Jordan" that involved moving your legs fast in these shuffle-like movements. And most of these kids just pretended to be into this kind of music, none of them ever went to a rave or anything, or at least that's what I suspected.

John fit in pretty well with the jock crew. He had his rolled-up stone-washed jeans, black untied Reeboks, tucked-in shirt with the collar up, and the "soccer-rocker" mullet. Both John and Carlos were pretty respected with the jocks, actually, as they were decent athletes in their own right. John started on the varsity soccer team, and Carlos was a starting wrestler. But they were not as outgoing and could never fully fit in with the popular crowd. (My theory is that the cool kids' families were generally much better off than ours, so they didn't need to work like we did, so maybe that had something to do with it.)

We were just at the turn of the decade, and although grunge rock was beginning to get popular, and some kids were into new wave bands like Depeche Mode and New Order, the

Maine West crowd was still mainly listening to the hair-metal bands. That night you would've heard music from bands like Great White, Poison, Guns N' Roses, Cinderella, Motley Cru, Skid-Row, Warrant, Tesla, and maybe a little Led Zeppelin, The Eagles or Aerosmith.

Colleen, the girl from the cafeteria, came running up to me and gave me a great big hug saying, "Alex, where have you been all my life?!" She was very pretty, to say the least, and drunk. I found it strange that she was all of a sudden so nice to me. Was it just because I helped out Jaime? I didn't know. I thought maybe I'd try to hook up with her, but then I found out that she was Andy's girlfriend. There were all sorts of other cute popular girls around that smiled and said nice things. After a few beers I stopped thinking about why I was getting the attention and just started enjoying it. Girls I'd always thought were beautiful were there and talked to me, like Kristen, Nicole, Amanda, this girl Kathy with really big boobs, and even Candice was there and said hi to me. Jaime introduced me around and I thought it was all pretty cool; I'd never been around so many nice-looking girls before, so it was kind of like a wet dream come true. John and Carlos were off on their own talking with some other not-so-cool kids (but cool enough to be at the party). Jaime was putting his arm on my back, as if I was his long-lost buddy.

I had a beer from the keg, then another, then another, and then another. I don't think I'd ever seen a keg until that party. Since Jaime was Andy's best friend, he would get a drink whenever he wanted to and each time he was getting mine as well. We were, or at least I definitely was, getting drunk. And the drunker I got, the better the music became.

Andy's house was on the outskirts of a small forest preserve. His backyard basically went into the woods and the back of his house had a great big wood deck that I thought was almost the size of my house. People were out there talking, drinking, smoking, being loud. I gathered that Andy's parties were known for being loud, and he could get away with that because of the woods in the back. I guess the neighbors to either side didn't care either.

Eventually pockets of kids started to sing-along to the songs that were playing. Andy and his friends started doing a great big sing-along to songs like "More Than Words" by Extreme, and "Sweet Child o' Mine" by Guns N' Roses. You can't forget that great guitar intro, arguably one of greatest introductions to a song. From the first notes it's unmistakable, and even to this day it brings a chill up my spine when I hear it at a bar and a bunch of 30-something's break into the first verse. It's like our fucking generational anthem.

Remembering this party and all the sing-alongs we used to have makes me reflect on today's music and wonder what the hell happened. My friends and I don't have any music today that we can all listen to and sing along with—we don't know the entire lyrics to any one song like we did back then. Sure, everyone can chime in and sing the chorus to something like 50 Cent's "In Da Club," but no one that I know knows all the lyrics.

I listen to some really good shit today, or so I think I do, but none of my friends know what the hell it is, so there's no way we could sing along to the stuff I like. I mainly like stuff with inaudible lyrics or none at all, as in bands like Explosions in the Sky, which you've probably never heard of before. Additionally, I don't know what the hell my friends like anymore, if they like anything at all. My friends and I have become so dispersed with our interests in music, movies, and books that we hardly have anything in common anymore. I like to think it has something to do with today's access to information over the Internet. You'd think it would have the opposite effect, but it seems to also have turned us all into isolated, individual consumers downloading whatever we want and not really sharing anything. I miss the days when we would make tapes for each other in order to share albums or songs. It could also be that we, including myself, are just getting old and crusty and are completely losing touch with what kids are into these days.

We seemed to be more carefree back then, less restricted. Things like underage drinking and smoking didn't seem to be much of an issue. Back then, the Cold War was just ending, the "evil" Soviet empire had crumbled and we were all proud to be American. But come to think of it, even before the Berlin Wall came down, although we were supposedly under the threat of nuclear attack all the time, we never seemed worried about it, it didn't matter.

Back at the party I went outside to get a beer and these girls, Amanda and Nicole, started talking to me.

"Alex… How come you don't have a girlfriend," Amanda asked in a drunk, slurred voice.

"Um, I don't know. Well, I had this one girl."

"You know, you're a good-looking guy," she quickly interrupted, and this dude named Kris and some other guys standing near kind of laughed. She then yelled at them, "Oh, shut up. Some guys just need to hear that… fuck you Kris…"

"Yeah," said Nicole, sort of jumping in, "Alex, you are cute."

"Yeah, Alex, you're so cute," said Kris in a girly kind of way, making fun of Amanda, and people standing around started to laugh.

"Shut up, you fuckers," responded Nicole, hitting him on the shoulder.

"Here, Alex, have a tequila with us," chimed in Kris, and then they started pouring and handing out shots in plastic cups to everyone. At that point I was already drunk, so I did it and then a few more.

After those shots and another beer, I only sort of remember hearing people talk, faces going back and forth as if watching a train go by, or something like that. I remember talking about the history cheating thing that happened with some guys, discussing how we might do it again. At one point, I was debating music with Kris the tequila guy. I was slurring, telling him about how music in the U.S. actually sucked compared to stuff over in Europe, bands like The Jesus and Mary Chain, stuff that kids I knew in my nerdy classes had recently turned me on to. He was saying that he didn't have any idea what the fuck I was talking about when Jaime came in and interrupted us. "Hey Alex, smart-ass, what's that poem you said last year in class?" Jaime was in my sophomore year American Studies class, but I never really talked to him. We were starting a session on poetry and the teacher asked if anyone wanted to recite a poem that they liked and had memorized. No one responded, but I knew a few and offered to recite one. I had forgotten all about it.

"Um, you mean that Pablo Neruda poem, 'Poetry,' right?"

"Yeah, whatever the fuck you want to call it. Recite it, will you, right here for all of us, fucking loud, like you mean it." After I just stood there for a bit Jaime started chanting "Poem. Poem. Poem," and soon was joined by Kris and others who were nearby and now listening in. I wondered whether he was being sincere or just trying to make fun of me. In most circumstances I would have been blushing like hell, gotten all flustered and red in the face, and refused to do it, but being that I had drank over 10 beers and done a bunch of shots, I guess I didn't give a shit.

"Well, I don't know if I remember it right now..."

"Bullshit, you know it," exclaimed Jaime. "Come on, recite it man. Poem, poem…"

"Um, well, it's something…ok…like… One night… no wait…um, oh, okay, it's…" I paused, took a breath and then exclaimed, "And it was at that age, poetry arrived in search of me!!!"'

"Yeahhhhh!!!!!" exclaimed everyone who was around me. To my surprise, I was now on top of a table in the back yard, just off the deck, staggering, with my arms raised over my head and with a good deal of the party looking on. I remember looking out over the crowd, spotting John and Carlos, who both had big smiles, pointing up at me, John with his typical, sort of disapproving face (he always seemed to disapprove of me). I stood there, wavering, trying to fight back all the alcohol that was in me, seeing Jaime's big face as he was pumping his arm up into the air and cheering me on.

"I don't know, know where it came from… From winter or a river, from the branches night, abruptly form the others, or returning along, I was without a face and it touched me…" I yelled out, with my hands still raised in the air.

"Yeah, haaaa…." some people screamed as I said that, with others just looking at me confused or laughing. I knew that I was already fucking the poem up; I had skipped an entire line and bastardized another…. So I put my arms down and stood there for a minute without saying anything, trying to gather myself again.

"Poem, poem, poem," some started to chant again.

And then I yelled "Friends, people, I have another poem to recite," gathering confidence, lifting my arms up again.

"Yessss!!!" they started to scream.

"This is a new poem, one of my own, are you ready????"

"Yeah!!!!"

"Are you ready???"

"Yeahhhh!!"

"One night, when the moon was green, around the corner came a shit machine."

"Ohhhh…"

"A shot was fired."

"Haaaa!!!!"

"A scream was heard… A man was hit… by a flying turd!!!"

And the place erupted. It was the first time I'd ever done anything like that, and probably the last. I've never been the center of attention like that at a party—and all for a stupid poem. The poem was something I read once in the bathroom stall of a truck stop up in Janesville, Wisconsin.

After my poem recital, people were cheering, laughing at me, demanding another poem. Someone handed me a shot, which I drank, after which I almost fell off the table. Hands came up to catch me, but I regrouped and slowly made my way down. At that point I could hardly walk, and I remember stumbling through the crowd with people patting me on the back. I remember a girl grabbing me and saying "Alex, are you ok?" but I kind of smiled and continued on with some kind of dude dragging me along. More shots continued, and then I was kind of talking to Kathy, the big breasted girl, who had this reputation of being a slut, and come to think of it had been giving me eyes all night. I don't remember at all what we were talking about, but I do remember that as we were making out I vomited all over the rail of the deck, just barely missing her. People kind of dispersed, it caused quite a commotion.

All I remember after that is sitting down on this rocking chair and then having everything black out, and then waking up in the front seat of someone's Maxima and the sun blaring down on me through the windshield and sweat running down my face. My body hurt like hell from apparently being in that seat for a while. When I looked down I noticed mud and grass all over my jeans, shirt, and hands.

I had no idea what the hell I was doing in the car and it really freaked me out. I lifted my head and felt this awful shrieking pain run through the back of my neck up through to the top of my head, as if someone had driven a nail in there. My mouth was dry, my lips sore, and I began to notice scratches and dirt all over my hands. I had no idea what time it was. I didn't have a watch or anything, but looking around I thought it had to be early morning. There was no one around, so I slowly and quietly opened the door and made my way out of the car, closed the door, crept back along the driveway over to a bush, stopped and looked around. Noticing that still no one appeared to be looking out from the house or was out on the street, I made it onto the sidewalk and started walking down the street as if I was just taking a stroll or something. It reminded me of The Velvet Underground's song "Sunday Morning," about this guy walking along some sidewalk early on a Sunday morning after being out all night, being completely hammered, and walking by innocent people all dressed up on their way to church.

As I walked down the street, I finally noticed that I was only a few houses down from Andy's. I had driven there the night before, and I still had my keys. I walked directly to where my car was, didn't even bother thinking about where John and Carlos were. I didn't dare go into the house to find out what the hell had happened to me, I just got in, started the car, and drove home.

When I finally got home, my mom freaked out at me. "Alex, what happened? Oh my God, I was so worried about you... you didn't even call..." I heard the typical lecture from her husband Doug on alcoholism and condoms and that I could talk to him about anything. They meant well, my mom and Doug, and they trusted me, I knew that. So I always listened, did my best to act like the good kid, but that day I ended the conversation short and crashed out.

Later that evening, I was on the phone with Carlos, who said, "Man, where the hell did you go you last night?"

"I don't know, I mean, I woke up in a car down the street from the house."

"What? What do you mean?"

"Well, I woke up in the driver's seat of this car a couple of houses down the street from where the party was at. I have no idea whose house or car it was, or how I got in there. I guess

I'd been sleeping in the car."

"Ha, ha, ha!! Fuck man, that's fucking crazy. You don't remember how you got in there?"

"No, no idea at all. I was freaked out actually."

"Shit man, we were worried sick about you!!"

"Why, what happened?"

"Dude, do you remember the poem 'n shit?"

"Yeah, and I think I remember throwing up after too."

"Yeah, holy shit! You all of a sudden puked all over the edge of the deck, but like a shit load, like the Exorcist or something. After that you sat down on the rocking chair and like passed out for a while."

"Yeah, I sort of remember sitting down on that chair, but then not much more after that.

"Well, you were passed out on the chair for a good hour or so. Girls were coming up and seeing how you were doing. Andy was fucking pissed off as hell 'cause you puked, wanted to throw you out of the party, but people kind of backed him off and eventually they let you just sit there."

"No shit... what else happened?"

"People were taking pictures of you, someone tried to put a cigarette in your mouth to take a picture, and it stayed in for a bit and then you all of a sudden stood up and spit it out and screamed, and then just sat back down went back to sleep. We were fucking cracking up man."

"Dude, you guys weren't looking out for me?"

"Yeah, but it was just sort of funny," Carlos said laughing as he was talking.

"So," he continued on, "the party kept going, and then all of a sudden the cops pulled up and somebody screamed

'Cops!!' People started making their way out, and we were going to get you but then, just like that, you jumped up out of the chair with this crazy look in your eyes, looked around, and then boom, started on this crazy sprint, and I mean full dead sprint with your head up, legs kicking, right off the deck, through the backyard and into the woods.

"People were like 'Holy shit!!!' John and I were standing there stunned. We started walking out back yelling your name and looking for you, but couldn't find you. We were going to go out in the woods to look for you, but then the cops started kicking people out and since we didn't have a ride home we grabbed one with Matt who showed up right before the cops came. We were all drunk, so we thought it was funny 'n shit, and just kind of left without thinking of it. Later on, on the way home, we started joking around that maybe you were passed out in the woods or something."

"Yeah, I don't know how I got there, but I woke up in that car, with dirt and shit all over my pants, my hands and knees…"

"Shit dude," laughed Carlos, "you ran into the woods and you must have like hid behind trees, got onto the ground or something. I guess you made your way through the woods and you must have found your way to that car, got in somehow and passed out.

"Yeah, I guess so. I'm surprised that car was unlocked like that."

"No shit. Or what if an alarm would have gone off or something. That would have really sucked."

"No shit, you probably would have run off again, into the woods and really passed out there."

So that's what happened. Needless to say, Andy was kind

off pissed off about the throwing-up incident, but the story and the pictures ended up being pretty funny. Jaime wasn't as friendly to me anymore, but my friends and I seemed to get into parties easily after that. We went to a lot of parties—at people's houses, at the woods, and we were chased around by the cops a lot. When I said before that we were more carefree back then and no one seemed to mind that we were always getting fucked up, that's true, but the cops did harass us. They were nice about it though and generally waited until toward the end of the night to either give us a warning or break up the party and take our beer. They would sometimes arrest or fine someone, but that was extremely rare. I think they saw us as a good, consistent, and cheap beer supply and so they didn't want to do anything to disrupt that.

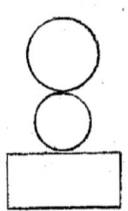

Cartoon Pornos, 10-Foot Bongs, and Parenting

Besides partying at houses when parents were gone— or sometimes even when they were there—we partied in the woods, under the viaducts, in the parking lots of factories, and even at the tip of runways at O'Hare Airport. Back then it was easy to get onto the service roads that went by the end of runways. We would drink and smoke joints while lying on the hood of a car or on the grass as the planes blasted over us taking off to who knows where. Security guards would sometimes tell us to leave, but that was about it. I have a feeling we wouldn't be able to get off that easy these days.

Parties in the woods became the way to party, especially during my senior year of high school. They offered spontaneity and freedom and taught great organization management skills:

getting a bunch of people together at the last minute, figuring out how to buy beer and deciding in what part of the woods to meet—all without e-mail or cell-phones. We would find a spot and use it for a weekend or two until the cops would catch on and bust our party up and, of course, take our beer.

The parties would be at one of the many clearings in the woods accessible by trail paths that were fairly easy to follow at night with the aid of flash lights. All the spots had some sort of name passed down by generations of Des Plainers, such as the Bon Spot, the Moon Cliff, the Drag, and so on. And there were always rumors of people finding dead animals in the woods that were supposedly slaughtered by Satan worshipers. Kids would swear to find them along with pentagrams and shit like that. It was usually kids that were into bands like Megadeath and Slayer. My friends and I never found any such things. We also had various ghost stories, like one about this old white sinister-looking house that would suddenly appear and disappear in the middle of the woods. I've heard that story told of many other woods in suburban Chicago, so who knows where it first started. But, again, my friends and I never saw it.

Anyway, the parties were generally lots of fun. All sorts of kids would show up. The woods parties were usually organized by the burnouts, who didn't mind if anyone else came. They were cool about that kind of stuff and were just interested in their music and getting fucked up. There always was a boombox, a radio or tape player (later CD player) at the woods parties. Some of the burnout kids would bring acoustic guitars and play songs like "Stairway to Heaven" by Led Zeppelin or "Hotel California" by The Eagles. And of course people would get high.

Sometimes I would get into conversations about colleges and stuff like that. Many kids were not sure what they wanted to do and thought about going to the community college for a couple of years or just start working.

I was set on going to the University of Illinois at Urbana-Champaign. The only real reason I was so determined to go there was because I loved the Fighting Illini basketball team. I didn't even visit or apply to other colleges. Neither my parents nor any relatives I knew ever went to college, so I had to figure it out on my own. Also, U of I was offering me a full-ride scholarship because I was one of only four Latino students in my high school that had above a B grade average and scored well on the ACT test.

When my friends and I went to these parties, Carlos and I dropped our friends off and then would go get alcohol and come back to meet them. That's how the parties generally worked—as opposed to the woods party the kids had in the movie *Dazed and Confused*, where they brought kegs to the woods and everything, our groups were generally on their own, kind of BYOB style. Kids would bring cases of Old Style and Bud Light, malt liquor such as Mickey's Big Mouths, 40s of Ole English or Colt 45, and nasty stuff like Purple Passion or Cisco—which was always good to get girls drunk with.

Carlos and I always went to a little liquor store not too far away called Packy's, which was owned by this old Indian guy. For some reason, the guy would not card Carlos, who I guess passed for older than 21, even though we were only 17 at the time. We would generally pick up a couple of 30-casers of Old Style, which was our favorite back then because it cost only $9.99 per 30-caser.

Sometimes when the cops would catch on to the spot where we were partying, they would make a dramatic bust— so by the time Carlos and I would be getting back with our beer, we'd arrive to find a paddy wagon and a few other cop cars parked along the road with a few cops leading a bunch of kids out of the woods, coming out single file with their hands around their heads, being ushered into the paddy wagon. The cops would usually just give out tickets for underage drinking and take all the beer, and then a few weeks later we'd end up finding a different place to party at.

One time I had a party at my parents' house. I held several small parties, get-togethers really, but this was the only all-out bash I've thrown. It was the summer after my freshman year at U of I. My parents totally let me have it; they even agreed to leave the house for the night. However, they were not aware that I planned to have a bunch of kegs, a 10-foot beer bong, a bunch of pot, and a kick-ass stereo system going in the back-yard.

The Wiley brothers brought over their huge stereo system, and we set this audio stand in one of the corners of my back-yard. The Wileys were both big meathead kind of guys who had gone to Maine West. It was rumored that their father gave them illegal growth hormones he bought somewhere overseas when they were little in hopes that they'd grow to be profes-sional athletes. Although the father's plan never panned out, the brothers were beefy and muscular. The older one, Rob, may have benefited a little more from the hormones because he was much taller. He's always had a goatee, short shaved hair with a long mullet-tail in the back, and he always wears sleeveless shirts, for like every occasion. The younger, smaller brother,

Steve, was like a little replica of Rob. They were a few years ahead of us, were really popular in their days in high school, seemed to linger around Des Plaines, as many Maine West graduates seemed to do, and pretty soon melded in with the rest of the stoner and party crowd. They still go to high school parties today, and now hold the market in terms of pot sales in Chicago's near northwest suburbs.

It was pretty damn impressive, the Wiley's stereo system, but I didn't really get involved too much in the music that night. I figured since they were bringing the stuff, I would let them run with it. Besides, no one that came to the party would have liked the kind of stuff I was starting to get into at the time, like the *Loveless* album by My Bloody Valentine, Nirvana's *In Utero*, Stereolab's first album, *Peng*. Instead, the Wiley boys played hardcore rap from that time, stuff like Cyprus Hill, NWA, and Too Short. I was amazed at how many kids back then loved gangster rap—especially kids like the Wiley brothers, who were as racist as could be. They constantly used the word "nigger" for anyone they were trying to downgrade, and they made fun of black people in general—but they loved rap and hip-hop.

We had Christmas lights up all over the backyard, televisions playing pornos sticking out through the windows of my house—one playing "regular" pornography and the other cartoons. All the guys were standing around watching and cheering. A ton of people came, mostly from Maine West—the younger kids that were still in high school and were now entering their party phase, us recent graduates, and the older kids who, like the Wiley brothers, were still around. I charged $4 for a cup to get in. Some of my friends' fathers came and even paid for a cup.

Someone brought this crazy 10-foot beer bong that, in order to use it, people had to climb a ladder to the top of my garage with a bunch of beer and fill it up there with the hose coming down to someone on the ground holding the other end to their mouth. At first it was kind of just a novelty; no one really used it until this little guy named Alberto, a small Mexican kid we all used to hang out with in high school until he got involved in some crazy shit, stepped up demanding to do a bong. So a couple of guys got up there, started filling up the beer bong as Alberto held the other end to his mouth, with the rest of the party cheering him on, and—whoosh!! The guys unleashed the bong, and he started drinking it down, but it was way too much and came down too fast. He had a few good gulps until it started spurting out of his mouth and he finally had to pull away. This, of course, started a whole slew of 10-foot beer bong challengers.

As the party went on, people started doing keg stands—20-, 30-, 40-, 60-second keg stands. The drunker everyone got, the longer the stands seemed to last. These legendary kids—usually smaller, burnout types who had practiced drinking a ton—had the ability to pull off the longest keg stands, slam a beer or do a "shotgun" the fastest. I, in fact, could slam a beer faster than most anyone, and it always amazed the big guys—kind of like that short, skinny Japanese guy who kills all the huge guys in the hot dog-eating competitions. There might be a correlation between being thin and small and consuming things efficiently.

For a moment I was kind of standing off in the back, observing my own party. All the burnout guys were lined up by the garage to do the 10-foot bong, as if they were lined up for communion; the young kids were in the middle, looking on—

with a few also finally daring to step up. The Wiley brothers and their gang were all standing around the stereo system in a corner of the yard, smoking blunts, sporting their L. A. Kings, Miami Heat or Charlotte Hornets baseball caps and jerseys. All the older cooler kids were up off to the side, probably talking about what was going on after and whether they were going to stay or go somewhere else, and then there were all the fuckers watching the constant stream of pornography streaming out of the windows of the back of the house. As I stood there, I noticed people smoking cigarettes whom I'd never seen smoke before, girls who weren't all that good looking in high school who all of a sudden were gorgeous, and also vice versa. At one point the fucking limbo even got going.

This kid, Raphael Alaya was there, and he was trashed beyond belief. Raphael was kind of quiet and nerdy back in high school, but really athletic—kind of like a muscular nerd. However, you never saw him at any parties or anything while we were in high school because he had this really controlling mother, who meant well by promoting school above everything else. And he in fact did do really well in school—he had great grades, went to Yale, being like one of the few kids from Maine West to go to an Ivy League school. However, at school he apparently began to party like hell. Eventually he smoked so much pot and drank so much that he failed out. He started going to community college, then Illinois State University to major in English. Raphael is one of the few people I know from Des Plaines that still lives in Chicago, and we hang out sometimes. He and I always have good conversations, the few intelligent ones that I have with anyone, about writing, religion, and politics. We love the philosopher David Hume and his attack on rationality, and all the existentialists who wonder whether there is any meaning in the world except for what we give it. He has always been working on a novel, though I've never read any of it.

The night of my party, he got there early as I was preparing my contribution: a punch that was simply jugs of Hawaiian Punch with lots of Everclear. It's the kind of drink that tastes pretty sweet but fucks you up completely. Raphael showed up, talking up all the partying that he had been doing at Yale, trying to show how cool he'd suddenly become, and he drank a shit load of the killer punch. At first it was fun to see him like that, to see someone breaking out of their shell. But then it sort of became depressing as he got drunker and drunker, eventually to the point where he was stumbling around on my porch as people were walking into the party, until he was eventually standing around in his boxers with people throwing stuff at him. After we got him to pass out on my bed, I was afraid that he would throw up on it so we arranged to have someone drive him home and drop him off on his front yard, pull away, and honk the horn a few times so his parents would come out and recover him.

The next morning, his mother called me, thoroughly upset, screaming "What the hell did you do to my son? He couldn't talk, walk, was throwing up. I know he was going to a party at your house, right?" She went on like that, threatened to call the police, call my parents, but when I told her that they had given me permission, she was even more upset and wanted to have them jailed. I was hung over, irritated, and finally I was like, "Listen, Mrs. Alaya, I'm sorry about how you found your son, but please don't question my parents' character. I have a very good relationship with them, they trust me, enough to let me have friends over and have fun, even if there is alcohol involved. Everyone had fun, it was great, I'm sorry, but your son was the only one that was like that. If I were you, I would stop yelling and blaming me and focus on your son and find out what the hell's wrong with him, why he can't have fun like the rest of us." It was kind of harsh; I wish I wouldn't have reacted like that in retrospect, but I hate it when parents try to blame the rest of society for all of their children's faults. Societal influences play a significant role in everything we do, but they can only be blamed to a certain extent. Anyway, those are my thoughts on parenting.

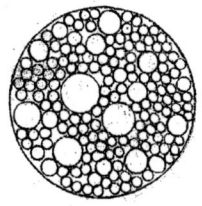

The Universe

After observing my party for a while and smoking a joint with a few people I barely knew, I lay down on my back and stared off into the night sky. It wasn't until my senior year in high school that I began to appreciate the universe we live in. I was in advanced physics, and the only part I remember well was when we studied the composition of our solar system, our galaxy, and our universe. We touched on concepts like the Big Bang, the expansion and evolution of the universe, how mind-boggling huge it is, and briefly on Einstein's Theory of Relativity. It fascinated me enough that I wanted to be an astronomer, briefly. I never became one, but I did take an astronomy class at U of I during my freshman year.

So as I lay in the backyard, I was thinking about the other galaxies, possibly like our own Milky Way, with its billions and billions of stars, many of which we can't see but all of which probably have planets like the ones in our solar system. Back then scientists hadn't discovered the first planet outside of our solar system; they just theorized that every star had to have planets orbiting it like our sun does.

I was wondering whether another young person like me on one of those planets could also be looking up at the sky during his own party, wondering the same thing I was. Or, I wondered, could it be that I, by chance, was the only living thing on this planet or any of those planets in the night sky—in the freaking universe—doing exactly what I was doing at that very moment in time and, therefore, I was fucking "unique" as one could be right at that moment.

This girl Heidi, whom Carlos met at a mall, was at my party with her friends. Carlos wasn't quite dating her yet, but I knew he really liked her. I guess she saw me laying like that and walked over and asked if anything was wrong. I was like, "Oh, no, nothing at all, I'm just laying here, looking up at the stars." (I think you could see stars back then in Des Plaines; I can't anymore in Chicago.)

"Oh, really? That's funny," she said, also looking up.

"Come lay down here and check it out for yourself; it's pretty cool," I said to her, speaking without really thinking about it, mainly because I was high. She kind of smiled at me, looked up, and then sat down.

"No, lay down; it's so much better when you're lying down and looking up. You can almost imagine yourself hanging from the earth, as if lying on the ceiling of a room and looking down at the floor."

Smiling even more and looking at me quizzically, she kind of brushed her shoulders and then in a "what the fuck?" kind of motion lay down next to me and looked up.

As we were both lying down and looking up, you could hear the party chatter going on—a shout, a cheer here and there, someone rooting someone else to drink faster or longer, shouts and laughter from the guys watching the pornos. I think that song by Blind Mellon that played all over the radio back then was playing at the moment, you know the one about the guy just liking rain? For some reason I remember hearing that the lead singer was Axl Rose's cousin, but I never knew if it was true.

"What are you looking at?" Heidi asked me, and so I told her that I was looking at the constellations, specifically at Orion the Hunter—the only one I really know by sight, except for maybe one of the dippers—and how he was sent by Zeus to shoot Taurus, the bull who was about to attack the Pleiades, the seven women that were bathing in a pond.

And then I told her about the whole universe thing I was thinking about, about whether another guy up there was doing the same thing as me, or that maybe I was unique at that very moment.

"Wow," she said, now turning over on her side to look at me with those great big eyes all cute girls seem to have when they're looking at you. "Did you make all that up, or did you read it somewhere?"

"What? Well, not all of it. I mean, it's true that there could be someone else up there doing something similar to what we're doing, or even some other type of life form we could never comprehend. That's all probably more speculation than anything else. But maybe the idea of someone up there just like me thinking the same thing, that might be an original idea although I doubt it."

"You're funny, the way you talk… what, do you study a lot or something?"

"Well, I guess, yeah, I like to read," I responded, looking up, enjoying the attention, and wondering if Carlos would mind if I made out with her…

"Do you really think there are other people out there, like aliens and stuff like that?"

"Yeah, I mean, it almost doesn't make sense that there aren't, if you understand the universe and how it's made up. I don't think the 'aliens' are necessarily monsters or these little people with big heads, like all the movies make them seem to be, but I tend to believe that they're just like us, just up there, living, raising their kids, cheering on their sports teams, making out and listening to music, going to the movies, getting into wars, wondering why the hell they're alive and whether the God they believe in is real. Or who knows, you know, maybe they're like great big blobs or smart dolphins or bugs or something?"

"Doing beer bongs, like all those guys over there?"

"Well, maybe not that. I would hope that they've evolved a little bit."

"Listening to Tesla and Cinderella?" who happened to playing, as the party music had reverted back to our hair-band roots.

"God, I hope fucking not. But, you know, maybe there are planets in which Tesla and Cinderella are actually Gods, and they're worshipped 'n shit."

After she laughed, she paused, then looked at me and said, "Hmm… I don't know, what makes you so certain that there are other people out there? I mean, wouldn't they have contacted us already, or do you believe in all that conspiracy stuff, about the government hiding UFOs and aliens from us?"

"I don't know about that conspiracy stuff. I mean, maybe aliens haven't contacted us yet because they haven't been able to figure out how to travel that far yet, or maybe it's not possible. But even if they have visited, there maybe are many reasons why they haven't made themselves known, like they want to observe another race for science purposes without interrupting us, just to see how we progress. Or maybe they're like secretly observing us in order to plan their attack, you know? Who knows… It seems silly to me why the government wouldn't want us to, uh, know if they have proof that life exists out there, I would think it'd give us have a better perspective on things. But who knows, the government has done dumber things. But why am I so certain that life is out there? Well, the odds are with it."

"How so?"

"Well, I mean, look at all the stars up there?"

"What does that have to do with it?"

"Well, do you know what all the stars are?"

"Um, no, not really, I mean I never really paid attention in class."

It's interesting how many people you meet, even in today's age when we're supposed to be so much more civilized, don't appreciate or understand some of our supposed great scientific facts. In the days in which people started going around saying that the world was round, not flat, there were tons of people walking around thinking that the world was flat for a long time after. They had no idea and died having no idea that we live on a big round rock that is circling a huge ball of gas and heat. I mean, Galileo got jailed for going around saying that the sun, not the Earth, was the center of our solar system (and the presumed universe back then), and this now-common fact wasn't widely recognized until like over 100 years after his death.

Understanding how long it took Galileo's ideas to get accepted, it's no wonder that many people like Heidi don't know that when we stare up into the night sky and see stars, we are actually looking at billions of suns like our own, some bigger and some smaller, all probably with planets orbiting them. Scientists believe that planets are the result of how solar systems like ours form. They believe that solar systems start out as one huge ball of gas, heat, and debris and, because of gravity, it all starts circling—with the inner part collapsing on itself, eventually forming the star, the nucleus of the solar system. The remaining materials continue to flatten out and extend off, with clumps of matter in between condensing to form planets, and matter condensing around the planets to form moons, and the rest of the stuff forming asteroids and comets. Therefore, all those stars or suns out there should have planets. It's like one continuous pattern: a core, surrounded by protective material being orbited by objects which all, collectively, orbit something else. Based on this theory, our galaxy, which is made up of billions and billions of solar systems, should be full of Earth-like planets.

All this theory about the planets and how our solar system formed is all fairly new, in terms of being widely accepted. It wasn't until 1995 that the first planet outside of our solar system was observed using sound or something. The scientists who, over the centuries, understood and theorized this stuff were probably considered eccentrics, way out of the mainstream. Nowadays, every scientist believes this, but even though this is taught in schools, it still is taking time for these concepts to catch on. For example, I didn't know about the first planets being discovered until a few years ago, and not many of my friends today know.

So as we lay there, Heidi on her side, no longer looking up but looking at me, I finished telling her what the stars represented and why I was convinced we were not alone in the universe, and she said, "That's beautiful Alex. Are you always like this?"

"Only when there's a pretty girl laying next in me in the grass under a moonlit sky and there's beer around," I responded, smiling, as she smiled back.

When women aren't accustomed to hearing stuff like that, they melt in your hands, and you can be like the most beautiful guy in the world, even if you're not. Either that or you can come off as a big fucking cheese-ball, it depends on the kind of girl or how you present it. In this case, Heidi loved it. For a guy like me, who usually doesn't get outright attention from girls, it's a great feeling when the shit I spend so much of my free time on actually helps me pick one up.

Then Carlos was standing over us saying, "Hey, what's going on, guy?" while smiling so much that he had a crazed kind of look, knowing that something was wrong.

"Oh, nothing," said Heidi, "Alex is just teaching me about the stars."

"Oh, well, *that's* cool," said Carlos. "Well, I'll be over by the keg if anyone wants to join me," he said as he walked away, giving me a lasting kind of stare as I was lighting up another cigarette.

"Well, I should go see what's wrong with him," said Heidi.

"Cool, no problem. I'm going to lay here a bit more, finish

this cigarette, and then get back to the party myself."

"Ok. Thanks for the stories, Alex. It was really interesting," she said, getting up. "Hopefully you can tell me more some other time."

"Sure thing," I said, and then she got up and walked away. She stopped seeing Carlos soon after that night, and I never saw her again.

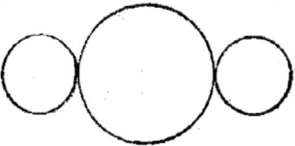

Trends and Raving

The cops ended up coming to my cartoon pornos party later that night, made the party disperse, and let of few of us take the remaining keg to a neighbor's across the street where it would be quieter. And of course some of the cops came back to join us for a few beers and tried to talk to some of the girls that were way under age. They were impressed with the stereo system, saying that they could hear and feel the music from a couple blocks down the street. My parents came home later that night and were blown away by the whole scene, which I had to clean up the next day.

Remember that girl Kathy—with the big boobs—that I almost threw up on at the Green Shit Machine party? Well, she was at the party and came with us to the Johnson's across the street. Although she got bigger in college, which I guess happened to a lot of us, she still looked really seductive, especially to the eyes of a drunk 19-year-old, so we started making out. I tried to take her into the back seat of my friend's car, but she wouldn't and instead wanted me to call her the next day, so she gave me her number. We kept making out though, and at one point I had her over the hood of a car parked across the street from my house, allowing my parents to watch the whole thing. They were there at the front door when I eventually stumbled my way across the street and walked in. They demanded some sort of explanation, asking who that girl was, etc. I simply said "hi," "goodnight," and that I needed to go to sleep. Then I passed out on my bed. The next day we talked again about condoms, that I should feel free to talk to them about anything. I never called Kathy.

At the party I noticed how, in only a matter of a year, the kids I graduated with were all changing. Our little cliques in high school evolved with the times, adopting new trends. Some kids, on the other hand, seemed to stop giving a shit about trends and just started looking "older." After high school a lot of the cooler kids turned into punks or punk wannabes because in 1993 being "alternative" was trendy. It started toward the end of high school and then seemed to explode after. In high school it was easy to tell the "head-bangers," "burnouts," "stoners," "jocks," "nerds," "theater kids," "housers"—they all wore whatever uniform those groups required. The cool kids, though, were just the kids who looked good, had the most expensive clothes, and were the star athletes or cheerleaders. They could look like a houser or burnout if they wanted to. They were social amebas I guess, so it makes sense that when the "alternative" movement was embraced by MTV they all of a sudden looked like they were born listening to angry, disenchanted rock and roll.

There were a few cool kids that caught on to punk or grunge rock toward the end of high school, just when it seemed to start getting popular, when all the Seattle bands like Pearl Jam and Nirvana were becoming best selling bands. Nirvana's *Nevermind* was released in 1991, making grunge rock a trend, and it started to be cool to be into "alternative" music and culture and against the mainstream. Out of nowhere these kids seemed to be into the bands that the Seattle grunge bands said they idolized, like the Sex Pistols, The Clash, and the Pixies. With money from their parents to buy instruments, and time to play them, they stopped wearing their Z-Cavaricci's and IOU shirts, started wearing Converse sneakers and ratty shirts, and started bands.

After several name changes and internal struggles, the band formed by the kids we knew became Radical Emperor. They started gaining an audience, first amongst the cool kids at one of their garages, and then at bowling alleys and roller rinks where other little punk bands from the Des Plaines, Mt. Prospect, and Park Ridge suburbs would come and play. Radical Emperor was not initially selected as one of the groups to perform in our high school's variety show during our senior year. Rumors circulated in the hallways that there was a conservative conspiracy that sought to mute the radical lyrics of the group. After enough protests, complaints, and petitions, Radical Emperor was allowed to perform, and when they hit the stage they exclaimed: "This is what your teachers didn't want you to hear!!!" and proceeded to rip through their three-chord song that involved a few slow parts cascading to explosions of sound and catchy verses and choruses that no one could understand but I'm sure were about how it sucks to be a kid, trapped in this society with no one to talk to, and so you just have to say fuck it and rock. During the song they even threw around a bunch of stuffed animals that were ripped open so that their stuffing flew all over the place. It was all very punk rock.

Radical Emperor's following started to grow and soon you saw some of the cool girls start to change. At first it was only slight changes in attire—the occasional retro look like something resembling Cindy Lauper or Pat Benetar, and then that skater-punk look with ragged skirts, studded belts, old worn out Converse shoes and ripped fishnet stockings. As we all went away to school and punk really became mainstream—and bands like The Smashing Pumpkins, Green Day and Nine Inch Nails continued making the "alternative" scene seem like the new revolution and hating yourself be the cool thing to do—you really saw a change in the cool kids. You started seeing colored hair, multiple piercings, heavy drug use, and lots of cigarette smoking. Oh, and suddenly everyone was an art major at their respective school and was, like, into doing really trippy shit. Most of them eventually became restaurant or bar managers.

There were certain kids, though, that never really seemed to follow the trends. Like my crush Candice, for example. Sure, she had her bangs sprayed up in the earlier years of high school, had her share of cardigan sweaters, even had an I.O.U. sweatshirt or two, maybe also a pair of those awful skin tight pants that came down to the calves with those little white slip-on shoes, whatever they were called. And these days I'm sure she would look great in her expensive faded jeans with stiletto heels, a sleeveless shirt and a little blazer jacket. But she more or less always looked nice, dressed more contemporary than the rest of her friends, so when it was apparent that being punk was the cool thing to be, Candice pretty much stayed the same, with maybe minor adjustments such as wearing her hair down and looser, cutting down on the hair spray, and losing the cardigan sweaters.

I like to think that I've always dressed the same. My everyday outfits have always consisted of jeans, shirts and sneakers. Back then I wore Airwalks, Pumas, Adidas, Converse, the occasional Nike sneaker, and toward the end of high school, Doc Marten's. My shirts usually were solid black, gray or dark blue, with a few boyish-looking, horizontal multi-colored striped numbers and an assortment of concert shirts. I liked concert shirts back when it was really cool to have them, back when we were 11 and 12—when it was cool to have the newest Iron Maiden or Metallica shirt. I still like to buy them, but infrequently and only if they're of obscure bands and you can't really tell it's a concert shirt—you know, with minimal actual reference to the band's name.

Well, I guess I have to admit that I've also had a few embarrassing clothing trends. I went through phases where my jeans were rolled up. I had my pairs of black and white Reebok high tops and an I.O.U. sweater or two. There are a few tie-dyed Grateful Dead concert shirts still in my closet. (However, none of us really got into their music, and I totally hate it today.) I also wore the houser look at times, had what some called a "Mexi-Mullet," and went to house dance parties at suburban hotels hosted by B96 DJ's like "Bad Boy Bill" and "Jammin Julian Jumpin Perez." Matt took me a couple of times to teenage dance clubs, such as Toto's out in Schaumburg, where he and his friends would try to pick up slutty girls from the far west suburbs, like Elgin and Hanover Park, and get into fights with their boyfriends.

I've also had my share, more than my share, of interests that I've started and stopped—starting when I was little, like eight, with remote control cars. After much crying and sobbing on my part, my dad finally bought me an expensive one that took forever to put together. It was called the Hornet, and the fucking thing kept breaking down and pissing my dad off, and eventually he trashed it while drunk. I then got into models, like tanks and helicopters, and I started a few but never completed them—same thing with puzzles. Later it was sports; I wanted to be a baseball or football player. I was pretty good at baseball, played it until I was 11, but then I got beamed in the back of the head by a pitch and was like "fuck that." I played football my freshman year until I got lambasted by a big freaking guy during a game and was like "fuck that" also. After my parents separated, I got into reading books, lots of them, encyclopedias even. I still read, but I don't read as much as I used to, and now I start to fall asleep when doing so. At one point I wanted to be a historian but once I saw how boring it actually is to study history, like for a whole semester at college, I decided I didn't like history all that much. I then wanted to be a philosopher and studied it, but decided only to minor in it because I didn't know how the hell I would make any money. Since then I've dabbled in painting and drawing, lifting weights (along with consuming the protein shakes), running marathons and triathlons, smoking and drinking, and playing the guitar—I have like three guitars that I no longer really use.

Out of all the interests or fads that I've dabbled in, the one that has been with me most consistently now is music.

I didn't grow up in any sort of musical family or any-thing. However, I remember the loud Spanish music my parents would play at the few parties from back then, and the sad Mariachi music they would listen to when they missed their country and their families. My father listened to stuff like Neil Diamond and Elvis Presley, at super-loud volumes, when we would visit him on the weekends, and he would get drunk and cry about my mother.

I don't really remember the first music I actually liked or the first band I was into, except for maybe the Chipmunks, especially their Christmas album in Spanish. I do remember the first rock and roll album I wanted—Kiss' *Destroyer*, the one with them all on the cover jumping up in the sky with their fists up in the air and you could see their crazy outfits, make-up, and Gene Simmons' tongue sticking out and all that. I didn't even know what it sounded like, but I wanted it because it looked cool I guess. I asked my mom to buy it for me when we were at a K-Mart, but she said no, so I snuck it in the shopping cart. That didn't work either, and I just ended up crying at the check-out line after my mother found it and told me to put it back, with the checkout girl saying, "Ohhhh, he's so cuuutteee…"

The first album I got was Michael Jackson's *Thriller*. My mom got it for my sister and me, and also bought us this cheap little record player from Toys R Us for our room. The three of us sat in our bedroom listening to it the first night. Me and my sister sat on our beds while the record played, taking turns passing the album cover back and forth, bobbing our heads, and my mom stood by the door smiling and crying for some reason. I remember the record had a big picture of Michael himself on each side, back when he sort of looked normal.

I'm not sure where the *Thriller* era led to, some kind of weird stuff like the *Grease* soundtrack, the band Survivor, the *Rocky* movies, my Dad's oldies albums, Debbie Gibson, Belinda Carlisle, Prince, A-Ha. After that weird phase, which coincided with early puberty, some of my friends and I got into heavy metal.

Metallica had transformed heavy metal in the early 80s, creating what I guess some call the first "thrash" album in *Kill 'em All*. We didn't know that, had no idea what was going on, had never even heard of heavy metal before, but we just liked it, mainly because some of my friends' older brothers liked it so much and because the albums were so cool looking. Then we got into AC/DC, Iron Maiden, Megadeath, Motorhead, Black Sabbath, DIO, Man O War, and later the hair metal bands like Motley Crue, Poison, Guns N' Roses, etc. We bought all the tapes and copied and traded them with each other. I remember the debates as to who was Satanist or not and whether the bands had secret, evil messages in their song lyrics or album covers. We debated whether AC/DC's name really stood for "After Christ the Devil Comes," whether the band DIO's name was code for devil, and whether the Black Sabbath albums, when played backwards, contained Satanic messages. We tried to play records backwards but only ended up scratching the shit out of them. Some of my friends would refuse to listen to the stuff because their parents told them it was the devil's music; we called them pussies. This was mainly a Southside Des Plaines thing because when we got to junior high school the other kids were like "what the fuck?" We scared the hell out of them.

This fixation with heavy metal made some of us try and look like head-bangers, but we really didn't know how. We all wanted long hair but none of us had the balls to grow it—either that or our parents didn't let us. We desperately wanted studded belts, spiked bracelets for our wrists and necks, big black leather boots, but we didn't know where the hell to buy any of it—K-Mart certainly didn't have that shit. Somehow we heard of a store called The Alley, which sold the stuff. Through tales from older siblings, we found out that it was down "in the city," which is how we referred to Chicago.

With Des Plaines so close to Chicago, many of us were fairly familiar with the city. I would go almost every weekend to visit my father, but I never traveled there on my own. My dad lived in an area called Albany Park, which back then was mainly Latinos and Middle Eastern immigrants, so they had nothing like The Alley there. All we did was eat burritos and tacos at the local hole-in-the-wall restaurants or go to Montrose beach to watch soccer games. So it was a big deal when we got up the balls to take the suburbanite bus (the Pace) to the Blue Line train all the way downtown and transfer to the Red or Brown Line that would then take us up to the Belmont stop. We set out like we were on a quest to find the Holy Grail or the lost city or something. It was scary—all sorts of people were on the trains. After maybe a few botched attempts where we just rode the train down a bit and then returned back, we finally made it to Chicago's Lakeview neighborhood at Belmont and Sheffield.

It was a like a totally different world than the suburbia we lived in. There were people walking around versus just driving or sitting in their houses. Everyone looked a lot different than what we were used to seeing. There were some who wore the bracelets we wanted. We saw lots of bums, people smoking, concert posters and stuff tacked up everywhere. I remember seeing my first skinheads there, bald dudes with bomber jackets and boots on. It was dirty—so dirty—and we loved it. The Alley was located literally in an alley off of Belmont Avenue near Halsted Street, bordering the gay neighborhood of the city. It was surrounded by cool little stores that sold all kinds of odd stuff like edible underwear and dildos. The Alley sold paraphernalia that would go great in any gothic, industrial, or punk person's house, such as black gargoyle statues and figurines, candles, studded arm bracelets and belts, nose rings, earrings, dog chain necklaces, whips, leather outfits, hand-cuffs, leather boots, and the greatest collection of shirts with sayings on them like "Fuck Off and Die." And there were loads of concert shirts. Some of us bought stuff, like I bought a few Iron Maiden and Metallica shirts, and a few posters—like my Police *Synchronicity* and Iron Maiden *Number of the Beast* ones that I still have today. I even bought a studded bracelet.

I never really wore the bracelet, though, out in public—I only wore it in my room listening to my tapes. It was like I was too embarrassed to wear it outside, like I felt it was just some sort of costume, like I was a poser, that people would think I looked stupid.)

We ended up going back to The Alley a few more times and eventually discovered Gramophone Records. We found it by accident after wondering south on Clark St. Finding Gramophone was kind of a transformation for me—I like to say I owe my life to the place. Back then, it was a long, slim, dusty, dark store. The store has since reopened further north. It is now nice and bright, sells mainly the same kind of stuff, but it isn't quite like I remember it. Back then it was primarily a DJ's store and sold mainly vinyl records. In the front there was a tape and CD section with all sorts of dance mixes made by the resident DJs who worked there. The DJs played in the back, spinning records, all sorts of records: hip-hop, R&B, house, deep-house, techno, industrial, ska, reggae, African beats and new-wave.

When I first went to the Gramophone I had no idea that there was so many styles of music. I still don't quite understand them all, and they seem to change all the time. All my friends and I knew was that we liked music. Before discovering Gramophone, we liked the loudness and pace of those Metallica albums, the "thump, thump, thump" of the drums behind the blaring guitars and roaring vocals. We never knew how similar that was to the constant thumping of fast-paced techno music, which is electronic music with all sorts of crazy sound effects. It was all new to us—it was like discovering a whole new world.

It's hard to explain, the feeling you get when you first listen to something through a good set of headphones and are totally blown away because it's unlike anything you've ever heard before. The sound from a good set of big, fat headphones just doesn't compare to small ear plugs. It's like your whole head is enveloped in the sound, like you can almost feel the music playing in different parts of your brain or something.

When we first started going to Gramaphone, the owner, Charles—this 40-something balding gay English man—would give us annoyed looks, like he didn't want a bunch of teenage suburban kids hanging around. But we started buying tapes, and soon he started talking to us, asking us why we would buy a certain tape. When he realized that we didn't know what the hell we were doing, he started giving us stuff to listen to.

The first stuff that we liked, because of the heavy metal we were listening to at the time, was the hard, pulsing sounds of techno. We used to buy tapes made by some of the local DJs, like DJ Psycho-Bitch and DJ Terri Bristol. I was fascinated with the trance-inducing effect the music had on me, with the multiple layers of pulsing sound. The DJs would let us listen to their headphones while they spun their records. Their mixes always had a really cool introduction, like a war speech or eerie dialogue of aliens overlooking the Earth, followed by the slow build up of keyboard melodies that suddenly, as if you were flying over the edge of a cliff and spiraling down over a massive landscape, were joined by thunderous bolts of bass, and layered on to that, all sorts of sounds like chirps, squeals and screaming hymns that, altogether, produced a crazed sort of symphony.

At first it was just dance music that we were listening to. Then another DJ there, Simon, this quirky Latin guy who always had on oversized round spectacles and big platform shoes, started talking to us as we listened to him spin. After seeing how we liked the heavy metal and techno stuff, he got us into bands like Ministry, Big Black, Naked Raygun, and Front 242. These were fast, loud bands that were metallic sounding, mixing guitars with synthesizers, drum machines, distorted screaming voices, all creating a disturbing sound that made you want to dance in a fury and tear something apart. He mixed this type of music in with the techno and the heavy metal we liked, and then with stuff like Sonic Youth, just to demonstrate the similarities in the beats. It was the closest that maybe I've felt to some sort of Buddhist trip or something, where it all seemed to make sense. We then started getting into trip-hop from England, bands like Massive Attack and later Tricky, which was like house with a deep bass sort of background, but instead of sounding soulful, it was more eerie sounding, dreamlike, with soft female vocals and hip-hop mixed in. Simon then showed us older stuff like Einsturzende Neubauten, Neu!, and Kraftwerk, which was German electronic music from the 70s that he said was the roots of the stuff we liked. According to Simon, most modern music, whether electronic dance, post-punk, Reagan era rock 'n roll, art rock like Sonic Youth, and even the punk rock from the late 70s, can be traced back to the Velvet Underground.

I took his word and bought all four of the original Velvet Underground albums. I immediately fell in love with the music and appreciated Simon's viewpoint. I vividly remember staying up until 2 a.m. on a school night listening to *White Light/White Heat*, from the mayhem of the first song, to the eeriness of the spoken word song recounting a guy shipping himself to his girlfriend—who accidentally drives a large set of shears through his head—to the ghastly rendition of a man undergoing a sex transplant, and finally to the climatic 17-minute "Sister Ray" that almost made me not want to listen to music ever again.

I mainly went with John, Matt, and Carlos—Jig was too scared to go with us because he thought he would get in trouble. John, Matt, and Carlos liked it, but eventually they seemed to get bored and stopped wanting to go, so I started going by myself. During my junior year in high school, though, I met Hassan Aldawari, Paul Berg and Carla Radinski. These kids were in what was considered the "theater geek" group back then. They were also the smartest, and I knew them because I happened to have Advanced Physics with them my junior year. They acted in the school plays, played in the school bands, went to fucking band camp, had braces for way too long, and had bad acne and moppy hair. They didn't play sports and didn't work out and were skinny and wore funny-looking clothes.

I ran into Hassan and Paul at Gramophone on a random Saturday afternoon, and we started talking. I had never really talked with them before in class. They seemed surprised to see me there and came up to me as I was thumbing through records. They were friendly, apparently had been going there for years, and recommended a few things to me. After that, we started talking in class, and they soon started inviting me to do things with their friends—but I didn't really admit it to anyone in my group because they would have made fun of me. There was something different about the stuff they were into that I found refreshing. Not just the music but the movies they liked that none of my other friends were into, like David Lynch's *Eraserhead*. And the parties they went to were of an entirely different breed than the kind I'd gone to.

Hassan and Paul and their friends partied by going to raves in the city. Back then the raves were true raves—in the sense that they were pretty much illegal, held in abandoned warehouses in the old warehouse districts west of the Loop and in the Southside. The spaces were dark, packed with kids, and the DJs blasted techno and house music through these massive speakers. Everyone danced in the flashing lights and stayed out all night. They would end up at the Belmont Harbor, parking their cars together and blasting more techno out of the windows, making fun of annoyed-looking joggers running by and watching the sun rise across Lake Michigan. I loved it all, the whole scene.

Sure, we did some drugs, mainly smoked pot, but we didn't drink much like my other friends did. Back then, there was not much ecstasy, or at least it was not that widespread. It really bugs me today when I see the city trying to crack down on raves. It's really expensive to throw parties like that now because they're so regulated and all because there have been a few deaths due to bad ecstasy. I agree that it's in the best interest for kids not to be doing drugs like that, but the point is that a minority of the kids are into it for the drugs; the vast majority just love the music. There's got to be a better way to regulate these parties and allow kids to have their fun, sort of how we do with adults who get shitfaced at sporting events.

We were mainly there for the music, for the sake of being out, enjoying our youth and freedom. I soon found that it was a great place to meet girls and fool around. I received my first blow job after a rave, in my car after I had given one of Carla's friends a ride down to the lake, but instead of going down to Belmont Pier, where everyone else was meeting up, the girl asked if we could go somewhere a little more private. So I took her up to Montrose Pier, where we parked and made out and she taught me what the hell oral sex was all about.

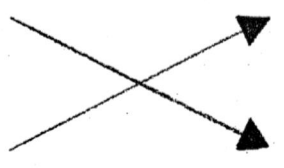

Hello and Goodbye

After the whole Miki incident, I entered a period of my life that was sort of like my Middle-Ages period, my dark years. At first, I did some heavy introspection and really concentrated on my interest in art and music. For a second there, I thought I was really starting to figure myself out. But then, I met this girl named Heather.

Heather was in her late 20s when I met her at this small manufacturing company I worked at briefly in Chicago's northwest side. I took the job a few months before Heather's first day, after spending about a year off pursuing my "true" interests in music and art. This year of soul-searching was triggered shortly after the Miki ordeal when PricewaterhouseCoopers laid me off after the fall of the dot-com economy—the economy that Bill Clinton always takes credit for. And then September 11 happened, and everything really went to the shitter.

During this year off I began to paint and draw again. I also smoked lots of weed in a spacious loft in Chicago's Humboldt Park neighborhood that I shared with Caleb, who I met through my ex-girlfriend Erica because he was dating her best friend. Both girls eventually broke up with us, but out of that whole mess our friendship continued. During this year I also interned for free at WXRT – 93.1 FM and was by far the oldest intern. I thought this would be a great way for me to make my inroads into the music industry. Instead I found myself populating a database with the significant events of every year since 1960, going out to get lunch for the radio staff, stuffing gift bags for events the station would hold called "Corporate Takeovers," and handing out fliers to concert goers before a "WXRT Show," hoping not to see anyone I recognized. After a few weeks of that kind of shit, I decided that I didn't want to work in the music industry, and never showed up for work again.

I never traveled the world, as I thought I would—as I sometimes tell people I did, especially during interviews when I'm asked about this year—so when a former boss of mine called me about a job five minutes away from my loft, I took it and ended my year of so-called soul-searching. A few months later, this blonde walked into the office. She looked smart, almost nerdy, but had the body of a stripper.

I say that I fell in love the instant I met her as she was being introduced around the office. I fell in love with her lazy blue eyes and soft, powdery, lips, and those long legs. She made a lasting impression on me, mostly because of her beauty but also because of her apparent shyness. She was the kind of woman most guys would have labeled as "hot," but she had no idea how hot she was. We all had offices with glass walls, and when

I was in meetings with the middle-aged men in my office, you could tell when Heather was walking by because all conversation suddenly ceased, and all of our heads slowly rotated from one side to the other.

I had no idea whether she was single or what, but it didn't matter. I was positive I was going to get to know her and that something would happen. I did the whole office flirtation thing and would find reasons to go by her cube and ask her things about work, even though we had no real reason to talk. At first she only answered my questions and turned back to whatever she was doing, but eventually, after much persistence, she warmed up to me and we started talking about personal stuff. I soon found out that she had spent some time traveling after being laid off from her previous job. We would talk while she sat in her office cube, her legs crossed, while I stood with an elbow raised and propped up on her cube, trying to sneak in a glimpse of her legs whenever I could. Her time off seemed to have been a lot more productive than mine; she spent most of it learning Spanish in Spain and traveling through Europe and even taking up smoking a little, which interested me even more. I asked her to come to lunch with a bunch of us once, and although she hesitated, she came with, and I made sure to sit across from her.

Eventually this girl who worked with us, Julia, told me that while she was with Heather on a trip to our offices in Seattle, when my name came up in conversation, Heather remarked I was a good dresser and that I was cute. Julia also confirmed that Heather considered herself to be single. Although she had recently met a guy and was sort of dating him, he had gone to Europe for work and would be there for a couple of months.

That was good enough for me. I became bold. I started inviting her out for drinks with the group. We did shots of tequila; we smoked cigarettes—I would light two at a time and give her one, which made her smile. We talked about how my parents were born in Mexico and that I knew Spanish pretty well. We started writing e-mails to each other in Spanish, which she liked so she could continue to practice. These e-mails became long, back-and-forth, all–day exchanges about personal shit like our families and what we were interested in. It became so intense that soon I couldn't sleep at night. Julia would come by and see me typing in Spanish and would laugh at me, shaking her head. It interfered with my job, which I didn't give a shit about anyway. I started looking forward to coming to work in order to continue with our e-mails and hope that I would see her.

Heather eventually started inviting me out with her friends. I was convinced we would start dating, and I felt like I had met the woman I would marry. Yeah, I said shit like that to my friends, stuff that I'd ridiculed others before for saying, stuff like "Dude, I think she's the one, truly, she's the one." I wanted to play it cool though, take my time, and not screw anything up. I especially didn't want to freak her out with the whole work-dating thing.

As we started hanging out I became more and more anxious. I badly wanted to do something about it, tell her how I felt, be brave and tell her that I wanted to take her on a "proper" date. There was a moment once, when I was dropping her off after a night out, where she looked at me and paused in the way girls do when they're hinting there is an opening for you to try and do something but holding back to let you know there are no assurances. I almost said something, almost leaned toward her to try and kiss her, but I hesitated. And so she just said goodbye and left.

I blamed it on work. I didn't want to make working at the same place awkward. I thought I learned something from the Miki / Erica bullshit. The e-mails started slowing down, but we were still hanging out, though not as frequently. I was freaking out that she was starting to date someone else, but this never came up in our conversations or e-mails. One night, in a state of delirium, I wrote her a four- or five-page letter that rambled on about how I felt about her and why I had held off on doing anything about it, how I wanted to see if she shared any of the same feelings and if she did, that I wanted to try and work something out. I never sent her the damn letter, and I still look back at it today and am disgusted.

I decided to get another job, with the plan being that after I did, I would finally bust it all out. But eventually I found out through Julia that the fucker who had gone to Europe had come back, and they had picked up their relationship and now it was serious—and I became devastated. I could see that she was tired at work, probably after staying up late with the bastard. I didn't know him, but I hated the asshole. I still kept some hope though—I persevered. I decided I would continue to be her friend. For the next few years, I indeed was her friend, and we went out a lot, especially when her boyfriend was out of town. I loved it when he went out of town.

I kept on like that, inside believing that it would be a matter of time before her relationship with that other guy would end and it would be my turn. And then suddenly, they broke up; he left her.

Not only had he left her, he suddenly moved out of the damn country. She was devastated, and I tried to be supportive, but I was secretly ecstatic. We started spending more and more time together. We went out to dinners, movies, and I thought things were looking good, but I didn't want to press anything so I played it cool. I had a plan. Then one day she said she needed to talk to me. I was nervous, I thought maybe she was going to say she also had feelings for me, or worse, that maybe she knew I had feelings for her but she didn't reciprocate them. When she told me that night that she was pregnant with the asshole's child—and that's why he fled to Europe and was now engaged to some Swedish girl he probably had been seeing the whole time they were together—I was fucking shocked. I hadn't expected it and was too dumb to have read the obvious signs, like that she had stopped drinking and smoking. I thought she was just trying different ways of coping with her break-up.

During the pregnancy I tried my best to support her. I knew how difficult it was for her. I was the only guy at her baby shower, and I bought her a bunch of baby books. Her mother remarked at how sweet and thoughtful my gifts were. I thought I was so fucking in. The pregnancy never sidetracked me, I never stopped thinking we would end up being together, which some guys thought was crazy, especially knowing that she was giving birth to someone else's child. It didn't matter to me at all. I took her to my company's holiday party at the Brookfield Zoo that year. I made her a painting of a silhouette of a couple hugging in the backdrop of a colorful horizon and had it framed. To this day I consider it one of my best paintings. Again, though, I held off on doing anything about my feelings—how the hell could I tell her? Who puts the moves on a pregnant woman?

After the birth, she moved back home to Duluth to have her parents help with the baby. She left Chicago, and I never did anything about my feelings. I almost did the day she was leaving, but her baby was less than two weeks old and crying the whole time we spent together.

A few months later, I convinced, Caleb, who was now living in New York, to fly into Saint Paul and go with me to visit Heather and her friends for the July 4th weekend. We stayed with her friend Ellen, who had a house in the woods. It's a beautiful area, overlooking the lake. Plus the band Low is from there, which made visiting extra cool. Caleb and I were playing their album *The Great Destroyer* as we rolled over the roads on the way to Ellen's house.

We had fun that long weekend. Caleb and Ellen hooked up; we saw Heather a few times although she was still recovering from the pregnancy. She met us at the big festival the towns were having and had a beer and danced a few polkas with us. The next evening we went to her house and had dinner with her family on their porch, with its beautiful view of the forested hills and the lake. Again, I was convinced more than ever about my feelings.

Later that night as Caleb, Ellen and I lay on the beaches of Lake Superior, drinking beer and staring up at the stars, we began talking about Heather. Ellen asked me if I had feelings for her, and then it all came out. For the first time I told someone—even Caleb had not known, not totally. Ellen then told me, with some hesitation, that when Heather first met me, she told her that she was going to marry me. I was fucking flabbergasted at hearing that, completely fucking shocked. I started drinking like a madman and got drunk and stoned. Ellen and

Caleb persuaded me that I needed to do something about it the next day before we left, that I couldn't hesitate any longer, that it didn't matter that she had just given birth, that I needed to have some balls and stop being a sissy already.

That night I went back and wrote Heather a letter in a card I had brought (just in case something like this happened). I planned to drop it off at her house the next morning before we left and headed home. I woke up the next morning hung over and nervous as hell about doing what I had planned, and I even considered just leaving and then mailing the card, but I gathered myself and eventually headed off, with Caleb and Ellen giving me encouragement. On the way there, driving through the winding forested roads, I had "Fix You" by Coldplay playing in my Jeep. I hate that band, but their bland, cheesy love songs just felt appropriate at the time. It was weird; I was nervous but glad this day had finally come. I felt that this was just the first step in what would become our life-long relationship.

At Heather's, we talked for a bit while the baby slept in the next room. I gave her the card and wanted to talk to her, but I could hear her mother in the kitchen. Heather almost started to open the card, but I told her not to, that she should read it later, after I left, and she said ok, but the vibe was sort of weird and my head started to perspire. I started to leave, got my stuff, and she went to see me off at the door. Just after we said goodbye, I asked her to step outside and close the door because I needed to say something to her. (Caleb later remarked that it was a slick move—guys just need to take control sometimes.) She closed the door, and after a few awkward seconds, with my heart pounding like hell in my chest, I blurted it all out in what seemed like a nervous fit. I said it all, all that I was feeling over the last three years or so, in a matter of minutes but what seemed like a blur. She sort of laughed or giggled nervously, and admitted that she had similar feelings years ago when we first met. I wasn't sure what I had expected, if we were going to make out or what. In the awkwardness of it all, she ended up saying that she would read my card and then give me her response. I said that was fine. Her response made me feel like I was in a Jane Austin story, and before I knew it we hugged and said goodbye and I was back in my Jeep with that Coldplay shit playing as I headed to pick up Caleb.

A few days later, more like a week later, after not hearing anything and wondering whether I should call or something, I finally heard back from her in the form of a short, cold e-mail saying that although she might have had feelings for me, that was many years ago and she no longer could see herself feeling anything different for me than just being friends. She also wrote that she valued my friendship and didn't want to see it go away. I wrote back a long winded e-mail trying to explain my feelings, thought about driving there or something, but instead just sent the e-mail—to which she responded pretty much in the same way. She said maybe we could talk about it sometime.

I wanted to talk to her live. I was convinced she would come around. I had all these ideas of how I would arrive there and we would talk and something would spark in her. But instead I convinced myself again that the timing wasn't right, it was still too close to her pregnancy and that I needed to give her some more time.

So, weeks, months went by and I didn't attempt any further communication on the subject. I thought about her all the time though, and I wondered if I was becoming delusional. I even saw her again when she came to Chicago and saw how pretty she was looking, but I didn't say anything. After that, I started going fucking crazy about it. My friends said it was completely stupid. It was long past time I either let this go or go all out. So I finally called her saying I needed to talk, and after a few times trading voice-mails, she finally called me back.

"Hello," I said, answering my office phone a little after 6 p.m., acting like I didn't know who was calling even though I could see the number on the display. I even let it ring a few times, just to pretend like I wasn't waiting for her call.

"Hi Alex, it's me, Heather," she said. I could hear the sound of the wind rushing up against her car windows; nowadays she only called me while driving. I could already feel my face warm up and the sweat glands at the top of my forehead begin to swell.

"Heather… what's going on? Glad to finally hear from you," I said still acting surprised.

"I know; I've been bad at keeping in touch lately," she said, with a little bit of a laugh.

"That's all right, I know you've been busy; I've been busy as well," I responded as I always did when she said that, acting like I understood and was super busy myself, like I hadn't had time to think about her at all. "Heather, I know it's been many months now, almost nine in fact, since last summer when I told you how I felt about you."

"Yeah…" she said, with the sound of the car driving along in the background.

"But, well, at the time, I wanted to talk about it more, but we, um, didn't. I was, ah, hoping we could, you know, actually talk face to face, versus going back and forth in e-mail, but at the time I decided to drop it and let go for the time being… I felt it was inappropriate, you know, given how close it was to the birth and all? And, um, actually… I, ah, am sorry for springing that stuff on you then, at that time, you know, I shouldn't have been selfish and I should've thought more about you then, you know…"

"Ok…" she responded, with that giggle again.

"Yeah, well, um, you know, I just wanted to say that, ah, that I still have feelings for you Heather, and as I tried to explain last year, I've liked you ever since I met you but for various reasons I couldn't ever act on my feelings, you know?"

And with her not saying anything, only hearing the noise of her driving, I felt that the conversation was going to shit, but I continued on and said, "And, well, although I wanted to talk about this in person, I just feel like I can't wait and, well, I just want to say that I really do feel like we could have a great relationship together… I know we've been friends, I don't want to change that, but, well, I just see that we could have a lot more and, well, if you feel this way too, we should try and, you know…"

"Alex, I don't know what you want me to say," she finally interjected.

"Well, nothing, I mean, I don't expect you to say anything, just, well, just I guess tell me whether you think you could ever reciprocate these feelings at all. I just, you know, I just need to…"

"I can't, I'm sorry, but I just don't. I've known you for how long now? I mean, we've been friends, or so I think we've been, and I can't change that… I mean, it would be weird even," she said and was now giggling again. "And also, I mean, it makes me kind wonder about your friendship, whether you've been sincere, or whether you had ulterior motives."

I was stunned at the comment about my sincerity, but I didn't fully comprehend it at the time and just said, "Well, ok, I guess, if that's how you feel, I guess I just needed to know… but as far as friends go, please don't think I've been trying to persuade you into liking me or anything, I truly have always wanted to be your friend, but I just thought maybe there could be something more…"

"Alex, I think you're a great guy, I know you'll end up with a great girl who will appreciate you one of these days, and I hope we continue to be friends, but that's all I can give you, is friendship. Ok? I'm sorry, but I hope we continue to be friends…"

"Yeah, I mean, I've been your friend Heather, it's just…"

"Alex, I'm sorry, but I really have to get going, Angela is fussing around here in the car and we're almost home. I'll talk to you soon, ok?"

"Ok, yeah, sorry, yeah I guess we'll talk soon."

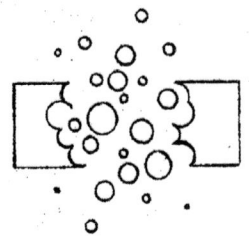

All Regrets

The one good thing about the Heather situation was that it took my mind off Miki. Years went by and I never saw or spoke to her. Nor did I really speak much with Erica. However, as luck would have it, just weeks after being shot down by Heather, I ran into Erica at a bar and for some reason we made plans to meet up for dinner.

The dinner with Erica became pretty awkward pretty fast. I quickly realized that I could still be with her if I wanted to. I discovered that Miki never told Erica anything about what happened between us. Miki was still with the boyfriend she met when she put an end to things between us and was "in love." Miki and Erica were now the best of friends, and somehow I felt left out. I also felt like shit for Erica because her "best" friend was almost going to break her heart by telling her that she slept with her boyfriend repeatedly while they were still going out. After all my troubles to not let anyone get hurt, the two girls continued on with their friendship, and I had no part of it. I was lonely as hell and about to embark on many years without any sort of girlfriend. In the end, I guess I got what I deserved.

After a while Erica decided to move back to Memphis as she had always wanted to do. At her going away party, I saw Miki for the first time in over three years. She had those same big, watery eyes and her body looked better than ever. I was crazy about her again instantly, and deeply regretted my handling of the whole situation. "What the fuck was I thinking?" I thought to myself. The girl basically threw herself at my feet and I fucked it up, and there I had been chasing dreams of being with a pregnant girl who didn't want me. Miki was there with her boyfriend, who was now her fiancé, and at first I deliberately didn't go near her and instead made my way over to Erica, politely said hi, gave her a kiss on the cheek, and started talking with some of her friends. We bought each other drinks and smoked cigarettes. Then after a while, after Erica had left me to talk to some other friends that had arrived, just like the night at the Field Museum, Miki came darting over toward me, looked me in the eye and gave me a huge hug with what looked like tears in her eyes.

"Alex, it's been so long since I've seen you. How long, like four years?" said Miki after pulling away from me.

"I think so. Yeah, about that. Crazy, huh?"

"Yeah, so crazy. This is crazy here, huh?" she said. She used the word "crazy" now for some reason. Everyone around us swirled, drank, and made senseless noise. We were at a bar called McGees up on Webster and Sheffield, by DePaul University, full of drunk frat guys drinking bad beer and doing shots.

The bar made for a loud, smoky, hazy backdrop, with its neon signs and televisions.

"Yeah, this is kind of crazy," I responded, sort of quiet, feeling really timid, looking over her shoulder to see if anyone was looking, feeling like I was cheating on Erica all over again and wondering where all this was headed, if anywhere.

"Alex, I can't believe that we're talking here. We really screwed up didn't we, huh? We really fucked up."

"Yeah, but Miki, it was such a long time ago, and we all fuck up every now and then, don't we?"

"But we really fucked up. Tom said he was going to shake your hand really, really hard if he met you."

"You told him about us?" I asked, shocked, looking around to see if anyone was looking our way. Even though I'd never met Tom, I thought I recognized him, standing off to the far side of the bar—sort of a meathead hanging out with Miki's sister and her sister's husband. You can always spot the angry, jealous boyfriend. There he was, all angry, all jealous knowing that I had been able to lure his now fiancé into bed with me and betray her best friend. He must have known that she had to have been really attracted to me, enough to put her relationship with her best friend on the line and have sex with me, not just once, but many fucking times. God that must have really pissed him off. But it made me happy thinking about it.

"Yeah, he can't believe that you and I, especially I, would've done such a thing to Erica," she said.

"No shit," I responded, all bothered now, especially because I knew she had the balls to be that way. "I can't believe that you're still like super friends with Erica, and I can't believe you told him. You're crazy. Well I don't want to meet him then. But

Miki, I mean, come on, things happen, some really crazy things happened between us. But that's that. You know? That was a long time ago."

"Yeah."

"I've just wanted to get past all that," I said, continuing with, "I'm really happy to see you now."

"Oh, me too." I could see tears fill up her big round, watery eyes as she said that.

"Alex, it's really good to see you," she continued, choking up. "You know, I often think of you. Think of how I was willing to give it all up, give up my friendship with Erica, probably lose other friends, and become the biggest gossip in the office. I was going to give it all up."

"Yeah, but you just weren't patient enough."

I said almost in self-defense, kind of feeling watery-eyed myself. "We would've worked it out, you know, we could have waited just a little longer…"

"Bullshit. It was all there, all there for you to take and you didn't," she said angrily, looking back behind her to see if anyone was listening, but no one really was, except maybe Mr. Angry, but he was far off. "You're right, it could've worked out, but you, in the end, didn't do anything about it. I was sick of waiting for you to take control. You're a wimp, Alex. And that's all there's to it." And that kind of brought out a giggle in her, it kind of pissed me off, but I laughed also.

Again, she was right. In the end, I didn't do anything about it. Oh, sure, I convinced myself of many reasons why I didn't do anything, most of all that Miki, ultimately, wasn't my type. After a while I'm sure I would've freaked out about how many guys she's had sex with; I can't handle knowing that kind of stuff about a girl I'm dating. But, in the end, well, I'm not sure. Just like with Heather and many other situations, I couldn't make up my mind, so I took no action.

Worrying that her fiancé would start to freak-out, Miki left me; we exchanged hugs and a kiss, not quite on the lips but close enough that if her fiancé had seen, I probably would have gotten my ass kicked. After talking with Erica some more, smoking more cigarettes with her friends, doing another shot or two, we all ended up leaving to go to another bar. I left with them, and on the way out, Miki and her sister were standing there by the exit. I said goodbye to Miki's sister, her sister's fiancé, some other people I had known only in passing, and then gave Miki one last, overly dramatic hug. I looked her in the eyes and she looked back. We held that gaze for just a moment. Out of the corner of my eye, I could see her fiancé staring at me like he was going insane; I smiled, and then I left. That was the last time I saw her.

Toward the end of the night Erica began telling me how she wanted all her different groups of friends back here in Chicago to continue hanging out even though she wasn't here anymore.

"Yeah, I think it would be great if you all hung out together. I would love nothing more than to see you all go out when I'm not here. You know it's weird that different groups of people, you know, can't come together and just become friends."

"I know what you mean," I responded, trying to be agreeable. "It's like you have all these different groups of friends who are afraid, or something, of breaking each other's barriers and comfort zones."

"Yeah, really," She said in her normal, happy tone, with a bit of a Southern twang, with her head slightly shifted to the right and her long wavy strawberry-blond hair coming slightly across her face and over her shoulders. "You know, I'm supposed to go camping with Miki and Sophia this September, I would love nothing more than if you and Tricia and them all came with. We always have such a great time and there shouldn't be any reason why you and everyone else can't come with, you know."

"Yeah, you're right. I mean, we're friends, I've always loved hanging out with Tricia and Andy, there's no reason why we shouldn't all be able to hang out with Miki and them."

"Yeah," she said, "you and Miki used to be such good friends, and there's no reason why you still can't be friends now, you know?"

I stood there agreeing, listening to her give me her idealistic vision of having all her friends come together while she was gone. Although I totally agreed with her view on trying to bring different groups of friends together, something I've always struggled with, that night listening to her tore me to shreds, especially listening to her wanting me to hang out with Miki. It was worse than being in a situation where you know you're about to be caught telling a great big lie and you have no way of being able to stop it.

On the way out, Erica and I hugged. She was pretty drunk and told me how much she loved me, that she had always loved me. My reaction was pretty weak. But then again, what the hell was I was supposed to say? It's like she was trying to set up a sort of dramatic exchange:

There, on a lamp lit street at 2:30 in the morning, with cabs passing by, she finally let it all out and told him that she still loved him...

It takes a lot of courage to speak your mind and heart, and it hurts even worse when it's not returned.

I finally left after muttering some useless, almost apologetic reply trying to be nice. I said something like, "Yeah Erica, I'll miss you. I know we'll keep in touch. I'm sorry how things worked out between us. Call me when you're back in town." And I pretty much ran off in the first cab I saw and never looked back.

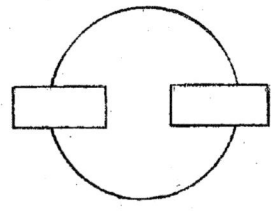

Uptown Nightmares

Not long after the quasi-finality I achieved with respect to Miki/Erica, I made plans to go to France's wine regions with a bunch of co-workers at the corporation I was now an accountant at. I didn't have much in common with this new group of work friends, except I suppose that we were all in our 30s and as single as we could be. We also had a bunch of extra money and nothing to do with it except buy plane tickets, spend it on expensive food and wine, be drunk, and maybe—just maybe—hook up and have sex. Initially I was really excited about going, just to get away, and especially because the hot Polish girl Asiaa was going, and I still thought maybe I had a chance at hooking up with her. I had even booked my flight and made arrangements to go. Just before going though, I started getting anxious.

I had started to feel more and more anxious as I entered my 30s, and this was especially compounded by the thing with Heather. I found myself dissatisfied with my life, unfulfilled, and bored. I felt a growing desire to try and accomplish something beyond being a passive participant, just another accountant. I'd come up with ideas and at times feel like taking a risk, but I'd always find an excuse to not leave my job or convince myself that I'd have time to do something "different" later on. The excuses were always the same: I'm still young; there will be plenty of opportunities; after I've saved enough money to quit work and focus on my "passions," I'll just do it. There was always something, and this time it was to go on this wine-drinking trip for about a week.

Most people would be absolutely jealous at the opportunity to go to France, and I can't help but to think that I'm crazy for not going. Maybe that was my only opportunity to hook up with Asiaa, and I fucking blew it (but probably not). The thing was, I just kept feeling like it was just another trip, another opportunity to get laid, and in the end I would return home and feel the same way: unfulfilled.

For maybe the first time in my life, I felt a genuine sense of urgency. So on the Thursday morning before I was supposed to leave, I cancelled my flight. I emailed the people I was supposed to go with and told them something personal had come up. I freaked out and made a last-second decision.

I stayed home and didn't tell anyone. My parents and friends thought I was off in France. I debated telling people, but I just wanted to be left alone so I could try and see if I could finally spend time trying to do something creative, maybe draw or paint or write. After squandering that whole year after

I left PricewaterhouseCoopers, I felt like I needed to try again, and for a few days I did just that.

But on the fourth day of not talking to anyone I got a little bored. I'm a social person, in a way. Although I don't particularly enjoy talking with people, I feel really insecure when I'm not around them. So I finally felt like I needed to go out, and on Sunday I called Carlos and Raphael, two of the few Des Plaines friends I have who still live in the city. They are also two of the few people I know that would be going out on a Sunday night. In fact, they were planning to go sing karaoke at a bar called the Uptown Lounge up north. So at around 10 p.m. I picked them up at Carlos' place, and we drove up and parked somewhere close to the intersection of Lawrence and Broadway, in Chicago's Uptown neighborhood.

Uptown was supposedly the hip part of town back in the 1920s and 1930s, when the infamous crime bosses ruled the city. The area is home to some great clubs that started back in the 20s, such as the Riviera Theater—a cinema/theater that had movies and dancers—and the Aragon Ballroom, which is this cavernous concert hall that holds almost 4,500 people and, from the inside, looks like the middle of a Spanish town center. The Green Mill, on the other hand, is this little jazz club with a long curving bar, big paintings in golden frames, and small booths along the wall. It draws a lot of out-of-towners who come to get a vision of Chicago back in the swinging 20s. It's said that Al Capone and his gang would hang out there and that there are underground tunnels, which the gangsters would use to elude the cops. That's what people say anyway; I've never seen them.

I'd only been to the Uptown Lounge once before, while I was waiting to go into a show. The night I was there, the customers at the bar were mainly 30- or 40-somethings who seemed resigned to a certain position in life, to hang out in a bar in a seedy neighborhood waiting for life to kind of move on by. There also were aging gay men and tattoo-covered women, with a handful of young hipster-ish people who I assumed were there waiting for the concert like me.

On Sunday nights, though, the Uptown Lounge hosts a karaoke night.

Carlos is a karaoke junky, which is something sort of new since high school—although he always wanted to be a singer. Also, Carlos is absolutely obsessed with girls, now more so than ever. Most men are, to an extent; I certainly am. But Carlos thinks about women like 99.999% of the time. He's a fairly good looking guy, draws the attention of women when walking down the street, but it's like he knows it and therefore that's all he thinks about—to a point where it's damaging. He has grown to be so shallow that when a girl with any sort of personality meets him, she generally thinks he's a freak and doesn't want to talk to him. Many of his fights with ex-girlfriends have resulted from the fact that he has a massive porn collection and is always getting busted masturbating, or that he can't help but to give out his number to girls whenever we're out, then they inevitably call and he gets busted for that.

Or he does things like go to strip clubs and charges outrageous tabs on his credit card, forgets about it, then complains to his girlfriend that he doesn't know where all these charges are coming from as they're reviewing his credit card statement—and while he's complaining, he remembers, then she keeps asking until he admits what the charges were for, at which point she gets pissed because he lied. When we're out, he constantly looks at pretty girls who are with guys and hates that they're with guys who he thinks maybe aren't as hot as he thinks he is, and he gets pissed that he's not with a hot girl.

Carlos has had many long-term relationships, but they're always the same. They fall in love and move in together right away, date for years with the growing anxiety of whether he's going to propose, until the girl comes to not trust him anymore and they eventually break up. After the breakup he always goes through a bout of depression, with heavy regret, second guessing what he did and if he was wrong and that all he wants to do is get married and have children. He says he just can't find that right one, and he's afraid that he'll grow old by himself. But then when he's with a girl, he tells me how much he misses the feeling of hooking up with a new girl, that he has never been interested in anything other than trying to hook up with girls, and doesn't know if he can stay monogamous forever. He also says as soon as he does settle down and gets married, he's going to move straight out to the suburbs because there's way too much temptation in the city. He doesn't understand why anyone would want to live in the city besides to look at, and try to hook up with, girls.

Carlos recently broke up with his girlfriend of about four years, Linda. She was this young, sweet girl that Carlos met at Illinois St. when Raphael was going there. I met her a few times and easily could see why they were together. She had a simple personality, laughed at anything that Carlos said, but seemed to be the kind of girl with whom you could never have a deep conversation. Forget talking about death, marriage, the meaning of life, etc. with her. Carlos said that was one of the things missing, they never talked about anything substantial, so he was bored. What bothered me though was that I've never talked to Carlos about anything substantial—he's the same way she is. It's almost as if he and Linda were meant to be together, equally shallow in their conversation. But I guess it leaves something of a void, when you have two people like that in a relationship, and Carlos had to know it. Linda lived with him for four years, but she would sleep on the couch because he snored too loud. When he was talking about breaking up with her, he also cited that she lacked certain qualities he liked in women, like having big breasts and liking to give blow jobs. Additionally, he said that she kind of smelled funny in the evenings after coming home from work. Who doesn't smell funny after coming home from work? Who says those kinds of things?

So they broke up, and Carlos was all depressed about the thing, always thinking that maybe he screwed up and let go of a really special person that he should have married, and so on, just like in his previous relationships. About a week after their supposedly traumatic break up, Linda started dating some guy who is now her serious boyfriend—who she, within a matter of weeks, took home to her parents. Carlos was furious, but had sex with at least two girls in those weeks following the break-up.

Before going into the Uptown Lounge, we stopped at a liquor store on Broadway just next to the Green Mill. In the store were a couple Latin women in small tight shorts and tank tops, with chunks of white powdery deodorant hanging from their armpits, buying cigarettes and booze. Raphael and I waited for Carlos outside as we had a cigarette. A bum walked up to us asking for money, putting his face practically into mine after I said that we didn't have any for him. Raphael got up to him, giving him a bump and moving him out of the way and told him to fuck off. (Raphael now works in hardcore construction, so although he'd always been athletic, he's more intimidating than ever—kind of a good guy to have as a friend.) I calmed the bum down, told Raphael to back off, and offered the bum a cigarette. Finally the bum took a cigarette and left. Carlos then walked out with a disgusted look on his face from the deodorant girls and we walked off.

Now if you're someone like me, an accountant who holds a steady day job, you notice that there are only certain types of characters out late on a Sunday night: people who work at bars or other service jobs, like artists or performers—who, for them, Sunday, Monday, and Tuesday are their "weekend" nights—or those who don't work at all and are your plain old alcoholics. Out on a Sunday you indeed get a sense that you are with the fringes of society, those who are not at home in bed with their spouse watching the local news, getting the forecast for the week in order to know whether or not to bring an umbrella on the way to the train station.

At about 11p.m. we walked into the bar, and "Oh, What a Night" was blasting from the speaker system. There was a television monitor playing the lyrics and this little flamboyant gay guy dancing around in the middle of the bar singing the words. The guy singing was the host of the Sunday Karaoke Night and goes by the name "Gay Willy."

"Hey Carlos," Gay Willy yelled amidst his singing as he saw us enter. He ran up to us, giving the microphone to Carlos so he could belt out a quick verse. Then he winked at me as he ran off singing.

"That guy's crazy, man," said Raphael in his typical, stoner kind of deep voice, "but he's cool. If you were to ever think of a perfect karaoke host, he'd be it."

"Yeah, I can see that," I responded as we made our way to a couple of empty seats at the bar. The bartender—this woman named Veronica, in her late 20s, with pulled-back dark reddish hair and tattoo-covered arms—came up and said hi to Carlos and Raphael, met me, and served us drinks. I had a Newcastle, as did Raphael, and Carlos ordered a Red Bull and vodka. Two cute girls walked by and said hi to Carlos, and then left for the door saying that they would be right back.

"Who are those chicks?" I asked.

"Oh, just two girls that usually come here on Sundays. I think I could've had a chance with the curly haired one, but I moved too fucking slow." Carlos always seemed to say something like that when talking about cute girls he knew.

"Are they coming back?"

"Yeah, they just go out to get high, that's all. They'll be back." Apparently, it was customary for the Sunday night karaoke crowd to go out and get high in the alley next the bar. Carlos had said earlier in the night that he brought a joint with him to smoke on the way back, in case I was interested, as it usually helped him get up easier Monday morning.

Carlos works in human resources, recruiting people to work for some corporation downtown—which suits him because that's pretty much a salesman kind of job where you have to like talking bullshit to people. He says he's in the business of "buying people," which I always thought sounded kind of creepy, but I guess it's sort of true. He had to be at work at eight in the morning on Mondays but always went to the Up-town on Sunday nights as it was one of the few places that had karaoke that night. He seemed to do karaoke like four nights a week, starting on Thursday nights.

Carlos has a decent voice, although he overdoes it, and probably one of his biggest moments was in high school when he sang a duet with this little girl in our senior year variety show. I don't recall the song, but it was one of those cheesy 80s romantic songs like "Wind Beneath My Wings" by Bette Midler or something—something you're bound to hear at a wedding reception being danced to by the couple or the fa-ther and the bride or some shit like that. He loved it because he was in front of a fairly large audience and garnered a decent applause—although a lot of us, especially me, couldn't stop laughing for some reason.

I like watching karaoke singers, and I admire them because I can't sing worth a shit but would love to. I do get up there and sing sometimes, but only with someone else, like with Car-los, and only when I'm stumbling drunk. I like when you see singers that are really, really into it, and it means a lot to them, to sing and be noticed—kind of like it's the closest thing they'll ever get to being famous. Like this one guy we used to see at this bar downtown called The Blue Frog. He had a pretty good voice, good tone and melody, seemed to know all the lyrics by heart, but he over exerted his effort to the point where it was sort of comical and embarrassing. All his effort was evident in his exaggerated facial expressions and the bouncing around he did to dance to the song he was singing.

When Carlos lived with Linda out in the suburbs, they

went to karaoke a lot at this bar in Mount Prospect and, apparently, Carlos brought the house down when he rendered his version of Ricky Martin's "Livin' La Vida Loca," so much so that it was typically demanded by the crowd whenever he walked in. I never made it out to see this performance, but for some reason I wish I had.

As we started our drinks, Carlos hurriedly scribbled on small pieces of paper a few songs—some of his staples such as "Wonderful Tonight" by Eric Clapton, "In My Life" by the Beatles, and "Satisfaction" by the Rolling Stones. Raphael insisted that we all sing "Time is on My Side" by the Rolling Stones, "Alive" by Pearl Jam, and "In the Ghetto" by Elvis Presley. We agreed, and Carlos ran off to submit the requests, after which he got into some conversation with what I guessed were other Sunday night karaoke regulars.

"Why do you think Carlos loves this shit so much?" I asked Raphael as he gave me a cigarette.

"I think it's the attention, you know, kind of like trying to experience the attention real singers must experience," he responded, brushing his long nappy hair to the side. It was kind of like an afro, but more wavy and almost as if he had dreadlocks, but not quite. He was a lot different from the Raphael I knew back at my Cartoon Pornos party.

"Do you think all people who karaoke do it for the attention?"

"I don't know man, but, well, I guess there are a couple different karaoke types, like the kind that are just doing it for the fun of it, because it's stupid, like the host, and there are others who use it for attention. I mean, look at Carlos when he sings. Sometimes I've been like 'Hey man, tone it down, you know? There aren't any agents here, man,'" he said laughing.

"Scream, motherfuckers," yelled Gay Willy through the microphone as someone finished a song, "Scream, motherfuckers…"

"Ha, ha, that dude always says that when someone finishes a song; it's funny as shit," said Raphael.

At that point, Carlos came back from talking to his friends and sat back down.

"So, hey, how was that party you all went to last night down in Bloomington?" I asked.

"Oh, man, it was cool," said Raphael. "You know, I expected it to be a lot worse than it was, man. Like, there were a bunch of girls there. I mean, it was like maybe 60/40 girl-to-guy ratio 'n shit, right Carlos?"

"Well, I don't know about that, but there were quite a few," responded Carlos, kind of looking away, to see if there were any girls around.

"Did you get lucky?" I asked Carlos.

"Well, not really. Well, almost," said Carlos, still kind of looking around, almost as if ignoring the subject.

"Yeah, Carlos almost hooked up with this 18-year-old freshman girl," said Raphael, laughing, slapping Carlos on the back.

"Eighteen years old?" I said, in a shocked kind of way just to be a smartass, "What, are all the freshmen starting at school now?"

"Yeah, it was their first weekend," responded Carlos.

"Dude, you guys are in your 30s, man, that's border-line criminal, isn't it?"

"Whatever, as long as they're 18, I don't give a shit," said

Carlos. "It was funny, because she and her friend were the only two freshmen there, and of course, they were the drunkest. The one girl, Stacey, the one I was with, kept saying the whole night 'This is so great! I'm away at college, and I'm drinking and smoking…' That was pretty fucking great, huh, the first weekend you were away from home, at school, getting fucked up?"

"Yeah, that was pretty cool. So what happened, what were they drinking?"

"They were just pounding beers, like out of control style. She was pretty hot though. I totally thought I was going to get in there dude," said Carlos.

"Yeah, but tell him what happened, man…" interrupted Raphael, slapping Carlos on the back again, and Carlos just kind of shook his head looking pissed, then Raphael turned to me and continued, "So, Carlos was all over this girl, you know, and she was getting all fucked up, and then next thing you know they're on the couch and she keeps passing out and putting her head on his shoulder, and he's like trying to lift her head up and trying to make out with her, but it just kept falling back on his shoulder. Everyone around was like talking about it 'n shit."

"Yeah, I didn't know what to do, I was trying to make out with her but she was seriously passing out," said Carlos.

"And then, out of nowhere, she looked up at Carlos and then fucking threw up all over his face and shoulder man, right in the middle of the fucking party!!"

"No way," I jumped in, "What happened then?"

"Dude, I freaked out, people rushed in and grabbed her, we ran into the washroom," said Carlos, finally getting into the story.

"Did you wash up there or something?"

"Yeah, I practically took a shower."

"What happened to the girl?"

"It was fucked up, she continued to throw up in the washroom, and was like in convulsions 'n shit. At first I was like pissed off at the chick for puking all over me, but then I felt bad after seeing how she was. I don't think I've ever seen anyone like that."

"Yeah, Carlos was totally pissed," said Raphael, "he was like screaming 'that fucking bitch' in front of everyone 'n shit, but then he finally calmed down."

"So, what happened to her, was she taken to the hospital or something?"

"Umm, I don't know," they both kind of said after looking at each other and laughing. "Yeah, I think she was taken away by a couple of friends, but I'm not sure what they did with her," said Carlos. "We just continued to get fucked up, pretty much, and laughed about the whole thing."

"Yeah, and boy, you should have seen the beer we were drinking man. We had Grolsch, Guinness," said Raphael.

"No shit?"

"Yeah, man, and Boddingtons too. We were drinking it up at that campus, with all these college students who could only afford cases of Miller and Bud Light, you know?"

"You were drinking like champs. I love Boddingtons.

"Yeah, I can't drink pilsners anymore, man; I can't stand that light shit. I need a real beer, you know."

"Yeah, I can't stand that shit either," I said although I really do love pilsners, prefer them to any kind of ale, usually. So the conversation went on like that, talking about how they crashed out on some kid's couch, Carlos got up early because he wanted to get home and get a massage at the Asian place down the street from his place in the city, which I think was one of those shady places where they finished you off for an extra tip because he all of a sudden started going there like every weekend.

"Scream you motherfuckers!!!!" shouted Gay Willy as someone finished their song. After some cheering he called Carlos' name, "And now we're looking for Carlos…come on Carlos baby, sing for us baby!!" Carlos went up to present his interpretation of The Beatles "Let It Be." It sounded kind of good but a little over dramatic as he sang loud with his face all tight, eyes closed, fist clenched.

"So, man, what have you been up to lately?" Raphael asked me as Carlos continued to sing.

"Oh, you know, not much man. Just working, working out when I can, you know, same old shit."

"Yeah man, I know what you mean."

"What about you man, you still writing 'n shit?" I asked Raphael. Raphael had gone to Illinois St. to be an English major after failing out of Yale. I liked to talk to him about this kind of stuff; despite his intimidating look and heavy drug usage, he was really smart.

"Hell's yeah man, I got some shit going."

"Like… what kind of stuff?"

"Like, I've been writing lots of poems, essays, short stories 'n shit. Mainly flow of consciousness stuff, you know, commentaries on this fucked up world we live in. Observations, you know."

"You should go and recite some of your stuff at the Green Mill. They have their Sunday Night Poetry Bash."

"Yeah, man, I've been thinking about going sometime,

man, and throwing some shit down."

"Hey, recite one of your poems now man," I said as Carlos was getting back from his song.

"Yeah, man, I can do that. Let's see, here it goes…"

"What are you guys doing?" asked Carlos as he was coming back from his song.

"Reciting poems, man. This one is called 'Frustration.'"

> We all talk to each other and try to understand
> God is among us and with us
> We run, think, place our heads down and are lost
> Truth is an idea that was conceived
> We butcher, hug, cry and laugh
> Insanity is often the safeguard that protects us
> We seek to fulfill, to help, to rampage and dance
> Music is the seed that taught the soul how to smile
> We get married, divorce, fight and talk about it
> Children are seldom seen as the ideal standard that they are
> We like to complain about what we don't have
> Virtue has been bastardized, taken down like a dirty curtain
> We write these movies and books to communicate
> Intelligence likes to frustrate us and be snide
> We will fight the aliens and see the parallel universes
> Sex is the drug we advertise and legitimize
> We love to hide in the shade of sadness.

"Man, that's some good shit," I said, though I was kind of lost half way through it.

"Word, man, thanks, I appreciate it. It's kind of like my observation man, we all try and do and say all this shit, you know like all those protestors at the Republican convention when good old Bush got re-elected, but it's all for shit man; we never back our words with real, substantive action man. We're a walking realization of hypocrisy man."

"Well, I can see your point." I responded, "At times, it does seem like all this is for nothing, nothing can be done about anything, any of our problems. We never seem to discuss real issues. Still, I like to think that our destiny is in our hands, though, you know? I guess I'm an optimist that way. I like to think that all the small steps, although they might seem ridiculous at times, over time they accumulate and in the end, our individual actions go toward making change, as do our inactions."

"Truth, man," answered Raphael, "I know you know that shit, and coming from someone like you, I respect it. What I don't understand is all this blind action, man, just for the sake of acting, when really the longer term goal hasn't been thought through you, know?"

"Hey, let's do a shot," Carlos announced, trying to get into the conversation, "How about a car bomb?"

"I'm in man, I'm in," agreed Raphael.

"Not me man, I'm not into shots anymore," I said, as the bartender came up and gave me a sad look, rubbing her eye as if wiping a tear from her face. I finally succumbed and agreed to do just a shot of tequila while they did car bombs.

"So, who did you vote for back in 2004?" I asked Raphael.

"No way, man, I didn't vote for nobody, for shit man. I'm not going to let myself be part of this system, man, always having to choose between the lesser of two evils man. Like they say, if it made a difference, they'd make voting illegal, you know? You know, it's a shame, that the United States, man, the world's supposedly leading democracy, only has two parties to choose from, man, only two parties!! It's a fucking mockery, man. And they're pretty much the same, one arm to the other of the same damn party."

"True," I answered, "I mean, I guess they supposedly stand for different things, but they don't really ever deliver on anything, I guess, besides lowering or raising taxes. But still, I feel like we should vote, especially being citizens, and I knew I couldn't vote for Bush, regardless if Kerry was sort of a loser. I mean, Bush has to be one of the worst Presidents ever, you know?"

"I agree with you there," jumped in Carlos, "I voted for Kerry although I'm a Republican. I think Bush has just been the most fiscally irresponsible President and with that war in Iraq, fucking lying out of his mouth. He's just awful... a fucking jackass."

"Well, from my perspective," I interjected, "he fucked up an opportunity to show true leadership in the world, to support the idea that democracy is a natural movement that is based on principles and to lead the world not through the use of military strength but through strong leadership—working with the rest of the world to reconcile our differences while, at the same time, pursing the terrorists that were truly responsible for 9/11. We shouldn't have gone and started a war with a leader we thought evil just because we thought they were a threat; it just doesn't make sense. The only way that war makes sense is when you think of how much we depend on oil—it really only makes sense from that perspective."

"He's also plain fucking dumb, inarticulate and thick headed," said Carlos, "I mean, just look at *Fahrenheit 9/11*, it was beyond ridiculous how much of an idiot he looked like in that movie."

"See, that's what I mean, man," exclaimed Raphael, "its all bullshit, even that fucking movie. Give me all the footage ever taken of John Kerry, or any other person for that matter, and I could make him seem like a big fucking idiot as well. It's all editing, slick production backed by a bunch of money. It's all bullshit, there's never any real discussion, anywhere, of the real issues man, what the alternatives are and which one makes sense. Like, all these people who didn't say shit when the war was starting, like all the fucking Democrats, like Hillary Clinton and John Kerry. They didn't say shit and voted for the war. And, now that the war is unpopular, they all of sudden are quick to point the finger and demand that we pull the troops out. Hey, like it or not, we're there man, and we have to fucking figure out if we'll ever be able to leave, and if we do, how to in order not to make it worse. That's what no one talks about man."

"Yeah, but you have to admit, we are in an illegitimate war right now," I responded, "It was unprovoked, unsupported by the world, backed by bunch of bullshit assumptions, that they had all these weapons, and we couldn't afford to wait because of 9/11, and all that shit. It's unheard of. Yeah, I agree that we have to carefully think through how to end this mess, but I think the President should be taken out of power, if not just for starting a bullshit war, but because he is leading this country away from its founding principles in the name of fear."

"Yeah, but to Bush's credit, Saddam was a fuck-head," interjected Carlos, "it was still good to have gotten rid of him, we just fucked up the planning for the war."

"Saddam was a menace to his society," I responded, "and yeah, his people might be relieved that he's gone, but you can't just go and instill democracy on a country like that, by forcibly removing their leader and then telling them to go and start a democracy. Democracy is a grass roots movement. It's born from revolution, and if it's not supported by its people, it's destined to not succeed. I'm not saying that the Iraqis don't want or deserve democracy; it's more that we can't instill it on them or anyone else. We can't build nations. It's ludicrous that our country, whose democracy was born from revolution, radical revolution against the fucking Brits, would fail to recognize that. I mean, we're becoming an empire, right?"

"Truth," said Raphael, "we're failing to learn lessons from history man. Time and time again, all the empires, when they were at the height of power and started feeling the pressure of challengers and started having small defeats man, panicked and responded with blind violence, which lead to their downfall. Plus they all end up bankrupt—it's too fucking expensive to keep expanding an empire man. The Romans, the British, the Soviets, in these situations, they reacted with violence, presuming that force by itself would stomp revolutions, man, but it can't; it won't. Violence breeds violence, you know? It breeds revolution, and that's what we're in right now. We control the world, have our military all over, including in the Middle East, and they don't like it. They're fighting back, whether you call them terrorists or whatever, they're revolting man, and we fail to realize that we're just fueling them man, we're exerting our violence in the name of democracy."

"I completely agree with you, man." I said, "That's exactly what's going on, and the majority of this country still wanted to support Bush, they seemed to be convinced that in the face of fear the only viable action is reaction with force. I guess it's almost a human instinct, isn't it, to react like that in the face of fear instead of being strong? And, what about all these Republicans who hide behind their veils of Christianity to justify the war and their way of life, when in fact this kind of action is condemned by Christ. Talk about being hypocritical, huh? And, look at the Iraqi Soccer team, you know, how great they did in the Olympics... A few Bush campaign ads came out at that time showing images of the Iraqi team doing well, and there was something to the effect that now, along with Afghanistan, there will be two more free countries competing in the Olympics. And, after one of the games, the Iraqi players were interviewed and asked what they thought about the commercials and they said that their brothers and cousins have died and, sure, under Saddam's regime they might not have been free, but they at least they could go outside and not fear being bombed. The captain, Sadir, I think, number 10, even said that one of his cousins who fought with the Mujahadin was killed by American soldiers and that if he wasn't there playing soccer he would be fighting to liberate their county."

"Truth, man, I hear that, and it's true," agreed Raphael, "They're not dumb people, man."

"But then why wouldn't you go ahead and vote against such a President," I asked him.

"Man, but that's just it," he answered, "who was John Kerry? Who would he have been if he was elected man, but yet another supporter of the same shit? It's the system that's broken, man. Remember Kerry's fucking convention speech man? When he acted all like 'I'm the military leader,' and shit, hoping to be able to win the votes of the conservatives, man. It's all politics. If he had more balls and came out straight away condemning what the President did, state that the war was wrong, is wrong, and had the balls to say so when the shit was starting, then I would have voted for him. But I refuse to be part if it, man, I refuse to be part of the system. We'll see though man; we'll see what happens this next time. I don't keep myself blind, man, if something happens this next time, if someone legitimate comes around, who really will be different, to convince me that I should use my right to vote, I'll do it man. But I will not if I don't see any difference."

"Well, I admire your viewpoint dude. I guess I feel that the appropriate 'small step' here is to at least vote when you can, we have that right and should take it."

At that point, Raphael offered me another cigarette, which I took and lit.

A couple in the background were singing "Total Eclipse of the Heart" now, and Carlos was pissed because he thought they sucked—that the guy couldn't sing worth a shit, and that he and Linda did a much better job. Then he started mumbling about how he fucked that whole relationship up and how he didn't understand how she could be dating such a fucking loser now.

"What else are you writing, man, ever think of writing a book?" I asked Raphael.

"Hell's yeah, man, I got a book going. I've written about a 180 pages. It's kind of scattered, hand written, in different journals and shit, but its coming together man."

"What's it about?" I asked, as Carlos was talking to the stoner girls who were seated at the bar—apparently he had snapped out of his brief Linda breakup funk.

This old man named Jeremy, who I was told had been coming to karaoke at the Uptown every Sunday night for years now—who always wore this big black cowboy hat that matched his thick leather vest over his white button-up shirt, and had long lanky gray hair down his neck—was singing his usual song, "The Gambler" by Kenny Rodgers.

"It's about this heavy shit, stories between these characters that are in their own way coming to epiphanies, realizing and coming to grips with their place in the world, their connections with each other. Some of them are enduring friends, others unknown lovers, and others bitter enemies, man. It's about the stink of humanity, the void that is at the center of us all, man, that we try to fill with religion, and the darkness that continues to smother and hide what's beautiful and pure in this world. It's an epic man, spanning generations. One of the characters is named George Jeroviches, and then there's Antoine Gray, and then there's Elena Stravagona, and others man, it's evolving 'n shit."

"Sounds heavy, man. You should go ahead and organize it, put it together and have it be readable. I would love to read it when you're ready with it."

"Yeah, man, I will," continued Raphael, "but you know, it's going to be challenging, man, there's going to be some heavy references to Oscar Wilde, Milton, man, others. I'm going to expect a lot from my reader, man. I want my shit to be criticized, discussed. I've read a lot of shit, man, I know how a good story has to be written, and I have a lot invested in this. I've written a lot of essays, discussing my story as if it were finished and read, and I've used these essays as feeders to the story, man."

"That's interesting, man," I said, "You know, I've been

writing some shit myself. You know how I stayed home from France, right? Well, as I stayed home, I started writing, just started writing some stuff, you know, about my life and shit. I think I'd like to try and write a book myself one day."

"Cool man. What would you want to write about?"

"Not sure, you know. I've often thought about writing a book that would have characters that were intellectuals, studied the great writers and philosophers, and basically debated issues the whole time. They'd discuss issues from religion, to death, to truth, romance, politics, and evolution, you know, the whole gamut. I saw it as somewhat technical, but basic enough for the layperson. Like not getting too into the details behind classic philosophical debates, but just far enough to highlight the importance of the issues, kind of like a *Brief History of Time*, you know, the Stephen Hawking book discussing complicated scientific theories in layman's terms? But mine is for philosophy."

"Word, man. I can dig that."

"Yeah, but then also, when I though about it, I thought what better way to highlight philosophical issues than through recounting ordinary life, you know, what goes on during real everyday experiences? You know, I've always enjoyed stories in which the characters were real, ordinary people, versus stuff like Ayn Rand in which her characters are these super human intellectuals who I always thought were sort of freaky. I mean, some stories featuring truly extraordinary individuals are great and all, but sometimes I feel that a mediocre life is too easily dismissed as uninteresting and it's never examined, or not enough anyway. So, I guess I'd like to just try and take a snapshot of a life from the viewpoint of ordinary individuals that maybe have the ability to appreciate issues that elite intellectuals debate—but never achieve anything really much more than an appreciation, almost like you're butting your head against a wall and know it's there but can't do anything to get through the wall, you know? Like you're in a car stuck in mud."

"Man, truth man. We should collaborate, exchange our shit, man, give each other criticism you know?"

"Cool, yeah, that'd be great."

"Yeah, man, you know, that's the thing, at school I had a group of friends, man, and we would challenge each other, stay up all night discussing wild shit, taking acid, smoking pot. When we would go out to cafes or bars, man, we would bring our notebooks because you never know when that shit's going to hit you, man, when all of sudden you got the shit to write about and bam!! You have pages pouring out of you, man, pages. You know what you should get, man, a tape recorder. That's what I use, man. I just talk into it, just talk about my ideas, where I see the stories going, and I'll get pages out of that shit man. Pages."

"Huh, that sounds like a good idea."

"Hey man, we got to hook it up," Raphael said. "You know, its hard with Carlos, all he ever wants to do is go to these loud clubs, man, or go sing karaoke, he doesn't know how to discuss anything else except for getting laid."

"Yeah, I know. But the ironic part is that he often complains that his relationships are shallow, that they never have anything to talk about. Even the shallowest of people desire something deeper, you know, something of substance to talk about, but instead they usually, like you said, fill this need with religion, right?"

"Truth. God is the ultimate scapegoat, the ultimate excuse

humanity uses to escape the pursuit of truth, to justify pred-ator-like actions that are easy to fall back to, all the wars and violence we wage against each other, they're ultimately justified by religion, man."

"Carlos, do you believe in God?" I asked him as he had re-turned and was now listening into our conversation.

"Ummm, yeah, I believe in God," he said, straightening up and nodding confidently with his response.

"So, you actually believe that when you die you're going to be judged and then either go to Heaven or Hell?"

"Well, no, not really, I mean, I know I'm going straight to Hell… ha, ha. Actually, I don't think so, I just think when you die, you die, and that's it."

"Then what's the point in believing in God?" I asked.

"It just doesn't make any sense otherwise, in terms of why we're all alive, everything around us. There had to be a creator or something. I just can't believe that all this, us, the world, was just created by pure chance."

"Well, that's just it, the idea of a God or creator has been used to try and explain the unexplainable, but it itself is an idea that can't be explained. It's like, although we've progressed sci-entifically, we're still left with the question of 'why?' Why do scientific principles exist at all? Since we can't answer that, many still resort to believing in a God. But even if you do be-lieve in God, you're still left with the question of 'why?' Why does God exist? So there's still always a 'why' that's left unan-swered, and personally I think we'll never be able to answer."

"You guys are too deep for me right now; I'm fucking smashed, man," said Carlos.

"Yeah, man, fucking God, dude," interjected Raphael. "Like

I said, it's the ultimate excuse to be lazy, to avoid deep searches, man, you know, real inquiry? 'Just have faith in God,' you know? Fuck that. This one time at Yale, man, this fucking annoying religious chick always wanted to talk to me about God, about Jesus, you know? She kept saying, 'Raphael, you just need to open up. Ask Jesus into your heart and he'll talk to you. Jesus listens, he understands, he loves you and wants you to love him... So, finally one day I was like 'O.k., I'll let you talk to me about Jesus, man, but only if I can talk to you about Lucifer first.' That's what I said, man, and she looked like she saw a ghost, man, like she saw fucking Satan himself, you know?"

"What about Lucifer?" asked Carlos, sort of confused.

"Lucifer man, Lucifer was the most beautiful angel, the most powerful, the closest to God, you know. And when God created Man, put Man on the Earth that Lucifer thought was so pure and beautiful, Lucifer grew furious. He couldn't understand why God wanted to taint the Earth with a vile creature like Man, with so many imperfections. Lucifer begged God to reconsider and when God didn't listen, Lucifer led a revolution against God in order to protect what he thought was pure and beautiful. He was beaten back by God and the other angles and expelled from Heaven. Ever since though man, Lucifer has continued to wage his war, but against humanity, using humanity's own vices, own imperfections, against itself, in an effort to have us win his goal, which is our eradication, fucking extermination. He wants to rid the world of the taint of humanity. And in that sense, Lucifer is actually the protector of what is good and pure in this world, and we are the sin, man. So I told that girl man, that she couldn't tell me to believe in God, in good, without understanding evil, and how it's on the same continuum as good, they're one and the same, and what we really should talk about is on what side of the divide God and Lucifer are really on, man."

At that point Carlos burst out laughing, and said "That's some fucked up shit man!! You really said that to her? She probably thought you were a Satanist or something. What'd she say?"

"She fucking looked at me as if I was the devil, Lucifer, himself, man, and the girl nearly pissed in her pants, man; she never tried to talk to me about Jesus again. So the next time someone wants to talk to you about Jesus, man, tell them they can, but only if you can talk to them about Lucifer first, man, ask them that."

"That's *Paradise Lost*, right?" I asked kind of recognizing what he was saying from somewhere, though I had never read it myself, so I was guessing.

"Hell's yeah, man. *Paradise Lost* indeed; and you should read it if you haven't, because it's fucking great man, fucking great."

And the night continued on like that, along with a couple more rounds of shots. I found out that the bartender Veronica's tattoos running up her back were of two dragons, facing off against each other, with the Japanese symbol of honor in the middle. The three of us got up to sing "In the Ghetto" by Elvis Presley, which I'm sure sounded really great. Carlos eventually started feeling sick, as if the hangover from the night before was not mixing in well with the drunkenness of the current evening. Raphael, of course, didn't give a shit, and neither did I, though I was pissed at myself for getting drunk. At around 2 a.m. this really cute girl with a soft face—really thin but with an attractive body, bright red lips, dark eyes, and gorgeous black wavy hair—came walking in and sat next to us. She told us that she was wasted and all of sudden Carlos started feeling better and tried to make conversation with her, but he was slurring too bad, so he gave up. I asked her what she was doing there by herself and she said she came to sing a few songs. She eventually got up and sang the best version of Neil Diamond's "Forever in Blue Jeans" that I've ever heard. It was slow, sexy, but with that flare of a girl just having fun. It kind of reminded me of the singer/songwriter Cat Power from out west who sings with this soft, almost whispery and scratchy voice. Anyway, she came back over and we all talked more, and I tried to start some conversation with her, but she turned and said, "Look, I'm not going to suck your dick, all right?" And with that, I gave up and decided it was time to leave—besides, Carlos was practically passed out at the bar. We stayed long enough to watch this black guy named James do what appeared to be his weekly rendition of "American Pie," which was pretty damn good, I have to admit.

We never sang "Alive." Raphael said that he would call me the next day to start discussing "writing 'n shit, you know, man," but I didn't hear from him. On the way home, I listened to "More Than This" by Roxy Music a few times, especially the second verse where he's singing about a relationship or an encounter that is just fine, perfect, but also fleeting in the sense that just as it's getting good, it's slipping away. I've been stuck on that song ever since it was used in that movie *Matchstick Men*, when the character played by Nicolas Cage and his daughter go bowling.

I relate to the song now because that's how I feel, and I really felt that way on the way home that Monday morning, with only a few cars passing by along Western Ave. from who knows where—probably home from some awful late-night job, the kind my mother used to have to work when we were young to earn barely more than minimum wage, or maybe to a lover's place, or out to get drugs, or just out driving, trying to figure it all out.

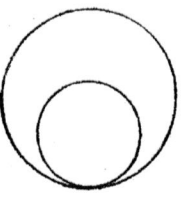

On Being Mexican-American – Part II

I've always wondered why Mexicans never smile in their pictures, whether it's because they're trying to show pride or self-respect or something. Or maybe it's just that they're more honest, somehow, about how tough their lives are.

Here in the U.S., whenever you see pictures of people in their homes or online at networking sites, it's like there's a smiling competition going on—everyone's trying to outdo each other with how big they can smile and how many of their big white teeth they can show.

Whenever you walk into someone's home here, the first thing you usually see in the front hallway are pictures of the couple, the children, the family all together, with everyone always smiling—even the dogs and cats seem to be smiling. It's like you walk into the house and there's a big sign there exclaiming "Look, see how happy we are!!! We have absolutely no problems in this home!!!"

Aside from straight-faced photos, the first things you see when walking into a Mexican's home are all sorts of symbols declaring the family's Catholic faith. You see big crosses hung up on the walls, over the beds, some with a dead Jesus hanging with a crown of thorns on his head, blood running down his body from his head and the holes in his hands and feet. You see great big framed pictures of the *Virgen Maria*, with her head down, a halo on top of her head, and her robe pulled apart to unveil a beating, bloody heart.

Whenever you talk to one of my aunts they invariably throw in a reference to God. Like, when they ask how you're doing, and you say fine, they'll respond by saying *Hay, gracias a Dios*. ("Oh, thank God") Or when you tell them you're sick they'll say *Hay Dios mio!!* ("Oh, my dear God!!") And when you say goodbye, they always say *Que dios valla contigo*. ("May God go with you.") Whenever we walk into a church, even ones that we visit as tourists, my family immediately does the Catholic prayer thing with their thumb after dipping it in holy water and kissing it.

Mexicans are open about their faith, and they really do believe that Satan and his army of demons are here to battle for our souls. And they really do believe that when people die, their souls don't always make it to Heaven or Hell right away, and instead they sometimes wonder the Earth and torment the living, for good reasons, and sometimes for bad. Come to think of it, Mexico can be one scary place.

Everyone in Mexico has really good ghost stories to tell. People are always haunted by dead relatives, dead friends, dead pets, famous ghosts (like *la Llorona*), and even by *el chango* (the monkey), as the prince of darkness is commonly referred to in Mexico.

All of my uncles, at some point, have told me a story of *el chango* appearing to them, or someone they knew. Especially in Ciudad Hidalgo, it seems like *el chango* was a permanent resident there. My uncle Arturo, the oldest brother, says back when the grandfather first moved the family there, they had no electricity in the streets, and so it was extremely dangerous to be out in the field when the sun went down because that's when *el chango* would appear, and to see *el chango* usually meant death.

Arturo says he even saw *el chango* once, when he was 18, and though he survived, he thinks and prays to God about it every single day. Although the story has changed slightly every time I've heard it, the following is the account as I understand it:

One day Arturo was working in *el cerro* with the grandfather and his friends, and he got separated from the group because he became careless. When the sun started going down over *el cerro*, he looked up and noticed he was alone. His heart raced as it was suddenly very quiet. After gathering himself to turn around and head back into town, he saw out of the corner of his eye a shape standing behind him in the path through *el maizal* (the cornfield). He felt like screaming but couldn't, and instead turned around to see a short man-like figure with deathly skinny, black limbs sticking out of dark, torn, work-man-like clothes. The figure wore a battered hat, and though Arturo couldn't make out its face in detail, he could see its beaming, gold-red watery eyes piercing through him. As he stood there, he could feel the wind gust through the path while bugs and rats started coming out of *el maizal* all around him. He then saw the figure motioning him forward with a clawy hand, and heard a deep voice say in his head *ven, mi hijo, ven aqui a morirte conmigo,* ("Come here, my son, come here to die with me,") at which point he somehow managed to let out a scream, the scream of his life, and the next thing he remembered was lying in a bed at the house, with the town's priest and nuns there praying for him. Apparently, just as he screamed, the grandfather and the others came running and found him lying on the ground with his mouth and eyes wide open. Though they didn't see *el chango*, they said they could smell its stink.

Recently, I asked my uncle Javier if he believed Arturo's story, and he responded by saying that Arturo drank a lot, so he wasn't completely sure, but then again he probably believed him because it had happened to so many other people he knew. He then looked at me and said that he knew us Americans thought Mexicans were stupid, and less civilized, that they're a bunch of *burros* (donkeys), and that he agreed with this assessment sometimes. However, he said (at which point he became somewhat serious, as serious as he would ever seem to get), it is true, the devil does exist, and he torments us here on Earth, especially when we least expect it. Then he lightened up again, slapped me on the back and told me not to be such an American and go to church sometimes, and we went back to drinking our tequilas.

Friday Night High School Football Games

It was a few weeks into our senior year. I came home from soccer practice, ate one of my mother's homemade meals—which I never fully appreciated until I went away to college—and there I was, getting ready to go to a Friday night high school football game.

As I was waiting for John to pick me up, I was lying on my bed staring up at the ceiling with something playing in the background, probably *Dirt,* by Alice in Chains, because that's what I often played back in those days when I was on my bed staring at the ceiling. I loved Alice in Chains—something about how painful-sounding their music was (though at the time I had no idea they were singing about heroin.)

It was the first home football game of the year, and although I'd been to plenty in the prior three years, I was conflicted as to whether or not I should attend. That summer I had talked so much trash with the theater kids about things like football games that I felt hypocritical going now—but I wanted to go. It took me about 15 minutes that Friday night before I eventually called John and asked him to come pick me up. I kept dialing his number and hanging up before it rang.

Except for Brian and Hassan, whom I saw everyday in my physics class, I didn't hang out with the theater kids much once school started. It was like I knew that I'd probably be going to football games and stuff, and since they weren't into that, I felt awkward hanging out with them. When I ran into Carla in the hallway that Friday and told her that I was probably going to the game, she responded by saying, "What? Uh, why would you want to do something like that?"

"Don't freak out." I said, all defensive, "I'm just going for the hell of it, it'll probably suck but at least it should provide some, um, good comedic relief, you know, some good people watching."

"Whatever! I wouldn't be caught dead at that shit. But that's cool Alex, if that's what you want to do. If you change your mind and feel like doing something *fun* tonight, we're going to a dance party down somewhere in the Pilsen neighborhood. We're meeting everyone at the Taco Burrito Palace Number 3 on Clark tonight around 10."

"Yeah, I'll see. The game will probably suck and I'll end up leaving early, so maybe I will meet up with you guys."

"O.k. Alex, we'll see. Have fun at your game," said Carla in a dry, sarcastic way as she shook her head and smiled. I thought then that maybe I should try hooking up with her; she was kind of cute and especially so with that little sarcastic smile, but I hooked up with a few of her friends over the summer, so that was probably out of the question.

I was fine with going to the game until that fucking conversation.

John pulled up in his Maxima; I swear the kid has had that car forever—he still drives it now. Jig was in the passenger seat. He, like John, had a varsity jacket on. Our Maine West Warrior varsity jackets were in our school's colors: ugly baby blue with ugly gold-yellow leather sleeves. Those jackets were the ugliest fucking things, but every guy wanted one—and, more importantly, to have the big blue varsity letter M on it—because it showed that you were a jock.

I bought one, but I never told my friends about it. I also don't even think I ever wore it in public; I was never comfortable wearing it. The real reason that I never wore it was because I wasn't awarded a big letter M until the end of my senior year. I played football my freshman year and wimped out and didn't go out for the sophomore team. Then I decided to go out for soccer, figuring that I would have a better opportunity to earn the varsity letter because I was Latino, even though I hadn't played soccer in years. I played with the varsity team, but I mainly sat on the sidelines, never playing enough to actually earn a big letter. I guess you actually needed some skills and practice to be a good soccer player instead of just being Latino. Who knew that shit? Anyway, I never told anyone that I never got a big letter M, and after a while I threw the fucking jacket away, telling my parents that I lost it. After that, though, I decided to join track during the second half of my senior year, and finally got a damn letter M at the end of that year. Jig and John, though, had earned their varsity letters earlier, both for playing baseball. Despite their nerdiness they were decent athletes.

"Hey Dude!" yelled Jig as I walked up to the car. He had a big old grin on his face with one arm out of the window, hanging over the door. John was in the driver's seat, looking annoyed, shaking his head, as he usually did. It's like he always had something against my attitude. I remember we used to go up to his parents' summer house in Wisconsin and fool around with these local girls, who really liked me, and I remember John saying "What the fuck do these girls see in you anyway? Some Mexican or something?" I don't know, he would say that kind of shit, but still we always considered ourselves best friends. Maybe his attitude had something to do with him thinking I slept with his high school girlfriend, which I sort of did, and maybe also with the girlfriend who's now his wife—but that's another story.

"What up, dude?" I responded to Jig as I strolled out to the car with my hands in my pockets.

"Come on, get the fuck in," said John in a sarcastic-yet-serious voice. "We're going to be late."

"Chill out, dude," I said opening the door and getting in the backseat. "You're not playing or anything like that."

"Yeah dude," said Jig to John as he patted him on the back, "Chill out man, we're just hanging out and seeing what's up with the chicks."

For a guy that was not very popular at all and never got laid until he was married—or so I think, but he'll say that's not true—Jig was always a happy-go-lucky sort of guy. I never understood, and still don't quite know, how much of it was forced or if maybe he's a naturally happy person. I know I'm pretty damn bitter most of the time when I'm alone, and when I'm with people I try to put on a show and act like I'm happy—although sometimes I don't even bother and just act pissed, like I am.

We pulled back out of the driveway and headed up Pratt Avenue and over to Manheim to make our way north toward Maine West. John had a tape playing in his car, a mix of some the hair-rock gems we listened to back in those days. "Slave to the Grind" was playing by Skid Row. That song sounded good driving through Des Plaines with the windows down and the words "We are the youth gone wild" blaring out of the speakers—especially with two guys in the front of the car wearing ugly high-school varsity jackets, their heads bobbing and soccer-rocker mullets in full tow. Even though grunge rock was starting to take over the mainstream, John, Jig and most of my non-theater geek friends were still listening to the 80s hair bands we all loved; it was like we just couldn't let go. And today when we hang out we prefer Def Lepard to, say, Pearl Jam or U2 any day. John was the kind of guy who played his music really loud and had a fake marijuana leaf plant hanging from the rear-view mirror, but he would turn the music down and take the plant off whenever he stopped at a light or stop sign and there were other cars around.

We drove up the driveway that leads into Maine West, up to the parking lot close to the stadium that was filling up by then. As was typical for Friday night high school football in the northwest suburbs, the game had a pretty good sized audience. However, our stadium was small, in comparison to some of the other high schools we played against. It was also pretty shitty-looking, again in relative terms. Our team always sucked;

we were like tackling dummies for the all the rich schools in our conference like Deerfield, New Trier, and Highland Park, but the games were still pretty fun.

That year was different though. Our friends had finally made it to the varsity level and were seniors. They were out there, and we knew they would make a difference. Our team had already started out 2-and-1—which was amazing—and was a touchdown away from being undefeated. We had a winning record for like the first time in eight years or something, and we had one more game before the conference season started. We were playing against Glenbrook South, one of the snotty teams in our sister conference, the Central Suburban South. (We were in the North). They were also off to a 2-and-1 start, but that was typical for them. This game, though, would be the telling if we were for real or not. There was a feeling in the air, we walked up to the stadium with an extra jump in our steps and our heads held up a little higher. The cheerleaders looked cuter that night, despite their ugly baby blue-and-gold uniforms, and the dads were extra pumped up. It was going to be a different year.

You know, despite my anxiety over it, I really liked the whole the thing—the whole high school sports scene. I especially enjoyed going downstate to Peoria to see our girls' basketball team play for the championship several times. All our teams sucked, except for girls' basketball for some reason, and they were like the best team in the state. They won 70- something games in a row, but we never went to go see their games until they would go the championships—and then we mainly went because it was a road-trip, and we would get hotel rooms and get fucked up. Our senior year we all packed into Pat's "Happy

Van," which is what we called an old emptied-out utility van he picked up somewhere. We pre-partied in it before the championship game by drinking Mickey's Big Mouths and pulling bongs. I don't even remember if they won that game or not.

I have to admit that I like sports in general. I love watching the Chicago Bears, hardly ever miss a game. I watch the NBA playoffs and watch when U of I plays major games. I've shelled out some big bucks to go watch the Illini play at bowl games. But I act like I'm not that avid of a sports fan because I'm really into music, the arts, literature, and it seems to me like that stuff and sports shouldn't mix for some reason. These days I'm a *little* more comfortable mixing the two worlds, but back in high school and later college it was a constant struggle. I guess I always felt like I couldn't admit to my theater friends that I actually enjoyed the games, and I couldn't admit to my other friends that I loved going to raves (which according to them were full of "freaks") or liked to read and write.

We walked up into the stands, looking around for our friends. We found Pat, Carlos, Jason, Mike, and others and made our way over by them, yelling "Pat... Mikey..." I like how guys do that, acknowledge each other by just yelling out each other's name; it feels sort of tribal to me. As we sat down, I spotted Candice sitting with the rest of the pom-pom girls on the sidelines, looking as beautiful as ever, with her soft blond hair pulled back in a pony tail, swishing over her back as she laughed, her lips red, and her cheeks soft and flush. Fuck, I could look at a face like that forever. She then started cheering frantically, waving the poms around and kicking her legs as her asshole boyfriend Jaime, the team captain, was getting ready to lead his team on the field.

"Hey you fucking pussy!" Pat yelled at me as he patted me on the back, and I turned to see what they were all talking about. He had a flask of whiskey, of course, and turned and gave it to me under cover. I took a sip. It was fucking Jameson; the shit sucks, but I always drank it with him.

That was the best part about the games, getting trashed drinking that shitty Irish whiskey, or smoking weed with Matt when he wasn't playing. We would get trashed at the game, and then hopefully afterward there would a party at someone's place or, better yet, at the woods. Or we would somehow get alcohol and just drive or walk around drinking until we were shit-faced and started doing stupid shit, like throwing eggs at each other in one of our backyards, mostly at Pat's or Carlos'.

Matt was on the team again our senior year. He had cut back on smoking, was working out, was bench-pressing 300 pounds, almost twice his weight, and was the starting left corner back. Glenbrook South supposedly had two standout players, a running back and a wing back, who were probably going to play at the college level. Matt had talked about how he was ready to bust their ass should they come running around one of the ends, or if the little wingback tried to come out of the backfield for a pass, as he was known to do. Their big play was faking a run to the running back, with the quarterback pulling back and then hitting the wingback, who would come screeching out of the backfield, too fast for the cornerbacks and safeties that were usually frozen by the fake run. Matt and our friend Vassant, who was the safety, had talked all week that they wouldn't fall for that shit, that if that little fucker came out of the backfield, he would be taken out.

So that night our team was all pumped. I remember Matt

running out onto the field hitting his helmet, head butting with some of the bigger players on the team, he was fucking psyched. We kicked off to them, the little wingback taking the kick and returning it until he was tackled like hell by Matt and some others. They were excited; we were pumped; I took a shot of the Jameson from Pat's flask, gave it back to him, and he took a swig. Glenbrook South handed off to the big running back on their first play, and he was gang-tackled by our guys after about four yards. Matt hit the little guy who had lined up across from him. After the play, Matt started talking all sorts of shit to him. The running back took it again for about another two yards. It was third-and-four; this would be a big stop, set the tone for the game. We weren't taking shit; this was the year to reverse Maine West's fortunes in football. Glenbrook South lined up in a tight format, the fullback, the running back, tight-ends, and the little wingback off to the side of the fullback, the L position or whatever. Our defense was pumped, the linebackers up, our corner backs up to prevent the fucker from bouncing around and trying to race outside of the defense to a first down. He would have no choice but to run up the middle and get fucked. They hiked the ball, the fullback came crashing in, followed by the running back, the quarterback going to hand it off to him, everyone crashing in the middle, our defenders had pushed the offensive line back yards behind the line of scrimmage; they didn't know what the hell hit them. Matt raced in toward the middle to prevent the guy from breaking through; we were all standing and cheering.

All of a sudden, you could see their quarterback standing back, still with the ball. He faked the hand-off, and next thing you know, he was lofting up a pass to the wingback who was wide open and racing down the field. Matt realized it and tried to turn around, but it was too late. The guy was already catching the ball, uncovered, sprinting down the field now with Vassant, who was also faked out by the play, about 10 yards back chasing him. But Vassant was not fast enough, and the guy ran 70 yards untouched into the end zone for an easy touchdown. Glenbrook South's fans who were packed into our tiny visitor's section were jumping up and down. And so it was, Glenbrook South went on to win 49 to 7. The running back ended up rushing for over 200 yards; the wingback had another 200 yards in total offense, breaking a few more big plays with Vassant and Matt chasing him down the field. Maine West only won one more game that year, and Matt was kicked off the team a few weeks later for throwing his helmet at one of the coaches during practice and telling him to fuck off.

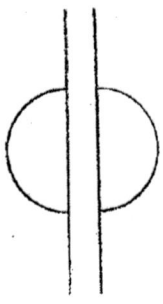

Close Calls

My friend Matt is a phenomenon, of sorts. He's someone truly too smart for his own good and too out of control with his emotions and lusts. He's always been very athletic. He is short but supposedly with a huge dick, per his own account. When he commits himself, he excels—as he was doing in football our senior year up until the Glenbrook South fiasco, after which it all fell apart. He always seems to lose focus and he falls into the shitter—hooked on drugs, girls, all sorts of shit.

During our junior year, Matt was suspended from the team for getting into a fight at school. He fucked this guy Martin's girlfriend, a pretty hot girl named Rachael, while drunk at a party, and Martin was all pissed and wanted to kick his ass. Matt was trying to stay out of trouble, was focused on football, and avoided making contact with Martin—who was a 6'4" lanky basketball player and notorious for being a loudmouthed, tough acting "wigger." Matt wasn't afraid of Martin—in fact he believed "a guy isn't that tall once you get him on the ground with you." He just didn't want to get in trouble. Martin, though, started talking about how Matt was a pussy, that he was going to get his ass kicked, that he was a fag. One day walking out of our home-ed class, the only class I actually had with Matt in high school, we heard Martin yelling shit from behind us down the hallway.

"Shit," said Matt, who started shaking his head. "Hey you little fucking pussy," we could hear Martin yelling. "What, you're too cute and faggy to come take your shit like a man, huh?" At first Matt ignored him, but then Martin threw a pen that hit the back of his head. Matt stopped, froze for a second, then turned around, dropping his books. I tried to stop him, but it was too late; he was running toward Martin, who all of a sudden had this pale ghastly face and was cowering back. Martin tried to swing down at Matt, who quickly ducked and tackled Martin by the legs and lifted him up and down on his back in a matter of seconds. He was then on top of him, punching the hell out of his face. It was finally broken up; the security guards came running, grabbing Matt who then punched one of them. He couldn't be stopped. He snapped. Martin was on the ground with blood gushing out, squirming like a 6'4" baby. Matt was suspended from school and the team. While on suspension he decided to quit the team all together. So he started coming to games with us, and he always brought a few joints. That was sort of the cycle I guess, he would play for a few games and then somehow end up leaving the team. At the games our junior year Matt would come up and whisper to me, "Hey man, I got a joint, let's go smoke it back behind the stands." He was secretive because he didn't want to share with the rest of the kids. "Cool," I would always respond, and off we'd go. Although I liked smoking weed, I never carried it myself. Therefore I liked friends like Matt who always seemed to have it.

"Hey man," Matt said to me one night during junior year while we were smoking a joint behind the stands and our team was getting its ass kicked.

"Yeah?" I responded.

"You know Vanessa and Kristen, right?"

"Umm, yeah I think so, what about them?" Vanessa and Kristen were these girls that had a reputation for being slutty. Matt hung out with them, but I barely knew them.

"Vanessa's parents aren't home tonight, they want us to ditch out of this game and go fuck them back at her house. I've been fucking Vanessa, and Kristen said she wants to fuck you. She thinks you're cute; I guess she digs that Mexican shit. What do you say we finish this and get the fuck out of here?" he asked, then took a drag of the joint and handed it to me. I wasn't sure if he was just making all this up just so I would come with him, as he was prone to do.

"No shit man?"

"Yeah, pussy, let's go."

"What about the game?" I asked.

"Dude, fuck the game. In fact I told them to meet us by my car in 10 minutes. What, are you fucking scared?" asked

Matt in a mocking tone, furrowing his brow at me.

"No, that's cool, let's go. Should I tell the others?"

"No, don't worry about it; we'll probably be back before the game is over."

"What do you mean? Aren't we going to hang out with them?"

"No dude, they're fucking sluts. We're just going to get them high on the way and get over there and start fucking; you'll take one of the extra rooms or something. We'll be back before you know it, unless you plan on pulling a fuck marathon or something you dirty spic..."

I swear, that's always how shit would be with Matt. I don't know how he's always done it, but whenever he's been focused on getting laid, he's always found a way, and I've been lucky enough to benefit from it on occasion. And so we finished the joint and headed out toward the cars and there they were, smiling and standing next to Matt's car, just as he'd said they'd be. Seeing them standing there made my heart start to race.

"Hey ladies," said Matt as we approached the girls. He was walking slightly ahead of me, smoking a cigarette, his polo shirt tucked into his jeans, his collar up and his short blond hair all spiky with a semi-mullet and his sides practically shaved.

"Hey," both girls responded in a shy sort of giggly tone. "Hey Alex," said Kristen as she turned toward me.

"You guys know Alex, right?" Matt asked, even though Kristen had just spoken my name and according to him she'd already requested to have sex with me.

"Of course we do," responded Kristen, "How are you, sweetie?"

"Good, not bad..." I said, in sort of a slow, muffled shy

tone, looking the other direction, trying to keep my composure.

"Come on, let's get the fuck out of here," said Matt as he opened the driver's door and got in. We all followed as if on his command, with Vanessa taking the front side passenger's seat and me sitting in back with Kristen. Vanessa gave Matt a kiss on the cheek as he started up the car, finished off his cigarette, and flicked it out the window.

Most girls back then still had rolled up jeans and big hairsprayed bangs. Vanessa and Kristen sort of wore that style, but they were a little different. Their hair was more flowing, sort of like the way girls wear their hair today, but puffier and with a little more curls and hairspray. They almost looked like a couple of head-banger chicks based on their jean skirts and high heels. I was trying hard not to look at Kristen's legs. Kristen puffed on the joint and then handed it to me. She had long dark brown hair. Her face was thin and sort of hard looking, almost intimidating, and she looked older than 17, but when she handed me the joint, she gave me a little smile, just a little twitch of the lips, which instantly made me a little more comfortable. I took the joint and dragged in a long breath, inhaling and then closing my lips to let it rest in my lungs for a couple of seconds before I let out a long stream of grassy smelling smoke.

Kristen and Vanessa smelled nice. I was nervous but the weed was helping. The car ride was fun as we sort of maneuvered our way through the Villas, back on the other side of Lee Street, on our way to Vanessa's house. She lived up north in Des Plaines, close to the border of Arlington Heights, practically on the border of Maine West's limits.

As I said, they both had reputations of being sluts, which to us meant they easily gave blow jobs and would probably fuck you without you having to be their boyfriend. Not that the other girls didn't, but it seems like girls who were termed sluts back in high school were the ones that were more open about it, acted like 30-year-old girls do nowadays. Maybe they were ahead of their times. I heard many rumors of Vanessa—how easy she was, how she gave great head—from various guys bragging about their conquests in gym class locker rooms, many of which I assumed were probably not true. I never heard stories about Kristen, and she definitely seemed to be the quieter of the two. I thought maybe she had the reputation of being a slut because the two of them were always together and they dressed alike. They didn't seem to be friends with many of the other girls; they were just off on their own and always seemed to be a prime target for older guys at parties.

As we pulled up to Vanessa's house we were all pretty high, at least I was. I tend to get all smiley when I'm high, don't say that much unless directly spoken to, and then tend to go on long discourses about whatever subject comes up. I've been called "concrete face" while high many times.

Matt and Vanessa were stumbling and laughing as she struggled with the keys and finally flung the door open. Kristen and I looked at each other and laughed also.

When I'm high I tend to fixate on things. When we were at the doorway, I stared into Kristen's eyes as she stood there laughing and looking at Matt and Vanessa for what seemed like minutes. I stared at her dark eyes glistening as she smiled, with the corners of her eyelids curled up, her eyeballs shiny, almost watery looking as if she was crying. Eyes are funny to me, how fragile they seem, how if you take away the surrounding skin and stuff, they're essentially the same for everyone. They make me feel humble I guess.

"Get some beers if you want; they're in the fridge. My old man drinks Old Style, so I hope you guys like that," said Vanessa once they opened the door and we walked in.

"Yeah baby, we love that shit, $10 30-packs, right Al?" Matt said as he headed for the fridge. I followed him into the kitchen as the girls went to the living room. He seemed to know his way around the house. I didn't know what was really going on between him and Vanessa, but she seemed to like him. He would only say to me that they had been fucking, you know, he'd been fucking that slut.

"What do you think, pussy?" said Matt, as he opened the fridge door, sort of whispering.

"Yeah man, it's cool," I responded, looking around the kitchen, looking at the way it was arranged, wondering how the parents decided what to put where.

"Cool? Not the kitchen you fuck—the bitches. We're going to get fucking laid, that's what's cool motherfucker," he said a little louder but still in a whisper, and then we walked off with the beers back into the living room.

We decided to head downstairs into the basement. Matt raced and jumped onto one of the couches, with Vanessa plopping down beside him, both of them laughing. Kristen and I sat on the couch across from them, and we all opened our beers. Vanessa got up and turned the stereo on and played *Siamese Dream* by the Smashing Pumpkins—back then the new up-and-coming band from Chicago, at the beginning of the so-called "alternative era." Although I was familiar with the genre of music—and among my theater geek, rave-dwelling friends, I acted all snotty at the fact these kind of bands were becoming popular now—there was something refreshing about sitting in that basement and hearing the blaring of those distorted guitars and Billy Corgan's squirmy voice coming from the speakers. It's said that he played all the instruments in the recording of their early albums, was a perfectionist, but I'm not sure.

"Tell me all of your secrets… Cannot help but believe this, is true…" screamed out Matt singing along to the first song of the album *Cherub Rock* with Kristen humming the words also, and my head bobbing along. I stared off at the ceiling, and Kristen handed me a freshly lit joint. I puffed on it and handed it back with the sound of the guitars and drums still pulsing through my head, intently listening to every chord, everything got hazy as the pot really began to take hold. It seemed like forever had passed when I realized that only the second song on the album was starting. I noticed Matt whispering into Vanessa's ear and then puffing on the joint. He then whispered something else and started licking her ear. I looked away and started wondering whether she had any siblings; I didn't think so but wasn't sure. And then I was wondering where the fuck her parents were; I mean the fucking stereo seemed to be blasting, and we were passing around a joint, smoking cigarettes, and drinking beers. What the fuck? I knew they were out for the night, but if I were her, I would be freaking out. What if they suddenly came home out of nowhere? My parents would have freaked if they came home and my friends and I were all smoking dope and drinking in the family room. I decided I would go scrambling up along the far wall and out that little window. It would be tight, but we would squeeze through; I would lunge first and then help Matt out, but then we would have to scramble and make it to the car and get the hell out of there before the old man came and got a hold of us.

"Dude, wake the fuck up!" Matt yelled at me and everyone started to laugh. I snapped out of my stoned daydream and smiled back at everyone. "Concrete face man," said Matt and they all started laughing again. After a bit Matt said, "We're headed upstairs, you lovebirds," and then he and Vanessa got up and headed for the stairs.

"Don't do anything naughty…" said Vanessa smiling at me and Kristen.

"Or anything she would do, dirty slut," said Matt slapping her on the ass as she glared back at him, hitting him across the shoulders, laughing.

They were gone, up the stairs, while the Smashing Pumpkins continued to play "Today is the greatest day I've ever known. Can't live for tomorrow, tomorrow…" from the third song from the album, "Today," their great single playing all over Chicago radio at the time.

"Don't you just love this video?" asked Kristen. Holy shit, I had practically forgotten she was there. "You know, the one with them driving around in an ice cream truck?"

"Yeah," I managed to respond while straightening up, "it's pretty cool." I don't know if I recalled it really being that great. I was never really into videos. I always thought there was something weird about videos, the concept of a band filming itself, making themselves seem like badass rock-stars, super sexy or seductive, or trying to be ultra-artistic. It all just seemed really vain to me, like propaganda, like long advertisements. I do remember liking the Tool videos, though, because they were so damn creepy, but that's about it.

I looked over and noticed that Kristen was lighting a cigarette, had taken her heels off, and was sitting with her legs up on the couch, her feet off to the side underneath a pillow. I wanted to see them. I also tried to see if I could smell them. Weird, huh? I don't think I have a foot fetish or anything like that. I'm not sure I know what one is, but I'm assuming guys with one do some crazy shit. I just have always found it interesting that women, as beautiful as they are, with such pristine feet, beautifully manicured toes, can still have smelly feet like guys, or worse, so I always check when a woman next to me is barefoot.

"Do you want a cigarette?" she asked, handing me her pack of Parliaments. "Sure," I said and reached out for one, and then she lit it for me with her pink lighter. I puffed on it and then looked back at her as we both sat there in silence. She seemed to be staring off at the stereo, puffing on her smoke, bobbing her head a little.

I normally like to sit in silence like that all stoned and listening to music, but sitting there with a strange girl seemed weird, I felt like I needed to start up a conversation. Not really knowing what to say, I asked her, "Do you like the Smashing Pumpkins?" as the song "Rocket" started to play.

"Yeah, you know, they're pretty cool, better than some of that other stuff on the radio. My older sister went to see them at the Metro last month," she said.

I only saw the Smashing Pumpkins once, at Illinois State University when I was at U of I. I like to think that I went to their last show at the Metro, before they called it quits and Billy

Corgan came back with his band Zwan. I say I went to their last show at times, even though I never did. I don't know why; I guess I just like to think that I was really there, it must have been cool.

"Cool," I said, continuing to puff on my cigarette. "Does your sister live at home with you? Isn't she at college?"

"No; she was going to UIC, but then dropped out. Now she's living in the city with some older guy, she doesn't like to come home that often."

"Why, she doesn't get along with your parents?" I asked. I normally don't ask such personal questions, except I guess when I'm stoned. She seemed to giggle a little, kind of running her fingers through her hair.

"No, my father's an asshole and is always moping around about this or that, and my mother just doesn't care. So, no, it's not much fun at home. Anyway, what's your story? What about your parents, siblings?"

She obviously wanted to get off the subject. It's not fun to talk about something bad you're going through, I know very well, especially about your parents or siblings.

"Well, my parents divorced when I was young. They both remarried. My mother married a guy named Doug she met at the grocery store, and my father married another Mexican woman, much younger than he is, and from the same home-town that my mother is from. It's a very small town in western Mexico, so it was quite a coincidence, I guess."

"Really? That's weird."

"Yeah. My father had three more children. They're much younger than me and my sister."

"Huh. Do you like them?"

"Yeah, they're pretty cool. I see them almost every weekend."

"What about your sister, the one you grew up with, how old is she?"

"She's 15."

"Really, so does she go to Maine West?"

"No, she did for a little, but then kept trying to run away from home, off with this loser guy, so finally my parents shipped her off to this boarding school for children with problems far up north in Wisconsin."

So there we were, talking like that, or at least I was doing most of the talking which was strange for me. But I was stoned, and I sensed that she didn't want to talk about herself and she was looking so fucking pretty.

"You're sweet," she said, interrupting me mid-sentence as I was going on about visiting Mexico every summer as a child, how many aunts and uncles we had because my mother's family was so big. "You're not like those other pricks that Matt hangs around with."

"Oh, yeah?" I said, not knowing how to respond. "Well, his friends are pretty cool, aren't they?"

"No, they're assholes, trust me." Matt and I hung out mainly when he wasn't out with his other friends who I didn't know that well and were much more popular than me and my friends. I was sort of his back-up plan most of the time.

By then, we could hear muffling and moaning from upstairs, I guess Matt was getting laid after all. She smiled at me and I smiled back in return, feeling sort of awkward all of a sudden while the Smashing Pumpkins continued to play along in the background—although now I couldn't quite hear the lyrics and melodies anymore and instead heard the sounds from upstairs.

"Hey, we don't have to screw around," I suddenly said out of the blue. I could smell her perfume and shampoo. She looked at me with a surprised sort of look, and then smiled and looked intently at me, like a dog noticing that you're scared. As I saw her looking at me, I turned and focused on the stereo.

"You're not a virgin, are you Alex?" I wasn't. I had definitely had sex before, but never quite with a girl like her, or at least that's what I assumed. I felt inferior, like I wouldn't be able to satisfy her, and I also felt like it would be awkward to break this sort of bond we had started to develop, like I was standing on higher ground or something.

"No, um, you know, I'm not," I uttered nervously as she continued to stare at me with a smirk on her face. "But I was just saying, you know, that we don't have to if you don't want to. I'm not saying I think you even want to or anything, you know, I don't know if you do or don't, I was just saying."

"You're too cute," she said now smiling even bigger, with her head now slightly tilted to the side. And then she scooted over on the couch right next to me and slowly got on top of me, putting her hands on my shoulders, her lips on mine, with her hair flowing down over our faces as I fell on my back. "Don't worry, I don't bite," she said and we continued to kiss. "Holy Shit!" I thought as I lay there, now in full blown make-out mode—tongue, saliva and all—tasting her smoky breath, smelling her sweet scent, feeling her feet (did they smell?) rubbing along my jeans. I wanted to stop, be better, and not feel like I was taking advantage of this girl, but it felt more like she was taking advantage of me, and the guy instinct was taking over. I was in full motion, with an instant erection

I could feel rubbing up against her. I knew she could feel it, and it embarrassed me. What if she thought I was too small? I felt like I was going to explode. The fucking Smashing Pumpkins were still playing, I couldn't hear what song it was, maybe that long one toward the end that everyone skipped over but I thought was pretty cool, the best on that album in fact. "I can't understand what the hell he is singing in this song," I thought to myself. I put my hand on one of her breasts, they were small, but felt nice and firm, especially along her lanky body, and my other hand was running through her hair. God damn I loved that long dark hair. I've always been into blondes, but I really loved that dark hair that night. "Fuck," I thought as I remembered that I didn't have any condoms. I rarely carried one with me, never have, and I wondered if she had some but then thought that it would be fucked up if she did. Or, I wondered if we would just fuck without one right there on the couch. I would pull out, unless she asked me not to; maybe she would want me to leave it in, and maybe I would leave it in and come real hard into her, hold her tightly, stare into her eyes, still kissing, maybe we would fall in love. What the fuck was I thinking? This is crazy, this is how 17-year-old kids end up getting pregnant and all crazy and shit. Then I felt her rubbing my stomach, reaching for my belt and the thoughts of me coming inside her started all over again. She unzipped my pants. I prayed I wouldn't make an ass out of myself and come.

Then suddenly, we heard a bunch of banging, and stomping from upstairs and then a girl's voice screaming "Get the fuck out of here, asshole!"

"Fuck you, bitch, slut!!" I could hear Matt yelling back.

More banging, and then I could hear Matt saying "Al, let's

get the fuck out of here, these fucking bitches are whacked, man!"

"Get the fuck out here!!!!" I could hear Vanessa scream. I sort of looked back at Kristen as we both started getting up with bewildered looks on our faces. "What the hell is going on?" Kristen shouted as she got up and started up the stairs. I could hear Matt yelling "bitch" at someone. I sort of sat there, more yelling going on, back and forth between Matt and Vanessa, and Kristen now, not really hearing what they were saying. I then saw Matt at the top of the stairs yelling down at me, "Al, come on, let's get the fuck out of here man! What the fuck are you doing?

"What?" I said, utterly confused and slowly getting up.

"Dude, let's go, you spic."

I finally got up and made it up the stairs, and we headed toward the front door. I couldn't see the girls around, I wanted to say bye to Kristen, but she wasn't there. I assumed she went upstairs to talk to Vanessa. I stopped right before the door and hesitated, looking toward the stairs leading to the second floor, thinking of going up there to see if everything was ok and saying goodbye, maybe getting Kristen's number or something, when Matt pulled my arm and said, "Let's get the fuck out of here." Then we left the house and got into the car and drove away.

I never got a chance to say goodbye to Kristen, in fact I never spoke to her again. I would see her occasionally at school, once she even waved at me and I shyly waved back, but for some reason I hesitated going over and talking to her. I still wonder what having sex with her would've been like. I imagine it would've been really good, for me anyway.

Later on in the year she was never at school anymore. Apparently her father hung himself in the upstairs attic after he had set the house on fire. She and her mother were all right, but I'm not sure what happened to her, whether she dropped out of school, went somewhere else, or what. Several times I thought about asking one of the teachers what happened to her, but I never did. I thought then that I should have restrained myself more that night, should have gone back to see if she and her friend were all right, and asked to see her again. I still remember wanting to come inside her. I wish I could have been there for her when she went through that horrible experience of her father committing suicide. I watched as my father threatened to kill himself in front of me, my mother and my sister when I was like 12. It was horrifying, so I can only imagine how it would have been had he actually slit his wrists in our kitchen and died in front of us that night.

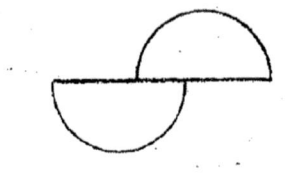

Advances and Retreats

As we drove back through the Villas on our way to Maine West, Matt was laughing as he was telling me what had happened. I sat there, sort of motionless, still stoned, feeling the breeze blow on my face through the window.

"Ah dude, I was fucking railing her," Matt was explaining as we were driving through the dark winding suburban streets, "and then I turned her over and started doing her doggy style. I was in a fucking groove, man, and she was moaning 'n shit, wet as all hell, I was pounding it, and I decided I wanted to go for the ass. We talked about it before and she never said she wasn't into it or anything, so I figured it was cool, you know? So then I took my dick out and started to slide it in her hole. Then she like turned around and said 'Wait... what are you doing?' I was like, 'Relax baby,' and started sliding it more man, but the shit was fucking tight, and then I just sort of rammed it in," he said, laughing. "She started fucking screaming 'n shit. I thought she was digging it, you know, fucking whore, so I kept going, fucking pounding it, it was so fucking tight that I came right away, pulling it out and spraying my shit all over her ass." As he continued, he kept on laughing, face turning red. "Then she all of a sudden turned around and started punching me, throwing pillows, yelling *'GET THE FUCK OUT'* like she was crazy or something!!"

"Dude, that's practically rape," I said.

"Rape? Whatever fucker, she was playing hard to get. She wanted it in the ass; she just felt like a slut when it was done and then freaked out. If she didn't want it, she would have stopped it. Fucking slut. Rape... Don't ever say that again you fucker. Hey, your zipper is still down pussy!!"

I'm not sure if he really raped her or not, or, like he said, whether she was just feeling bad about it when it was over, but she sure was freaking out in the house, the way I heard her screaming. We never really discussed it again. In fact, I think after a while he started fucking her again, so who knows. That night he kept recounting the story to our friends while we were drinking in the parking lot of some factory in Des Plaines, one of our fallback places, but his version of the story was that he fucked her in the ass so hard that she was crying from the pain, and after he was done, just left her like that. "Fucking slut," is how he kept referring to her over and over.

Besides practically being witness to a rape, the next most awkward moment I've had to endure with Matt was when I ended up taking his underage girlfriend to get an abortion. That was our senior year during wrestling season. Matt had met this 15-year-old girl from a western suburb called Hoffman

Estates out at Woodfield Mall. He kept telling me how he was fucking her, talked me into giving him a ride out there a couple of times, wanted to set me up with one of her friends, but the fact that she was only 14 sort of freaked me out. Anyway, one week Matt called in a panic, telling me how she was pregnant and that she was getting an abortion and that it was scheduled for the upcoming Saturday. However, that day he had an important wresting tournament that would dictate whether he would go downstate and therefore couldn't miss it. He begged me to take her and for some reason that I can't fathom today, I agreed, and there I was, with this young, scared, cute freshman girl I didn't know, walking into the Abortion Access Health Center in Des Plaines. I think there might have been one or two protestors along the way in, but I pretty much ignored them and mainly remember just sitting in the waiting room, not talking to anyone, not really even to her. (I didn't know what the hell to say, and I don't even remember her name.

I like to think of Matt as a microcosm, a living example of how humanity functions. He has so much energy and potential, makes progress, and has moments of almost pure brilliance—only to experience significant failures and setbacks. But then he rebounds and tries again. Like that night of the football game, Matt had a girl that wanted him, all to himself, an opportunity any young guy aims for. But then it totally ended up in disaster. I know this happens to all of us. I've had my share of promising things that seem to start out good but only lead to failure. Matt just seems to embody this pattern all the time.

I remember when my friends and I started getting jobs when we were kids. It was exciting for all of us. Matt especially seemed to be excited and eager to start so he could save money for clothes, afford to take girls out for dates, save up for a car. He talked about it over and over. In fact, we both trained together for our first real job when we were 15, finally old enough to work at the grocery store. Man was he pumped during the training, learning how to put the groceries in the brown fucking bags, produce with produce, meat with meat, the big heavy cans on bottom followed by the softer stuff on top so that nothing would break, then saying "Thank you for shopping at Dominick's" after we put the bags into the cart. But then we went out into the store and tried it for real. Matt looked across at me smiling and acting tough as we bagged those groceries quickly and efficiently but strictly following the rules we'd just learned. We were really good; the manager told us so. We were about to start working and making money for real, you know?

So we started working at the Dominick's, making $6.50 an hour, working up to eight hours at a time on the weekends, and then going out with our friends. We imagined what it would be like to earn $10 or more an hour. It was great until it started getting really fucking cold and we had to go outside and get the carts, dragging them around for hours at a time. Eventually after the glamour of our first job wore off, we started taking turns running off and hiding out at the Little Caesar's pizzeria there in the strip mall, or in one of our cars while the other guy would pull the carts around freezing his ass off.

One night we were out pulling carts and it was Matt's turn to hide out at the Little Caesar's. There I was, out with the fucking carts, and after about half an hour I looked back at the store to make sure I wasn't being watched and went over by the Little Caesar's window to wave at Matt so he could work the carts and let me get out of the cold for a little bit. Matt saw me but didn't pay any attention because he was talking to a group of older girls that went to our high school. I opened the door and called out for Matt, who turned around and acted all cool and told me he was busy and that I should continue pushing the carts around because I was much better at it than he was anyway. I was like, "Hey, it's freezing out here," and I started getting all flustered, standing in my winter coat with my Dominick's apron over it. The group of girls was staring over at me and laughing as Matt was like, "Oh, you poor baby," and again told me he was busy and took a bite of a pizza slice. He could be a real asshole that way. They all started laughing again and so I was like fuck it, left the store, and started pushing carts around some more.

After a bit I finally had it and went inside. When our manager asked me where Matt was, I was pissed, so instead of covering for him I just said that I didn't know. Another kid that Matt picked on a lot was nearby and overheard and told the manager that he was probably in the Little Caesar's where he usually was. The manager, this man in his late 30s, partly balding with a mustache and fairly good-sized belly, walked over to the store and went inside. I followed out to see what was happening.

I'm not sure what was said inside, but soon after, Matt came busting out with the manager following behind him and Matt screaming, "Fuck you, I'm out of here, this place fucking sucks!" making a big scene probably so the girls would notice. He threw his apron and name tag back up in the air behind him toward the manager. Then he got in his car, started it up a couple of times until it finally stayed on, and sped off—again as if trying to make a big scene out of it all. But then the car started sliding because it was icy and snowy and he lost control. The car hit this snow bank in the parking lot at full speed and jumped the fucking thing, sailed off and landed on the other side, bounced, and then smashed into a parked car. By this time, all sorts of people—shoppers, the manager, the kid who was coming out for relief, the fucking girls from Little Caesar's—they all seemed to be watching. Matt was ok, but his car was wrecked, he had lost his job, and he got into all sorts of shit from his parents.

That was the first of many jobs that Matt would get excited about and then abruptly get fired or quit. One time he was excited to be working for the city in a construction job, making $15 an hour, which was like a fortune for us at that time. He didn't go out the night before, told me that couldn't go out anymore as he needed to rest up for his job, and that he had different priorities nowadays—he was done being a dumb kid. I was like, cool man, go for it, it's good money, and I wished I could do it. Then the day after he started his job, he came walking into the swimming pool we hung out at during the summer, and we asked him what the fuck happened. He said he went to the job and the next thing he knew, he was wearing a hard-hat, standing next to some big fucking guy who was banging away at a concrete sidewalk with a huge jack-hammer that was loud as hell. Matt was standing there picking up and throwing huge slabs of concrete into a truck, which he did for like two hours and then realized that he would be doing that all day, all week in fact, and finally said fuck it and took off his hat, goggles, gloves and stuff and threw them on the ground and walked off, with the guys yelling back at him, calling him a pussy and all sorts of other things.

Next there was the lawn-mowing job we both worked at, where we would get paid $10 an hour to ride around in this truck and jump out and kick ass with these huge mowers and blowers. The guy who ran it gave us cash and bought us dinner every night from places like Burger King or Arby's. We ate that stuff so much that I haven't been back to one since high school. The job was going great, until Matt ran over this lady's rose bush by accident as he was talking shit to some kids he knew across the street. The lady happened to be watching and started screaming at him and Matt started telling her she could fuck off, and then our boss overheard and told him to get the fuck out of there, to walk home and not come back to work for him again. Then there was his job as an assistant custodian at an elementary school during the summer, which lasted until he kicked one of the other custodian's asses for making fun of Jews.

After high school Matt went to Southern Illinois University, saying how he was going to take that fucking place by storm, was going to play football there and probably wrestle as well. Again, he was really excited about it, but when I talked to him over the phone a few months after we started college and asked him how it was going, whether he'd tried out for the football team as he'd planned, he told me that he had dropped out. "Yeah, fuck that place," he said when I asked him what happened. He said he just didn't like the place, it pissed him off, and besides, he could make big money with his dad at the carnival, so why bother. (Later it turned out that he was really kicked out of college for getting busted with weed a few too many times in the dorms.)

Matt's dad was this old, tough-looking Jewish man with a big nose and big bushy eyebrows, who always seemed to have a cigar in his mouth. He worked at the carnival. It was the traveling type that went from city to city, state to state. We kids loved it when it came to town. We would all go and eat nachos and ride the rides for free. There always seemed to be something shady going on though with the whole carnival business. The neighborhood would talk about how big trucks would come driving through Des Plaines and over to Matt's house in the wee hours of the morning. They seemed to have good money for families in our side of Des Plaines, but who knows; maybe the carnival business is lucrative.

After his failed attempt at the family business, in his 20s, Matt got hooked on cocaine and ran off to Los Angeles with this coke-head, hot blonde that had big fake boobs. They had ideas of surfing and going into acting. He said he was never fucking coming to back to shit-hole Chicago—he was sick of the place—but two months later he was back living with his parents because he had run out of money and the coke-head girl left him for someone that had money. I've heard rumors that Matt acted in a few pornos while in L.A., but I've never tried to confirm them.

I know it's just my friend Matt, and it's a huge leap, but I really do see him as an allegory of society. Although hopefully in society, like the philosopher G.W.G. Hegel argued, amidst a stream of advances and failures, overall progress is being made.

I guess it's the old trial-and-error technique used in science; you try, fuck up, and try again until something works. But then when something works, something else breaks apart and you start again. Maybe it's all necessary for humanity, the universe, whatever, to progress and fulfill itself. I've been thinking about this stuff ever since high school—seeing Matt accomplish things, then fuck up real bad, and then try again. I also think of this whenever I see a newborn baby. We're born, we're tiny and helpless. We grow; we mature (maybe), and then we start destroying ourselves through drugs and alcohol as we supposedly become wiser. And if we make it far enough, we're back to being a baby and eventually die. And we keep reproducing, like we're hoping that the next round of humans will be better somehow.

I wonder whether it's something that we can fix or even should. I guess we shouldn't because if it is part of the evolutionary process, we wouldn't make any progress on some macro level. The scary thing is, with all the deadly weapons humanity has created, it really only takes one major fuck up by one part of society to shatter everything the collective "we" have worked toward—like some asshole terrorist or government regime setting off a nuclear bomb in the name of some insane political or religious idea. Maybe humanity would recover from a major nuclear catastrophe—who knows?—and somehow come ahead better because of it. But if we didn't survive, like the dinosaurs before us, maybe something else better would come along, like the insects. Maybe it's the fucking insects that are destined to take the torch of progress. We humans have only been on Earth for less than 1% of the time it has existed, so if we kill ourselves off it's no big deal, in the grand scheme of things.

However, unlike the dinosaurs that went out because of a big-ass comet, what's fucked up if we do kill ourselves off is that it would be of our own doing. Stephen Hawking has said that a reason why we haven't met any extraterrestrial life is that maybe once life becomes intelligent like us it creates deadly weapons and kills itself off. American politicians talk about how we're failing to protect ourselves from nuclear or biological attack, and that we need to beef up our land and sea borders, but no one talks about how to rid the world of this menace that we've created. The United States continues to be the world's largest holder of nuclear weapons, but we don't do anything about it—instead we're paranoid of Iran and North Korea having them. If we ever do go extinct because of some crazy shit like war or terrorism, or because we've polluted the Earth so badly, we have no one to blame but us.

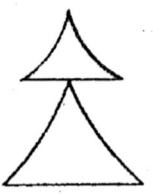

Candice

Except for a few smiles in the hallways or at parties, I didn't interact with Candice until my senior year, when she was in the same Advanced English class as me.I remember the first day in class, when I realized that Candice was going to sit in front of me.

I was sitting there doodling on my notepad when she walked in. She said hi to the teacher. As she was about to sit in a chair a few aisles down from me, she looked up, smiled and walked directly toward me. (The "Crimson and Clover" song started running through my head.) Although I never really talked with her, I guess I was the only person she knew in the class.

As Candice walked toward me with her arms wrapped over her books and notepads in front of her chest, with her blond hair pulled back, I pretended not to notice and put my head down.

Nowadays, I do the same thing. Say I'm sitting on an airplane, and as people are boarding I see an attractive woman come walking down the aisle. I start to panic as I think that maybe she's going to sit next to me, so I focus on whatever book I'm reading or on my headphones—anything to avoid eye contact.

(In the rare case that a woman does sit next to me on a plane or on the train, I'm often too preoccupied with thinking of what I should say to start a conversation. I never want to make any kind of effort, in fear that she'll say something completely rude like, "Um, that's great, but I really don't feel like talking to you; I would, maybe, if you were at all attractive. But seeing that you're not, I prefer to just sit here and read the airline-supplied magazines stored alongside the puke bags.")

As I sat there, doing my best not to notice her, I looked up and there was Candice, standing in front of me with her nice smile saying, "Hey Alex, how are you?" greeting me like we were old buddies, just like her boyfriend Jaime had.

"Fine, good, thanks, Candice. How are you?" I answered straightening up a little, turning my notebook, suddenly a little nervous and sweaty.

"Great, you know, I'm excited for my first day of classes, especially this being our senior year, ha, ha." It's funny how only a girl can talk to you like that… "I'm going to sit right here by you, if you don't mind," she continued as she took off her purse. As she sat down in the chair in front of me, she whispered while looking away over the rest of the class, "I don't really know many of the other people in this class, so I was excited to see you in here!"

"Oh, really, well, that's cool," I said, sitting a little straighter still.

"Yeah," she continued as she crossed her legs and turned to face me, "I'm actually pretty excited about this year. I finally have an AP class, I begged Mrs. Thomas to be in her class, versus Mr. Edwards, and she finally let me in. I started liking English last year, and toward the end I loved it. I'm thinking about majoring in it at college now. I've heard Mrs. Thomas is good."

"She's really good, I like her. She's enthusiastic, reasonable, challenges you and usually picks good stuff to read. I think you'll like the class, especially if you like English now."

"Oh, I hope so. I'm just worried that it'll be hard. But at least I have you here to help me!" she said, with a great big smile that any guy in his right mind would smile back to. And I'm not just saying that because Candice was beautiful, though she was, but I find it difficult not to smile back when any woman smiles at you. It's like getting tickled, a pure reaction, like when a little baby smiles at you.

"So, how was your summer, Alex? Did you go to any fun parties or anything?"

"Yeah, I went to a few, but I worked a lot. Also I hung out a lot in the city, with my friends Paul, Hassan, Carla and them. I don't know if you know them, but I have physics and history with Paul and Hassan."

"I think I know who they are. They're in the band, right? I didn't know you hung out with them; I thought you hung out with John, Carlos, Matt and those guys."

"I do hang out with those guys as well, but I guess this summer I spent a lot of time with the other group also."

"Hmm… what'd you guys do in the city, like, go to raves?" she asked, kind of jokingly.

"Yeah, actually we went to raves, dance parties, stuff like

that, staying up all night," I said feeling really cheesy and turning red in the face. "It was fun, though I'm not doing much of it anymore these days with soccer practice and school now."

"That's interesting, Alex. I'd never think of you as a 'raver.' But I'm sure it's fun," she said, smiling, and then she turned around as Mrs. Thomas started class, and I was glad the conversation was over.

Mrs. Thomas was, in fact, a pretty cool teacher. I really liked her classes. During our junior year we read the *Lord of the Rings* trilogy, and we really got into it and dissected it, all the mythology, religious and allegorical interpretations. She always emphasized character analysis, trying to understand the motives of the characters, what drove their actions, and, furthermore, the author's objective in creating such motivations. An overarching theme in her class was to analyze why humans told stories—was it purely for entertainment, or to pass on history, or as an extension of our pursuit of enlightenment by exploring situations, conflicts and characterization in order to understand how different people deal with situations such as death, love, fear, desire, etc. She liked to say that writing stories and then reading them was our collective way of role-playing, imagining how we would act in all sorts of situations.

She used to draw parallels between literature authors, historians, and philosophers. I remember her saying that philosophers were writers who explored the ideas of meaning, logic, science, truth, and ultimately their goal was to lay out a framework under which the fields of mathematics, science, ethics, and personal fulfillment would operate or co-exist.

"Their writing is more technical," she would say, "first person in nature, discussing subjects in an analytical fashion. Authors of literature, on the other hand, analyze similar issues, though in the form of storytelling, dialogue. And a historian's main objective is to recount our past, but also to analyze it so we can learn and better prepare for the future. But in the end," she would argue, "the purpose of all different forms of writing is ultimately the same—to make sense of our existence. And in many cases, such as with Fyodor Dostoevsky, certain writing is studied under multiple disciplines. His writings, *The Idiot*, *Crime and Punishment*, *The Underground Man*, are often studied in literature classes because of his beautiful writing style and also in philosophy classes because of the painstaking detail in which he explored the moral and value dilemmas his characters faced."

Mrs. Thomas told us she was excited to teach us English for our last year before we headed on to our new adventures, whether to college or wherever. We were going to read *Frankenstein*, *Dracula*, *Zorba the Greek*, *The Picture of Dorian Gray*, *For Whom the Bells Toll*, *The Great Gatsby* and others, but the exact books might change as the class went on, based on where our "adventure" together was taking us. She especially was looking forward to *Zorba the Greek* because she and her husband had just returned from Greece and visited Crete while they were there.

I had read *Zorba the Greek* before, loved it, and was excited to read it again. I also saw the movie, in which Anthony Quinn played Zorba. Although it diverged a lot from the book, I felt it did justice to its spirit. From my teenage years through now, I've loved to re-live experiences, like re-reading books, seeing movies multiple times, trying to grasp all the different nuances and perspectives. Same thing with music, I love to listen to albums I like over and over again. Many people that know this about me think I'm crazy and that I have nothing better to do with my time, which I guess is sort of true.

As the class was ending, Mrs. Thomas indicated that she wanted to have us do a few group papers, probably in pairs of two or three, and a few other such projects, and was even open to a few suggestions from us if we had any ideas as to how to liven the class up. "It's your class just as much as mine," she would say. "You're the best in your graduating class; it'll be my honor to teach you this year and make sure you get all you need prior to going off to your next adventures." I'm a sucker for that cheesy, inspirational sort of stuff...

It was time to go and as we were getting up, Candice said to me with a big smile, "So, you'll be my partner, right, if we need to do some group writing?"

"Of course I will," I responded as we started walking out.

"Oh, here, I want to give you my number, in case, you know, you want to get together and study sometime, once class gets going." She wrote it down in her notepad, ripped out the page and handed it to me.

"Great, yeah, definitely. Um, here's mine also. Feel free to call me as well, you know, in case you have any questions or anything, or whatever..." I wrote mine out on a piece of paper and handed it to her. Mine was written out in this barely legible scribble. Hers, on the other hand, was written in a very bubbly and neat sort of way that only girls seem able to write in.

"Ok Alex, thanks. This should be a fun year. Well, I'm off to gym class. Where you headed to?"

"Um, I'm not sure," I said, and I really didn't have a clue. I was just dumbfounded, shocked actually at what had just happened. I could only imagine Candice changing for gym class…

What kind of great fucking opportunity, I thought to myself, as if I had won the lottery and was suddenly a millionaire. I knew that she had a boyfriend—that meathead Jaime fucker, who all the teachers thought was so great but who I knew was a fraud. During my sophomore year, I was in an American history class with him. It was an experimental thing; the school was trying to combine history and English. That year his group won the first-place prize for a contest our teachers made us do in groups. Our goal was to select an item we thought best represented the American Dream and make a presentation about it. I didn't really have any good ideas; I was like what the fuck kind of project was that? What the hell was the "American Dream" anyway? Jaime's team won first place with, what else, but the goddamned television… I couldn't believe it, but there he was up in front of the class talking up the television: "We all watch it; it tells us our news, our sporting events, all our stories and dreams, great and sad ones, our entertainment."

The fucking teachers were going gaga at his presence, his swagger. I'm sure the one female teacher wanted to fuck him.

Finally I gathered myself and remembered where I was going, "Oh, yeah, I'm going to math now," I said to Candice.

"O.k., well, I'm going upstairs this way," which was the opposite way, "Well, have fun in math Alex!"

"Thanks, I'll talk to you later," I said, and off we went.

The funny part was, all through the summer, with the theater kids, I had talked about how bullshit all the popular kids at school were, how fake they were, and how the pretty girls were all shallow and that they would end up getting knocked up and fat and shit like that. I would say that the guys were all a bunch of assholes, laughing at their own stupid jokes, thinking they were the shit and basically prepping to take the places of their fat, beer guzzling, football watching suburban fathers.

Additionally, I hated studying with other people. I would maybe get together with other people only if I knew that we had all read the material and were prepared to have an intelligent conversation to exchange ideas, perspectives, challenge each other, but that rarely happened because I was generally procrastinating and needed to cram it all in at the last second. Cramming was something I was good at, but I needed to have absolute quiet in order to properly concentrate.

"You don't really think you are going to hook up with her, do you?" Paul said to me one night as Hassan and I were at Paul's house listening to records. Though I had hesitated telling anyone, I eventually told them about Candice giving me her number. "It might seem like she likes you or something, but she's really just going to use you for grades. Chicks like her, they're so fucking selfish. She'll never see anything in you except that you get good grades and that maybe you can help her."

"Those bitches all suck, man. They have no taste; they're dumb, and they're sluts," Hassan chimed in. Its funny how all guys can talk like that, regardless if they themselves are not at all good looking. Hassan was skinny, nerdy, kind of an ugly fucker, who happened to have great taste in music and art.

"Candice is not a slut, and she's really not that dumb," I responded in her defense. "I was surprised, but she's actually pretty smart. Fine, she might not have the greatest taste in stuff like movies or music, but it's not that awful, I'm sure. There's a lot worse in our school." Of course, I didn't know what kind of music Candice listened to.

"Yeah, but still, look at her fucking boyfriend, that guy's a joke, man. And that's all they want, these hot rich girls, a guy who looks like that. That's all," added Paul.

"He is a fucking joke," I agreed. "But the truth is your pussy-ass would squeal if she would ever even come within two inches of you, and it'd be over before you even had your dick out of your pants."

"Hey, go for it then. Study with her and see what happens," replied Hassan, shrugging his shoulders. "Maybe you can pull it off and sweep her off her feet, you know? That'll be funny if you end up banging her and that asshole Jaime freaks out and rampages, kicks your ass and does himself in or something. We could write a play about it, you know?"

And that's how my conversation with Paul and Hassan went on the subject. Anything is excusable among guys if there is a possibility of getting laid.

Even though I hated studying with people, I didn't hesitate before taking Candice's number and offering her mine. Not even for a second. She was too cute, too hot, too nice to look at. Despite her boyfriend, I just couldn't pass up that kind of opportunity. It was like I was trying to quit smoking and all of a sudden someone offered a few cartons for free. Just thinking about studying at night with her made my skin tighten up. What the hell would it be like, where would we study? Not my house, surely not, she would think I was a freak with all my Iron Maiden, Metallica, and Black Sabbath posters. Her house? I would freak out. I assumed her parents were these perfect mannered white people. They would eat me up. I pictured me reading *Zorba the Greek* to her while she was lying on her bed in nothing but a long white undershirt, panties and slippers. I started getting pissed at myself for thinking like that and tried to shake it out of my mind, but I couldn't concentrate the rest of the day or even at soccer practice after school.

That night I ate dinner fast and immediately went into my room, played REM's *Murmur*, and began flipping through *Zorba the Greek*. I was already preparing for my study sessions with Candice. As I flipped through my copy of the book—in which I had written in the margins, highlighted and underlined favorite sentences, passages—I came across this one where Zorba's telling his friend why he needs to go to bed with this widow, explaining that no matter what, even if he doesn't feel true love for her, he has no choice because God frowns on men who, when called upon, don't go into a woman's bed because that's what we, men, are made for:

> "My boy, if a woman calls you to share her bed
> and you don't go, your soul will be destroyed! That
> woman will sigh before God on judgment day, and
> that woman's sigh, whoever you may be and what-
> ever your fine deeds, will cast you into Hell!"

And I thought to myself that, see, I was right to give her my number, even if I had no chance in hell to hook up with her—she asked me for it and I needed to oblige. Zorba, if he were here with me, would be patting me on the back, saying, "Good job, my lad."

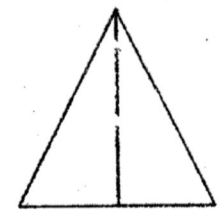

For the Greek

I've really only had four girlfriends—Jackie, the girl whom I lost my virginity with; Sandy, whom I dated my junior and senior years during high school; Sarah, whom I dated on and off during college, and then Erica, the cute southern girl whom I really didn't want to date and then cheated on. I've gone through long spells of not having a girlfriend—recently as long as like five years. Chuck Klosterman wrote that Billy Joel is lonely and depressed partly because he's never received critical acclaim, but mostly because of his lack of success with girls. I'm like that I guess, but without his money and fame.

My high school girlfriend Sandy was about 5'4, had short black hair, and was very cute. She was nice, had nice parents, listened to fairly good music, and made a great pizza. We hung out a lot and, of course, Matt had sex with a few of her friends. I took her to my senior year prom, rented a Ford Taurus to pick her up because the rusty gold 1970s Grand Prix I was driving was a big piece of shit and I couldn't get anything else last-second. I had sex with her that night at the Embassy Suites downtown; it was supposedly her first time but I had my doubts. We broke-up shortly after that, and she immediately dated a younger guy—who was cuter than me but a dumb-shit—and of course I was a jealous mess... even though I wanted to break-up with her because I was going away to college and needed my space. I saw her a few times after high school and even had sex with her again—in her bed-room, which was right next to her parents' bedroom (that was cool but weird)—but then she faded away. She recently sent me an e-mail through this web site where people join and try to get in contact with people they knew from high school. My friend Carlos told me about it. He always had this fantasy of getting in touch with high school people who thought he was a fucking loser and impressing them somehow. Anyway, Sandy e-mailed me, saying she saw me on the site, that it had been such a long time, and she wanted to say hi and see how I was doing. I responded back saying it was cool to hear from her, asked her how she was doing, and told her that I kept busy with my career, international travel and all that bullshit I usually say to impress someone and make them think I do something im-portant for a living. I told her I wasn't married, was living the single life in the city, and asked her what she had been up to. She responded by saying she lived out in some suburb, way the fuck out there, just had her third baby, had been married for like five years or something. She also said it would be nice to keep in touch, maybe meet up for drinks or something. I never responded back after that. What was the point? We'd lost touch over 10 years ago, had nothing in common, what the hell were we going to keep in touch about?

On the other hand, Candice, who's not anywhere close to being a former girlfriend, is a girl I would love to get in touch with again. There was just something about the girl that created a warm feeling when she spoke to you. I'm sure every guy has had a girl create this feeling in him, in fact some guys, if not most of them, feel this way any time a moderately good-looking girl talks to them, including me. But Candice was pretty— very fucking pretty—and also so goddamn nice, which can be a rare combination. I mean she would talk to you and genuinely smile. She was like that to me but also like that to other nerdy kids in our class, to the teachers, to her hot friends, and also to that fucking asshole Jaime.

Jaime wasn't really that much of an asshole per se. He was just your typical tall, blond, muscular, outspoken, all-American guy with perfect teeth. He always cracked jokes that I thought were stupid but everyone else laughed at, especially girls who would get all pie-eyed. One thing though about guys like Jaime that I admire is that they tend not to change much with the tide. I mean, their style might change here and there to keep up with current trends, but overall it's consistent. He could be a real prick too, especially to the weaker kids in school, but he was generally nice to me though, especially when I helped him out with history. He was especially nice to me my senior year after I started studying with his hot girlfriend. Jaime's the kind of guy that goes into politics.

When Candice first made good on her offer and actually called to discuss what we were reading in class, I almost shit in my pants.

I was lying on my bed during a school night, flipping through my math book, doing a problem here and there, and scribbling in my notebook. I had my headphones on listening to something loud, like Ministry or Front 242.

I hated math, was never really that good at it. I think it's too organized for me, too logical. I always liked the "fluffier" stuff, like my English and history classes. I've always been an organizational mess. Although I hated it, I always did ok at math—usually ended up getting a B if not an A—but it took me a lot of time studying and thinking about it. To study math, I would have to dedicate long hours to having my math books in front of me and doing the problems slowly, trying to absorb them. I somehow became an accountant, so go figure. But still, that's one of the biggest stereotypes, that to be an accountant means you're good at math. You only need to know very basic math, which is why I guess I became one.

"Alex!" I finally heard my mother yelling in the doorway to my room. I could barely hear her because of the music coming through my earphones.

"What?" I said to her, loud and acting annoyed because she was interrupting me, even though I saw a phone in her hand and knew it must be a call for me.

"Some girl's on the phone for you," she said in her semi-broken English. After running, crawling, and walking across the border illegally in her 20s, she was now a proud citizen and we pretty much spoke English to each other all the time, as we still do.

My mother handed me the phone. It was one of those cordless phones, which was a big deal back then because I never had a phone in my room. Before we had cordless phones, I went through hell trying talk on the phone from my bedroom in private, having to drag the cord from the phone socket in the living room through my sister's bedroom and then into mine. I'd have to talk with my back against the door because the chord was barely long enough. It's amazing how far we've come with respect to telecommunications. I remember going to Mexico with my mom when we were young and having to go to the one neighbor's house on the block that had a phone, and he would charge us for making calls from their house.

"Hello," I said, in the soft girly voice I still use when I know there's a girl on the phone. I don't know why I've always done that, but when I talk to a girl, I all of a sudden take on this girly voice, sort of like trying to imitate them; they seem to think it's cute for some reason. I thought this was going to be Carla or someone like that; she usually called to bullshit during the week.

"Hi Alex," said this super feminine voice that I didn't recognize at first. I'd never heard it over the phone. "It's Candice," she said after a second, and it still didn't quite register, but then I stopped my Walkman and started paying attention knowing that some crazy shit was about to go down.

"Are you busy?" she asked, probably because I was being awkward.

"Um, no, I'm not, I mean, I'm just studying some math, you know?"

"Oh, well I don't mean to interrupt you. I can let you go if…

"No, no it's fine" I said, now fully paying attention, sitting up and looking around the room. "Hi Candice, what's up?" I asked her, feeling the sweat glands bulge on my forehead.

"Oh, it's just, I don't know about this Zorba guy…" she said with the cutest little laugh. That shit just kills me, when girls say something and they laugh like that, it fucking kills me.

So, just out of the blue, she called to talk about Zorba the Greek, which we were reading in class. Yes, we had exchanged numbers like the first day of class that year. But I never called and neither did she. No fucking way was I going to call her, though I kept thinking about whether she would call me. I became obsessed with it in fact. I always saw her in class, she sat right next to me, would always say hi when she sat down, would smile at me, ask me how I was doing. I would rush to get to class early so I could see what she was wearing when she came in. I fantasized what it would be like to make out with her. When I told my "regular" friends that we exchanged numbers, they told me that I was a loser and I should just fucking call her, but I never dared. I never had the balls for that kind of shit, to just out-of-the-blue call someone, even when they had given me their number. Every girlfriend I've ever had was because they pressed the issue and called me.

At first I stressed out about whether she would call. If she did call, it would only be to use me for grades, so I decided to be standoffish and brush her off when and if she ever called. I started trying to ignore her in class too, like when she came in and said hi, I would say hey softly, not really even looking at her. I thought it was smooth, but really it was dumb.

My whole plan of blowing her off went out the window the instant I recognized her voice on the phone, and I began to think about the book immediately. I was not reading it yet. We were given like three weeks to read it. During class we would talk about it, read passages and then discuss them, and then after the three weeks we were tasked to write a short paper concerning the topic of our choice. I would suffer on the quizzes our teacher would give on the book, depending on how detailed they were, but I would try to make up for it on the papers. I'd already read the book a few times; I felt like it was my fucking life statement, my anthem, and I still do. Zorba is one of my heroes.

"What about Zorba?" I said after a second.

"Oh, I just don't know if I get him, what to write about here, you know?" she said, sighing. Candice was apparently working on her paper already, and it wasn't even due until next week; that's how crazy organized the girl was. I wouldn't even start to think about my paper until the day before, and fuck it if I used an outline or anything. I would just jump in and start writing the thing. I would re-read the first few chapters of the book and skim the rest and end up bullshitting my way through the paper. You learn so much about a character right in the beginning of a book. The author is just fucking making stuff up, so why couldn't I? (My teachers didn't always agree with me.)

"Yeah, he's an interesting fellow, isn't he?" I said.

"Well, yeah, but I just don't know if I get him. I'm trying to think of what he stands for, you know? There seems to be some sort of contrasts the author's trying to make by pairing him with the stuffy English guy, but, I don't know… Maybe I'm not as smart as you and all the others in class," she said. I wondered what she was wearing; could I really be talking to Candice while she was in some kind of nightie and lying on her freaking bed?

I wasn't sure why she waited until this book to call. The other books we read in class maybe were a little more straight-forward or something, and I guess Zorba the Greek might come off as different to people. I guess you can consider it a guy's book; that's what I've heard people say although I think it has a universal appeal.

"Stop it. Of course you're as smart as everyone else," I said. "If not smarter."

"Oh, you're too sweet," she responded laughing again. "What do you think Alex? Have you read it yet? I know you have a thought or two."

"Well, I like to think that Zorba represents, like, real passion for life, you know? He's passionate for life, all of it. He loves women, war, work, food, chaos, you know? But he also represents a true dichotomy, the balance between excess and discipline."

"You see!" she said, all excited. "How do you think of things like that?" I was red in the face and flattered, but I laughed to myself because I thought what I said was stupid. I've tried to imagine what really smart people think like. Have you ever been engaged in conversation with a fucking smart person who really knows his or her stuff? I'm always amazed by the TV talk shows, the political ones in which people sit around and debate. They all talk in perfect sentences—no "ums," "ors," "hms," "likes," or stutters, but just one word to the next. You can almost see the fucking commas, semicolons, dashes and periods come out of their mouths.

"Well, I mean, that's what it's about right? Zorba is like this guy who is full of energy, energy for life, all parts of it, good and bad. That's why he seems to self-destruct a lot, to us anyway. But to him, you know, he's just letting himself go to wherever life leads him," I continued. And I thought about Matt briefly; maybe he was like a modern day Zorba…

"Huh," said Candice. "So, is that why he's always cursing God and the devil too?"

"Yeah, I mean, it's like he doesn't see the barriers like the rest of us do."

"What do you mean?"

"I mean that, for Zorba, all emotions, feelings, events, memories, are expressions of life—they're what make up the energy that is just being alive and experiencing all of this stuff, regardless of whether it's considered good or bad. I think for Zorba there might be a difference between, you know, good and bad—but it's more like feelings or actions that are considered good or bad rest on some sort of continuum. Like, on each extreme there are clearly things that everyone agrees to as being good or bad, but there are certain things where it's not so clear, and it becomes a little hazy as to whether something is good or bad, and it depends on what definition you're using, or what the motivation is. And that's where the interesting stuff in life happens and where Zorba, in particular, spends his time."

"Hmm," said Candice. "So, do you mean that for Zorba, God and the devil, good and evil, are the same or something?"

"Yeah, exactly. Well kind of," I said, "I mean, he probably thinks they're of the same thing, just like all of the actions happening in ordinary life are part of the same process. God and the devil are aspects of the same thing. That's why he's, like, always cursing God and the devil, and in fact I think he often says there's no difference between them, that they're the same."

"Huh," she said. "That's why he seems to be angry all the

time. I mean is he like someone who doesn't believe in God or something?"

"Well, I don't know if Zorba believes in God or not. I think he just sort of thinks there's one God, you know, who is both good and evil, and there's barely a difference between good and evil. You know, to Zorba, good and evil just represent different aspects of life. The God that exists is fierce because life is fierce, you know—we fight, kill, cheat, steal, love, have sex, all that, to survive. And to live it, to battle with this God, one must tackle it just as fiercely, at all costs. And that's why he lives every day like it's the last, with all his energy."

"So, that's why he does things like go off and have sex with that young girl toward the end, the dancer, and spends all the money that the Englishman gave him for materials? Because it just happened upon him, and he had to be fierce and seize the moment?

"Yeah, but that's also the interesting part of this, right? Where's the balance? I mean, he almost destroys everything they were working for, just to have sex with this younger girl, right? I mean, just because it's there, is that justification for doing something? Where's the self-restraint?"

"Which is where the Englishman is, all the way on the other side, all restraint!" said Candice, laughing.

"Yeah, but where's the balance, or should there be? Or are we supposed to believe that one of them is right and the other one is wrong?"

"Or maybe they are working together to sort of create that character with the balance, where they come together in the end?"

"Yeah, something like that, that's great, that's where you should write your paper Candice, right there." I said.

"Huh, Alex, this was interesting. I'm so glad I talked to you tonight!

And so it was, we talked like that about Zorba the Greek that night. Then she started calling consistently, a few times a week, to bounce her ideas off me, to ask me questions, and I fucking loved every minute of it. Over the rest of the year, we talked about The Catcher in the Rye, Frankenstein, The Picture of Dorian Gray, For Whom the Bell Tolls. The funny thing was that I never told any of my friends—except for Paul and Hassan. I just knew that my other friends would've given me too much shit for talking to a girl like Candice every week and not trying to put the moves on her or something. I just didn't feel like dealing with any of it.

It was all good until she invited me over to her place one night close to the end of the year so we could study for our final exam. I hated studying with other people. I never studied with anyone, I fucking hated it. But that shit didn't even cross my mind at the time we were on the phone and I immediately answered, "Well, sure, that would be great.

"Yeah, you know, we could just spend some time gathering our thoughts, thinking about what we might have to write about. It'll be great, especially for me. I love your ideas," she said and then made that fucking little laugh, and I was going insane inside, getting a hard-on. What, me at Candice's house?

What the hell would it be like? What would it smell like? Would she have dolls, teddy bears, shit like that in her room? Would her parents be these perfect white people? What would she be wearing? I had this picture of Candice talking to me, lying on her stomach on her bed in her bra and panties, her hair back in a pony tail, making little puppy eyes at me as I put forth all sorts of profound thoughts on literature, with "Wouldn't It Be Nice" by The Beach Boys playing in the background.

Of course, none of that really happened. None of the fantasies I have before some sort of encounter with a woman ever really happen.

"How about tomorrow night?" she asked.

"Um, yeah, I guess that's fine," I said, sort of stuttering, "Um, just let me check and see if I have anything going on tomorrow night. I'm not sure, but I don't think I do, just, you know, I'm not good with keeping track of stuff sometimes…" I had nothing going on; I just always say that. I always say that when people ask what I'm doing to give off the illusion that I have things going on and that my time is precious. It's all bullshit. I always say that because I like to have an excuse in case I freak out and can't go through with the date. So, although this wasn't necessarily a date, it was very freaking close to one in my mind, and I was already freaking out.

"Um, ok, just let me know tomorrow, or just call me after school. I have poms practice, but then I'll be at home the rest of the night studying, so it's totally cool if you want to come over."

"Cool," I said, "I'll check my schedule and let you know tomorrow."

"Ok. Well, let's talk tomorrow. I'm going to do some more homework here and then hopefully hit the hay." How does a girl like Candice "hit the hay?"

"Ok, goodnight," I said, then we hung up, and I immediately put on "You Might Think" by The Cars, followed by "In the Name of Love" by U2. Then I called Hassan and told him what the fuck had just happened.

"You're a fucking idiot. Do you really thing the girl's interested in hooking up with you?" said Hassan.

"No, I don't know, well maybe. I mean, she fucking asked me over to her house. It's a start."

"Start to what? Dude, she's just using you, I mean, seriously."

"You're just fucking jealous, that's all. Besides, even if she is using me for my grades, I don't give a shit, it's still a fucking opportunity."

"Whatever, you're pathetic, but knock yourself out. I hope what's his name, that Jaime dude, kicks your ass."

"Yeah, fuck you. But hey, don't tell Carla and them this shit."

After hanging up the phone and sitting there for a second thinking about the whole thing, I thought that Hassan was probably right. Yeah, maybe it was stupid; I'm sure Candice really just wanted to study, but I still thought it was pretty weird. My own friends barely ever asked me to come over and study. No other girl, especially a gorgeous one like Candice, had ever asked me to before. Maybe I was the chump or nerd there at the right time. Even if she put the moves on me or something, I knew I wouldn't be able to handle it. I would probably super premature ejaculate and be embarrassed as hell. Maybe she would think that was cute or something. I decided that I should probably masturbate that night to relieve shit before I went over there—just in case—just like Ben Stiller's character in *There's Something About Mary*. And then I thought, so what if she was using me for her fucking grades. I almost thought of it as my duty to oblige her then, you know, like Zorba would encourage me to do. Yes, I needed to do this for Zorba the Greek's sake; he would tear my head off if I even hesitated.

I was freaking out about it all night though. I had all sorts of music on and forgot about the other homework I had going on for the next day. I don't even remember if I missed some shit or anything. I started flipping through the books we were reading that year that would be covered on the test, just reading passages here and there, thinking of the characters, the stories, jotting down notes.

Books are great in that way. They're our little accounts of history, whether they are nonfiction or not. I'm not talking about history in the typical sense, a factual account of events, but of the history of the human experience. What was it like to live in a certain time period, to be of a certain personality type?

That's what I thought as I flipped through our books. It made no sense to try to predict the questions we would be asked to write about. Rather, I thought it made better sense to just think about the stories, the characters, what was being drawn for us by these authors, what their motivations were in writing what they wrote. From Zorba and the Englishman dancing on the shores of a Cretan beach after their idea to bring wood down from the top of a hill to their mine ends in complete disaster, to Dorian Gray staring at his aged and torrid portrait in agony, to Merry Shelley's monster escaping to the far reaches of the Earth to escape humanity, the authors had their purpose, a story they were trying to tell.

My friend John used to pair guys and girls up based on the league they were in, and John encouraged his friends to never go for someone outside of their league. Well, I was way out of my fucking league in this case. I shouldn't even have been let in the stadium. If Candice was in the Major Leagues, I was still trying out for the little leagues. I was out of breath when I thought about it and started sweating. I've never been able to avoid this sort of feeling when faced with something to do. Even to this day, before I have a meeting or have to give a speech, no matter if I've given speeches a million times, I just completely freak out. When I'm about to go out with a girl, it's like insanity. I begin to sweat like I'm in a fucking sauna or something. My face sweats; I hate it. I always tell myself that there's nothing to fear; why the hell should I freak out? We're all just human, I have nothing to be scared about. The world and universe are vast, and these little things I get myself into ultimately pale in comparison to some of the other shit that is going on. I could easily be living in Baghdad right now, or have some sort of disability, you know?

At school that morning I was not really such a mess, but sort of in a daze. I vaguely remember being at my first class of the day. Two of the kids that sat next to me asked me if I was okay, and I was just sort of like, "Yeah, I'm just a little sick or something."

What was really freaky, what scared the living shit out of me, was walking down the hall after my first class and almost running right smack into Jaime, whom I had totally forgotten about in my silly delirium. I spent the whole night preparing, thinking and freaking out about how my night would go with Candice, and I had not one thought about him. I was just walking down the hall, my head somewhat down but more just staring into space, and I almost fucking put my face straight into his chest as he grabbed me by the shoulders.

"Hey!" I suddenly heard him yell practically into my face. I looked up and saw him staring down at me with a wide fucking smile on his face. If there ever was a devil, that fucking face I saw that morning would definitely be it. The beginning to

Iron Maiden's song "The Number of the Beast" would have been appropriate background music for that moment, "Woe to those of Earth and sea for the devil sends the beast with wrath because he knows the time is short…"

"Dude, what the hell? You almost ran right into me. Are you all right?"

"Yeah, you know, um, I'm just a little tired today 'n shit."

"Well, you better wake up man. I heard you're helping Candice study for English tonight. She's working hard for an A in that class; it means a lot to her."

"Yeah," I said, sort of still in shock that I was talking to him about this.

"But I know you'll help, you're a genius at this sort of shit—just like your little help for me in history," he said winking at me. He patted me on the back and said he would catch up with me later and then I took off down the hall.

"Motherfucker," was what I was thinking as I walked down the hall, no longer in the stupor I had been in all night and morning. Talk about a fucking wake-up call, as if somebody had splashed ice cold water on my head. It was more apparent now than ever, I was totally being used for grades, and not just by her—by fucking both of them, both parts of the Maine West super couple. Goddamn did I feel like a dip-shit. Hassan was right, that fucking asshole. I even forgot about my girlfriend Sandy the whole time; she called the night before, and I had totally blown her off. We were in some sort of fight or something and I didn't want to deal with it. But now I was thinking that I was fucked, and I better not fuck that up if I didn't want to end up single as all hell with no date to the fucking prom. I thought about totally blowing this Candice thing off, saying "fuck you" to all of it.

I was so pissed in my homeroom class, I just wrote in my notebook the whole time. I don't even know what the hell we did in homeroom anyway. I mean, we just sat around and were supposed to be quiet and do our homework. Isn't that what being at home was supposed to be? They should've used that time to teach us stuff like art or music, something productive, you know? Afterwards I blew right passed Carla, who was trying to stop and talk to me, and who called me a fucking asshole down the hall as I kept walking by. I remember seeing Sandy down in the hall at some point, so I slid into a classroom and hid for a second, until she and her friends had walked by. I didn't get a proper lunch in the cafeteria and instead went and hung around the tire shop where all the head-banger dudes hung out and got into a conversation about how Metallica sucked now. I didn't go to my English class. I was about to, but then flipped out and instead went to the nurse's office and told them that I wasn't feeling well, felt lightheaded, and asked if I could lay down—which they let me do. I was good at pretending to be ill. I wasn't really freaking out anymore; I was now just angry at the whole thing, pissed at myself, and I didn't want to deal with it anymore.

So after the 45-minute layout in the nurse's office, talking to her and telling her I was alright, I resolved to finish off the day, go to track practice, and then call Candice and just make up an excuse, tell her that I wasn't feeling well or something. I was a decent runner, not the fastest, but solid. I've always enjoyed running, and if it wasn't for how much I smoke, I'd probably still be running all the time. That day I especially enjoyed practice, and after building up a good sweat I felt much better about everything. I started thinking about Sandy. I knew she would be even more pissed at me than ever, but I would deal with that the next day. After practice we showered, and I was walking out toward the shitty Grand Prix my father handed down to me, when I heard Candice yell out my name.

"Hey Alex," I heard her say, and I turned around to see her walking toward me in the parking lot, in her ugly Maine West poms warm-up outfit, which looked great on her. Another surprise run-in, and again I could feel little sweat beads gather on my forehead.

"Hey," I said.

"Where were you today? You weren't in class."

"Yeah, I wasn't feeling well earlier today for some reason, I went to the nurse's office during class."

"Oh, that sucks. Are you still feeling bad?"

"No, I actually feel great now. Going to practice helps, you know?" I said, scratching my head now, starting to feel a little nervous.

"Oh, that's cool." She said standing there with her blond hair pulled back, her pretty blue eyes staring at me as she talked. "Well, you don't have to come over tonight if you're not up for it. I totally understand."

And despite my whole plan of saying fuck it and blowing her off and all that, I said "No, that's cool; I can still come by if you want."

"That would be great, but honestly, not if you're not feeling well, maybe another…"

"No, seriously, it's ok; I think I have things to do tomorrow, so tonight would be better."

"Ok, great!" she said, and then wrote down her address on a piece of paper and handed it to me and said that I could come over any time after seven.

"Sounds good," I said. And just like that, wondering what the hell had gotten into me, I got into my car, pumped on my stereo—which was playing a mixed cassette, a song by the Talking Heads. After dinner I got ready, and off I went to Candice's. Well, I did freak out a few times about what to wear. I finally just put on a shirt and jeans and a hoody.

I was all cool until I came closer to her house. It was crazy; I stopped short, pulled over, and tried to compose myself. I started up again and drove toward the house, but as I approached it, I sped up and drove past it. I thought about just fucking leaving and coming up with an excuse, but then I decided to turn back around. I did that a few times and started yelling at myself for being so stupid, started psyching myself up like a boxer does before a fight. I'd like to think that I acted like that because I was a 17-year-old, insecure male, but this shit still happens to me now that I'm in my 30s. I was always told that it all gets better when you grow up. However, I recently read that as you get older, your faults become exaggerated because you've worn them your whole life. I tend to agree with that assessment.

My anxiety, though, hasn't really prevented me from doing things. When I'm super anxious, I usually hit a point where it all becomes clear; the freaking out suddenly stops, and I carry on with whatever I am supposed to be doing. And that's what finally happened after a few drives past Candice's house. I drove up to the house, parked the car, and walked to the door and rang the bell.

As soon as she opened the door and said "Hi Alex!" with her big, beautiful smile—as if I was staring into the gates of Heaven and an angel was greeting me—every bit of anxiety I had been feeling suddenly rushed back.

After I walked in, I calmed down, and everything was fine. I got a reprieve from the little hell I was living in. Candice was nice; her house was nice, and her parents were fucking nice. I don't even remember if she had any siblings. I don't think she did, but I can't recall now. She introduced me to her parents, who seemed to be way older than mine but looked a lot healthier. Her father came up and shook my hand, saying it was nice to meet me. His wife also said it was nice to meet me, that they had heard so much about me, how good I was at school, and how important they thought school was. They asked me if I was going to college, and I said that I was going to the University of Illinois at Urbana-Champaign. It was close but yet far enough to be away from home, to which they laughed. The father thought it was a good school. For some reason I thought of what my father would think if he was standing in that living room, whether he would try to start a fight with Candice's father for some reason, perhaps accusing him of looking at us funny. They wished me luck and then said they better let us go off to study, and so we went.

The main floor of their house had a dining room, kitchen, living room, and family room—with every room full of all kinds of shit. We went to the basement, which was fully furnished, of course, and seemed to be as big as my whole house. We sat down on the couches. She had the radio on, 93.1 WXRT, which was a decent radio station back then. I wasn't paying too much attention to what was on the radio, but just listening to her talk, noticing how she looked at me when I talked, and I was just sort of in disbelief that I was sitting there in a somewhat private setting with such an attractive and smart girl.

We both had out our books, notes, and the papers we had written. I just sort of followed her lead. She proposed some kind of plan, to start in order through all the books we had read that semester. She seemed experienced in studying with people. We talked about all the books again, the characters, what they might have stood for, what the authors might have had in mind with different romances, scenes, moods, writing in the past or present tense. We talked a lot about *Frankenstein* that night because it was the most recent book we'd read. I really enjoyed the book when I first read it.

Frankenstein is a simple story about the yearning for eternal life, or moreover, our ongoing fear of death. Doctor Frankenstein creates life, but he realizes that it is hideous. Realizing his mistake, that humanity ought not to tamper with nature, the doctor comes to hate his creation, hate what he's done, and avows to destroy it. The creature, in his turn, becomes self aware, aware of his own imperfections, and thus begins to despise his creator. But ultimately the creature also begins to fear death, and thus the story ends with the ongoing chase, the creator seeking to destroy his creation, and the creation struggling to evade its creator and to hold on to the life it's been given.

I don't remember much of the book's details anymore, but the overall theme still resonates with me. People look at me like I'm crazy sometimes when I say that *Frankenstein* is one of my all time favorite books. They're like, "It's a monster story." In fact, I think that Merry Shelley was like 19 when she wrote it, at the request of a teacher for her to write a monster story. But I think she hit something on the head there.

Candice and I talked about stuff like that for hours. I think she had a good grasp on the books, probably more so than I did because she read them all in detail. I saw how all her books had highlights of different colors and notes throughout them. It's crazy how only girls seem to highlight in different colors, and their note taking is always much more organized than mine could ever be. We read some Jane Austen that year; I'm sometimes ashamed to admit that I enjoyed reading her stories. There was always something catchy, like a pop song, about her stories.

I'd like to say that something magical happened that night, but nothing did, not really. I was just surprised that after all my anxiety, all the bullshit from my friends, that in the end, she just wanted to study with someone she came to trust. Despite being fucking hot, she was smart and a hard worker. I now know how all those hot TV news anchors, like all those long-legged broads on CNN or MSNBC, get their start. They all probably were like Candice was in high school.

And you know, I don't ven remember what she was wearing that night. Not just panties and a bra though.

After a while, we had, or she had, decided we'd studied enough, and we laughed at how we were going to ace our essay test. We sat there, starting to put our things away when she asked about my girlfriend.

"So, Alex, you have a girlfriend, right? Sandy?" She and I had never talked about that kind of stuff. We'd always just talked about class, and other things about her, but never much about me.

"Um, yeah, sort of," I said, suddenly fumbling with my words, which I hadn't done at all that night.

"What do you mean?" she asked now smiling, laughing a little.

"Well, you know, we've sort of been dating, but it's a little weird now and then, you know, I'm just not sure where it's all going and stuff."

"Oh," she said, still smiling. "I know how that can be. I'm sure you'll figure it out Alex, you're a good guy."

"Yeah, but I'm not the best at this sort of stuff, you know, with girls and everything, when it comes to dating."

"Oh, come on," she said. "You're just saying that. Besides, none of us are really good at that. We're all learning how to date all the time. We're all still so young."

"Yeah, I guess, but I would have thought that like you and Jaime were experts at it. You seem to be at least."

"My gosh," she said with a loud laugh this time, "Jaime and I? I mean, he's great, but we have our problems, just like everyone else."

"Really? I would've thought that like you guys were like already certain you were going to get married, you know?"

With more laughter, she said "Alex, that's funny. I mean, we've had fun dating, and who knows what is going to happen in the future, but, like I said, we're all so young. I'm sure we're going to grow up in ways we didn't anticipate, and who knows what'll happen. I don't think any of us should be thinking we have any of this figured out yet."

"Candice, you're so smart…" I said, being serious, but I think she thought I was being sarcastic by the way she looked at me.

"It's my mother," she said, putting the stuff into her bag. She looked at me and said, "But seriously Alex, don't worry about Sandy, you'll figure it out, and most of all, have fun with it. Don't take it too seriously. You're young, smart, cute, and I know you'll end up making a great gal very happy one of these days." She then leaned over, put a hand on my shoulder, kissed me on the cheek, looked at me, like with her face fucking close to mine, smiled and said, "Alex, you're a really great guy. Any girl would be crazy not to want to have you as their boyfriend." Then she stood up and we got our things and went up the stairs.

I think I've been told that like a thousand times. I've heard it from my mother, my sister, girls who were just about to break up with me, girls who didn't want to go out with me, but that night, it seemed sincere. I think she meant that, and I was so fucking flattered by it. I've wondered whether I should've said something after she kissed me on the cheek. I mean her face was so close to mine. Was I supposed to grab the back of her head and pull her toward me and then give her a huge kiss? I could have; it was there, but then what if she freaked out, slapped me and everything? That shit would've been embarrassing... So, instead, I just like froze there, sort of smiled back without saying anything, and then got up to follow her up the stairs like her little puppy dog.

After saying goodbye to Candice and her parents, I got in my car and drove around the neighborhood, and instead of going home, I hit the highway and drove out northwest toward Rockford on I-90. I've always loved I-90. It's what we would take to get into the city, but if you went west you could keep going on it, straight up to Wisconsin, past Madison, west into lower Minnesota, through South Dakota, and into Wyoming. In high school that was one of my sanctuaries for some reason, driving up that highway at night, with some good music playing at full volume. That night, I put in the Smashing Pumpkins and drove along the highway, smothered in loud, early-90s rock and roll.

I made that same drive on other memorable occasions, like when my sister ran away, when my father threatened to kill himself again, when Sandy and I broke up, when I received my acceptance to U of I. I would always drive up the highway about half an hour toward the Belvedere oasis, park by the rail on the overpass above the highway, and sit on the hood of the car smoking cigarettes and listening to and watching the cars roll by.

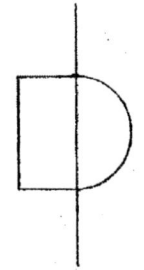

Schizophrenic Relationships

The blissful feeling I had after studying with Candice pretty much went away the next day. I started thinking back on the evening and felt a great deal of agitation. With such a great opportunity dropped on my lap, why the hell didn't I try and do something? Why didn't I grab her and kiss her hard on the lips when she said I was cute and kissed me on the cheek? What was I so afraid of? The logical side of me would insist that it was perfectly fine not to have done anything because it was the "gentlemanly" thing to do. At least, that's how I justified my action that night, and how I've continued to in countless similar situations that I've been in since then. Although it may be true that I have no confidence with women and that I'm just a wimp in general, I really do think that there's too much aggressiveness out there. Maybe my passiveness is not all that bad, and it's a welcome change of pace for women, isn't it?

As I said before, I believe that as we grow up we become more entrenched in our weaknesses and personality traits and, thus, they become more and more magnified. But I guess some of us deal with this better than others. Some people become comfortable with their traits and just go with them, use them to their advantage somehow. Others never fully cope and are always restrained by them or fall victim to them—as in full-out addiction to things such as drugs, sex, porn, gambling, whatever.

I remember being anxious and indecisive even as a little kid. Most of my toddler studio photos are of me cowering or holding a toy with a frown on my face because I was so scared of having pictures taken of me. I remember my mother being upset at me because I could never decide what kind of candy I wanted at the store, how scared I was when I first went to school, and how freaked out I was when I first kissed a girl.

In elementary school it seemed like me and my friends pretty much liked and did the same things. We played the same sports, video games, and rode the same bikes. Later we grew an appreciation for the nudie mags that some of our fathers hid in their garages and watched pornos for the first time and laughed at them, especially the time that our friend's dad suddenly appeared on a videotape wearing some kind of hat and smoking a cigar while his wife blew him. We were all dying of laughter, except of course for the kid whose parents starred in the tape.

My pre-high school days were also probably the hardest of my life. I don't remember much of the television shows or cartoons we watched, except for a stray Tom & Jerry or Flinstone's episode, or any of the childhood books I liked or songs anyone would sing to me. I have an acute memory, though, of the terrible fights I had with my sister, how mean me and my friends were to her, how my father abused us, mentally and physically while he was drunk or high. I hated the terrible yelling, violence, divorce. I hated my mother for leaving my dad, hated my father for being who he was, and hated Doug, the man whom my mother married. Back then I also hated being Mexican because of the name calling that came from the other kids, which pretty much lead to me stop speaking Spanish until I was a young adult—and now I can barely speak it.

My friends and I changed when we got into our adolescent years. Some of us started liking heavy-metal. Some of us started scoring with chicks, and some of us, like me, started reading the Encyclopedia Britannica and memorizing the Roman battles and Emperors.

Once we got to high school, it really all became different for us. Everyone seemed to join their own little clique. We suddenly had jocks, cheerleaders, losers, head-bangers, weirdoes, nerds, freckle-heads, yuppie rich kids, theater kids, housers, spics, polacks, sluts, white trash, and Hindus, to name a few. There was a little of this when we were younger, but it became pronounced in high school, like we were all now fully aware of our differences.

I never knew quite where I fit in and still don't today. I played sports, girls liked me sometimes, but I just wasn't aggressive or funny or had enough money to fully fit into the crowd of dudes that got a lot of action. If you were on a sports team you were supposed to wear your jersey to school the day you had a game, which I never did because I felt somehow insecure about it. It's funny to think back on how tough or cool everyone who played sports thought they were—strutting around Maine West with their jersey on for game-day, even though most of our teams sucked. It all seemed so important, though, to try and impress. Some of my friends, like Carlos, always say that they wish they were back in high school, knowing what they know now. I don't know if that would make a difference though. Being in high school requires that you know nothing; otherwise the whole system would fail. It's tacky and embarrassing on purpose, sort of like a four-year-long hazing to weed out those not tough enough to make it in our twisted society. Looking back, as I think about it, I guess *everything* about growing up was awkward to me.

My high school world revolved around sports and girls, learning to masturbate, trying to be cool, reading books, and listening to music. Half-way through though, I started going to the Gramophone and made friends with the theater kids in my physics class, which changed my perspective. It's funny how I refer to these kids as my "theater friends" because the truth is that only a few of them actually acted in the theater. Carla acted in the school plays, and last I heard she was living in New York, still acting in off-Broadway plays. Paul and Hassan just played instruments in the high school band that played with the theater. They did their own recitals; they were in the school's jazz band called "The Mean Green Jazz Machine." None of these kids were interested in sports, probably because they were not athletic. They were not very good-looking kids, and maybe as a consequence, they were all very talented and interested in things like music, art, books, and later drugs (though I guess we all eventually got into that).

Who's to say what's interesting and whether any one group is into "more interesting" things? Maybe sports, beer drinking, getting laid, having muscles, or knowing how to fix old cars is more interesting than being into obscure music and film. But for me, when I met these theater geek kids, I found it intriguing that they all still played instruments when all the rest of us had given them up long before. I played the violin when I was like 10—it was awful. I remember the recitals, playing the fucking *Star Wars* theme music for all of our parents. Imagine how terrible that must have sounded. But I'm pretty sure all my friends were playing along side me. We just, at some point, grew up and thought it was stupid or gay or whatever, so we gave it up and put our attention to sports, probably because we thought it a better way to attract girls. I remember the line from *Dazed and Confused*, where the one football guy is talking to the other, and he's sort of reminiscing and pissed about the football coach and wondering if they could have scored just as many if not more girls by being in a rock and roll band instead of playing football.

I regret that my friends and I never got into musical instruments or art or anything like that when we were in high school. None of us had any instruments, not even a drum kit or anything. We never knew anyone who did. I never had any older siblings, a parent or other family member who played any instruments, and neither did my friends. All our parents ever did was work at their factories. When I started hanging out with the theater geek kids in high school, I never really thought about trying to learn one of the instruments they played. It just didn't occur to me that it was something I could do. I finally started to learn to play the guitar in college, and now I can play ok, but I think it would've been a lot of fun had me and my friends tried back in high school. Maybe we all wouldn't have such fucking boring jobs today; I don't know.

I remember one day during my sophomore year, before physics class, when I asked Hassan what he was listening to on his Walkman. Instead of telling me, he handed me his ear phones and played it for me. It was a David Bowie song, from his *Low* album, called "Sound and Vision." I never heard anything like that before. The noise I remember hearing was surreal, all sorts of effects, kind of crossing through my head in between the earphones, and then David Bowie's unique vocals flowing over and through all those different sounds. I thought it was a more interesting experience than any I'd had with my other friends up to that point. And I had the best time, possibly ever, at the raves I went to with them during the summer after my junior year—especially when I started getting blow-jobs at Montrose pier.

The strange thing though is that although I made friends with people like Hassan, Paul, Carla—and later my idealist college girlfriend Sarah, and after college, the artist Caleb and writer Raphael—all the people who I found interesting and turned me onto new types of art, music or literature, these friendships have seemed to fade away. Or rather I've let them go, maybe even have been scared to continue on with them in some way or something.

During high school I wanted to hang out with Hassan, Carla, and Paul more than I did. When I did hang out with them it was more in secret without telling my other friends like John, Matt and Jig. If my friends called or wanted to do something, like go to one of the football games, I would feel compelled to go with them—even though I might have thought what they were doing was boring. I never invited any of them to hang out with the theater kids because they always remarked how "fucking weird" they were. It's like I had known my "regular" friends longer and knew what to expect, and I felt somehow comfortable and secure around them. John, Jig, Carlos and Matt are the ones I'm still friends with today—though I only see them a couple of times a year now as they for the most part live out in the burbs with their wives and children.

Actually, for the first time in my life, I've felt it easier to maintain friendships outside of my comfort sphere, but almost like I've been forced to. If they were still single in the city, I'm sure we'd hang out all the time.

In college, my core friends were some of my friends from high school, like Jig and Vassant who also went to U of I. They were business majors from the beginning of college and started hanging out with other business majors, who were mostly fraternity and sorority types. Hassan and Paul also went to U of I, so I sometimes hung out with them and their liberal arts friends who were majoring in things like art, English, history, music, and, of course, horticulture, but I didn't hang out with them much until my sophomore year.

When I was a history major at U of I, and then a philosophy major, my friends, my mother, everyone kept asking "What are you going to do with a history or philosophy degree?" I would say, write, or teach, or maybe become a fucking archeologist like Indiana Jones. I didn't know what I'd do actually—I just knew I liked it. My mother would also say things like "I knew this guy, very smart, very nice, who had a degree in history, but is now making $10 an hour working at our factory. He doesn't make any money, and I know he struggles, like I always have. What are you going to do making such little money? I don't want you and your sister to struggle like I did."

Well, at the end of the day, I had nothing to say to that. I longed to be able to say I didn't care about fucking money, but I couldn't. I just couldn't, and eventually I decided to transfer to the College of Business and major in accounting because it seemed easy. But I told others, told myself, that it would only be a security blanket, that I would continue to take philosophy classes and see how they went, and if I wanted to, I could then transfer back into the Liberal Arts College and get a degree in philosophy. I could then study it on the side after college while I worked in business and made "good money," and hopefully retire early to pursue my true passions.

I never transferred out of the College of Business. I secured a relatively high-paying job while I interned the summer after my junior year and any thought of staying longer to pursue further educational degrees quickly vanished. However, to my credit I guess, I studied philosophy all four years. I earned enough credits technically to minor in it, though the university never officially acknowledged it because the College of Business did not offer a minor in philosophy. But I always said I "concentrated" in it as I headed off into the business world. That's what I told my potential employers during interviews, which made for a few interesting conversations and garnered me a few awkward glances.

While taking my philosophy classes, I made some more friends that got along with the Paul and Hassan crowd. For example I met Sarah in one of my philosophy classes and she turned out to be my first and only meaningful relationship in college. She was cute, blonde, green-eyed, smart as hell, took a few philosophy classes but was really a cultural anthropology major.

We had fun, these other friends and I. We went to great shows at places in Champaign like Mabel's or the Blind Pig, watching bands like Big Head Todd and the Monsters, Hum, Urge Overkill, Veruca Salt, The Suede Chain, Blues Traveler, The Freddy Jones Band, The Flaming Lips. These little venues would be packed, sweaty and loud, but fucking fun as hell. I don't think any one of my business major friends ever even heard of these clubs that were right there by campus. Then there were the parties where we would be smoking pot, drinking, taking LSD or mushrooms while listening to albums like the Orb's *Adventures Beyond the Ultraworld,* My Bloody Valentine's *Loveless,* Frank Black's *Teenager of the Year,* Nirvana's *In Utero,* or the Beatles' *Revolver.* We would end up staring at the ceiling or rolling around in the backyard of the loft building Hassan, Paul, and I lived in during our junior year. Paul and Hassan were in a band with another kid, and I even learned the guitar enough to be able to play with them on occasion. The band was called Curbside Splendor. They played shows primarily in the loft we lived in our junior year, the coolest college loft you'd ever see. They were a three-piece punk band and were pretty good. Our place would be packed, kids standing on the stairs leading up from our living to my lofted bedroom, and more kids up in my bedroom looking over the railing. Paul grew his own weed in the water pipe closet located in the basement, and it was the best I'd ever had. His system was unbelievable. Lights and sprinklers would go on at pre-programmed times, it was like the *Ode to Joy* would play whenever you opened the doors. It lasted almost all year, until the landlord found the plants when he was fixing a washroom we were having problems with. The local plumber exclaimed "It's the Ganja!" as they opened the door. The landlord just made us throw the plants out.

Besides the music and drugs, I also got into things like vegetarianism and organic products. At the time it seemed to make sense, and it still does at times, to eat less meat and avoid mass- and artificially produced food in order to minimize global consumption, minimize damage to the environment, and not pollute the body with unnatural chemicals. I read books like *The Aquarian Conspiracy* by Marilyn Ferguson and was wide-eyed and idealistic. I even worked at the Common Ground Food Co-Op and the vegetarian restaurant called The Red Hearing and went to Rainbow Gatherings at Shwanee National Forest in downstate Illinois. All this stuff was pretty cool and refreshing, and some of the principles are still with me today. But suddenly, as if just turning off a switch, I abandoned most of this lifestyle (except for the music and drugs) during the summer of junior year when I interned and had my first job in the corporate world.

These friendships faded away pretty much by the end of my four years at U of I. My senior year I moved out of the apartment with Paul and Hassan, for no good reason, and moved in with one of my business major friends: Sal, this smart, fast-taking dago from New York obsessed with becoming a millionaire. I started ignoring Paul and Hassan and them. I would get invited to go to a U of I football or basketball game, to a fraternity party, a corporate recruiting event, an expensive dinner—and often if there was a conflict with an invitation to do something with Paul and Hassan and their friends, I would choose to hang out with the business friends. It was like high school all over again.

Don't get me wrong, hanging out with my business friends was fun, in its own way. We mainly got drunk and eventually started smoking some pot, which was shitty compared to the stuff Paul grew. We took turns hooking up with the same accounting major girls that all wanted to hook up with Sal; I would get what was left over. And we would go out and pick up other girls, cute sorority girls that really had nothing much to talk about and were generally easy to get into bed with, especially when offered weed. The music we listened to, though, was your typical shit, fun but with no substance. It felt safe. And that, really, is what it boiled down to for me again, the security. Like choosing to major in business, it seems like choosing friends was another example of me being scared to let go and really explore a different sort of lifestyle. Plus, in a way, it was almost necessary that I hung out with the same kind of people I would eventually work with. Working in the corporate world requires that you fit in socially, very much so.

I like to think I've tended to choose a "safer" group of friends and lifestyle because of my parents' background as poor immigrants. They came to America and lived meekly, working two jobs a day, getting beat-up, ridiculed by neighbors for barely knowing English, all so they could afford to give us a better opportunity than they had. I've always felt this as a burden, as a guiding factor. How could I ever just choose to say fuck it and take risks, maybe live like a bohemian when the chance of making money was there in front of me? I felt like I owed it to them to make more "rational" decisions. I still do; it's a constant pull.

Sarah and I continued to date through graduation, even though I alienated her throughout my senior year. She hated doing the things my business major friends liked, but she continued to date me and would even suck it up sometimes and go with me to certain events. At the end of school though, as we were discussing our futures after college, instead of going right into her master's program, Sarah decided to join the Peace Corp. and go to Africa for two years. I chose not to go with Sarah to Africa although she practically begged me, saying it would be great for us to go while we weren't pinned down—an opportunity we may never have again. She was right; she went, and I know it was the most rewarding experience of her life. But I just couldn't go, not when I had an offer to go work as an accountant in Chicago making a good salary. So I stayed and let go of our relationship.

Now I have my corporate friends whom I hang out with and do "normal" things with. Instead of going to music and art shows, I seem to choose to do things like go to a Cubs, Bears, or Bulls game. I don't know, maybe I am just a corporate, yuppie scumbag and don't want to admit it. Maybe it would be easier if I finally admitted and accepted it. I think about doing that sometimes but I always feel like something is missing, like there's a train going by and I know it's going somewhere cool, and it slows down for me to jump on it, but I don't and it just keeps going.

On occasion I've tried to mix my different types of friends although it never seems to work. It just seems awkward to me for some reason. I feel like these two groups are so different, so ingrained in their ways of life, that they can't possibly mesh. Maybe if I didn't feel so weird about it, it could work.

All the girls I've dated since Sarah, I've met from what I would consider the mainstream or business world—mainly ones I met through work, pretty much all Big Ten or Notre Dame alumni. These relationships usually began with some sort of drunken attraction, sex that came quickly after (usually lots of it right at the beginning), then a sudden ending. Many of them ended because I just lost interest and wouldn't want to spend much time with them other than to have sex. Sometimes the girls would freak out when they heard me talk about art, different sorts of music, philosophy, or that I didn't want to make a life-long career out of my profession, was just doing it to support my interests further down the road. Eventually they would conclude I was a weirdo or that I thought I was too smart for anyone else or something. Many of them, like Heather for example, accused me of being a snob, because I was so sure of what kind of music, movies, food, and art I liked. I thought it was fucked up to think that it was some kind of flaw to have a preference in things like that. Other girls caught on that I was just interested in having the sex and not being lonely. I never did the breaking up though; they always did, which was fine by me, most of the time.

Others still, like Erica and another girl I dated, this short little brunette, seemed to think what I was into was cute or interesting, but they thought I would grow out of it. They said things like, "You think you're like this artist guy, but you're really just as normal as everyone else... It's great that you paint, but come on, you're taking it way too seriously. Get over yourself."

I didn't draw, paint or read anything good at all during the two-plus years I dated Erica. That was probably the low point in my life. I think I was ready to really give it all up and settle for the house in the suburbs, having kids, getting bald and fat, and probably end up getting divorced. When we started dating, I tried to make time to pursue my interests. On the weekends she would invite me out with her friends, and I would say that I was staying home to draw or read. She would get upset and think I didn't want to spend time with her. She sometimes would say I should spend more time doing my things if I wanted to, but I always felt pressure to spend time with her. I don't know if it was real pressure or self-imposed in some way, but I felt it. It seemed like she never wanted to do anything on her own.

I would love to be in a relationship where the other person and I wanted to spend time together, a lot of time, but where we would always feel free to pursue our own interests. I didn't feel that; I hardly ever have in a relationship.

So it has always been like this, me not wanting to veer too far from center, but keeping tabs on those who do. This schizophrenic outlook confuses those I interact with. I've had many friends say that they would set me up with one of their girlfriends, but they never know quite what I'm looking for. Most artistic girls are not interested in me because I'm an accountant and I drive an SUV. Most mainstream girls get weirded out when I bust out the philosophy or art shit. Some of my artist friends here in Wicker Park call me the "Drawing Accountant" and think my drawings are "hilarious." My current co-workers are amazed when they come over and wonder why I'm an accountant.

As I've gotten older, it has gotten a little easier to have friends inside and outside of the mainstream. I've been drawing and painting a lot more recently, and think I'm getting okay at it again. I've even picked up a philosophy book or two. Although I still haven't read that much of them, but it feels good to at least have them back out on my coffee table. With age, I have gained a little self-confidence I guess. Maybe it's the money I've made—maybe my mom was right after all. But I debate with myself, over and over, whether I've made the right decisions. Was this money and security, in the end, worth it? Had I pursued my interests more when I was younger, as in high school and college, would I have had a more fruitful life?

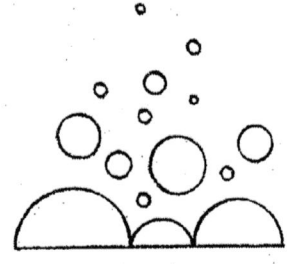

The Widow-Maker

Despite all the whining about being anxious and not pursuing my "true" passions, I have to admit that my life has been pretty damn good, from a materialistic point of view at least. I've made good money, grown "intellectually," traveled to different parts of the world, learned how to drink wine (although I never remember what kind I like), and stuff like that. I've read some pretty good books, been a fairly successful professional, and have had some success with women. When compared to other situations I could have found myself in, I know I really have no reason to complain, none at all.

But I have to say, all these moments that having good money has afforded me don't compare to moments I had during or right after high school—so much so that I sometimes really miss those days. My experiences as an adult seem to lack a certain vividness. Memories from high school are just more "real" in a sense. We were all coming out of our shells, our protective little homes for the first time.

The feeling I get when I'm high now is as close to how I felt when I was a teenager, when everything was dramatic, exciting, overwhelming, and embarrassing. When you're high, every detail is amplified, seems so vivid as if it were happening for the first time. You're able to focus on details you hardly notice while sober. While listening to music, the instruments jump out at you—you can focus on the guitars if you want, or the drums, the bass, the vocals, the keyboard or other crazy background noise, especially if you're listening to a band like Radiohead. While watching movies, it's like you're watching a movie for the very first time. You wonder how the director selected the first scenes, the music that is playing when the intro notes come across, how the intro notes are presented, what camera angles are chosen and why certain ones are held longer than others. Don't get me wrong, I sometimes think about these things when I'm sober, and I'm sure lots of other people do too, but these thoughts come out more naturally when I'm high for some reason. And sex is fantastic while high. Anyone who has ever said that aphrodisiacs are not real has never smoked pot and then had sex. Instead of Viagra men should be smoking pot.

I started smoking weed when I was a teenager. It was just what everyone else was doing back then in Des Plaines, or at least my friends were. We were warned against it in our health classes, especially of mixing weed with alcohol, but that didn't prevent us from trying and perfecting it. I still smoke it today but not frequently. Although the feeling is pretty much the same, today when I get high it seems to be all personal, individual to me, versus back then when it was more communal. Everyone around me back then was likely high also; we were all able to share that feeling together. As adults, most people are paranoid or more restrained, and it's hard to find people who want to smoke it just enough to enjoy it. People I know that still smoke tend to abuse it, like get high all the time.

With all the money, the nice clothes, nice cars, expensive homes that me and my friends have, I still haven't been to a better party than the one fucking Jaime (of all people) threw on New Year's Eve back in 1994. I don't even know if it was the best of the parties from those years (it probably was not as good as my cartoon pornos bash for example), but it was one of the last great ones I remember.

I was a sophomore in college and back home in Des Plaines for Christmas break. A lot of my high school friends still lived in Des Plaines. A few of them went away to school like I did, but others went to Oakton Community College, the local option.

During our high school senior year and the summer that followed, the line between the "cool" and "not so cool" groups began to fade. Everyone started going to the same parties. The woods parties helped that bonding process because it wasn't like you could kick someone out of the woods or anything. Woods parties were just sprawling parties anyone could attend.

Everything started to depend on who could get alcohol and weed, which a lot of my friends could. Once kids starting getting high, it didn't matter if you were "cool" or not, just whether you had the weed. Jaime, along with his jock friends, started smoking weed our senior year after football was over, and the next thing you know they were hanging out with a lot of my friends. All of a sudden everyone was at the same parties. Especially after we graduated—it was as if everyone who stuck around Des Plaines after high school suddenly had been the best of friends forever.

During these years we cultivated our pot-smoking skills. We moved on from your standard joints to more elaborate pipes we bought up north across the Wisconsin border in towns like Racine or Kenosha, where pipe and porn shops could be found at every exit from the highway. From those, we moved on to large bongs purchased at these same shops or handed down from older brothers or sisters. Then we got to the point where we constructed our own devices. These devices were not bongs exactly; they were more like contraptions, monstrosities built out of large pipes, buckets, and hoses. They held a lot of water and had big sliding pipes that would burn almost a quarter ounce of weed at a time. One was called the Black Hole because after you took a hit, if you were strong and experienced enough to hold in the smoke, once you exhaled all you would see was black for the first few seconds—you had gone into the black hole and would emerge to a hazy world of blurry lines and buzzing in your ears.

My favorite, though, was the Widow-Maker. It was built out of a large water jug that had a plastic skull on top of it along with two arms that stuck out of the sides made of some twisty plastic tubes that had rubber like hands at the ends. The arms danced around as you sucked on the pipe due to the air that rushed around inside the clear jug. Inside the jug, plastic golf balls floated on the water for effect. The plastic skull—some sort of Halloween decoration gone wrong—was fitted to not allow air to escape and thus ruin your hit, but loosely enough so it would dance along with the arms. The pipe from which the slider was attached protruded from the basin of the jug, going up diagonally so it looked like you were sucking on the Widow-Maker's cock when you were taking a hit. We referred to taking hits from the thing as "blowing" the Widow-Maker.

The Widow-Maker became infamous. It was the main attraction at parties; the hits people would get from it were legendary.

One time, Suzanne, this girl that hung out with us the summer after graduation and liked to smoke weed, came late to a session we were having in Carlos' basement. Suzanne was pretty cool and was usually the only girl in our little group that summer. No one really fooled around with her; she just hung out and got stoned with us. She came running downstairs that day, pissed because she was stuck at work, was bitching about it, and wanted some fucking weed right away.

"Give me some pot you stoned fuckers," she said as soon she came downstairs.

We had taken a few hits from the Widow-Maker already, so we were pretty ripped at that point. The Widow-Maker hadn't received any play outside of our group yet, and Suzanne hadn't seen it. It was like a secret project for a while, the Manhattan Project for bongs. Only a few of us were able to test the early incarnations of it.

"Holy shit," she said when she saw it, "What the fuck is that?"

"It's the Widow-Maker," Patrick responded all stoned.

"What the fuck? I want a hit off of that!" she yelled and sat down in front of it. We tried to persuade her not to, as it had just kicked all of our asses—we needed to work out some wrinkles—but she insisted, so Carlos packed the pipe up with more weed. All of us looked on, laughing, blurry-eyed, heads swirling. *Physical Graffiti* by Led Zeppelin was playing in the background, and the Widow-Maker's skull face seemingly smirked back at us as it got ready to unleash its fury once again. So, with the pipe packed, Suzanne, who held her own with the rest of us when it came to bong hits, put her lips on the pipe.

Someone lit the weed, and she started sucking. As she sucked, the Widow-Maker's chamber began to fill with smoke. The water bubbled; the little plastic golf balls floating on the water danced up and down; the Widow-Maker's arms waved wildly, and its ghastly and sinister head shook back and forth. Suzanne was taking a large hit, a really fucking large hit, trying to outdo us, and we stared in disbelief at how thick the smoke inside the jug became as she kept on sucking. Carlos, who was there with his fingers on the slider ready to pull, stared at the thickening smoke, stared at us, stared at Suzanne with his eyes ready to bulge out of their sockets. Then he finally pulled the slider out.

For those of you who don't know, who have never had the luxury of taking a bong hit, it works like this: The weed is lit, and someone starts to suck on the pipe. There is a little slider that, while in its place, keeps the smoke that accumulates inside the bong's chamber. Once it's pulled out, the pressure is released and the smoke rises out into the sucking mouth. This is pretty intense with a normal bong, but with the amount of smoke that accumulated in the Widow-Maker, it was just fucking insane. When Carlos pulled, as we all stared, the smoke was unleashed through the Widow-Maker's pipe, and its arms and head seemed to dance as if it was exploding out a mammoth orgasm.

I remember seeing Suzanne's face, with her cheeks puffed out like a blow fish, turn instantly red, devil-red. Her hair seemed to frizz up, and her eyes expanded two fold and became watery. She looked like a cartoon. All of a sudden she erupted in this hideous, screeching, belching cough, with smoke seemingly puffing out of her eyes and ears. Then she fell off the couch, letting go of the Widow-Maker who continued his hellish dance. We all erupted in laughter, the hard, crying sort of laughter, some of us hitting the floor grasping our guts. This had happened to us all before she came, but it was funny as hell watching it happen to her, especially as she was so eager to take a hit. It was one of the many red-faced and watery-eyed coughs the Widow-Maker would unleash on its victims during its lifetime. We decided that the Widow-Maker didn't need any further modification; it was ready for the world.

(I'm not trying to preach the virtues of marijuana here, but you have to appreciate its qualities. Should it be legal? Sometimes I don't really care. Regardless if it's legal or not, whoever wants to get high pretty much can. I guess it doesn't make any sense that it's illegal. I mean, why are alcohol and nicotine legal? Why are man-made drugs like Ambien legal? I've heard and read stories of people sleep-walking while on that kind of shit to the point where they kill themselves by accident. These drugs are not just legal; they're promoted in society through constant advertisement. They're accepted and encouraged even though their effects on the body are equally bad if not worse than marijuana's. Have you ever been to the bars outside of Wrigley Field after a Cubs game and seen all the belligerent drunks there? Or all the drunks stumbling around on Saint Patrick's Day? And also, look at the millions that are invested in our sporting events that are basically huge advertisements for sex, alcohol, and fat, greasy food like hot dogs, hamburgers, and fries. So many adults die from a bad diet, stress, pharmaceutical drugs, and alcohol, yet it seems like all we do is promote the intake of this stuff. I don't know. None of this seems to make sense. But anyway...)

At the height of their popularity, the Widow-Maker and its companion bongs held their own at the corners of parties like Jaime's that New Year's Eve. They stood firm in the corner of the basement, with the Widow-Maker standing higher in the middle, the leader of the pack, and with the rest of the party goers keeping at least a few feet from them in a show of respect.

That's the first thing I saw when looking over Jaime's party that night from the staircase heading down into his basement. I was down there early with my friends when there weren't that many people at the party yet. We were doing hits off the Widow-Maker with a bunch of other guys, and later I went upstairs and passed out for a bit. The party was packed when I made my way back downstairs. A wall along the stairs prevented you from seeing the expanse of the room as you went down, but you could hear what was going on—the music, the chatter, girl laughter, a "Fuck yeah!" here, and a "Dude!" there, and so on.

It was dark and smoky, and there were people going up and down the stairs to the basement, but you couldn't really see their faces. As I turned the corner of the staircase, I could see the expanse of the party across the basement, and it seemed like everyone from our high school class was there—except for my theater geek friends who were never at these sorts of parties. I stopped and stared at the Widow-Maker and his friends;

they were right there in their corner opposite the winding staircase. No one was smoking from them anymore; they had done their job as they always did and now reveled in their mastery. I smiled to myself, laughing at the fact that we had created such things and given them such names, and wondered if kids in other Chicago neighborhoods—or in other cities or in other countries or on other fucking planets—made and smoked from such things, or if it was only us, a bunch of fuck-ups who were smart or lucky enough that we weren't in jail yet, but on the edge of total recklessness.

I spotted Candice, whom I hadn't seen since graduation, standing with some of her friends in the back of the room. We had talked after the big study night we had, but I never made any effort to see her, and she never really invited me over to study again. We graduated, and it seemed like whatever relationship we might have had faded away. At graduation she came up to me and gave me a huge hug. I still remember her hugging me in her robe, with her cap perfectly placed on her head, her blond hair in my face as she hugged me. Her father took a picture of us then shook my hand and wished me luck. Candice said we would stay in touch. She told me to write her at school; she was going to the University of Missouri to major in journalism. I never wrote her. I just didn't see the point. She was still with Jaime, and I thought she always would be with him, or someone else like him.

I snapped out of my thoughts of Candice when I heard someone say, "Alex, you pussy!" I wasn't sure who had said it, but I looked out ahead and saw many of my friends' faces there, looking up at me, pointing their fingers and laughing. I must have been standing there for a little bit.

I began to make my way through the sea of people at the party. All my friends were there, all huddled in their own group. They had become somewhat of a popular group now, especially because they brought the Widow-Maker and his friends to parties and because they were friends with some older guys, like the Wiley brothers. There were some younger kids there, still in high school, like the jocks and cool kids that were popular. They were learning and observing how to party so they could take the baton.

Walking through a packed party or club is quite an event. I've seen many movies try to capture the sentiment, and I guess the best that I've seen is the woods party scene in the movie *Dazed and Confused*. It's hard to recreate, especially from the perspective of a stoned and drunk 19-year-old like me that night.

You sort of stumble along, see faces all around you, see mouths moving, hear the voices going back and forth, see bodies moving to the music, see someone look at you and recognize you and kind of rock their head at you to the music, maybe hold up a beer or cigarette in a sort of toast, an acknowledgement that you're both there sharing in the same kick-ass moment. It's dark, hazy, and sometimes, if you're Mexican like me, you'll hear a "hey you dirty Mexican!" directed at you, like I heard Matt yell at me that night as he was grabbing me by the shoulder.

"Dude, what the fuck is going on man?" he said as I turned toward him. I hadn't seen him since the summer before going off to school. He had already been kicked out of Southern Illinois by then and was working with his dad's carnival. His spiky hair with shaved sides was now flatter, longer. He was wearing corduroy pants with a flannel shirt.

"What's up Matt?" I said as we hugged.

"Not much you spic, just back in town, been working like hell at the carnival. What about these fuckers?" he said laughing and pointing around at Carlos and the others. "They're fucking whacked! The Widow-Maker? That shit's crazy man."

"Yeah I know, right?" I agreed.

"That shit's crazy," he continued on laughing. "Fucking Pat made me take a hit off that shit right when I got here; fucking almost knocked my ass out."

"No shit," interjected Kris, a friend of Matt's who was standing next to him. Kris was this big Indian guy who had a good sense of humor, so he always seemed to be popular, and he had good access to weed through his older brothers. Tony, who I hadn't seen since high school, was standing with them. I actually hadn't talked to him much since he jumped through John's dad's car's window that Halloween night—which he never helped pay for. I'm not sure what he ever did after high school. He sort of nodded his head at me acknowledging I was there, but not really.

"That's some crazy shit, man," Kris added.

"Dude, everyone here is fucking stoned man. Are you, Al?" asked Matt.

"Yeah," I said, "I took a few hits from that also earlier. It's intense."

"Fucking pot-head," said Matt laughing and shaking me again by the shoulder. "Kris you fucking Hindu, light that stick you have," and then Kris took out this huge, big joint that looked like a monster white cigar.

"Alright, chill you Jew-bag," said Kris and held the thing up in the air and began moving a lighter underneath it to warm it up, a trick used by steady pot-smokers when lighting a joint in order to prevent it from "running," or burning down one of the sides and thus fucking it up.

As soon as he lit it up, it was like all eyes in the immediate vicinity turned and locked on the monster joint, kind of like flood lights zeroing in on an escaping inmate. It took him a few puffs to get the thing going. It was finally lit and he gave it to Matt, who took a few huge puffs and then handed it to me, and I took my turn. I took a big hit that made me cough and get teary eyed, which made Matt, Kris, and Tony laugh. By that time, my friends were around us, talking to Kris and praising him on his excellent rolling job, and he in turn asked about the Widow-Maker, how it was keeping up, and shit like that—good back and forth banter between fellow pot smokers.

"Man, what are these fucking wiggers listening to?" asked Matt. Some rap music was playing. Evidently the Wiley brothers had gotten hold of the stereo, as they always seemed to, and started playing rap music. Playing rap versus playing alternative music always seemed to be the debate at these parties; we would go back and forth between playing the popular rap of the time—stuff like Cypress Hill, Public Enemy, NWA— and alternative music, bands like The Smashing Pumpkins, Belly, Blues Traveler, Spin Doctors, Soul Asylum.

"I don't know, it's just some rap shit," I said.

"Dumbasses, they don't even like black people."

"Yeah, I know, it's all pretty weird, huh?"

"Hey, fuckheads," jumped in Tony who had gone to get beers.

"What's going on?"

"Oh, nothing, just getting stoned, wondering who I'm going to fuck tonight," answered Matt, when I noticed he was making a face and scratching his balls.

"Matt, what's up? Are you all right?" I asked.

"Dude," answered Tony, laughing and patting Matt on the back hard, "he's got fucking crabs from that trailer carnival bitch he's been fucking."

"What?" I said.

"Yeah dude, he's got fucking crabs from what's her name, Lisa?"

"Fuck off dick-head," yelled Matt, still scratching his balls, looking around, "It's not crabs, it just fucking itches some-times." Matt had been living with this 27-year-old girl named Lisa. They were sharing a trailer together, she had two kids, and according to Matt, she gave great head.

"Yeah, but she's got like four kids, you dumbass."

"Two, fucker," said Matt.

"Whatever, they're probably from different fathers. You're shit is going to fall off if you keep that up, daddy.'" "Fuck you... but yeah, you're probably right," answered Matt as he kept scratching and looking around. "Fuck, I probably do have crabs, goddammit... fucking bitch."

"What about these bitches here?" asked Tony, sort at both of us, "Who's going to put out tonight?" he continued looking around.

"Let's go talk to Cindy and them," answered Matt, no lon-ger scratching his balls, now pulling out cigarettes, giving me one, lighting them both, and then pulling me in close and looking toward the group of girls he was talking about, who were a few years ahead of us.

"Alex, I heard that slut Amanda wants to fuck you, she's

kind of big but has monster tits. I'm sure she would rock your shit. I guess she wants some of that spic action," he said. I turned to see who he was looking at and I saw this girl who was kind of on the bigger side, had long brown hair, was in fact extremely well-endowed, and was smiling at us as Matt smiled and waved back.

"Come on, you fuckers," said Tony who then started walking over there.

"Um, I think I'm going to hang out here for a while," I said to Matt, suddenly not feeling like I wanted to hang out with those girls, feeling that I was too stoned to talk anyway.

"Insane in the Membrane!" suddenly jumped in Patrick, who was dancing and rapping along to the Cypress Hill song that was now playing. "Gone insane! Got no brain!!" he continued.

"What's up you fucking mick?" yelled out Matt.

"Not much Jew-boy," answered Patrick, who was still dancing along to the song. He was a tall, lanky, goofy-looking Irish kid with big dark curly hair who always seemed to be having the time of his life. He would usually end up getting super drunk at parties and make a spectacle of himself—end up with his pants-down, pissing in the corner of some basement, or passed out right in the middle of a party, stuff like that. He was the creative brain behind the Widow-Maker; it was like his little son. Patrick dated a girl named Kelly who was in our grade, who's last name was O'Malley like Patrick's (but no, they supposedly weren't related), and they dated for like all of high school and are now married with children.

"Alex, I'm going over there. Come along when you get some balls, we'll end up getting our dicks sucked tonight," yelled out Matt, leaving us to go join Tony who was already talking to the girls.

"Dude, what's going on man? I haven't seen your ass in a while," Patrick said to me as he was still doing his little dance but now to a different song.

"Not much man, just fucking hanging out, back from school, you know?"

"How's it going dude? How are them college bitches, huh?" he said, winking at and elbowing me. "Yeah, they're all right, pretty fucking great actually," I answered, but not honestly. My first year and a half at U of I was not that exciting, from a girl perspective anyway. I spent the majority of my social time going to fraternity parties and rush events although I swore I would never do that. I went, mainly got drunk out of my mind, and stumbled around staring at all the pretty girls and guys from north suburban Chicago. I had no chance in this crowd. I had nothing to talk with them about, never received any offer to pledge at any of their fraternities, but I did get thrown out of a few parties for doing things like pissing in a hallway or throwing up in the middle of a dance floor. I guess in hindsight it was fun, but when asked by my high school friends like Pat how college was, I would say that I hooked up with a lot of slutty sorority girls, received a bunch of pledge offers, and refused them because ultimately I was beyond the whole frat thing. It wasn't until my sophomore year that I started hanging out with the Paul-and-Hassan crowd again and not until after the winter break of 1994 that I would meet Sarah and things got better for me at U of I, for a little bit.

It seemed like everyone in Jaime's basement was dancing, or swaying. The rap was still going on, but now some Arrested Development was playing, which, at the time, was on the border of rap and alternative. Everyone was having a good time. Jig was also there doing his dance that he would do, which always garnered lots of cheers. Like Patrick, he would do the same sort of dance for every song. It was like a mix of what people called the "Air Jordan" and some sort of break dancing moves, but it was faster and crazier the drunker he was. He had no rhythm, but he tried really hard and sort of mastered his little dance.

Jig also was known for getting really emotional when he was drunk. He was famous for hugging and telling everyone "I love you man!" and then crying or passing out. He was a short Indian dude, but in college he suddenly got huge somehow, bulked up, and then started looking like a meathead. We all thought he was on steroids, though he claims he just had a late growth spurt. My favorite memory of Jig was when we went to Mardi Gras and he did his dance in the middle of Bourbon Street and got into a huge dance battle with a bunch of black kids from the University of Georgia. They took turns battling him in the street, and he held his own, busting out these crazy moves that complemented his standard routine. It was all good fun, and they were impressed with his dancing ability. He eventually ended up pulling down his pants for beads from this older woman, and we lost track of him and didn't see him until 7 a.m., stumbling down the street in dirty clothes. I don't think I've ever smelled anything as nasty as the way Bourbon Street smelled that morning after Mardi Gras. It was like the smell of bad breath, a sewer, and chicken shit all combined.

At the party, Patrick, John, Carlos, Vinny and I were all egging Jig on. Suzanne was there, all fucked up. Patrick's girlfriend Kelly was also there with her skinny cousin, Amy, who was a few years younger than us. Amy was a gymnast who would also go to U of I, and would eventually marry John, but that party was the first time they met. John and Amy ended up going to back to Patrick's house that night and apparently they all woke up in the same bed the next morning, fully clothed except for Patrick, who was buck naked for some unexplained reason.

Jaime came up to us and started talking. Jaime's blond hair which used to be short and spiky, was now long and down over his neck, with bangs sort of. He was wearing an untucked shirt and jeans, a flannel over the shirt, sporting a version of the grunge look but not all the way. At this point, the 80s look was pretty much gone. He was still huge and ripped as hell.

"Alex, you geek, what's going on?" he asked me, which made me snap out of it. I had been zoning out in the crowd of people and the smoke cloud that was hovering over the party.

"What's up Jaime?" I said.

"Dude, I finally got the stereo back from those fuckers," he said, making a reference over his shoulder at the Wiley brothers. The tall one was clearly visible over the crowd, with his goatee and tail hanging down over his neck. He was wearing a sleeveless shirt, even though it was like zero degrees outside. The littler one was standing besides him, looking mean also, like a smaller version of the bigger one. They were smoking blunts, hanging out with other kids who seemed kind of like their disciples.

"Yeah, they seem to monopolize that shit." I answered.

"Dude, do you like this shit? I fucking dig this band," he

said, referring to the Sugar album *Copper Blue* that was now playing, which I actually did like. The third song "Helpless" was blaring through the speakers. Jaime seemed to have a newfound interest in music; a lot of kids did at that time. For some reason, music felt more relevant to everybody then, like ground-breaking stuff was being created. Many people, like my theater geek friends, argued that the music of the early 90s was just ripping off the true pioneering of post-rock bands from the 80s—bands like the Pixies, Naked Raygun, Ministry, Sonic Youth, Mudhoney—and these new guys like Nirvana, Pearl Jam, later Bush, were just reaping the commercial success. But still, there was something to it, or maybe it just seemed like it because we were living through it. The first Iraq war had happened; the Soviet Union had collapsed; Kurt Cobain would soon kill himself. There was something in the air, you know? It was probably just a bunch of smoke, but kids like Jaime suddenly were into music and being "alternative."

"Yeah, this is pretty cool shit. Have you ever listened to Husker Du?" I asked him. That was Bob Mould's first band, the guy who started Sugar. Jaime hadn't, so I recommended that he should, especially their classic album *Zen Arcade*. The thing I found funny about former jocks like Jaime liking bands like Sugar was that they had no idea how gay Bob Mould was. Not that it should matter, but it was sort of funny—kind of like how all the metal heads loved Judas Priest, whose singer (Rob Hatfield) is gayer than hell.

Jaime urged me to go with him to the stereo so he could show me the CDs he had assembled. It was all pretty cool stuff, stuff that was playing through the alternative radio stations. We put in the Nirvana CD, *Nevermind*, and played the first track, "Smells Like Teen Spirit," the so-called anthem of those times. Soon Jaime left me to attend to the music. I was glad I only had to talk to him a little bit. I never liked talking to him all that much, even now that he was a little cooler than he used to be. Off he went and started talking to some other guys who I recognized but didn't know very well, older former Maine West high school football player types. I'd noticed that Jaime seemed rather drunk already, he was sort of slurring his words and his eyes seemed extra small. My friends had told me that he took a bunch of hits off the Widow-Maker so he was probably super stoned at that point. Most people could only take one, maybe two hits from that beast. As I was looking through the CDs to decide what I was going to play, I realized it was approaching midnight, so I needed to pick out some good stuff to bring in the New Year.

I've always thought the song selection around a New Year's Eve was very, very important. I mean, you were saying goodbye to a whole year and ushering in a new one. Everyone at the party would be making New Year's Eve resolutions although they might not admit them. I always do. It was a chance to start over in a way, and it was an excuse to party hard. The music leading up to the midnight moment wasn't all that important, the song at midnight always had to be that fucking song that I never remember, Auld Lang Syne. Luckily, I saw that Jaime had a holiday CD there with the song on it, so I grabbed it to make sure I played it. The songs that really mattered, though, were the ones that followed and continued on for that first hour after midnight. They had to be carefully chosen, needed to start a new year off with a bang, and then keep the party going. This was the hour when everyone would party the hardest. People would get lucky and start to hook-up—after that it would be a free-fall and those who were getting wasted would begin falling off one by one.

So I decided that I would start this new-year off with an especially good one, one of my all time favorite first songs of the year, The Beatles' "Revolution." That song kicks ass, right? I mean, the rocking guitars, their screaming in the beginning followed by their harmony and all the references to non-violent forms of revolution—all that makes for a kick-ass rock song. I've heard people say that it was the first real punk rock song, and regardless if that's true, I can see why someone would say that. I've had a fantasy of me being able to play that song, like busting out a guitar at a bar, at a karaoke party, or at a work party, tearing off those first few chords and then doing the scream thing, having everyone get excited and be surprised by my hidden talents. I've always figured that everyone else had similar thoughts of themselves, but I'm not sure.

I continued planning what the next songs would be. I was thinking of playing songs like "Shook me All Night Long" by AC/DC, "Paradise City" by Guns N' Roses, "Legs" by ZZ Top, "Pump Up The Jam" by Technotronic, "Free Falling" by Tom Petty, "Looks that Kill" by Motley Crue, "Panama" by Van Halen, "Black Dog" by Led Zeppelin, "Cecilia" by Simon & Garfunkel, "Rock n Roll All Night" by Kiss, "Born to Run" by Bruce Springsteen, "Jack and Diane" by John Mellencamp, and "Alive" by Pearl Jam. I wanted to play an older song first, save the newer ones for later on in the hour, so I was really struggling between the AC/DC, Led Zeppelin, and Guns N' Roses songs, but was beginning to lean toward AC/DC.

Then, as I was gathering these CDs and preparing them

for their play, I felt these hands clasp over my eyes. I turned around, and there she was: Candice. Why the fuck she and Jaime always had to make these surprise entrances, I don't know, but that's how it always happened.

She had a huge smile, and her hair was a little straighter than it used to be. It seemed longer, her bangs were less pronounced, they seemed to fall over her eyes, but I could still see them, and her lips had this nice red lipstick on them.

"Alex!" she said as we hugged. "How are you?"

At first I didn't respond. I was still very stoned and surprised because I had forgotten all about her. I might have mumbled a "good" or something. When I was hugging her I was looking out to see where Jaime was. I could see him off in the distance still with his group of guys, who had been joined by some other friends. I could also see my friends, who were still huddled up, bobbing their heads and talking. Suzanne was all fucked up and in the middle of them. She was the only girl with them besides Kelly and her skinny cousin Amy, whom John now seemed to be getting closer to, planning his moves. I saw the fucking Widow-Maker off in the distance—his head also seemed to bob along to the music.

Candice was with her friend, Diane, who also was very beautiful, but I didn't know her at all. At some point I started talking, answering the questions she was asking me, but I don't quite remember the words very well. I do remember how nervous and anxious I started feeling. The whole day of the party I wondered if I would see her and stressed out about whether I should try to talk to her or not, whether she would even care and be interested in talking to me. I was telling her that school was good. She was saying that Missouri was great, she had met so many new friends, was really excited about her classes and teachers, and that she was definitely going to major in journalism, it was better than her wildest imagination.

(I can't remember how girls in general dressed in those days. Guys, yes guys, had the flannel, corduroy pants, and Birkenstock thing, but what about girls? I remember that in the last half of the 1990s, girls always wore all black, these tight black pants and shit like that, and for a little while, the hippie sort of look came back. But in the early 1990s? What the hell did girls wear? Flannels and Jeans? I seem to remember Candice was wearing a black skirt, with tall black boots on, and with a blue jean jacket and some kind of top on underneath.)

"Alex, are you ok?" Candice asked, putting a hand on my shoulder, kind of giggling.

"Ah, yeah, I'm fine," I said. "You know, I'm just sort of drunk and all." She laughed, Diane was also laughing, and then I started laughing also, we were all just laughing. I realized then that Candice was in fact drunk. Candice was never at the parties we used to have, or the ones I went to at least. The few times that I had seen her at parties she was always very composed, nice, not drunk and staggering around like a lot of the other girls at those things. So this was the first time I saw her drunk. She was herself, but just extra so, I guess. Her eyes glistened a little more, her head seem to be tilted to a side more when she smiled, her hair blonder for some reason. I don't know, maybe it was just how fucked up I was. Come to think of it, when you're drunk, it's hard to tell when others around you are also drunk—its hard to tell if they're acting weird because they're also drunk, or because you're drunk.

Jaime came staggering in behind the stereo saying, "Hey,

Candice, I need some help with the champagne!" Then, seeing me, he said, "Alex, it's almost midnight, get that New Year's song going buddy!"

"Yeah, I got it, like right here," I said, showing him the CD case. "It's in the player, all set to play."

"Good boy, good job, Alex. Candice, let's go, leave smarty pants to do his thing." He then slapped me on the back and took off. Jaime was now very drunk, was talking louder than usual, being more of his typical asshole self.

"Ok, I'll be right there," Candice said, sort of pushing Jaime off as he went back out into the crowd. "Sorry Alex," she then said to me. "He can be kind of an ass at times, especially when he's drinking and smoking pot."

"Yeah," said Diane in agreement, shaking her head. "He's been a real ass lately, along with all those guys."

"Alex, it's almost midnight. Come on, let's go get some champagne and bring in the New Year," Candice said as she grabbed me by the arm.

"Yeah," I said, pulling back my arm. "I'll be right out; I just need to get these songs ready in here, that's all."

"Ok, well, we'll be out there, come find me Alex," she said as they started heading out into the party.

"Save me a dance, ok?" I responded, to which she smiled, saying "you're too cute" as she left.

Fucking Candice, I don't ever remember such a good-looking smile as the one she had that moment before leaving me behind the stereo. I'm thinking of Kirsten Dunst, the way she smiled in *The Virgin Suicides*, that sort of smile.

After they left, I stayed behind and got the songs ready. Champagne, or some sort of cheap sparkling wine rather, was being passed around, beers were being poured from the fourth or fifth keg of the evening, and cigarettes were being lit. Kris the fat Hindu was passing around the second of his big monster joints, from which Jaime ended up taking a few huge hits that probably pushed him over the top. Matt and Tony were still with the group of girls. Matt was talking to Misty, a girl taller than him with long brown hair, long legs. He kept whispering stuff into her ear, and she kept giggling. Tony was talking to Amanda, the girl that supposedly wanted to hook up with me. John was talking to Amy as she shyly smiled at him, drinking from her plastic cup of beer.

I spaced out watching all the partygoers, so when I heard the countdown starting, I freaked out about the music. Luckily, I had already put all the CDs in place and I was ready to go.

"Five, four, three, two, one… happy New Year!!" everyone screamed, and I hit the play button, and off went Auld Lang Syne. People kissed; I saw Jaime hug Candice, practically burying her head in his shoulders. Matt was making out with Misty, as was Tony with Amanda. My friends were all hugging each other. Jig was telling everyone how he loved them.

People always talk about how the New Year's Eve kiss is the greatest, that's when you're really supposed to kiss someone. I've never had such a kiss at New Year's, I don't think. Sure, I've had some girlfriends during a New Year's Eve, and we hugged and kissed, but it was never very special. I've had some really great kisses, just not on New Year's Eve.

It was fun, though, watching the whole party erupt and the hugs and kisses, like a communal sort of bonding thing was going on. I lit a cigarette as I watched all this, and then after I let "Auld Lang Syne" play on for a bit, it faded it out and "Revolution" went off with a fucking bang.

People loved it, some serious dancing and head bobbing started going on. It was pretty great, I have to admit. The party was rocking. I was moving my head with a cigarette dangling from my lips as I looked out at the party from behind the stereo. Soon, the other songs I selected came on, and they were also smashing. I'm not sure I remember the exact order they came in, but they worked. Someone I didn't really know came back there and asked if I was the one playing the songs. "Yeah," I responded. And then he said speaking to me in the second person and shaking his head in agreement, "Alex knows what people want to listen to," and then left. I like to tell people I was a DJ in college, or in high school, that I used to spin house or techno back in the height of the rave scene in Chicago. But that New Year's Eve party was probably one of the few nights I was anything like a DJ at all.

I stayed back there for about an hour or so, just kept playing songs and watching everyone get more and more fucked up. After a bit, Jig came over and brought me beers and told me how much he loved me. He could barely stand, was slurring a lot, and eventually sat down and began passing out right there beside the stereo.

After a bit the party started getting kind of ugly. Too many teenagers had consumed too much beer and too much pot and they started falling off one by one.

Jig was the first to go. He kept passing out and then getting up to party more, but eventually was just passed out in the sitting position against one of the walls with people ashing on his head, calling him the "Human Ashtray." Next a slew of girls were carried out after puking in the washroom or outside in the cold. Then Carlos started stumbling around and knocked a tall lamp over and caused a stir. Jaime, who was really fucking wasted by this point, wanted to kick Carlos' ass and an all out brawl almost broke out. But instead Carlos was escorted out by a few of my friends who were going back to this kid Jason's house to "continue partying like real men unlike all these fucking pussies." The Widow-Maker was left behind by accident.

The Wiley brothers and their posse also took off to go to Jason's house to party. They were also like, "Fuck these pussies," and thought they would have a much better time with a bunch of dudes getting as fucked up as possible.

Matt and Tony eventually took off with the pack of girls they were with. By that point, I was out in the party here and there, still pretty much in control of the music, but having lined up a bunch of CDs to play. Eventually, though, I lost control as other people started going back there to play stuff.

"Dude, are you sure you don't want to come with us?" Matt asked me as he was saying goodbye, "Tony's fucking Amanda now; sorry, you wasted your opportunity. But Tanya over there is pretty horny, plus she's a slut, man."

"No, I'm cool," I responded while stealing a look at this Tanya girl who had big, bleach-blond hair and, in fact, did look pretty slutty—making me reconsider for a second. But I stood firm and said no again, to which he said, "All right you Mexican," and they started getting ready to leave.

And then, just before going up the stairs, Matt came back, put his arm around me, and whispered in my ear, "Dude, I think you should go for Candice man."

"What do you mean?" I responded.

"Come on you spic, the girl digs you, you can tell by the

way she acts when she talks to you. I was checking it out earlier, there behind the stereo." I looked at him confused, and he continued, "Yeah, I was watching. I'm fucking observant like that; she was giving you her 'fuck me' eyes. Trust me, I know." If anyone would've known it would've been Matt, but still, I thought he was crazy.

"Yeah, but," I started responding, looking around at the party which was dwindling down, and I could see Jaime talking loud to some people, staggering around. "I mean, Jaime's her boyfriend, and we're at his house…"

"Al, come on, that guy's a fucking loser and he's wasted," Matt interrupted me. "I don't know. Get her to somehow leave and meet you back at your place, or something, or at least get her alone and whisper in her ear that you want her. I gotta go get my dick sucked, but all's I'm saying is that if you had any balls, you could get a piece of that, that hot piece of ass, tonight even." He stared off to where Candice was standing, grabbing his crotch. "Damn, I might stay back and get some myself some if you don't stop acting like such a girl."

"Fuck off," I said, and then he punched me in the shoulder and took off, telling me to call him the next day.

After he left, I noticed that John and Patrick were still there, and that John and Amy were definitely flirting with each other. I thought it was cute. Good for John, I thought. He deserved it.

Another altercation broke out, and a bunch of guys started shoving each other. There was a bunch of yelling, and I noticed that the guys were holding Jaime back from this older Greek guy, who was known for starting fights at parties. I had no idea how it started or what was going on. The Greek guy was being taken away, and they started leaving up the stairs, with him and a few of his friends yelling "fuck you, you fucking pussies" back at Jaime and his friends. It was like drunk Maine West ex football players against other drunk Maine West ex football players. Who knew why these sorts of things ever happened, but they always did, and I always thought it was kind of funny.

As I got closer to see what was going on, Jaime was still sort of being held back, and then he started fighting with one of his own friends. Candice was there, looking disgusted. Everyone was drunk and or high. Jaime's friends tried calming him down, but he started telling everyone to fuck off and get out of his house. His friends started to take him upstairs so he could pass out somewhere, and as he was being dragged out he sort of took a swing at me when he was passing by. I staggered back to avoid it, and he yelled out, "You fucking spic, what are you looking at?" I saw his crazy drunk eyes, you know, those eyes that just look all fucked up and sort of evil. He was dragged away and up the stairs. I guess that's what you get for taking multiple hits from the Widow-Maker, I thought to myself. The Widow-Maker would kick your ass no matter how big and beefy you were.

At that point more people started to leave. I had no idea what time it was, but it was after 2 a.m. for sure. I was hanging around with John, Amy, Patrick and Kelly. They still had beers and were not yet leaving. One of Jaime's friends came back downstairs and said everything was cool and that Jaime was passed out. There weren't that many people left, but whoever was left was still drinking. Someone then put on "Sweet Jane," the version by the Cowboy Junkies, from the *Natural Born Killers* soundtrack.

I knew that "Sweet Jane" was originally written by Lou Reed, was on the last Velvet Underground album that was released after the band broke up, and had been covered many times since, so I was sort of a snob and had dismissed the Cowboy Junkies' version as lame. However, that night as I listened to the song, I decided that it was actually really great, that their spin on it and how it fit with the movie was awesome.

John and Amy started to dance at that point, as did Patrick and Kelly along with a few other couples. I took a step back and thought it was cool—people were actually slow-dancing; it was like we reverted to having one last school dance. I almost imagined our 6th grade teacher, Mr. Matteson, standing there in his bad teacher outfit chaperoning us. The basement had cleared out quite a bit; there was stuff everywhere. The lighting was right down there, dark and murky, and it was cold as hell outside, back when we had real winters.

"Hey Alex," I suddenly heard Candice say as she approached me. "Will you dance with me?

Without me even responding, she took my hands, put one of them on her waist and held the other one up with one of her hands as she put her other hand on my shoulder.

"My boyfriend kind of made an ass out of himself, so I need a dance partner," she said as we started dancing. I always thought of Candice as being such a tall girl, like taller than I was. But being up so close to her and standing up like that, with our bodies basically touching, I realized that I was taller than her. Her boots must have had like three-or-so-inch heels, and she still was an inch or two shorter than me. I could smell her hair also, through the smoke of the party.

She mentioned something like how pretty the song was, to which I nodded my head in agreement. We didn't talk much, just danced. I was pretty much spacing out, looking at her hair, feeling the curve of her body under my hand, looking off, thinking that other people were staring at us, but everyone seemed to be making out, passed out, or getting ready to leave. I saw John and Amy dancing, with Amy's head on John's shoulder. John, though, was staring at me and Candice with big eyes. Then I noticed that he was giving me the "pump" fist sign, our way of saying "go for it." I noticed Patrick was doing the same thing.

When the song ended, we all sort of stood around talking, and soon everyone started leaving. Patrick and John were going back to Patrick's. They invited me with them, but I asked them to drop me off at Jason's which was on the way. I figured I might as well get really fucked up.

I then turned around to say bye to Candice, who was leaning up against the wall, her head slightly tilted down, her hair sort of coming down over her face. She was pretty drunk, and again it was weird to see her like that. As I approached her, she grabbed one of my hands and murmured, "You should stay," to which I was kind of speechless. I stared, and she repeated, "You should stay," and adding, after a pause, "and chat with me. everyone's leaving now anyway."

After what felt like minutes, I let go of her hand and turned around and told Patrick and John that I was staying behind to help clean up. They nodded. Kelly asked if I was sure and how I was going to get home, to which Patrick pulled her back saying, "Come on, let's go," and John gave me the same wild eyes and fist pumping thing like he did before. And then they finally left.

I kind of slid back toward the stereo system and started putting CDs away, thinking it would be weird if anyone saw me there, but nobody noticed or people were too drunk to care. Candice said goodbye to a few more friends that left stumbling drunk. Everyone eventually left; then it was just me and Candice there in her boyfriend's basement.

I put on the *Singles* soundtrack, which I had pulled out earlier in the night. Candice came back behind the stereo with me and started flipping through a few of the CDs that were scattered on the table, when she asked me, "Do you want to get high with me?"

"Um, well, yeah I guess," I answered hesitantly—one because I was already as high as hell, and two, because I was thinking like, "What the fuck am I doing down here?"

"I've tried it a few times at college, but I've never told Jaime about it. He would freak out, even though he's such a stoner now. He's such a hypocrite like that."

"Ok, well, I'll have a little, but I don't have any with me…"

"That's ok, here," she said, pulling out a joint. "Someone gave me this earlier." And then she pulled a lighter out of one of her pockets and lit it. I was shocked, I mean, really fucking shocked. I never imagined myself doing something like this with her. What would Zorba say? He would be smiling from his Heaven or Hell. She smoked it and then gave it to me. Next thing I know, we were sitting down with our backs against the wall looking over the dim empty room, sharing a joint, with "The Battle of Evermore" by The Lovemongers playing on the stereo. The room looked so big now, so dirty, with plastic cups, cigarettes, and all sorts of other garbage everywhere—a wonderful post-party wasteland. And we both sat there, smoking the joint as the music played.

At first we didn't say anything—we just took turns taking drags off the joint. She then started talking to me about how school was going, how it was different coming back to Des Plaines; it just seemed like such a different place now after being at school for a year and a half. Nobody seemed to change around here, or if they did, they didn't change for the better, like Jaime. She started telling me how much of an ass Jaime was now, that she didn't really see how they were still together, but for some reason she found it hard to let go. They'd been dating for so long, but ultimately they just seemed to be growing apart. I sort of shook my head in agreement but didn't really say much, just sort of agreed with her observations. I've always found that just listening in these situations works miracles.

We didn't quite finish the joint, and she said she had had enough, so I took another hit and put it out. We talked some more, but it was hazy, especially after the joint. I can't really say I remember what we were talking about after that, but I do remember when she put her head on my shoulder and said something to the effect of how sweet she thought I was, and then her hand kind of clasped onto my arm and she started to rub it.

I didn't react right away. I was too nervous and thought I was dreaming or possibly hallucinating or something. I'd hallucinated when getting high before so I wanted to be careful I wasn't. It was like a good dream you're having and just when you realize that it's a dream and you're waking up, you fight to not wake up and keep it going. But the reality of it really hit fucking home when all of a sudden she lifted her head and started to kiss the side of my check with these soft kisses, just barely putting her lips on my cheek. I just sat there, not believing this was happening. Then one of my arms was like, "Fuck it, if you're not going to do anything about this then I fucking will!" and took control and started caressing the back of her head as she started to kiss faster and lick the side of my face, moving to my ear, and I turned to meet her lips, and there we were, in full make-out mode.

Yeah, full make-out mode, as in wet and sloppy with our tongues, teeth, and everything, soon falling to the floor. I stopped thinking about how fucked up it all was, how we were in her boyfriend's basement, and just let my instincts take over. And I was ballsier than I'd ever been with a girl up to that point. It was intense, full body making out with me feeling her legs, pulling up her skirt, feeling her perfect ass, and her feeling my back and chest. I didn't give a shit anymore, I didn't care if it was a fucking dream or not. This was it, all that time I had spent freaking out about our study date, how I was ridiculed for thinking I had a chance with her, this was my opportunity and I wasn't about to let it get away from me. "Fuck you, Matt," I thought and could almost see him off somewhere with that girl by his side, smiling in appreciation of what I was doing and saying with an approving smile and a wink, "Go for it you fucking spic. I told you so; don't fuck it up."

This was the first time I really learned how to give a woman oral sex, real oral sex. I'm telling you, after losing my inhibitions, I went all out, like I had been given vanilla ice cream for the first time, like this might be the one and only chance I would ever have to be with a beautiful woman. This was also the first time I gave a woman an orgasm, or so I think... I thought I had previously, but this experience made me realize how different the real thing was. I had her completely naked on the floor, and I'm not going to describe it here for you in much more detail, though I should—if you have a pulse you should want me to—but I have to say, thinking back makes me want to smoke a cigarette, like right now.

At one point, she asked me why I had my clothes still on, so I promptly disrobed. Soon we were both getting on a couch with a blanket she got from somewhere. I can't tell you how much I wanted to have sex with her, but I held back. I started thinking about how drunk and stoned we both were and also felt sort of inferior, like I wouldn't be able to satisfy her, or that I would ejaculate prematurely. I mean, come on, she was beautiful, and to top it off, what if fucking Jaime came down? It was all sort of crazy, so I slowed down a bit and told her we should chill out for second.

Candice kissed me, saying again how sweet I was, and laid her head on my chest so her hair was just under my nose, with her arm over my chest and one of her long legs wrapped around my waist. It was like she didn't even know where she was. I just lay there, ran my finger through her hair, feeling her wetness against my hip below, and just took in the moment for a second, stared off at the ceiling and thanked God, until I finally closed my eyes.

Upon opening them, everything was hazy; my head hurt like hell; my mouth was dry; the room seemed a lot brighter, and looking up at the windows at the top of the basement walls I could see that the sun was out. I had fallen asleep but I wasn't sure for how long. Candice was still in the same position. It seemed like she had barely moved, actually. I could hear her lightly breathing, so I knew she was alive. Then I heard some sort of moving or thumping upstairs. At first I just lay there listening to it, relishing that I was there with her like that, smelled her hair a little, but then all of a sudden terror ran through every inch of my body—we were in Jaime's basement, and I was laying there naked with his girlfriend. I panicked, but I didn't want to freak out. I slowly took her arm and leg off me and slid out from the couch. Candice was out cold. I was so scared she would wake up. She didn't, and then I scrambled around to gather my clothes, which were scattered all over floor. As I picked everything up, I was about to start getting dressed when I heard the door to the basement open and then heard a "Hello?

I was squatting there with my clothes in my hands in the middle of the room, like a fucking dog that's getting busted with a dead bird in its mouth. In seconds, but what seemed like minutes, I reacted and ran off, still squatting, toward a closet off to the side with my clothes in hand. I got in and closed the door as silently as I could. I wasn't sure what the hell was in the closet, but just put my body against the door still in the squatting position and listened.

After a minute or so I heard Jaime say "Candice?" He was clearly downstairs now and just outside of the closet where I was hiding. "Candice? What the fuck is going on?" I heard him say now louder and more frantic. After a few seconds, I could hear her voice and some movement and then Jaime saying even louder and in a panic, "Candice, you're fucking naked! What the fuck? Who's been down here?

"No, no one Jaime, I, uh, don't know, I guess I just passed out like this?

"Buck fucking naked, your clothes are all over the place!

What the fuck did you do?"

"Nothing Jaime, I swear!"

"Oh my God, I can't believe this! Is there someone down here Candice?"

"No! Jaime, my God, no."

"I can't believe this," he continued saying on and on in a frantic voice as my heart was pounding. There was more movement, and as Jaime kept muttering on, it almost seemed like he was crying or something. But I couldn't tell. I could hear him walking around, kicking stuff around. I could hear her saying stuff, and then I realized that he might be looking around for someone. I started thinking of the scene in *Blue Velvet* where the guy's hiding out in a woman's closet as her mobster captor is about to open the door and find him there. So I then backed up still naked and squatting into the closet against some wall and next to the furnace or something. If he opened the door, I would be fucking dead that was for sure. I stayed there like that, almost teary eyed myself, when I heard more movement and mumbling and then thumping up what I thought was the stairs as if someone was running up them. Then I heard some more thumping and muttering, and then silence. At that point I waited but didn't hear anything. It seemed like one of them had gone up the stairs for sure, but I wasn't sure if both had. I then took the opportunity to put my clothes on and then just stayed there for a second.

I wasn't sure if I should just take a chance and run out and try to make a break for it out of the door that was on the far side of the basement leading up to the backyard. What if one of them was still down there? If it was Candice that was ok, but if it was Jaime then I would be in trouble. I would have to make the run of my life and hope my Mexican instincts would pay off. Waiting still, not hearing anything more, I decided it was now or never, so I gathered my strength, opened the door and without hesitating ran right out, kind of looking around really fast and wildly as I ran through the room and toward the corner where the door was. In those crazy seconds, I was terrified that Jaime would be there and all of sudden tackle my ass or something, but luckily, the room was empty. The only thing I noticed was the Widow-Maker and his friends still standing off in their area as I ran to the door. As I was fumbling to unlock the door, I thought I heard noises behind me by the stairs, but I wasn't sure. I didn't care to find out, so I just unlocked the door, pulled it open as fast as I could, no longer caring if I made any noise, went up the stairs leading up to the backyard, ran across the backyard, and jumped the fucking fence in what was almost a single bound.

I never looked back to see if they saw me, or if anyone else did. I remember hearing a few dogs bark, but nothing else. I just ran straight through another neighbor's yard and finally down a driveway to a street, where I took a left onto the sidewalk and continued running. There was snow all over the place but I don't even remember feeling cold or anything. I ran so fast that I swear if I was trying out for the Olympics, for like the Guatemalan national team, I would have qualified.

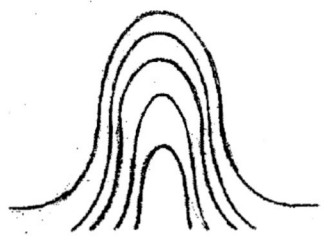

I - 57

I made my way toward Jason's house, which was not that far, thank God.

On my way, I kept repeating in my head, and then even sang out loud, the chorus to Pearl Jam's "Alive," "Oh Iiiiii, oh, oh, I'm still alive..." I'm not sure I've ever understood what that song's all about; I would like to talk to Eddie Vedder about it one day. It might be that simple, a song about someone barely escaping something, and just being thankful in the end that they were still alive. That's how I felt that morning. After the initial shock and sprint, I settled into a steady run. I had a sort of triumphant smile on and attitude going, a sort of swagger to my run. I mean, I had just hooked up with Candice, fucking Candice. And to top it off, on a New Year's Eve, in the basement of her freaking boyfriend's house, and to top it off even more, the fucker almost busted me—

almost. I was naked and hiding in the goddamned closet with him just outside. How cool is that shit? It might have been a little better if he had caught me, if I had to like fight my way out, run around the house ass naked or something, with Candice like screaming and crying in the background, shit breaking all over, me all naked fighting Jaime off with a lamp or something. I would have really had a reason to be singing "Alive" then, huh? But actually, I'm glad it didn't go down that way, I probably would've ended up in the hospital all fucked up.

When I got to Jason's, it was like walking into another post-party wasteland. There were guys passed out all over, some still up and drinking, some sort of rap playing in the background, the whole place smelled like shit. I swear I never understood where everyone's parents were in those days. Carlos and Jason were up, as was Jig, who was like half passed-out with something ineligible written on his forehead. Later I would find out that while he was passed out at Jason's they wrote "Carlos was here" on his butt cheeks. They were all still drunk. When they saw me, they all started asking what the hell was going on. At first, all I could do was laugh, I was hysterical. I asked for a beer and a cigarette even though I totally didn't need either. They all started laughing too, for no reason. I eventually told them what had happened and at first they didn't believe me, but soon we were all having a riot with it. We stayed up through the day, drinking more, watching the Bears beat the fucking Vikings. My parents knew I was staying over at a friend's and I'm sure they were worried, but I didn't care. I eventually headed home, hitching a ride with Jig who was still elated about my story, with his big white smile on the whole time, and the writing on his forehead.

When I got home, I went right to my bedroom, then the ugly truth began to hit. Jaime would eventually find out; he might even have seen me leaving and therefore already knew. But I also thought that if Jaime had seen me he probably would have chased me down—I was fast but I'm sure he was much faster. I was dumb to go to Jason's and begin bragging about the whole thing. What the hell was I going to do? I decided I needed to head back to U of I as soon as possible. I thought I would end up getting my ass kicked if I stayed in Des Plaines any longer. And what about Candice? Should I call her? No, I decided I couldn't. And as I was debating all that, my mom came into the room with the phone saying "A Candice is on the phone, Alex."

"Hello," I said, after having a brief freak-out and getting the phone and closing the door behind me.

"Hi Alex," she said in a soft voice. Was she calling to say she liked me? That last night was not a fluke? That this could be the start of something special? I wasn't sure what I would say in response. I would be little worried or scared, maybe even play it a little cool and act like I wasn't sure if I was interested because I wanted to know what she was going to do with Jaime first. But hell, I would be a big fucking idiot not to go for it, especially if she were the one to offer it up. Or maybe she could also have been calling to tell me that Jaime saw me running out and wanted to kill me and that I needed to get the fuck out of town.

We exchanged a couple pleasantries, about how tired we were, how fun the party had been, how much of an ass a lot of the guys had been, and then she got into the heart of shit.

"Alex, about last night," she said.

"Yeah, uh…"

"I'm so sorry about whatever happened, I wasn't myself and I vaguely remember what happened but I know something did."

"Yeah, um, ok…"

"Alex, did we have sex?"

And I paused for a second. Although I knew for certain that we didn't, for some reason I felt like saying we did. And I then I thought that I should have. After a few seconds though, I confessed the truth.

"No, we didn't."

"Oh, gosh, thank God. I was so scared we did something really, really stupid. Jaime woke me up this morning and I was completely naked on the couch in the basement. He was freaking out, and I couldn't remember what had happened. I convinced Jaime that I just passed out and must have taken my clothes off, but he's suspected something all day and he's still freaking out. All I remember is talking with you toward the end of the night and that's it."

"That's it?" I asked, feeling now more comfortable that she and Jaime hadn't seen me running out, and that I guess he didn't know, yet.

"Well, I guess I remember we started fooling around, or at least I think so, it's all kind of hazy, Alex. I was on some medication for a cold I've had and drank way, way too much. I guess I know something happened, but I'm just sort of hazy about it all. Although we get into fights from time to time, I love Jaime, and I would hate it if I ever did anything like that to him, you know?"

"Yeah, I understand. Well, you don't have to worry. I can

assure you that nothing like that happened."

"Ok, thanks, that's a relief."

"Candice, I'm sorry. I guess I didn't realize that you were not in a good state of mind, I had no idea. I mean, we talked a lot, I thought we had a connection, it was nice. I would never have done anything had I known you weren't all there." I thought about saying that she was even the one who instigated all the physical stuff, she's the one that first started licking my fucking face while I was just sitting there like a good stoned boy, but I didn't.

"Oh, I'm sure it was Alex. I've had a strong admiration for you. I think you're so sweet and smart, and deep inside I'm sure I would love to be with someone like you, but I just, you know, I've been with Jaime for a long time and, you know, sometimes you just can't explain things like love. We do have our problems that we have to work out, but I just, I wouldn't want to just throw it all away like that, I hope you understand."

"Yeah, sure, I do. Again, I'm sorry for whatever happened."

"Thanks Alex. I know you'll find a girl who you'll make very happy one of these days, and she'll be a lucky gal... Oh, and, please don't say anything to anyone about what happened, ok? You know..."

"Of course, don't worry."

"Ok, take care."

And that was it; it was over like that. She had just called to make sure we hadn't fucked because she felt bad. At first I felt like shit, like my whole night of glory, of triumph, was squashed just like that. I felt like putting something by the Cure or Pink Floyd on. To the other person that participated in my amazing moment, it was a blur, an accident that she regretted happening. But what the fuck? How could she not have remembered? That was bullshit, I thought. What we said to each other, how she fucking moaned during all of it? God, fuck, shit, I should have just fucked her. I didn't understand how she couldn't remember anything.

But, then, you know, I was like fuck it, whatever. How many bastards like me, passive, neurotic, spacehead and wimpy sort of guys ever get to taste what it's like to be with a beautiful woman like Candice? And besides, that shouldn't be the point. I had a great night, went to a kick-ass party, got into some trouble and almost caused a freaking catastrophe. What more could I ask for. I was still "Alive," right? Yeah, that was it, you know? But then I remembered that I still needed to get the hell out of Des Plaines and head back to U of I the next day. Although it seemed that Jaime didn't know, based on my conversation with Candice, I had told all those fuckers at Jason's what had happened, and I couldn't trust them. Maybe they all had forgotten already; I wouldn't be surprised if they had, based on how drunk and stupid they all were, but it was still likely, I thought, that Jaime would find out somehow.

So I left the next night telling my parents that I needed to get back and get a head start on the new semester. On the drive back, I pulled over about halfway down on I-57, off onto a small service road, and looked out at the moon that was out and just thought about stuff listening to the stereo and hearing the car running. I-57 is a highway that runs between Chicago and Urbana-Champaign, through stretches of farmland, which pretty much is all there is in Illinois outside of Chicago. Stretches and stretches of farmland, as far as the eye can see in either direction. People say it's boring, and maybe it is in a way when compared to other areas of the country like the rolling hills of Pennsylvania, or the mountains out west, the coastline of California, whatever. But, for some reason, the farms of Illinois and the Midwest have always been appealing to me. Something about the flatness is reassuring. I like the straight lines—it's all clean and calming to me. They remind me of The Orb's song "Little Fluffy Clouds" from their mid-90s classic ambient album that starts with a girl reminiscing about the clouds in Arizona she remembers seeing as a child living there. I guess because Chicago is so cluttered, although I like that about the city, sometimes it just feels nice to be around nothing. Also, we would all fucking starve if it wasn't for the flat lands of the Midwest, right?

I've had some great moments, a few epiphanies, driving up and down that highway and driving or biking around the farm roads outside of Urbana-Champaign. Like this one time when I thought that I had figured out what "God" was all about while I was driving back to school and thinking of what I was going to write my philosophy thesis on, and this other time when I realized that Sarah and I would not continue to date after college and how shitty that made me feel—even though I was the one pushing for us to agree to go our separate ways. A lot of other stupid shit happened on that highway, like our senior year when a bunch of us were driving to Chicago for the weekend and we were celebrating that we were almost done with college, had taken the CPA exam, were now old enough to go to the Chicago bars legally, and we were bright enough to bring a case of beer with us and drink it on the way, throwing the cans out of my shitty car's window until we were pulled over and given tickets for underage drinking. I was driving and I'll never know why I wasn't thrown in jail for a DUI.

That night driving back from Des Plaines to Urbana-Champaign, it was clear and starry. It was cold; there was snow on the ground due to the heavy storms we had all through the Midwest just before New Year's, but, thankfully, the roads were clean. The moon was out, bright and big, and I was listening to a mixed tape that had a compilation of U2 songs on side one and R.E.M songs on side two. I left without even saying good-bye to my friends or anything. My parents thought something was wrong, but I convinced them that I really just wanted to get a head start on stuff and that everything was ok.

The night before I was freaking out about what would happen if I got busted but still pretty pumped about the whole hookup. Now on the way back to school, the reality of it sunk in, that yeah, although the whole thing was fun, was crazy, I had hooked up with a hot chick and all that, it was now over, and she didn't really want anything to do with me. I thought again, as I did the last time I was with her and we studied, about what would happen if I really did try something with her. Maybe I could've insisted on meeting up with her to talk about it. When the hell does a guy try and "be a man" and force the issue with a woman? Everyone says that women want men to take control, to chase them around and make them feel wanted. Is that what Candice really wanted? From me? She sure as hell didn't sound like it. She was the one that instigated the whole thing, that's for fucking sure, but on the phone she was pretty clear that it was some sort of mistake on her part. I guess you have to know when they want you to chase them around and when they don't, but I hardly ever pick up on that shit. I could have tried though, couldn't I? I could've shown up to her place, announce my love for her, brought a boom box and played some cheesy love song like John Cusack's character did in *Say Anything*. Even if she would have kicked me out, or laughed at me, or whatever, I didn't have anything to lose, we never do, right? Then why the hell am I always such a chicken shit all the time? I'm always so fucking scared, so I must have something to lose, damn it!

So no, I didn't do anything like that. In fact, as it turns out, that phone call was the last time I would ever talk to her. That night, staring at the circular moon and thinking, while listening to Michael Stripe sing songs like "Talk about the Passion" and "Don't go back to Rockville," I thought about one of my favorite words, "evanescence." Not the stupid early-2000s rock band, but the feeling that things are all slipping away right before your very eyes. I think that's what it means anyway. When I reflect back, every great moment I've had has been great indeed, and I've had many of them and am very thankful for that, but ultimately, I can't stop from thinking that no matter how good the moment was, also present was that underlying feeling that it was slipping away as it was happening, before it was even over. And although I can remember these moments and write them down, they start fading away instantly until they're vague, distant thoughts and are finally gone forever.

As I recall memories about individuals that I've known, I often realize that those very memories were the last time I saw them. And indeed, that's how most stories about people I've known seem to end, from my first girlfriend Jackie, to my high school theater geek friends, to Sarah, to Erica, Miki, eventually Heather, and on and on. The ones that stick around are the ones I supposedly like the least, or that's what I tell myself. Whenever someone has told me they love me, I can't help to think that although their feeling might seem sincere, at the time, it's still transparent, like they could easily be saying that to someone else, or might easily say that to someone else in the future. Maybe that's just a fact of life. It's representative of how fragile it all is. We can never hold on to things forever because well, we ourselves are not forever, and neither is anything around us, so it's natural that everything seems to be fleeting. We live on a big rock that is circling around at some amazing rate, for crying out loud. I can't tell you how many times I've known people—friends, relatives, lovers—who, when parting ways after some time together, say that we'll continue to keep in touch and continue to talk. At the time we're saying our goodbyes, it seems so real, so heartfelt, like we really mean what we're saying and we're going to do all our best to stay in touch, write each other, call. But that never really happens, and it always just seems to fade away.

It's not just their fault, it's mine also; no matter how much I try, I inevitably let it go. And they are gone from my life, and the memories I've had with them get blurry as time goes on, to the point where I start to forget what the person looked like, and eventually all I have left is a shadow. It's kind of like death, I suppose, but a slow sort of death. It's weird because you know they're still alive, out there somewhere in the world, and maybe you think about them, but you can't really reach out to them anymore because to do so would be weird, or maybe you don't even have their contact information anymore. It's like you can almost feel it, feel that intangible thing we call "time" passing by, the one thing we can't do anything about.

Up until 1994, none of us had *really* experienced death. There were a few kids who died growing up, but their passing didn't hit home; they were an afterthought. Like Ed Botticelli, who died when we were young, but none of us really were told what happened—and I'm still not sure. For some reason I still can remember a little of what he looked like and can vaguely see him as a teenager although I think he didn't make it past like 14. He was just a kid, always around in our little groups, acted in our "Outsiders" plays, smoked cigarettes with us under the viaduct, and then suddenly he wasn't around anymore. It's unreal to think that he didn't get to experience his high school years like we did. And I know a few relatives who have died, but none of our immediate friends or parents has. Not even with our dogs have I experienced death, and that's what they're essentially for, to teach kids about death, right? My dad gave away the Husky we had for a year when we were little because no one ever trained him and he shit all over the place. My parents forgot my little Jackson outside after leaving for a trip to visit a friend in New York while I was away in college and we never saw him again.

I've been fortunate, I suppose, in that fashion, that I haven't experienced death directly—in that none of my direct family members have died, yet. But I'm not sure how fortunate that really is, though, because at times it feels like a lingering event. I know it'll happen one day; it's the most certain thing I know. It could be just around the corner, tonight or tomorrow, waiting there to happen when I least expect, like sometimes you just want to let it happen and get it over with. Like, when it does happen, I think I'll be in shock, but I'll probably think to myself that here, finally, like this, this is how it finally happened to me, like Grant Lee Buffalo sings in his song "Devastation," "Devastation at last, finally we meet…"

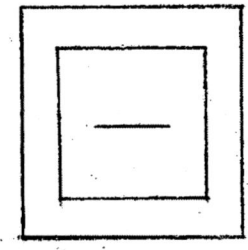

The End of Innocence

Well, when I said that I never talked to Candice again, it was partly because I was a big wimp and didn't want to try and express to her how I felt, but it was also because she died about a year after that infamous New Year's Eve party.

After I made it back to U of I, I never called her. I never wrote her although I thought about it many times during school, especially when drunk at bars or parties and that fucking song "Sweet Jane" played. I played the Velvet Underground's version to myself through headphones many times after coming home drunk and stoned. Even after I met Sarah that second semester of my sophomore year, and I finally fell in "love" with someone, with a great girl, I would still think about Candice and wonder how she was doing. I would wonder if she really did love Jaime the way she told me that night on the phone, or if that was just her panicking and she later came to her senses.

I began to lose touch with the Des Plaines people after that New Year's Eve. That summer after my sophomore year at college, I stayed in Urbana-Champaign, working, taking classes, hanging out with Sarah. I only went back to Des Plaines once; my parents mainly came to visit me. Sarah was from Omaha, so I went back there with her a few times and enjoyed it. It was this chilled out town with a really great music scene. Ska, punk rock, folksy stuff, bands like the Flaming Lips, cool people, and lots of weed. I had no reason to want to go back to Des Plaines, or so I felt at the time. I had so much fun that I went back to Omaha to spend Christmas and New Year's Eve with Sarah and her family that winter during my junior year.

By the time the summer that followed my junior year arrived, I had given up on my idealistic dream of being a philosophy major and found myself interning at a public accounting firm called Coopers & Lybrand with a bunch of other Big Ten and Notre Dame business majors.

However memorable that New Year's Eve of 1994 was for me, Candice had become a distant memory. Although I said I hated being a business major, that I was only doing it for the money and would continue to pursue my interests in literature and the arts, I secretly liked the lifestyle that my high-paying internship afforded me. I was already 21, could go out drinking in the Chicago bars—although the ones we went to were all shitty ones in Lincoln Park, Lakeview, and Wrigleyville (like John Barleycorn, Irish Eyes, Gamekeepers, The Hidden

Shamrock and Beaumont's), places I now avoid. I had money to spend, and I crashed at the apartments some of the other interns—the ones that were cute girls. It seemed that many of the other interns had never really interacted with a Latino before, so I was kind of a novelty, in a way. I was definitely the only minority in my intern class of 30-or-so college kids. Sarah was interning in Costa Rica, off observing monkeys, and I took some liberties, although I didn't consider it "cheating" as we didn't see each other for months.

I was trying to be a new person. The new friends I was making didn't know my past, what I was like, or what I had done. It really was like starting out with a fresh slate, a new canvas on which to draw new memories. When I was back home in Des Plaines, my conversation with friends always seemed to go back to things that happened between us all in high school and shortly after, mainly the dumb things we did while fucked up. With them, I could never escape the memories that they had of me. I started becoming scared to go back there; Des Plaines was becoming a place that grounded me as a kind of person that I was trying to grow apart from.

Thinking back, though, Des Plaines was humbling in a way. It was a reminder that no matter what I was studying, what kind of new music I was into, what sort of philosophy interested me, or whatever, I would always be a first-generation Mexican-American who drank, smoked cigarettes and pot, broke windows when I was young, and did a lot of other crazy things with other first-generation immigrant kids. Not that all that is necessarily a bad thing—and in the end, maybe it's actually a good thing to have a place like Des Plaines as a sort of anchor.

I also didn't go back to Des Plaines because I didn't want to run into Jaime at a party and have him kick my ass. I heard of parties going on through my friends whenever I would talk with them over the phone, but I never asked or heard about whether Jaime and Candice were there, and I assumed I would have heard if he was looking for me. Jaime never called me out the blue or randomly showed up at my college apartment like I thought he would. Eventually, it was like the whole thing that happened with Candice was fun conversation with my friends for a day after that party, but it quickly faded away. No one ever really brought it up anymore, and no one ever really does these days. Today it's as if Candice is just a part of my imagination.

Candice died just over a year after the New Year's Eve party, during my junior year. She was back in Des Plaines on her winter break just before it was time for her to go back to Missouri. She was driving home from somewhere by herself, maybe visiting friends or going shopping, something very innocent like that. It was snowy out, she was driving through one of the winding roads in Des Plaines that went through the woods where we all used to party, and by what people later called a freak accident, she hit an icy and snowy patch on a curve of the road, slid off, and slammed into a tree. The impact killed her on the spot, just like that, during the middle of the day.

There was a wake and a funeral; her family and friends cried, I'm sure. I'm also sure that it was talked about in Des Plaines, in the paper there called the *Daily Herald*, at Maine West, at the University of Missouri. They must have talked about how tragic of a thing it was, for this young, attractive, smart girl who was full of promise to suddenly have life pulled away from her, just like that.

I didn't find out about Candice dying until about six months after it happened, during the summer after my junior year. I wasn't around that winter because I was in Omaha, and when it happened, no one thought to call and tell me. But why would have anyone called? I had hardly been back to Des Plaines since that party, had only talked to a few of my friends since, and I was wrapped up in my own little world. Outside of my memories, what happened between us did not really exist, and there was no reason for anyone to think I would have wanted to know. By that time, my parents had already moved further west to Barrington and they didn't keep in touch with any of my friends' parents or anything, so they didn't know—and even if they had, they had no idea who the girl was anyway.

I first heard of Candice's death during a conversation we were having in Patrick's parents' backyard during a get together early that summer of 1995, during one of the few times that I had seen all my Des Plaines friends together since that New Year's Eve party. There was a bunch of us there, mainly guys, standing in a circle drinking cans of Miller Light—we had evolved from Old Style, I guess—talking about what the guys who were not going to college were doing now, what salary-paying jobs those of us who were in college were hoping to get once we graduated. We got to talking about what other kids from our graduating class were up to, and during this part of the conversation, Patrick mentioned how Jaime was now dating Colleen, one of Candice's best friends, and hardly six months had passed since her death. Nick then remarked on how fucked up that was, that he could have shown a little more respect, and then the conversation moved onto someone else. It came up and went like that, as if almost an afterthought. It almost slipped by me actually, but then I paused and thought to myself, "What did he just say?" The conversation went on, and I didn't want to interrupt the whole thing, so when I had a second, I turned to John, and asked him what Patrick was just talking about, asking him "Did he just say something about Candice dying?"

"Yeah, she died. What, you didn't know dude?" he responded with a surprised look on his face.

"No, I had no idea," I said.

"Yeah dude, she had an accident, was driving down East River Road during the winter while here on break this past January. It was snowing, and she lost control or something like that. They said she wasn't even going fast or anything, it was just a freak accident."

A few others overheard and jumped in with more details. No one seemed shocked that I didn't know; they just jumped in to explain how they felt about it, how I guess they were all bothered when they found out, how sad and tragic it was. Some of them, like Patrick, Nick and Carlos actually went to the wake and funeral, not really because they knew her, they didn't fucking know her at all, they just knew Jaime now that he was a stoner. They went but didn't bother to tell me about it. No one remembered that I had hooked up with her and that I fucking studied with her. Out of all them, I was the one that fucking knew her. I felt like none of these other fuckers had any business going there. If anyone did, beside Jaime and her family, it was me.

The weird thing is that although I was surprised and pissed off that these slobbering idiots went to her funeral while I had no fucking clue, it didn't feel real to me. The conversation went on, and I just kept on drinking, not saying anything else about it. I've never even talked to anyone about how it made me feel. It was just like something that happened, just like that, and I had nothing to do with it. And I honestly didn't know how I was supposed to feel. I thought I should be sad, horrified, pissed off, but I really wasn't. I was just kind of in disbelief and not very emotional. If anything, I was more pissed because no one had told me and I had no idea. I guess I felt that way because I was hearing about something happening many months after it happened. I hadn't talked to her in over a year, and her death happened, and I totally missed it. It also made me feel even more inconsequential to her life—no one, not a single person thought to tell me. I realized that was a very self-ish way to think, but I couldn't help it.

It's strange, isn't it? The concept of how we're supposed to react toward a dramatic event that you have no direct experience with. Like, September 11. I remember where I was and what I was doing when it happened. I was at home being lazy and taking my time getting to the office when I heard over the radio that some sort of plane had accidentally crashed into one of the World Trade Center towers, but they weren't sure why. I thought it sounded fucked up, but I'd heard stranger things. So I turned the television on to see if more information was available, and as I was watching I saw the second plane hit the second tower, still not really knowing what was happening. I remember watching that and thinking of a story from my child-hood about how the moon was cheese, and it was close to the Earth, and cheese was falling from the sky. I saw how the two towers ended up crumbling down, watched as they showed video of people jumping from the high floors to their deaths,

President Bush talking from a plane. I remember the rumors that planes were missing and that some could be on their way to Chicago, how they closed all the offices downtown and everyone went home, the speculation as to who did it and why, how many thousands of people were thought to be dead. I can say that the experience felt real to me; but would it have felt the same way to someone who didn't watch it like I did, who maybe only heard about it after, months or years after? Like the Holocaust in Germany during WWII or the genocides that are occurring in Africa. I know that these events are tragic, I can say that, but I honestly don't *feel* it, it's hard for me to relate, I've never known someone to suffer directly in these events, I've never been there, seen it, smelled it.

It was weird to see all the people who didn't have any direct friends or relatives die in the September 11 attacks mourn the loss of life over and over again for days, weeks, months, years after it occurred. At first I thought it was acceptable. But then it continued, over, and over again, all these people seemed to be stuck, obsessed with mourning victims they really didn't know. Am I a terrible person for thinking this way? It just doesn't seem appropriate, after a certain point, to mourn the loss of life, or tragic events, to which you have no direct experience in. Acknowledging the events happened, understanding the significance and trying, however you can, to learn from it all and help those who are grieving—all this seems to be acceptable. But there seems to be a point in which you leave the personal mourning and tearful grieving to those who had direct involvement with the lost ones. They are the only ones who really understand, and for someone to act like they do also just seems to intrude on their feelings to me.

I remember when my mother's mother died when I was 16. She had been sick for a long time. My mother used to run off to Mexico every now and then after emergency phone calls that my grandmother was on the verge of death, but every time my mother returned saying that it was just a close call. We didn't have that much money, so the travels took a toll, and therefore she stopped going every time—including the last time when it was for real. It was late at night and we were all home when my mother found out after a call from our aunt in Mexico. She cried, sobbed, wailed uncontrollably. I didn't understand. I was like, "She was old; she was sick; what did you think was going to happen?" That's what I told my mother as a form of consolation, to which she brushed me off in tears, telling me to leave her alone. I thought I knew, I thought I knew how she should react because I presumed to know how she ought to feel, but I had no clue, and I still don't to this day. No one will know how I feel when my mother someday dies, not even my sister will know how I feel. No one has had the conversations I've had with my mother nor known the counsel she's given me, the recipes she's taught me, they way she's looked at me, the regrets I have for the ways I've acted toward her.

But I know people will console me, will tell me how I'm supposed to act, will come to her funeral and will surprise me by being there because they didn't really know her. I guess that's fine; it's fine to acknowledge someone else's grieving, respect it, but don't act like you know it. Don't go to the funeral just because it's something you're supposed to do, because it somehow makes you feel better.

Maybe I'm just a terrible person for thinking this way. Maybe a stronger person does know how someone feels during a tragedy, like the death of a relative or acquaintance, and therefore can give counsel. But after my grandmother's death, and the way I treated my mother, I realized that I can never truly know how this sort of thing affects someone—so all I can do is listen but never tell them how it is they should be feeling. And not just in situations involving death, but in any which someone is hurting, whether because of a divorce, a falling out of some sort, whatever.

Though in truth I barely had a connection with Candice except for one study night and a drunken hook-up that she supposedly didn't remember, her death seemed to mark a sort of turning point in my life. A definite part of me ended there. As the 90s progressed, people started getting married, pregnant, and divorced. People started getting fat, losing their hair, losing their sense of style, listening to shittier and shittier music, revolving their lives around sports teams and fucking fantasy sports.

Soon after I learned of Candice's death, a kid from our high school killed himself after serving in the military. Soon after, another guy died in another car crash; another was thrown in jail for heavy drug trafficking; another was shot by the cops while they were trying to disrupt a drunken fight between him and his girlfriend. The list continues to grow every year. (None of my direct friends though have died or had something terrible like that happen to them, not yet anyway.)

I became fascinated with the stories I heard of who attended these funerals. As more deaths occurred, more and more of my friends in Des Plaines began attending these sorts of services, even for individuals who they hardly seemed to have known or hadn't seen or talked to in many years. It seemed like everyone attended any funeral service for anyone who died and happened to live in Des Plaines—and they acted all weird about it. It was almost as if they all had nothing better to do.

A few years ago, Jig called me and asked if I was going to Patrick's grandmother's funeral because he and all the guys were. He thought he should let me know. I was surprised. Although Patrick had been my friend throughout high school, and I got shitfaced with him drinking Jameson's many times, I had never met his grandmother, and he wasn't the first of all our friends to lose a grandparent. Shit, I only had one that was still alive. I didn't recall Patrick ever talking to me about her or anything, so no, I didn't feel it was appropriate for me to attend the funeral. I wouldn't have expected any of them to attend any of my grandparent's funerals. But evidently Jig and everyone else was going to the funeral, even though none of them knew her either. They were all going to a bar after, in case I wanted to join them there, to drink with Patrick in his grief. When I asked him why, he just said, "Because it's Patrick, man." He had this bummed out voice, like the suffering was hitting him personally.

I don't know, again, it just struck me as weird. I kept picturing all these 30-something, overweight, beer-guzzling and cocaine-snorting guys in their best tight-fitting suits, grieving over the death of a little old lady none of them knew, just because. It's like it was just another reason to get together and drink.

And then, a few years ago, a kid from Des Plaines named Tom—Little Tommy—died from a drug overdose. Tom was this short, blond kid, who was a year younger than us. He was the kind of kid that a lot of people in high school knew. He was funny, a bit of a trouble maker; girls thought he was cute, and if it wasn't for how short he was, he probably would have had a ton of girlfriends—but I think he did well for himself. I only knew him from little league when I was 12. Like most of my friends, I talked to him on only a few occasions, saw him at parties later on in high school, where he grew a reputation for drinking a lot and smoking a lot of weed, especially for a little guy. He even showed up at a few of the parties we had at the apartment I lived in my sophomore year in college, where every now and then a bunch of kids from Des Plaines would come down to party. They would end up stopping by my place simply because I was a former Maine West grad and they somehow knew where I lived. Other than that, I never knew the kid, didn't know what he was really like, what his family situation was like, what he aspired to do with his life, whether he went to college or not, what kind of work he did back in Des Plaines.

Apparently he, like a lot of the other kids who stuck around Des Plaines after high school, got into drugs like cocaine, meth, ecstasy and heroine.

I was probably 30 or so when Little Tommy died. I hadn't seen or heard of him since those college parties. I remember seeing the e-mails from my group of friends about a wake and funeral that they were all going to, about who was driving in case anyone needed a ride. I always skipped their e-mails because they were usually gross jokes about sexual organs or odors and other shit like that. When I went back and read the e-mails, at first I wasn't sure who they were talking about. The name sounded familiar, I remembered the person but couldn't picture the face. And so I finally called Jig to see what the deal was, asking him who was it that had died.

"It's Tom, dude, Little Tommy, you know?" responded Jig over the phone, sounding as if I should have known without a doubt.

Jig had returned home to live with his parents, after years of living in the city primarily as my roommate—he was my first roommate in the city after college. He graduated from U of I, also with a degree in accounting, to the shame of his father who desperately wanted him to be a doctor in order to make his grandparents, uncles and aunts back in India proud— apparently being an accountant wasn't successful enough. Jig told me that it was customary for the eldest Indian son to stay at home with his parents until he married, then have his Indian wife come live with them and the new couple would become the head of the household. It was also customary for the wife to be selected for the husband from the same area and religious sect that the son's family was from in India.

"Why date? Just get a girl, marry her, fall in love later." That's what Jig's dad used to say to me when I'd see him at weddings or parties we were all at. I've been told by other Indian friends that this is old-school and not so customary anymore, so I guess Jig's family's traditional. Jig always said he didn't want to conform to the Indian culture, that he wanted to date and marry whomever he fell in love with. When he decided to be my roommate in the city after college, his father refused to talk to him, turning his back on him as he left their house in Des

Plaines. After many years of unsuccessfully dating in the city, with constant pressure from his family, Jig decided to move back in with his parents, for what he said was only temporary. He started to hang out more and more with our Maine West friends and whoever else was still in Des Plaines. It was only a matter of time before he went to India, selected a girl from his mother's hometown, married her, and brought her back to Des Plaines where they now live with his parents, sleeping in his parents' bedroom. His wife's parents live there now, and their newborn son. I don't know how he does it.

"You mean the little blond kid? From little league?" I asked him, trying to clarify who we were talking about.

"Yeah man, Little Tommy."

"Did you even really know him? I mean, I hardly did."

"Well, you know, little league, I've seen him around town 'n shit, you know." Jig did live in Des Plaines again, so maybe he had a point.

"You're going to go to the funeral?"

"Yeah man, everyone's going; it's a big deal around here."

"But you hardly know him, why would you go?"

"Cause man, he died, it's tragic, and everyone's going."

"How did he die, anyway?"

"He overdosed on drugs. They were out partying and he crashed at a friend's place and apparently they left drugs out in the living room and Little Tommy took some more, and they just found him dead on the couch in the morning." Well, after more of that sort of conversation, I finally agreed to go the funeral, due more to curiosity than anything else. It would be my first Maine West funeral.

The funeral home was in downtown Des Plaines, which

has changed a lot. The original McDonald's is still there, but it's now a museum or memorial to the billion-dollar global franchise. The Sugar Bowl, a diner and sundae shop we used to go to, is still there, as are the few bowling alleys like Sims Bowl where we used to hang out. The Des Plaines movie theater is still there, though it now shows Indian movies 24/7, like the ones made in Bollywood. The historic town center is now overrun with cheap condos that are mainly occupied by old people and Russians, primarily single chain-smoking Russian moms whose Russian boyfriends stop by every now and then. And Des Plaines now annually hosts The Taste of Des Plaines, which I've heard is prime for observing sleeveless, mullet-sporting, beer guzzling white dudes.

I arrived at the funeral late, so the main parking lot was already full, and I had to park in the adjacent overflow lot. On my walk toward the entrance, I passed by a bunch of guys and girls all dressed up who were outside smoking cigarettes, what smelled like some weed, and drinking cans of beer, right there in the parking lot of the funeral home. It looked like there was a tailgate going on—I thought I was going to a wedding in Wisconsin. I recognized a few of them, all former Maine West grads now in their late 20s or early 30s like me. Some of them looked my way and nodded toward me as if in recognition, but I just smiled back at no one in particular and walked inside.

It was packed inside, standing room only. I recognized people here and there, kids now grown into young adults, everybody looking like hell. I didn't say hi to anyone. As I stood in the back, I saw all the pictures in the front of Little Tommy. Many showed his big bright smile and bright blond hair that he was known for. There was a blown up picture of him in his

Devon Higgins Little League Pirates baseball team uniform. I played on the Cubs in the same league. The Pirates were our rivals and we beat them 7 to 1 in the championship that year. I remembered that he was their leadoff man, a fast little guy; you always had to worry about him stealing bases if he got on. He scored the only run of that game by bunting his way on, stealing second and third, and scoring off a sacrifice fly. Looking at all the pictures up there, of him smiling and looking innocent, I wondered what happened that drove him into all the drugs and lifestyle that eventually killed him.

In the preceding days, I heard all sorts of stories that he was practically living on the streets, going from place to place, totally hooked on heroin, crack, any drugs he could get his hands on. The night he died, he and his friends were out partying it up, doing coke and other stuff at some bar in Des Plaines where that stuff might as well have been legal. When they got back to his friend's place, they were too coked up to fall asleep, and so his friend decided they should take some downers to help them. Apparently, the friend left a bottle of strong sleeping pills on the coffee table next to the couch where Tom was to fall asleep, and in the morning when they found him dead on the couch, the bottle was on the floor, empty. Who knew if Little Tommy killed himself or was just too fucked up to know any better? The family was trying to press charges against the friends for leaving the pills out there. Others wanted to kick their asses, while others defended them saying it wasn't their fault that Little Tommy couldn't control his drug-intake. I guess it was causing a big rift in Des Plaines; people were taking sides.

As I was looking up through all the people gathered there, many standing, listening to the eulogy, I saw Jig and them all standing up in the same row toward the middle. The Wiley brothers, the big one and the small one, both mean looking, were also there. I found that ironic, as they were the primary drug suppliers for kids like Little Tommy in Des Plaines—it was a known fact. But I guess they were there to pay respects to a former customer, a form of good old-fashioned customer service I suppose.

I heard the sobbing and crying all around, especially from the front, where I gathered the family was. I could see an older woman with a man's arm around her, and her head sort of buried in his shoulder. The eulogy was over quickly, and people started to walk up and pay their last respects to the body, which was up front in the coffin. I saw Jig and our other friends getting in line. At that point I decided to leave. I didn't feel comfortable there and felt like an outsider. My friends told me that everyone was getting together at Radish's afterward, so I figured I would go and hang out for a bit. On my way out, the group of people was still there drinking and smoking, and as I walked by on the way to my car I ran into Matt, who was standing there smoking a cigarette.

After college I stayed in touch with Matt although I only talked with him once or twice a year. There were a few years where I lost touch with him completely. He had run into some hard times, was doing his share of drugs, specifically cocaine, and he continued his trend of going in and out of jobs and schools. He was a bartender at some bar in the city and wanted to open up a restaurant of some sort, and he was married to a 37-year-old divorcee living off alimony. She lived in a condo down in the city's Gold Coast, and was expecting a baby from him and had one of her own from her previous marriage. As we were standing there, he was mainly doing the talking, all coked up, about his wife, how hot she was, their soon to be born baby, his other plans and ideas of ways to make money.

Then a fight broke out in the parking lot. It turns out that the guy whose apartment Little Tommy died at was there. He wanted to go in and pay his last respects; he and Tommy were good friends, but the family specifically didn't want him there. After some shouting, pushing, exchange of many vulgar words, all among a bunch of drunk and stoned guys, the guy and his buddies decided to leave, telling everyone to fuck off. They walked away with cigarettes in their hands. Matt told me to watch and see that one day soon, not that day out of respect, those fuckers would get their asses kicked for what happened to Little Tommy.

At Radish's it was like a high school reunion. The bar is down the street from Maine West, down the street from the McDonald's we got busted at for our attempt to egg freshmen on Halloween our senior year. The bar owner's name is also Tom, a life-long Des Plaines resident and Maine West grad. Tom also had gone to the funeral. He was behind the bar, helping to bartend as the place was at capacity. The shots were on the house that night, out of respect. As Tom served up the drinks and talked with my friends, who were frequent guests of the bar, he lamented that it was a shame what happened to Little Tommy, that he was such a good kid, spent a ton of time at the bar, and that Big Tom almost thought of Little Tommy as a son. So he had a drug problem, he said—we all got problems, you know? Shots and shots of Jaegermeister were ordered and passed around, with the biggest of the Wiley brothers leading the way, urging everyone to drink it up, for Little Tommy's sake.

I talked to a few people I hadn't seen in a long time. Some of Candice's friends were there. They were still fairly attractive girls although they looked older now, had bigger hips, and sported their new trendy $200 jeans. I didn't see Jaime there. My friends Jig, Patrick, Carlos, and John were there. Jig, Patrick, and John were married by this point and had children— Patrick leading the way with three, working on a fourth, following in the good traditional Irish family spirit. They all lived in big houses out in Schaumburg, with big yards for their children's birthday parties, full of stuff bought from Menard's and Home Depot, and all within a few blocks of each other. Carlos still lived in the city and was as single and neurotic as I was. I saw a guy named Gus, Big Gus, who used to play soccer with me and John. He was our big Greek sweeper in the back of the field. He was fat and newly married.

Everyone seemed to be getting fatter and fatter. I even had a little gut now and my six-pack was long gone. Gus came up to me and gave me a big drunken hug and asked me how I was doing and told me that everyone else looked like shit, that I was the only one who still looked young and good, while he was patting me on the cheek. (I ran into him again at a wedding recently, he was still married and expecting a child, but he kept asking my date, Stacy, if she wanted to go back to the kitchen and hook up with him. She just laughed at him, and later commented to me how fucked up everyone from Des Plaines is. I told her that it was something they put in the Des Plaines River, it had to be.)

I ran into big-breasted Kathy, the girl I almost hooked up with and then almost threw up on at the Green Shit Machine party and who I had bent over the car in front of my house after my Cartoon Pornos bash. She still was sexy looking, had her big boobs, but had gathered a rather big butt to go with them. She was dating this guy who was a former football player at Maine West, now big and round, with a Marine style crew cut. He was a police officer for the nearby suburb of Mt. Prospect. During our conversation, she kept looking back to see where he was, and he kept looking over at us suspiciously. He finally came by to see how she was doing, eyeing me while they were talking. She finally introduced me saying that I also went to Maine West and we graduated together, that we were just catching up and that she would be back over in just a few. He shook my hand rather hard without really saying anything and walked away looking back at me. As Kathy and I finished up our conversation, she gave me her card, again looking over her shoulder to check, and said I should stop by and see her up at the salon she was working at, or even just call her during the day to catch up, and that she sometimes came down to the city to hang out with her girlfriends and maybe we could meet out. She sort of rubbed my arm, squeezing it a little before she left. I never called her, and I don't know what happened to her card although I have to admit I think about it sometimes.

While up at the bar I finally did a shot of Jaeger, which was, and still is, the popular shot to do in Des Plaines. I was surrounded by all of my old high school friends, Matt was there and talking 100 miles an hour to whomever was around. Jig was there, and so was his little brother, Wajid. Wajid was about four or five years younger than us, was a freshman in high school the year after we graduated, but he was now part of the Wiley brother pack. Another round of Jaegers was passed around, and I did another with everyone else. I told Jig that I was going to leave after that because it was almost 10 o'clock and I needed to drive back into the city. He said that he would leave with me because soon his wife would get mad at him and, also, he had his brand new BMW with him that he didn't want to drive drunk. Our friends gave us shit and called us pussies for wanting to leave, but we did anyway.

Wajid and his friends stayed—Jig telling them to be careful and take a cab home if they needed to, to which they agreed, but that didn't prevent Wajid from smashing his car against a tree two blocks away from their parents' house that night. He woke up in the house not remembering what happened. On our way out, we saw a lot of Little Tommy's friends slurring their way through conversation and reflecting on the tragedy of his death, passing joints around, some of them crying. The cigarette smoking was legal inside the bar; the weed smoking was reserved for the parking lot. I thought it weird that so much alcohol and drugs were being consumed on the aftermath of a drug-related death, but then, I also thought that, well, you know, why would they change course now, right?

As I drove home that night, down I-94, or the "Kennedy," as we call it here in Chicago, I thought how in the 10 or so years that passed since the 1994 New Year's Eve party that climaxed my teenage bliss, so much had happened to all of us. The world at large had changed; another Bush was elected and another war in Iraq had started; girls for me had come and gone, and I was single and in "love" with Heather, who, like Candice, seemed to be another figment of my imagination. What stayed constant, though, was that all my friends and I got drunk every time we got together. When we were young, we used to get together to do things like bike ride, camp, discuss sophomoric philosophy, trade music, stress out about girls, and play sports. Eventually, though, we started to consume all these substances which in turn consumed us, like a disease, and that's how it's been ever since. All we did now—for every occasion, whether it was birthday parties, weddings, and now funerals—was drink and get fucked up. Sure, we are adults now. Some of us have wives and kids; some of us have money and own real estate; some of us have fancy BMWs like Jig, but we're bonded by alcohol—and some of us to other drugs—to a greater extent than ever. I and some of my friends who live in the city, like Caleb and Raphael, may smoke marijuana, but it seems different. It's like we use weed to help with creativity, or at least we say we do. With my high school friends though, it just seems to have taken the place of any other interest they might once have had. Instead of having any interests or hobbies, they now just get drunk, get high, watch TV, play fantasy sports, like its all a filler, a way to waste away the time. And maybe that's just it, we all waste time—what's different is how we waste it.

Except for an occasional wedding or maybe a child's birthday party, I hardly ever go to Des Plaines. However, I do see it often from a distance, from planes as I'm flying back home from some business trip out East or driving west on I-90 on my way to visit my parents. I always look and see if I can spot the woods and factory building parking lots we partied at, the viaducts we learned to smoke under, the street where my house was where my mother used to say our grandfather's ghost would come when my father was being especially violent. As we fly over Lake Michigan toward O'Hare, I look out my window at the orange and yellow glare of Chicago's massive grid that expands north, south and west. And as we go further west and descend down toward one of the runways, I try to look down and see if there are any kids laying there smoking a joint and looking up at the plane like we used to do back then.

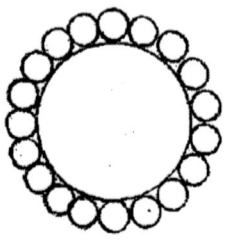

On Being Mexican-American – Part III

My aunt Nadia recently died. One morning while preparing to make the tortillas, she needed to get up on a ladder to reach something and, apparently, it gave way and she fell to the concrete floor, hitting her head. The girl that would come help her during the day had to leave that morning because her daughter became sick at school, and so Nadia was alone at the time. They'd always told her not to use the ladder as it was very old, but she never listened because it was built by her husband Pedro, *El Perrico*, who had died many years before.

Though I've had other family members die in Mexico over the years, I didn't go to any of the other funerals because as a teenager I had lost interest in going to Mexico—I didn't go there for over 14 years.

After my sister and I stopped wanting to go to Mexico, my mother kept going. She kept inviting us, but after a while she gave up. In my late-20s, after finding a book of poetry in Spanish my mother had from when she was little, I gathered an interest in Latin American authors such as Pablo Neruda and Gabriel Garcia Marquez, and I read some of their stuff, though in English. I bought their books in Spanish, but haven't touched them.

A few years ago, when she was talking about going to my cousin Marcela's wedding, although she didn't say anything about me going, I told her that I would go with. She didn't seem surprised and just said that it would be great, and we made arrangements to go. At the wedding I saw my cousin Roberto who I hadn't seen since we were 12, when we played soccer in the streets of Ciudad Hidalgo. He now lives in Mexico City, in *la Zona Rosa*, a wealthy neighborhood, and does well for himself as a real estate speculator of some kind. That sparked a series of trips for me, and over the next few years I kept going back to visit him. We spent our time partying in Mexico City, Cuernavaca, Puebla, Toluca, Zacatecas, and Acapulco. We also visited Ciudad Hidalgo a couple of times.

To get to the funeral, I flew into Mexico City and had to take a cab from the airport to the bus terminal that has departures west to Michoacan. There's no intra-state train system in Mexico, so you have no choice but to drive or take the bus. It was my first time traveling from Mexico City to Ciudad Hidalgo alone, so it was quite an experience.

Making my way to the cab stand in the airport was an experience in itself, with so many people going back and forth, people selling stuff all over, and all sorts of shifty eyes staring around. After grabbing a ticket from the taxi-stand, I got into a cab, holding my breath as I got in. Although I tried not to, I couldn't help but think if the guy wanted to do something like kidnap me, there was not much I'd be able to do to prevent him.

In Mexico the cars just feel and smell different, like they're cheap heaps of metal and you feel every bump the car goes over. There are so many shrines of the *Virgen Maria* all over the roads because people die driving all the time. And nobody seems to obey any sort of driving rules—the cabs just zig-zag down the streets, cutting from one to another, suddenly jumping off a main road and onto a little thoroughfare, and then onto another. Along the roads you pass all sorts of businesses, homes, more businesses, dogs, people selling stuff, young couples completely making out on benches, make-shift soccer fields, garbage, and clowns. (For some reason, there's always a bunch of clowns walking around Mexico City).

After eventually making it to the bus station and nervously buying a ticket, I ate a steak *torta* while sitting next to men drinking beers and smoking, and then after about an hour's wait I got on the bus and started the five hour trip to Ciudad Hidalgo. Though the buses have vastly improved since I was little, they're still of far less quality than the ones here. The seats are pasted together, there's little to no elbow room, no room to really lean back, no air-conditioning, and the cushions are stiff.

The bus station and the airport are located pretty much in the middle of the city, and since there are no straight roads that go from one place to another, traveling through the city by bus takes an enormous amount of time. Some of my cousins that live in Mexico City have work commutes of two or three hours each way, and that's just within the city.

Once you leave the city, the roads open up a bit, and finally the country becomes beautiful and you know you're entering (as my uncle Javier says when he's drunk) *la tierra donde los hombres comen chingon y las viejas son cabronas!!* ("The land where the men eat well and the women are tough as goats!!"). The view from the bus becomes marked with stunning forests, soaring mountains, valleys with creeks, town after little town, and dark-skinned people walking along the road carrying white sacks full of all sorts of stuff they're hoping to sell somewhere.

After arriving in Ciudad Hidalgo I was immediately reminded of how much the town has changed. On the way in you now see super-markets, department stores—I'm sure there'll be a Wal-Mart there soon, if there's not one there already. But the old bus station is still how I remember it—dark, meager, carved out of wood, and looks to be falling apart.

Roberto, with his dark hair slicked back, designer jeans, a black button-down shirt, black boots, and sunglasses, met me at the station, and after we hugged and all that, we got in a cab (they also now have cabs there) and made our way to the funeral home where the whole family was.

In Ciudad Hidalgo there are now newer, modern looking homes, mixed in with the old concrete-slab style ones I'd known. All the old churches are still there, as is the town center and the *Mercado* where they still sell all sorts of food (and live animals). But now, along side the beaten-down cars, young kids drive around in SUVs and Ford trucks, blasting rap or loud techno music. There are now a bunch of clothing stores that sell American style clothes, and there now is all sorts of graffiti on the walls. My mother told me that the town has grown so much because of all the money that people like her have sent back from the states over the years.

Despite all this modernity, the town still felt old and scary to me. When walking down the streets, I stared off at *el cerro* and wondered whether *el chango* hung out there waiting for prey. When looking at the butcher boys, I still felt like they would cut me up if they could.

I'm told in Mexico they used to hold wakes in people's homes, like they did for my grandmother, and they still do sometimes, but for whatever reason they chose to have Nadia's at the new funeral home in town. Upon arriving there, we immediately saw cousins that I hadn't seen in years out in front smoking. Roberto knew them all, and although everyone seemed to recognize me, he reintroduced me. They were all very nice and welcoming, though some of them gave me dirty looks. They all remarked how they remembered me and my sister from when we were babies. They asked how my sister was doing and when she was going to visit, and I told them she would soon although I knew that wasn't true. Before going upstairs, my uncle Gustavo talked to me a bit about money he was trying to raise for an investment, sort of but not really asking me if I wanted to invest.

When we finally made it upstairs, the actual wake was about to begin, after which the group was to walk to the town's cemetery, where Nadia was to be buried in the tomb our grandparents are buried in. Roberto told me that at the cemetery a mariachi would be there to sing during the burial and that it would bring out tears in me like I'd never experienced.

It's customary for the immediate family members to stay up with the deceased the whole night before the wake and funeral, with some staying back at the house in order to prevent the spirit of the deceased from returning.

As we made it upstairs, everyone started going into a room where the casket was, and once inside, everyone stood facing the casket that was surrounded by flowers and pictures of Christ and the *Virgen Maria*. It was dark, but with some light coming in through a window, and there was some distance between the observers and the casket.

Not all the family went inside—deference was given to the immediate family members who stood up front, with everyone else filed in the back and the rest peeking in through the door, or outside smoking. I was going to stay outside with Roberto, but my uncle Javier put his arm around me as he was walking in, and took me in with him.

Everyone just stood there, some silently praying. I thought someone like a priest or family member was going to get up there and speak or something, but then all of a sudden people started shouting stuff out about my aunt—they shouted her name, their memories of her, how much they loved her. Her sons and daughters, many who have now been parents for years, started to lunge up into the space in front of the casket to scream, moan, some falling to their knees with their arms outstretched. Tears started flowing down everyone's faces. The feeling overwhelmed me, and I stood there not knowing what to do. Eventually, as more and more people were yelling, Javier, my big jolly uncle, patted me hard on the back, pushing me forward.

At first I didn't do anything. I just stood there, but then

he patted me again, harder. I looked back and could see tears rolling down his big puffy cheeks, down through his long mustache, and although he was looking beyond me, towards the front and off into the distance, he gave me a reassuring face and nodded approvingly.

I turned around, and after a moment, I all of a sudden screamed out in my broken Spanish *Tia!! Tia, nunca olvidare tus tortillas, y la carne, y el queso que comiamos contingo!! Tia, nunca olvidare!!!* (Aunt!! Aunt, never shall I forget your tortillas, the meat, and the cheese we used to eat with you!! Aunt, never shall I forget!!!). My uncle patted me on the back again after I finished, as the tears were now flowing down my cheeks and onto my lips, leaving their stale, salty taste on my tongue. I didn't want to look back at him, and I felt like leaving the room, getting back on a bus to Mexico City, and then back on a plane to Chicago, far away from there, where I would feel safe again.

I'm not sure what it means to be Mexican-American anymore.

After growing up visiting Mexico every year as a kid, I lost all interest in anything Mexican when trying to fit in with all the white kids I went to school with—when that became ever more necessary. Suddenly I only wanted to speak English at home, and now we never speak Spanish anymore. We always talk about speaking in Spanish again, but when we try, we quickly revert back.

I think white, talk white, dress white, eat white, and I date only white girls. I've never had a Mexican, or Latin-American girlfriend.

All my friends are for the most part white. Some are of different backgrounds, like Indian or Irish, but they've also worked hard to be white. A few are Latin American, but we only speak English to each other, and if we speak in Spanish, it seems sort of trivial.

I met a few Latinos in college. They were all part of this organization called *La Rasa Latina* and hung out mainly with other Latino kids. I went to one of their parties, at someone's apartment, and though it was fun—everyone was dancing, moving the floor, chanting the lyrics of whatever song was playing—I though it was sort of weird. So I stayed with going to frat parties, drinking keg beer, and trying to hook up with white girls.

At work I've met other Latinos, but they're just like me.

Though I've enjoyed my recent string of visits to Mexico, it still seems awkward to me, like I know it will not last—I can almost feel my desire to go vanishing. When I'm there, I feel like I'm visiting a ghost, or a fading memory. I don't know what really prompted my interest to go back in the first place. I feel like I should think I wanted to save a part of me that's been lost because it's important, as an American, not to lose touch with what brought us all here. But I can't help from feeling that I'm only doing it for entertainment's sake, that somehow it really doesn't matter to me, and somehow it's left me feeling emptier than I was.

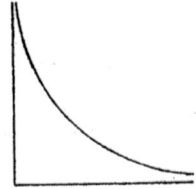

Love (sex) Stories

Caleb once remarked that every book, story, movie, song, work of art ever made is ultimately about love (or better, sex) in one way or another. And I think he's right.

Man is, after all, a conscious being who is aware of the need to procreate in order to continue his existence. We know how important it is, and therefore we think about it all the time. And we know it feels good, for most of us. We don't seem to know how to deal with the problems that really threaten our existence, like global pollution, global food shortages, affordable heath care, but we sure do know how to have sex and make babies—that's easy. It's like despite all the bad shit going on, we just keep going and going, expanding the number of humans on Earth hoping that we'll figure out the rest before we kill ourselves off. Sometimes I think we should call a timeout on baby making so we can focus on our freaking problems and a plan for solving them. Then again, maybe we are the problem, and we need to keep new generations coming that maybe will be smarter and able to deal with the problems prior generations created when all they were thinking about was how to expand humanity.

Sex and love are encouraged all around us, through the commercials and advertisements we're bombarded with, the movies we watch, songs we listen to, and the books we read. In our culture we're taught how we ought to fall in love. We've decided that meeting someone out in the world, versus having someone selected for us, is the appropriate way to find a mate. We're also taught that love should be some sort of fantastical, fairytale kind of thing. We're supposed to be "head over heals." Other cultures, however, promote economic and cultural matchmaking, suppressing all references to love and sex from popular media. It's almost like a tradeoff between seeking to promote diversity, and evolution versus efficiency and consistency.

Looking back at the countless times I've had sex, and the countless other times that I've just wanted to, I can say that I don't think it was because I wanted to make babies. In fact, except for some situations, my partner and I took every precaution not to. We're taught all about birth control from a very early age so clearly we, as a society, don't think of sex only as a way to procreate, but also something that's enjoyed. And it does feel good—it feels really fucking great actually. Not just the sex, but also the coupling aspect, to hold hands, to kiss, to enjoy basic things with someone. But still, I just can't help to think that all these things that feel good are just meant to entice us to "do it." Even if you have no chance of procreating, because maybe you're gay, you still wan to "do it." So, is that all our notion of "love" really is—an inducement for us to keep having sex and therefore keep the human race going? It's like we're all being duped by this fantastical notion of love so we can just do it and hopefully make babies.

I find words like "love" to be interesting. I wrote my one philosophy thesis paper, which was maybe ok at the best, on the topic of "truth." In the paper I analyzed when, and if, words like "love" can ever be considered to be "true."

If you think about it, words like "love" could be defined by individuals, by society, kind of like how we define crimes, laws, through a process of actively discussing them, the process of adjudication. And therefore love is not merely a subjective feeling people get that can't be explained and is different for everyone. I'm not saying that we should write into law what being "in love" means, and therefore dictate to everyone how and who they should love. I just think that emotions such as love are not so different than words like "rock" that we define by experience. Based on this logic, we shouldn't dismiss any responsibility for understanding why it is that we say we're in love with someone, and discerning, potentially, between different kinds of feelings, those that are harmful to us versus those that are positive. If we were able to better define what "love" means to us, I think we'd be better able to differentiate between feelings that are actually infatuation and are more likely harmful versus those that truly are "love."

I've always been troubled by how everyone tends to say that they don't know why they're in love with someone who is awful to them. They always say that they just are, and that no one can understand why you fall in love with someone, you just do. I've seen too many people, including myself, even at an early age, get hurt by this sort of behavior, and it just seems sort of irresponsible to me to shrug off bad judgment by saying that it's the result of instinctual reactions or feelings we just can't control.

I like to relate this thinking to the concept of God also, that it is a word we define through our cultural-specific experiences, and understanding this could lead to more open discussions among members from different cultures. If our beliefs are based on our own cultural-specific experiences, then doesn't that mean that none of our beliefs are necessarily "truer" than others? And through sharing our cultural experiences, one day we could collectively create a global belief system, and thereby establish a global, modern framework consisting of global definitions of things like "God," versus having all the disparate, individual, cultural-specific frameworks we have today. Back in history, not too long ago actually, the different cultures on Earth had no idea there were other cultures outside of their own. It makes sense that different cultures developed their own religions and ethical models. Why we hold on to such vastly different belief systems today seems insane to me. It's like we're brought up to accept that people have different religions, there's nothing we can do about it, just like we all say we don't know what love is because we're told it's so different for all of us.

What strikes me the most about the religions we have is how we continue to think that God looks like a human. It's crazy, but I guess it makes sense because we're so egocentric. It's funny to me that when we think of God we see a man who's white if you're Christian, Islamic-looking if you're Muslim, Indian-looking if you're Hindu, or Asian, fat and jolly-looking if you're fucking Buddhist. It's no wonder the government probably tries to hide any proof of extraterrestrial life—we're so used to thinking of God in terms of ourselves that if we ever met tiny little green people from another planet that were smarter than us, our very foundation would be shattered and we'd probably want to fight them instead of learn from them.

I'm all for individualism. I don't think we should force everyone to adhere to a way of thinking. I just think we need a better global framework than the broken, disparate ones we have today. Under a good framework, individuals would be afforded the liberty to make their own interpretations, to be creative, but also be encouraged to learn and adapt from others from different backgrounds. I just think the different frameworks all of our cultures have are no longer in line with the advancements we've made in the fields of science and philosophy—they haven't been for a long time.

I've used the word love in many different aspects. I've thought it to myself in situations where, looking back, I know it wasn't truly love (based on my definition). The first girl I had sex with, Jackie, I thought was really cool and maybe was my first love, but in all reality, we didn't know what the hell we were doing, I'm pretty sure I didn't put the condom on right.

I never thought I was in "love" with Candice; I just thought she was beautiful and nice and, although I'm sad that she died, I have to admit that I think more of how I ended up naked with her on a couch in the basement of her boyfriend's house and regret that I didn't have sex with her.

I told Erica that I loved her, but it was more to make her happy. She desperately wanted to hear me say that to her, even asked me why I wouldn't say it to her. And because I was a coward and couldn't end my relationship with her like I should have, I finally told her that I loved her and continued to do so for far too long. Then I cheated on her with Miki, her best friend, whom I also told I loved. We told each other that over and over like it was going out of style, especially while we were having sex. I now know that all we really loved was the amazing sex we were having. I thought I was a terrible person after that episode. I really thought that I would never recover. I feared entering into a relationship because I had this horrible predisposition to cheating. I had become the stereotypical cheating Latino male and would just break someone else's heart. What I learned from it was to never force yourself to say "I love you" to someone you don't, it only ends up in disaster.

I think I loved my college girlfriend, Sarah, and she loved me, but we were just too young, or maybe it was that I was too scared to take a chance. If there ever was such a thing as bad timing, I think that was it. Though if we truly did love each other, wouldn't we have tried to make it work? Ultimately though, because we didn't try to compromise each other's dreams and instead encouraged each other to do what we needed to do, we must have been in love, in a pure way, right?

And then there's Heather, the girl I thought I was in love with for the past five years. I thought I was so, so in love, and I thought she was the one. I continued to date other girls while I waited for her to come around, just like Florentino from *Love in the Time of Cholera* did. I had to continue dating to keep my body in fresh condition, but she was what I was waiting for at the end of it all. Looking back, I sometimes wonder if I was chasing a ghost. Heather eerily reminds me of Candice—tall, beautiful, blonde, smart, graceful. Whatever it was, I came to a rude awakening when she rejected me, after I finally gathered enough guts to lay out my feelings for her—the one time I've ever put myself on the line.

She accused me of using our friendship to influence her feelings. After the lashing she inflicted on me, she still wanted to be friends, and I couldn't resist; I just continued being her friend. So there I was, going up to visit her and her baby, pushing the stroller around, taking pictures, visiting with her parents. People assumed that I was the father all the time, with our awkward responses that no, we were not a family. I was the guy who was "just a friend.

Among people of the same sex (or sexual orientation), friendship is different. You don't have the awkward tension of knowing there could be something else. But among members of the opposite sex, it seems like friendship ends up being a way to get companionship from someone until you don't need it anymore. In almost every friendship I've had with a girl, at some point there was some sort of sexual tension, from one side or the other. To be frank, I've had sex with most of my "girl friends," except for Heather. Ultimately, the friendship fizzles out when one member meets someone else that can provide that same friendship, plus something more.

In my case with Heather, I finally realized that I was in the weaker position of someone who wanted more. I met another guy friend of hers who lived in Los Angeles, a friend from college that she talked about often but I'd never met. He was close in age to me, single, didn't really have any dating prospects, and seemed to really like being friends with Heather—and I hated hearing about him. I met him here in Chicago, and when we all were out, he posed for lots of pictures with

Heather and the baby, hugged and kissed her on the cheek, talked about how they should go places together, how she should come visit him in L.A. When I met him, I felt like I was looking in the mirror, and I wanted to throw up. He was a pawn just like me. She wasn't interested in him, just the male companionship he provided, and would soon dispose of him when she met a man that could be her lover.

So I realized that although I "loved" spending time with her, I would always want something more but it would never happen, and that was painful. The last time I was up in Minnesota visiting her, we went out to the bars and drank, went out for walks with her daughter, hung out on her parents' deck. I had conversations with her parents like a boyfriend would have with his girlfriend's parents. We hiked and took pictures. I remember posing with her off of a road with a beautiful view of the surrounding hills and lake. I set the timer on the camera, placed it on top of her car and ran back toward her to pose for our picture. I awkwardly repeated that as I kept screwing up the timer, but it finally worked. She was wearing jeans and a soft white blouse that she had to hold down because of the wind. She turned and smiled at me, and we both turned back and smiled at the camera. We talked about going to Mexico together, for her to visit when I next went to my mother's home town. I remember wondering what my family in Mexico would think if I showed up with a beautiful young lady that had someone else's baby and I told them that we were "just friends." It would have been an outrage. She wanted me to come back up and visit her during the July 4th festival, which was the same setting where I almost pissed in a my pants a few years earlier when I told her I loved her and she rejected me for the first time.

On my drive home that weekend, which turned out to be the last time I visited her, I felt like I was going crazy again. I decided to do something about it. I didn't want to continue on like this knowing that eventually our friendship would have to fade away, and the prospects of not spending the rest of my life with her just were too much for me to handle. So I decided I would tell her, once and for all, that my feelings for her were too great for me to just be friends. I would say that I didn't want her to question the friendship that we'd shared, that in no way was it a ploy, but I just needed to move on and I couldn't do that if I continued to hold on to feelings that she could never reciprocate.

When I got back to Chicago, I struggled with when and if to have this conversation. I began to contemplate whether I should wait it out a bit, to continue hanging out more that summer and then see what happened. I thought that maybe that July 4th I would visit and see how it went. I began to hash out a conversation with her in my head and even started writing letters that I would maybe send her...

And suddenly, just like that, I let it go. I was like, "What the fuck! Enough." I finally put a stop to all the madness and let it go. I felt like someone started to play "For Those About to Rock" by AC/DC, and I was finally let into some sort of club.

(It helped that soon after that trip I met a girl here in Chicago that I became strangely comfortable with, but that's a small detail...) I never had that conversation with Heather, I eventually told her that I was dating someone and with that, our friendship began to fade away. She stopped calling to chat with me; I no longer made the trips up north; she no longer came down to visit me—exactly how I thought our friendship would end.

I still wonder whether there was an alternate life—maybe in one of Stephen Hawking's fucking alternate universes, or in one of the dimensions we supposedly exist in according to String Theory—in which things between me and Heather worked out differently.

End Notes

After being shot down by Heather the first time, I went on a tirade of dating. I dated and dated—probably even dated you, if you're a girl.

I tried to expand my circle of friends and be more social with my work colleagues. I started going out to bars I never thought I could stand, like Can's on Damen, or Tavern on Rush, or lounges like the Fulton Lounge. I made friends with girls at work hoping to meet their friends—who were always perfectly dressed and manicured—but I realized I wasn't getting anywhere when I would overhear them say things with a giggle to each other like, "Yeah, I've been playing with this boy who has a boat on the lake and a place over in Vail, and if this 'play-thing' continues we'll be going on nice trips this summer…" It was like I was sitting with a bunch of girls pretending they were in an episode of *Sex and the City*.

I started hanging out with people who would wear and show off their expensive clothes, which I also started doing. They would talk about their expensive trips, their expensive cars and watches, and episodes of *Entourage*, *The Sopranos*, *The Office*, *Desperate Housewives* and *Grey's Anatomy*, or about how the Cubs or Bears were doing. I found myself watching these shows and sports just to try to fit in to the conversations, like a foreigner watching TV to try and learn English. I started going to work-sponsored sporting events and fundraisers. But I always felt awkward at these things, like I was an uninvited guest crashing the scene, only there on a temporary pass that would soon expire. I seldom talked openly about my interests in art, movies, music, and books, and if it ever came up, I felt embarrassed talking about it. The more this went on, the more I realized how corporate organizations are just like high school, with an "in" crowd and losers who never get invited to anything—and thus never get promoted and walk around the office pissed off all the time thinking everyone is after them. Progressing up the corporate ladder is highly correlated with whether you're invited to attend the company's skybox events. And these people's only friends were other people they worked with, like it was like an extension of their full-time job.

I also started hanging out with Caleb and his art friends more. I liked the parties, music, weed, and the whole scene of it all, but again I just felt like I didn't belong. After spending so many hours at work and out with my work friends talking about so much bullshit, I found myself with not much else to talk about with this other group. I also hated when someone, especially a girl I was trying to talk to, asked me what I did for a living. They were all artists, designers, and I would have to say "um, well, I'm an accountant..." to which they would say, "oh, uh, do you like that?" and I would respond with "well, it's ok, pays the bills and is sort of intellectually stimulating... but I also like to paint and draw," at which point I would get all anxious and sweaty and feel weird about it.

After 30-something years, after this balancing act of working as a professional but secretly wanting to pursue something else, something artistic or romantic, I found myself in some social purgatory, not really knowing where I fit in.

The last time I saw my college girlfriend Sarah in New York, she asked me to swear to never try online dating because it was a sign of the downfall of common human decency. She always said things like that, about cell phones, the Internet, even television. But soon thereafter, I was desperate and posted a profile on a Web site. All the women on the site were interested in the same things—they wanted the prototypical male, primarily someone who is nice, into fashion but a guy's guy underneath, into physical fitness but doesn't overdo it, has a great smile, and can hold a smart conversation—but is not cocky and over-confident (no, no, never that). And, most importantly, someone who is passionate about their job. And absolutely no smokers!

Of course, I said that I was all these things, that yes, I was indeed the super-male they were looking for.

At first I mainly got interest from older women for some reason. I went out with a 40-something suburban divorcee who was into Nirvana and philosophy, enjoyed good wine and was sexy, but she smoked cigarette after cigarette, like they were necessary for staying alive, which maybe they were for her. She intrigued me, we had sex a few times, but when we kissed all I could taste was the cigarettes she smoked. I went out with another older woman who, after a few drinks, whispered into my ear that she wanted to tear off my shirt, unbutton my pants and ravish me, and that was the last time that I, um, went out her...

I also went out with girls closer to my age. This one girl and I went out for a nice dinner and had a bottle of wine; she talked a lot but was cute, and after inviting me back up to her place and leaving me on her couch waiting for over 20 minutes, I got up to see what was wrong—only to find that she had passed out in the bathroom. This other girl liked to make her own clothes, collect vintage things, was into old records, and had a kick-ass body. She also tried to dress like Marilyn Monroe, literally, which was fun at first, until I kept feeling like we were going to a Halloween party every time we went out. Then I started dating another girl, an artist, who liked South American art, was an importer from Belize, and spoke Spanish. We had wild sex on her couch on the like first date to some sort of loud African music she was into, and she told me she loved me as she was bouncing up and down on me while I looked at her big old cat that was staring at me. We seemed to have some common interests and physical chemistry, but after a few dates, she kept asking me where the relationship was going, that she just wasn't sure of my intentions, wasn't comfortable, over and over again. I felt like we were going through divorce discussions even though we had only known each other a few weeks. I finally said that she was right, I also wasn't sure where the relationship was going, nor did I want to find out. She somehow ended up dumping me over e-mail.

And then I went out with other girls who were a little more normal. They seemed to like me. We talked about all the things we said we had in common, and after they would tell me to call them because they had a nice time. I would call, leave a message, they would not return my call, but instead, they would send me an e-mail or text message saying that although they had a nice time, there just wasn't any chemistry. And I would be like, "Well, why the fuck did you tell me to call?"

After countless episodes like these, I was frustrated and ready to give it all up. I felt ashamed that I had even resorted to this, felt that Sarah was off somewhere in Africa shaking her head at me in disapproval, so I chose to cancel my membership at the end of the month—which meant that I still had a few weeks left to find my mate.

I put up pictures of my art instead of the ones with me all dressed up and smiling. I switched my tag line from "Passionate Professional Male Seeking Companion" to quotes like "Circular cars, disco balls and cool guitars," from a Warlocks song called "Baby Blue," to "Prefers fighting to toil, drink to fighting, chasing women to booze or battle: may attempt all three concurrently," a line from Nelson Algren's *Walk on the Wild Side* and "I feel the comfort in being sad," a line from a Nirvana song. And instead of describing myself as the all-American prototype male, I listed my top fives in art (Richter, Monet, Picasso, Hurier, Duda), music (Stereolab, REM, The Flaming Lips, Radiohead, PJ Harvey), literature (*Love in the Time of Cholera, For Whom the Bell Tolls, Realism with a Human Face, The Virgin Suicides, Zorba the Greek*), and movies (*Do the Right Thing, Dazed and Confused, Mulholland Drive, The Royal Tenenbaums, Pulp Fiction*). I said 'Yes' to the "Do you smoke?" question and that I drink all the time to the "Do you drink?" question. I didn't receive any e-mails after this change, which was fine with me. And then, just before it was all over, this girl who lives in Logan Square e-mailed me saying "hey, you're pretty..." She looked cute, and in her profile said she only was looking for someone who didn't like to kick dogs. After a few e-mails, I agreed to meet her at a bar one night for drinks.

I almost didn't go but was like 'fuck it,' and just showed up in my raggedy jeans, a black shirt and hoody, and was unshaven. I met her at a bar called Cleo's on Chicago Avenue, which was her choice. It's a simple, dark place, has a long bar, tables, all sorts of things up on the walls, good beer selection, and when I walked in the song "Blitzkrieg" by Metallica from their *Master of the Puppets* album was playing, so I immediately felt at home. Looking down the bar for her, I spotted a girl at the end with pig tails, jeans tucked into her boots, and a nice big smile and big eyes. She noticed me and waved, so I walked over, ordered a beer, and we began to have a nice, simple conversation, probably the most comfortable setting I've ever had on a date. I started sweating a little at first—no matter how comfortable I was, I still couldn't help it—and did the hand-in-my-hair thing to try and calm it, at which point she remarked that my hand thing was "cute," after which all anxiousness finally left. We talked for hours mainly about her experiences growing up in rural Illinois and her fascination with the band Cheep Trick, that her dream was to get dressed in good old white-trash garb and go see them play in Rockford, Illinois where they're from. After I walked her home, we hugged, and she told me to call her later in the week, saying "bye pretty." I called and told her that I was going to the Empty Bottle with Caleb to see a band called The Secret Machines and that she should meet us if she wanted to. She did, and we've been spending almost all of our free time together ever since.

She's a stationary designer and baby-sits. She seems to like what she does and is good at it, although she doesn't make much money. She struggles with what she wants to do yet with her life, says things like "I'm not sure I know what I want to do when I grow up," practices the philosophy of living in the moment, in the now, which many people say they do, except I think she really does. She's short, has light brown hair, wears it often in these pig tails or pulled back, doesn't use much make-up but has very plushy skin, soft and smooth like a baby's. I catch myself just staring at her when she's not looking at me, like when we're at a show or a live recording of one of the many NPR shows she likes to go see. She reads mostly non-fiction and likes music that I normally can't stand, like the Dixie Chicks, Rufus Wainwright, and the Indigo Girls, but I don't mind, I guess. I feel comfortable doing things that I like around her, like drawing, painting, daydreaming, and reading. She makes fun of how I tend to zone out of conversations. Truly, for once, I feel comfortable being who I am with her—as of now anyway. She grew up outside of Peoria, Illinois, on a farm, and her parents are Harley bikers. They go on long road trips with their biker friends, and each summer they throw an all-out bash on their farm with things like volleyball, horse rings, kick ball, bon-fires, kegs and skinny dipping. She wears shirts that say things like "My mom is a biker bitch," "I'm an Eager Beaver," and "Homecoming Queen." She has a big old mutt whom she calls Kelly—I love using people names for dogs. She likes paintings of birds and whimsical art, and she says she has Flintstone feet, though I think they're just cute little girl feet. And she's tired and cranky after work and needs her time to "decompress.

I've always liked to think of potential wedding songs, just in case I ever get married, which I really don't plan to do, it's too "formal" for me and I would feel like a hypocrite if I ever did. However, I've always liked the Beatles song, "Here, There, Everywhere." You could get more creative and choose a song like "Hey Now It's the Sun," by the Polyphonic Spree, which is a glorious, spirited song simply about how beautiful the sun is. I also like the song "Here Comes Your Man" by the Pixies for when the groom walks down the aisle and "American Girl" by Tom Petty for the bride.

We've only been dating for a few months, but it seems longer as we spend practically every day together. Sheryl's been late on her period now for over two weeks, she's been feeling nauseous every day, and so we're going to take a pregnancy test tonight, which is something I've truly never done before. I'm not nervous—not a lot anyway. We haven't been careful with sex, but for some reason I didn't care. Perhaps all the practice I've gained having sex has finally panned out, and I'm getting ready to make my contribution to a new generation that will hopefully be better than ours. She would be a great person to raise a child with, so I think I'm okay with however it turns out…I think.

Even though I'm comfortable with this girl, I still have many unanswered questions. I still don't know what God truly is. If he, she, or it is really out there, looks like a human or is some kind of aura. If he, she or it is listening and judging, then well, then I'd like to ask he, she or it if he, she or it is lonely or bored. I don't know whatever happened to the Widow-Maker, but I'm sure he's out there somewhere, maybe in bong-heaven, maybe in some young Des Plaines kid's basement, watching and observing all the amateurs. Although I'm the most confident, most comfortable with myself than I can ever remember being, I still have the same shitty career with no prospects of getting out of it, and I still perspire whenever I have to give a presentation or a good-looking girl talks to me.

I'm not sure how much longer my father is going to live, but I've forgiven him for what he did, and I hope my sister will soon before it's too late. The experiences that my friends and I shared in Des Plaines were fun; I can't believe we did what we did and wonder how I'll handle it when my children do the same things. These experiences affected us all in many different ways, some for the worse and some for the better.

When it comes to love and dating, though, I've figured something out. I've figured out that the old adage "just be yourself," the biggest cliché of them all, the most sophomoric statement ever, is true. If I could go back and re-write my philosophy thesis, I would argue that that statement is a fundamental concept we all can hold as true, self-evident, along with statements like Descartes' "I think therefore I am." When love happens, it's not magical, it's not like U2 or Coldplay starts playing in the background. Though I haven't come up with a real definition of "love," I feel like I'm fairly comfortable with my notion of it.

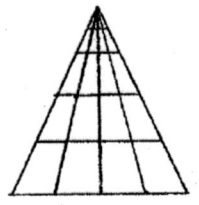

Please visit www.curbsidesplendor.com for further literary fiction, poetry, and other musings.

CPSIA information can be obtained at www.ICGtesting.com
Printed in the USA
244045LV00005B/1/P